JO'S BOYS

Jo's Boys

and How They Turned Out

Louisa May Alcott

GRAMERCY BOOKS
New York • Avenel

Foreword copyright © 1994 by Random House Value Publishing, Inc.
All rights reserved.

This edition is published by Random House Value Publishing, Inc.,
40 Engelhard Avenue, Avenel, New Jersey 07001.

Printed and bound in the United States of America

Library of Congress Cataloging-in-Publication Data
Alcott, Louisa May, 1832-1888.
Jo's boys and how they turned out / Louisa May Alcott.
p.   cm.
Summary: Recounts the further adventures, successes, and failures
of the numerous young men of Plumfield school. Sequel to "Little Men."
ISBN 0-517-11830-0
[1. Boarding schools—Fiction.   2. Schools—Fiction.   3. Family
life—New England—Fiction.   4. New England—Fiction.]   I. Title.
PZ7.A335Jo   1994
[Fic]—dc20   94-14794
                                                          CIP
                                                           AC

8 7 6 5 4 3 2 1

CONTENTS

FOREWORD vii

1 TEN YEARS LATER 1
2 PARNASSUS 17
3 JO'S LAST SCRAPE 33
4 DAN 51
5 VACATION 69
6 LAST WORDS 91
7 THE LION AND THE LAMB 107
8 JOSIE PLAYS MERMAID 123
9 THE WORM TURNS 137
10 DEMI SETTLES 151
11 EMIL'S THANKSGIVING 163
12 DAN'S CHRISTMAS 171
13 NAT'S NEW YEAR 183
14 PLAYS AT PLUMFIELD 195
15 WAITING 211
16 IN THE TENNIS COURT 219
17 AMONG THE MAIDS 233
18 CLASS DAY 245

v

19 WHITE ROSES 257
20 LIFE FOR LIFE 269
21 ASLAUGA'S KNIGHT 283
22 POSITIVELY LAST APPEARANCE 295

FOREWORD

W$_{HEN}$ Louisa May Alcott wrote *Jo's Boys* in 1886, she was completing a trilogy begun with the now-classic *Little Women*, the story of the March sisters, Meg, Beth, Jo, and Amy, and their parents. The family saga continued with *Little Men*, which took the surviving Marches further along in life and also focused on the Plumfield school for boys that Jo ran with her husband, Professor Fritz Bhaer.

Jo's Boys is the conclusion to the story of the sisters and the people at the center of their lives—their children, the former students of Plumfield, and a handful of students at Laurence College, the successor to that school.

Most of the book is devoted to the separate but interlinked stories of Jo's boys, whose adventures filled the pages of *Little Men*. Now, some years later, these "boys" are in their early twenties, just entering adulthood, searching for a path in life, and looking for, and usually finding, a suitable soul mate. (The March sisters' children—young men *and* young women—get their own share of attention, with their fortunes more often than not intertwined with those of the now-grown Plumfield boys.)

To open the covers of *Jo's Boys* is to enter a world very different from our own. Life in small-town New England more than a hundred years ago was simpler, quieter, gentler, and more civilized than what we know today of urban or suburban living. It wasn't an era of complete innocence, of course: the country had experienced the horrors of slavery and the Civil War. But as yet unknown were the ravages of world war, atomic weapons, and the terrible social ills that beset families and communities today.

This was a time when a family picnic or an outing to the beach was considered the greatest fun; when a party for young people (in their late teens and early twenties) was heavily chaperoned by parents, and the party activities might include elaborate skits, poetry recitations, a performance of small satires—or a lively co-ed debate about a compelling topic of the day, such as women's suffrage. For—oh yes—this was one other significant difference between then and now: at the time *Jo's Boys* was written, women still had not been granted the right to vote!

Louisa May Alcott was a staunch early feminist and quite outspoken—even by modern standards—and her insistent championing of equal rights, as well as several other causes, comes across loud and clear in her books. In *Jo's Boys* the most obvious bearer of the feminist torch is Meg's daughter, Nan, who is studying to be a doctor and who is determined to forego marriage to devote all her energy to her calling. It is Nan who declares that she is "ashamed of America" for not extending the vote to women.

She also states emphatically that she is "very glad and grateful that [her] profession will make [her] a useful, happy, and independent spinster." (The term "spinster" didn't carry quite the same negative meaning then as it does now.) There is much lively discussion about the positive value of so-called "superfluous women"—among them, widows and spinsters. Other characters also give voice to Louisa May Alcott's own opinions

about the value of women's contributions to society. Jo's son,
John, for example, attributes the "high state of culture" to the
preponderance of women in society, to which Jo replies:

> It is a merciful provision my dears; for it takes three or
> four women to get each man into, through, and out of
> the world. You are costly creatures, boys; and it is well
> that mothers, sisters, wives, and daughters love their duty
> and do it so well, or you would perish off the face of the
> earth . . .

It is obvious from this quote that Jo is the character who most
clearly speaks with Louisa's voice—in fact, she is her creator's
alter ego. The two share many life experiences: Louisa acted as
a surrogate mother to her large family and supported them
through her writing, the profits from which also helped maintain the progressive school run for some years by her father in
Concord, Massachusetts. Jo mothered many boys at Plumfield,
a progressive school she helped her husband run, and she shep-
herds a mixed flock at Laurence College, where she espouses
her (and Louisa's) belief in "the right of all sexes, colors,
creeds, and ranks to education. . . ." And Jo, too, is a successful but beleaguered author of novels for young people; she, like
Louisa, had turned to writing out of financial desperation and,
also like Louisa, succeeded beyond her wildest dreams.

Although Louisa was very forward-thinking for her own time,
it must be remembered that she was also a product of that time.
So, although she was anti-slavery and pro-equality, she could
still include in her book a fragment of Black "minstrel" dialect
and not imagine she might give offense. Or, despite her senti-
ments concerning the rights of Native American Indians, she
could still have a character who strongly *sympathized* with the
Indians' plight joke about scalping "a few red fellows."

Jo's Boys ends as it begins, on a somewhat wistful note.
Louisa seems to have been both sorry and relieved to end the

saga of the March family and their extended brood. Also, there is true sadness when she mentions in her preface to the first edition that if she appeared to neglect the character of Jo's sister, Amy, it was because "the original of that character [Louisa's sister] died," and the same held true for Marmee, the beloved mother in *Little Women,* who was modeled on her own parent. But, she added, "the folded leaves are not blank to those who knew and loved them. . . ."

Louisa's affection for her characters glows in these pages, and cannot help but touch the reader. She closes on a final note, stating, ". . . let the music stop, the lights die out, and the curtain fall forever. . . ."

In 1888, two years after she saw the March family disappear from the stage she had set for them, Louisa May Alcott herself died. But her characters live on, and through them their creator, too, has achieved an immortality she could not have imagined.

NAOMI KLEINBERG

New York
1994

Jo's Boys

To
DR. CONRAD WESSELHOEFT
This Very Inadequate Tribute of Affection and Respect
is Gratefully Inscribed
by His Friend and Patient,

THE AUTHOR

CHAPTER 1

TEN YEARS LATER

"If anyone had told me what wonderful changes were to take place here in ten years, I wouldn't have believed it," said Mrs. Jo to Mrs. Meg, as they sat on the piazza at Plumfield one summer day, looking about them with faces full of pride and pleasure.

"This is the sort of magic that money and kind hearts can work. I am sure Mr. Laurence could have no nobler monument than the college he so generously endowed; and a home like this will keep Aunt March's memory green as long as it lasts," answered Mrs. Meg, always glad to praise the absent.

"We used to believe in fairies, you remember, and plan what we'd ask for if we could have three wishes. Doesn't it seem as if mine had been really granted at last? Money, fame, and plenty of the work I love," said Mrs. Jo, carelessly rumpling up her hair as she clasped her hands over her head just as she used to do when a girl.

"I have had mine, and Amy is enjoying hers to her heart's content. If dear Marmee, John, and Beth were here, it would be

1

quite perfect," added Meg, with a tender quiver in her voice;
for Marmee's place was empty now.

Jo put her hand on her sister's, and both sat silent for a little
while, surveying the pleasant scene before them with mingled
sad and happy thoughts.

It certainly did look as if magic had been at work, for quiet
Plumfield was transformed into a busy little world. The house
seemed more hospitable than ever, refreshed with new paint,
added wings, well-kept lawn and garden, and a prosperous air it
had not worn when riotous boys swarmed everywhere and it was
rather difficult for the Bhaers to make both ends meet. On the
hill, where kites used to be flown, stood the fine college which
Mr. Laurence's munificent legacy had built. Busy students were
going to and fro along the paths once trodden by childish feet,
and many young men and women were enjoying all the advantages that wealth, wisdom, and benevolence could give them.

Just inside the gates of Plumfield a pretty brown cottage, very
like the Dovecote, nestled among the trees, and on the green
slope westward Laurie's white-pillared mansion glittered in the
sunshine; for when the rapid growth of the city shut in the old
house, spoilt Meg's nest, and dared to put a soap factory under
Mr. Laurence's indignant nose, our friends emigrated to Plumfield, and the great changes began.

These were the pleasant ones; and the loss of the dear old
people was sweetened by the blessings they left behind; so all
prospered now in the little community, and Mr. Bhaer as president, and Mr. March as chaplain, of the college, saw their long-
cherished dream beautifully realized. The sisters divided the
care of the young people among them, each taking the part that
suited her best. Meg was the motherly friend of the young
women, Jo the confidante and defender of all the youths, and
Amy the Lady Bountiful who delicately smoothed the way for
needy students, and entertained them all so cordially that it was
no wonder they named her lovely home Mount Parnassus, so

full was it of music, beauty, and the culture hungry young hearts and fancies long for.

The original twelve boys had of course scattered far and wide during these years, but all that lived still remembered old Plumfield, and came wandering back from the four quarters of the earth to tell their various experiences, laugh over the pleasures of the past, and face the duties of the present with fresh courage; for such homecomings keep hearts tender and hands helpful with the memories of young and happy days. A few words will tell the history of each, and then we can go on with the new chapter of their lives.

Franz was with a merchant kinsman in Hamburg, a man of twenty-six now, and doing well. Emil was the jolliest tar that ever "sailed the ocean blue." His uncle sent him on a long voyage to disgust him with this adventurous life; but he came home so delighted with it that it was plain this was his profession, and the German kinsman gave him a good chance in his ships; so the lad was happy. Dan was a wanderer still; for after the geological researches in South America he tried sheep farming in Australia, and was now in California looking up mines. Nat was busy with music at the Conservatory, preparing for a year or two in Germany to finish him off. Tom was studying medicine and trying to like it. Jack was in business with his father, bent on getting rich. Dolly was in college with Stuffy and Ned reading law. Poor little Dick was dead, so was Billy; and no one could mourn for them, since life would never be happy, afflicted as they were in mind and body.

Rob and Teddy were called the "Lion and the Lamb," for the latter was as rampant as the king of beasts, and the former as gentle as any sheep that ever baaed. Mrs. Jo called him "my daughter," and found him the most dutiful of children, with plenty of manliness underlying the quiet manners and tender nature. But in Ted she seemed to see all the faults, whims, aspirations, and fun of her own youth in a new shape. With his tawny locks always in wild confusion, his long legs and arms, loud voice, and continual activity, Ted was a prominent figure at Plumfield. He had his moods of gloom, and fell into the Slough of Despond about once a week, to be hoisted out by patient Rob or his mother, who understood when to let him alone and when to shake him up. He was her pride and joy as well as torment, being a very bright lad for his age, and so full of all sorts of budding talent, that her maternal mind was much exercised as to what this remarkable boy would become.

Demi had gone through college with honor, and Mrs. Meg had set her heart on his being a minister—picturing in her fond fancy the first sermon her dignified young parson would preach, as well as the long, useful, and honored life he was to lead. But John, as she called him now, firmly declined the divinity school, saying he had had enough of books, and needed to know more of men and the world, and caused the dear woman much disappointment by deciding to try a journalist's career. It was a blow; but she knew that young minds cannot be driven, and that experience is the best teacher, so she let him follow his own inclinations, still hoping to see him in the pulpit. Aunt Jo raged when she found that there was to be a reporter in the family, and called him "Jenkins" on the spot. She liked his literary tendencies, but had reason to detest official Paul Prys, as we shall see later. Demi knew his own mind, however, and tranquilly carried out his plans, unmoved by the tongues of the anxious mammas or the jokes of his mates. Uncle Teddy encouraged him, and painted a splendid career, mentioning Dickens and other celebrities who began as reporters and ended as famous novelists or newspaper men.

The girls were all flourishing. Daisy, as sweet and domestic as ever, was her mother's comfort and companion. Josie at fourteen was a most original young person, full of pranks and peculiarities, the latest of which was a passion for the stage, which caused her quiet mother and sister much anxiety as well as amusement. Bess had grown into a tall, beautiful girl, looking several years older than she was, with the same graceful ways and dainty tastes which the little Princess had, and a rich inheritance of both the father's and mother's gifts, fostered by every aid love and money could give. But the pride of the community was Naughty Nan; for, like so many restless, willful children, she was growing into a woman full of the energy and promise that suddenly blossoms when the ambitious seeker finds the work she is fitted to do well. Nan began to study medicine at sixteen, and at twenty was getting on bravely; for now, thanks to other intelligent women, colleges and hospitals were open to her. She had never wavered in her purpose from the childish days when she shocked Daisy in the old willow by saying, "I don't want any family to fuss over. I shall have an office, with bottles and pestle things in it, and drive round and cure folks." The future foretold by the little girl the young woman was rapidly bringing to pass, and finding so much happiness in it that nothing could win her from the chosen work. Several worthy young gentlemen had tried to make her change her mind and choose, as Daisy did, "a nice little house and a family to take care of." But Nan only laughed, and routed the lovers by proposing to look at the tongue which spoke of adoration, or professionally felt the pulse in the manly hand offered for her acceptance. So all departed but one persistent youth, who was such a devoted Traddles it was impossible to quench him.

This was Tom, who was as faithful to his child sweetheart as she to her "pestle things," and gave a proof of fidelity that touched her very much. He studied medicine for her sake alone, having no taste for it, and a decided fancy for a mercantile life. But Nan was firm, and Tom stoutly kept on, devoutly hoping he might not kill many of his fellow beings when he came to practice. They were excellent friends, however, and caused much amusement to their comrades by the vicissitudes of this merry love chase.

Both were approaching Plumfield on the afternoon when Mrs. Meg and Mrs. Jo were talking on the piazza. Not together; for Nan was walking briskly along the pleasant road alone, thinking over a case that interested her, and Tom was pegging on behind to overtake her, as if by accident, when the suburbs of the city were past—a little way of his, which was part of the joke.

Nan was a handsome girl, with a fresh color, clear eye, quick smile, and the self-poised look young women with a purpose always have. She was simply and sensibly dressed, walked easily, and seemed full of vigor, with her broad shoulders well back, arms swinging freely, and the elasticity of youth and health in every motion. The few people she met turned to look at her, as if it was a pleasant sight to see a hearty, happy girl walking countryward that lovely day; and the red-faced young man steaming along behind, hat off and every tight curl wagging with impatience, evidently agreed with them.

Presently a mild "Hullo!" was borne upon the breeze, and pausing, with an effort to look surprised that was an utter failure, Nan said affably, "Oh, is that you, Tom?"

"Looks like it. Thought you might be walking out today," and Tom's jovial face beamed with pleasure.

"You knew it. How is your throat?" asked Nan in her professional tone, which was always a quencher to undue raptures.

"Throat? Oh, ah! Yes, I remember. It is well. The effect of that prescription was wonderful. I'll never call homeopathy a humbug again."

"You were the humbug this time, and so were the unmedicated pellets I gave you. If sugar of milk can cure diphtheria in this remarkable manner, I'll make a note of it. O Tom, Tom, will you never be done playing tricks?"

"O Nan, Nan, will you never be done getting the better of me?" And the merry pair laughed at one another just as they did in the old times, which always came back freshly when they went to Plumfield.

"Well, I knew I shouldn't see you for a week if I didn't scare up some excuse for a call at the office. You are so desperately busy all the time I never get a word," explained Tom.

"You ought to be busy too, and above such nonsense. Really, Tom, if you don't give your mind to your lectures, you'll never get on," said Nan, soberly.

"I have quite enough of them as it is," answered Tom, with an air of disgust. "A fellow must lark a bit after dissecting corpses all day. I can't stand it long at a time, though *some people* seem to enjoy it immensely."

"Then why not leave it, and do what suits you better? I always thought it a foolish thing, you know," said Nan, with a trace of anxiety in the keen eyes that searched for signs of illness in a face as ruddy as a Baldwin apple.

"You know why I chose it, and why I shall stick to it if it kills me. I may not *look* delicate, but I've a deep-seated heart complaint, and it will carry me off sooner or later; for only one doctor in the world can cure it, and she won't."

There was an air of pensive resignation about Tom that was both comic and pathetic; for he was in earnest, and kept on giving hints of this sort, without the least encouragement.

Nan frowned, but she was used to it, and knew how to treat him.

"She *is* curing it in the best and only way; but a more refractory patient never lived. Did you go to that ball, as I directed?"

"I did."

"And devote yourself to pretty Miss West?"

"Danced with her the whole evening."

"No impression made on that susceptible organ of yours?"

"Not the slightest. I gaped in her face once, forgot to feed her, and gave a sigh of relief when I handed her over to her mamma."

"Repeat the dose as often as possible, and note the symptoms. I predict that you will 'cry for it' by and by."

"Never! I'm sure it doesn't suit my constitution."

"We shall see. Obey orders!" sternly.

"Yes, Doctor," meekly.

Silence reigned for a moment; then, as if the bone of

contention was forgotten in the pleasant recollections called up
by familiar objects, Nan said, suddenly, "What fun we used to
have in that wood! Do you remember how you tumbled out of
the big nut tree and nearly broke your collarbone?"

"Don't I! And how you steeped me in wormwood till I was a
fine mahogany color, and Aunt Jo wailed over my spoilt jacket,"
laughed Tom, a boy again in a minute.

"And how you set the house afire?"

"And you ran off for your bandbox?"

"Do you ever say 'Thunder-turtles' now?"

"Do people ever call you 'Giddy-gaddy'?"

"Daisy does. Dear thing, I haven't seen her for a week."

"I saw Demi this morning, and he said she was keeping house
for Mother Bhaer."

"She always does when Aunt Jo gets into a vortex. Daisy is a
model housekeeper, and you couldn't do better than make your
bow to her, if you can't go to work and wait till you are grown
up before you begin lovering."

"Nat would break his fiddle over my head if I suggested such
a thing. No, thank you. Another name is engraved upon my
heart as indelibly as the blue anchor on my arm. 'Hope' is my
motto, and 'No surrender,' yours. See who will hold out longest."

"You silly boys think we must pair off as we did when children, but we shall do nothing of the kind. How well Parnassus
looks from here!" said Nan, abruptly changing the conversation
again.

"It is a fine house, but I love old Plum best. Wouldn't Aunt
March stare if she could see the changes here?" answered Tom,
as they both paused at the great gate to look at the pleasant
landscape before them.

A sudden whoop startled them, as a long boy with a wild
yellow head came leaping over a hedge like a kangaroo, followed by a slender girl, who stuck in the hawthorn, and sat
there laughing like a witch. A pretty little lass she was, with

curly dark hair, bright eyes, and a very expressive face. Her hat was at her back, and her skirts a good deal the worse for the brooks she had crossed, the trees she had climbed, and the last leap, which added several fine rents.

"Take me down, Nan, please. Tom, hold Ted; he's got my book, and I *will* have it," called Josie from her perch, not at all daunted by the appearance of her friends.

Tom promptly collared the thief, while Nan picked Josie from among the thorns and set her on her feet without a word of reproof; for having been a romp in her own girlhood, she was very indulgent to like tastes in others. "What's the matter, dear?" she asked, pinning up the longest rip, while Josie examined the scratches on her hands.

"I was studying my part in the willow, and Ted came slyly up and poked the book out of my hands with his rod. It fell in the brook, and before I could scrabble down he was off. You wretch, give it back this moment or I'll box your ears," cried Josie, laughing and scolding in the same breath.

Escaping from Tom, Ted struck a sentimental attitude, and with tender glances at the wet, torn young person before him, delivered Claude Melnotte's famous speech in a lackadaisical way that was irresistibly funny, ending with "Dost like the picture, love?" as he made an object of himself by tying his long legs in a knot and distorting his face horribly.

The sound of applause from the piazza put a stop to these antics, and the young folks went up the avenue together very much in the old style when Tom drove four in hand and Nan was the best horse in the team. Rosy, breathless, and merry, they greeted the ladies and sat down on the steps to rest, Aunt Meg sewing up her daughter's rags while Mrs. Jo smoothed the Lion's mane, and rescued the book. Daisy appeared in a moment to greet her friend, and all began to talk.

"Muffins for tea; better stay and eat 'em; Daisy's never fail," said Ted, hospitably.

"He's a judge; he ate nine last time. That's why he's so fat," added Josie, with a withering glance at her cousin, who was as thin as a lath.

"I must go and see Lucy Dove. She has a whitlow, and it's time to lance it. I'll have tea at college," answered Nan, feeling in her pocket to be sure she had not forgotten her case of instruments.

"Thanks, I'm going there also. Tom Merryweather has granulated lids, and I promised to touch them up for him. Save a doctor's fee and be good practice for me. I'm clumsy with my thumbs," said Tom, bound to be near his idol while he could.

"Hush! Daisy doesn't like to hear you sawbones talk of your work. Muffins suit us better." And Ted grinned sweetly, with a view to future favors in the eating line.

"Any news of the Commodore?" asked Tom.

"He is on his way home, and Dan hopes to come soon. I long to see my boys together, and have begged the wanderers to come to Thanksgiving, if not before," answered Mrs. Jo, beaming at the thought.

"They'll come, every man of them, if they can. Even Jack will risk losing a dollar for the sake of one of our jolly old dinners," laughed Tom.

"There's the turkey fattening for the feast. I never chase him now, but feed him well, and he's 'swellin' wisibly,' bless his drumsticks!" said Ted, pointing out the doomed fowl proudly parading in a neighboring field.

"If Nat goes the last of the month we shall want a farewell frolic for him. I suppose the dear old Chirper will come home a second Ole Bull," said Nan to her friend.

A pretty color came into Daisy's cheek, and the folds of muslin on her breast rose and fell with a quick breath; but she answered placidly, "Uncle Laurie says he has *real* talent, and after the training he will get abroad he can command a good living here, though he may never be famous."

"Young people seldom turn out as one predicts, so it is of little use to expect anything," said Mrs. Meg with a sigh. "If our children are good and useful men and women, we should be satisfied; yet it's very natural to wish them to be brilliant and successful."

"They are like my chickens, mighty uncertain. Now, that fine-looking cockerel of mine is the stupidest one of the lot, and the ugly, long-legged chap is the king of the yard, he's so smart. Crows loud enough to wake the Seven Sleepers, but the handsome one croaks, and is no end of a coward. *I* get snubbed; but you wait till I grow up, and then see." And Ted looked so like his own long-legged pet that everyone laughed at his modest prediction.

"I want to see Dan settled somewhere. 'A rolling stone gathers no moss,' and at twenty-five he is still roaming about the world without a tie to hold him, except this." And Mrs. Meg nodded toward her sister.

"Dan will find his place at last, and experience is his best teacher. He is rough still, but each time he comes home I see a change for the better, and never lose my faith in him. He may never do anything great, or get rich; but if the wild boy makes an honest man, I'm satisfied," said Mrs. Jo, who always defended the black sheep of her flock.

"That's right, mother, stand by Dan! He's worth a dozen Jacks and Neds bragging about money and trying to be swells. You see if he doesn't do something to be proud of and take the wind out of their sails," added Ted, whose love for his "Danny" was now strengthened by a boy's admiration for the bold, adventurous man.

"Hope so, I'm sure. He's just the fellow to do rash things and come to glory—climbing the Matterhorn, taking a 'header' into Niagara, or finding a big nugget. That's his way of sowing wild oats, and perhaps it's better than ours," said Tom, thoughtfully, for he had gained a good deal of experience in that sort of agriculture since he became a medical student.

"Much better!" said Mrs. Jo, emphatically. "I'd rather send my boys off to see the world in that way than leave them alone in a city full of temptations, with nothing to do but waste time, money, and health, as so many are left. Dan has to work his way, and that teaches him courage, patience and self-reliance. I don't worry about him as much as I do about George and Dolly at college, no more fit than two babies to take care of themselves."

"How about John? He's knocking round town as a newspaper man, reporting all sorts of things, from sermons to prizefights," asked Tom, who thought that sort of life would be much more to his own taste than medical lectures and hospital wards.

"Demi has three safeguards—good principles, refined tastes, and a wise mother. He won't come to harm, and these experiences will be useful to him when he begins to write, as I'm sure he will in time," began Mrs. Jo in her prophetic tone, for she was anxious to have some of her geese turn out swans.

"Speak of Jenkins, and you'll hear the rustling of his paper," cried Tom, as a fresh-faced, brown-eyed young man came up the avenue, waving a newspaper over his head.

"Here's your 'Evening Tattler!' Latest edition! Awful murder! Bank clerk absconded! Powder mill explosion, and great strike of the Latin School boys!" roared Ted, going to meet his cousin with the graceful gait of a young giraffe.

"The Commodore is in, and will cut his cable and run before the wind as soon as he can get off," called Demi, with "a nice derangement of nautical epitaphs," as he came up smiling over his good news.

Everyone talked together for a moment, and the paper passed from hand to hand that each eye might rest on the pleasant fact that the "Brenda," from Hamburg, was safe in port.

"He'll come lurching out by tomorrow with his usual collection of marine monsters and lively yarns. I saw him, jolly and tarry and brown as a coffee berry. Had a good run, and hopes to be second mate, as the other chap is laid up with a broken leg," added Demi.

"Wish I had the setting of it," said Nan to herself, with a professional twist of her hand.

"How's Franz?" asked Mrs. Jo.

"He's going to be married! There's news for you. The first of the flock, Aunty, so say good-bye to him. Her name is Ludmilla Hildegard Blumenthal; good family, well off, pretty, and of course an angel. The dear old boy wants Uncle's consent, and then he will settle down to be a happy and an honest burgher. Long life to him!"

"I'm glad to hear it. I do so like to settle my boys with a good wife and a nice little home. Now, if all is right, I shall feel as if Franz was off my mind," said Mrs. Jo, folding her hands contentedly, for she often felt like a distracted hen with a large brood of mixed chickens and ducks upon her hands.

"So do I," sighed Tom, with a sly glance at Nan. "That's what a fellow needs to keep him steady; and it's the duty of nice girls to marry as soon as possible, isn't it, Demi?"

"If there are enough nice fellows to go round. The female population exceeds the male, you know, especially in New England, which accounts for the high state of culture we are in, perhaps," answered John, who was leaning over his mother's chair, telling his day's experiences in a whisper.

"It is a merciful provision, my dears; for it takes three or four women to get each man into, through, and out of the world. You are costly creatures, boys; and it is well that mothers, sisters, wives, and daughters love their duty and do it so well, or you would perish off the face of the earth," said Mrs. Jo, solemnly, as she took up a basket filled with dilapidated hose; for the good Professor was still hard on his socks, and his sons resembled him in that respect.

"Such being the case, there is a plenty for the 'superfluous women' to do, in taking care of these helpless men and their families. I see that more clearly every day, and am very glad and grateful that my profession will make me a useful, happy, and independent spinster."

Nan's emphasis on the last word caused Tom to groan, and the rest to laugh.

"I take great pride and solid satisfaction in you, Nan, and hope to see you very successful, for we do need just such helpful women in the world. I sometimes feel as if I'd missed my vocation and ought to have remained single, but my duty seemed to point this way, and I don't regret it," said Mrs. Jo, folding a large and very ragged blue sock to her bosom.

"Neither do I. What should I ever have done without my dearest Mum?" added Ted, with a filial hug which caused both to disappear behind the newspaper in which he had been mercifully absorbed for a few minutes.

"My darling boy, if you would wash your hands semi-occasionally, fond caresses would be less disastrous to my collar. Never mind, my precious tousle-head—better grass stains and dirt than no cuddlings at all." And Mrs. Jo emerged from that brief eclipse looking much refreshed, though her back hair was caught in Ted's buttons and her collar under one ear.

Here Josie, who had been studying her part at the other end of the piazza, suddenly burst forth with a smothered shriek, and gave Juliet's speech in the tomb so effectively that the boys applauded, Daisy shivered, and Nan murmured, "Too much cerebral excitement for one of her age."

"I'm afraid you'll have to make up your mind to it, Meg. That child is a born actress. We never did anything so well, not even the 'Witch's Curse,' " said Mrs. Jo, casting a bouquet of many-colored socks at the feet of her flushed and panting niece, when she fell gracefully upon the doormat.

"It is a sort of judgment upon me for my passion for the stage when a girl. Now I know how dear Marmee felt when I begged to be an actress. I never can consent, and yet I may be obliged to give up my wishes, hopes, and plans again."

There was an accent of reproach in his mother's voice, which made Demi pick up his sister with a gentle shake, and the stern command to "drop that nonsense in public."

"Drop me, Minion, or I'll give you the 'Maniac Bride,' with my best *Ha-ha!*" cried Josie, glaring at him like an offended kitten.

Being set on her feet, she made a splendid courtesy, and dramatically proclaiming, "Mrs. Woffington's carriage waits," swept down the steps and round the corner, trailing Daisy's scarlet shawl majestically behind her.

"Isn't she great fun? I couldn't stop in this dull place if I hadn't that child to make it lively for me. If ever she turns prim, I'm off; so mind how you nip her in the bud," said Teddy, frowning at Demi, who was now writing out shorthand notes on the steps.

"You two are a team, and it takes a strong hand to drive you, but I rather like it. Josie ought to have been my child, and Rob yours, Meg. Then your house would have been all peace and mine all Bedlam. Now I must go and tell Laurie the news. Come with me, Meg, a little stroll will do us good." And sticking Ted's straw hat on her head, Mrs. Jo walked off with her sister, leaving Daisy to attend to the muffins, Ted to appease Josie, and Tom and Nan to give their respective patients a very bad quarter of an hour.

CHAPTER 2

PARNASSUS

IT WAS well named; and the Muses seemed to be at home that day, for as the newcomers went up the slope appropriate sights and sounds greeted them. Passing an open window, they looked in upon a library presided over by Clio, Calliope, and Urania; Melpomene and Thalia were disporting themselves in the hall, where some young people were dancing and rehearsing a play; Erato was walking in the garden with her lover, and in the music room Phoebus himself was drilling a tuneful choir.

A mature Apollo was our old friend Laurie, but comely and genial as ever, for time had ripened the freakish boy into a noble man. Care and sorrow, as well as ease and happiness, had done much for him, and the responsibility of carrying out his grandfather's wishes had been a duty most faithfully performed. Prosperity suits some people, and they blossom best in a glow of sunshine; others need the shade, and are the sweeter for a touch of frost. Laurie was one of the former sort, and Amy was another; so life had been a kind of poem to them since they married—not only harmonious and happy, but earnest, useful,

and rich in the beautiful benevolence which can do so much
when wealth and wisdom go hand in hand with charity.

Their house was full of unostentatious beauty and comfort,
and here the art-loving host and hostess attracted and entertained artists of all kinds. Laurie had music enough now, and
was a generous patron to the class he most liked to help. Amy
had her protégées among ambitious young painters and sculp-
tors, and found her own art doubly dear as her daughter grew
old enough to share its labors and delights with her; for she was
one of those who prove that women can be faithful wives and
mothers without sacrificing the special gift bestowed upon them
for their own development and the good of others.

Her sisters knew where to find her, and Jo went at once to
the studio, where mother and daughter worked together. Bess
was busy with the bust of a little child, while her mother added
the last touches to a fine head of her husband. Time seemed to
have stood still with Amy, for happiness had kept her young and
prosperity given her the culture she needed. A stately, graceful
woman, who showed how elegant simplicity could be made by
the taste with which she chose her dress and the grace with
which she wore it. As someone said, "I never know what Mrs.
Laurence has on, but I always receive the impression that she is
the best-dressed lady in the room."

It was evident that she adored her daughter, and well she
might; for the beauty she had longed for seemed, to her fond
eyes at least, to be impersonated in this younger self. Bess inherited her mother's Diana-like figure, blue eyes, fair skin, and
golden hair, tied up in the same classic knot of curls. Also—ah!
never-ending source of joy to Amy—she had her father's handsome nose and mouth, cast in a feminine mold. The severe
simplicity of a long linen pinafore suited her, and she worked
away with the entire absorption of the true artist, unconscious
of the loving eyes upon her, till Aunt Jo came in exclaiming
eagerly, "My dear girls, stop your mud pies and hear the news!"

Both artists dropped their tools and greeted the irrepressible

woman cordially, though genius had been burning splendidly
and her coming spoilt a precious hour. They were in the full
tide of gossip when Laurie, who had been summoned by Meg,
arrived, and sitting down between the sisters, with no barricade
anywhere, listened with interest to the news of Franz and Emil.

"The epidemic has broken out, and now it will rage and ravage your flock. Be prepared for every sort of romance and rash-
ness for the next ten years, Jo. Your boys are growing up and
will plunge headlong into a sea of worse scrapes than any you
have had yet," said Laurie, enjoying her look of mingled delight
and despair.

"I know it, and I hope I shall be able to pull them through
and land them safely; but it's an awful responsibility, for they
will come to me and insist that I can make their poor little loves
run smoothly. I like it, though, and Meg is such a mush of
sentiment she revels in the prospect," answered Jo, feeling
pretty easy about her own boys, whose youth made them safe
for the present.

"I'm afraid she won't revel when our Nat begins to buzz too
near her Daisy. Of course you see what that all means? As
musical director I am also his confidant, and would like to know
what advice to give," said Laurie, soberly.

"Hush! You forget that child," began Jo, nodding toward
Bess, who was at work again.

"Bless you! She's in Athens, and doesn't hear a word. She
ought to leave off, though, and go out. My darling, put the baby
to sleep, and go for a run. Aunt Meg is in the parlor; go and
show her the new pictures till we come," added Laurie, looking
at his tall girl as Pygmalion might have looked at Galatea; for
he considered her the finest statue in the house.

"Yes, Papa. But please tell me if it is good." And Bess obedi-
ently put down her tools, with a lingering glance at the bust.

"My cherished daughter, truth compels me to confess that
one cheek is plumper than the other, and the curls upon its
infant brow are rather too much like horns for perfect grace;

otherwise it rivals Raphael's Chanting Cherubs, and I'm proud of it."

Laurie was laughing as he spoke; for these first attempts were so like Amy's early ones, it was impossible to regard them as soberly as the enthusiastic mamma did.

"You can't see beauty in anything but music," answered Bess, shaking the golden head that made the one bright spot in the cool north lights of the great studio.

"Well, I see beauty in you, dear. And if you are not art, what is? I wish to put a little more nature into you, and get you away from this cold clay and marble into the sunshine, to dance and laugh as the others do. I want a flesh-and-blood girl, not a sweet statue in a gray pinafore, who forgets everything but her work."

As he spoke two dusty hands came round his neck, and Bess said earnestly, punctuating her words with soft touches of her lips, "I never forget *you*, Papa; but I do want to do something beautiful that you may be proud of me by and by. Mamma often tells me to stop, but when we get in here we forget there is any world outside, we are so busy and so happy. Now I'll go and run and sing, and be a girl to please you." And throwing away the apron, Bess vanished from the room, seeming to take all the light with her.

"I'm glad you said that. The dear child *is* too much absorbed in her artistic dreams for one so young. It is my fault, but I sympathize so deeply in it all, I forget to be wise," sighed Amy, carefully covering the baby with a wet towel.

"I think this power of living in our children is one of the sweetest things in the world, but I try to remember what Marmee once said to Meg—that fathers should have their share in the education of both girls and boys; so I leave Ted to his father all I can, and Fritz lends me Rob, whose quiet ways are as restful and good for me as Ted's tempests are for his father. Now I advise you, Amy, to let Bess drop the mud pies for a time, and take up music with Laurie; then she won't be one-sided, and he won't be jealous."

"Hear, hear! A Daniel—a very Daniel!" cried Laurie, well pleased. "I thought you'd lend a hand, Jo, and say a word for me. I *am* a little jealous of Amy, and want more of a share in my girl. Come, my lady, let me have her this summer, and next year, when we go to Rome, I'll give her up to you and high art. Isn't that a fair bargain?"

"I agree. But in trying your hobby, nature, with music thrown in, don't forget that, though only fifteen, our Bess is older than most girls of that age, and cannot be treated like a child. She is so very precious to me, I feel as if I wanted to keep her always as pure and beautiful as the marble she loves so well."

Amy spoke regretfully as she looked about the lovely room where she had spent so many happy hours with this dear child of hers.

" 'Turn and turn about is fair play,' as we used to say when we all wanted to ride on Ellen Tree or wear the russet boots," said Jo, briskly. "So you must share your girl between you, and see who will do the most for her."

"We will," answered the fond parents, laughing at the recollections Jo's proverb brought up to them.

"How I did use to enjoy bouncing on the limb of that old apple tree! No real horse ever gave me half the pleasure or the exercise," said Amy, looking out of the high window as if she saw the dear old orchard again and the little girls at play there.

"And what fun I had with those blessed boots!" laughed Jo. "I've got the relics now. The boys reduced them to rags; but I love them still, and would enjoy a good theatrical stalk in them if it were possible."

"My fondest memories twine about the warming pan and the sausage. What larks we had! And how long ago it seems!" said Laurie, staring at the two women before him as if he found it hard to realize that they ever had been little Amy and riotous Jo.

"Don't suggest that we are growing old, my lord. We have only bloomed; and a very nice bouquet we make with our buds about us," answered Mrs. Amy, shaking out the folds of her rosy muslin with much the air of dainty satisfaction the girl used to show in a new dress.

"Not to mention our thorns and dead leaves," added Jo, with a sigh, for life had never been very easy to her, and even now she had her troubles both within and without.

"Come and have a dish of tea, old dear, and see what the young folks are about. You are tired, and want to be 'stayed with flagons and comforted with apples,' " said Laurie, offering an arm to each sister, and leading them away to afternoon tea, which flowed as freely on Parnassus as the nectar of old.

They found Meg in the summer parlor, an airy and delightful room, full now of afternoon sunshine and the rustle of trees; for the three long windows opened on the garden. The great music room was at one end, and at the other, in a deep alcove hung with purple curtains, a little household shrine had been made. Three portraits hung there, two marble busts stood in the corners, and a couch, an oval table, with its urn of flowers, were the only articles of furniture the nook contained. The busts were John Brooke and Beth—Amy's work—both excellent likenesses, and both full of the placid beauty which always recalls the saying, that "Clay represents life; plaster, death; marble, immortality." On the right, as became the founder of the house, hung the portrait of Mr. Laurence, with its expression of mingled pride and benevolence, as fresh and attractive as when he caught the girl Jo admiring it. Opposite was Aunt March—a legacy to Amy—in an imposing turban, immense sleeves, and long mittens decorously crossed on the front of her plum-colored satin gown. Time had mellowed the severity of her aspect; and the fixed regard of the handsome old gentleman opposite seemed to account for the amiable simper on lips that had not uttered a sharp word for years.

In the place of honor, with the sunshine warm upon it, and a green garland always round it, was Marmee's beloved face, painted with grateful skill by a great artist whom she had befriended when poor and unknown. So beautifully lifelike was it that it seemed to smile down upon her daughters, saying cheerfully, "Be happy: I am with you still."

The three sisters stood a moment looking up at the beloved picture with eyes full of tender reverence and the longing that never left them; for this noble mother had been so much to them that no one could ever fill her place. Only two years since she had gone away to live and love anew, leaving such a sweet memory behind her that it was both an inspiration and a comforter to all the household. They felt this as they drew closer to one another, and Laurie put it into words as he said earnestly, "I can ask nothing better for my child than that she may be a woman like our mother. Please God, she shall be, if I can do it; for I owe the best I have to this dear saint."

Just then a fresh voice began to sing "Ave Maria" in the music room, and Bess unconsciously echoed her father's prayer for her as she dutifully obeyed his wishes. The soft sound of the air Marmee used to sing led the listeners back into the world again from that momentary reaching after the loved and lost, and they sat down together near the open windows enjoying the music, while Laurie brought them tea, making the little service pleasant by the tender care he gave to it.

Nat came in with Demi, soon followed by Ted and Josie, the Professor and his faithful Rob, all anxious to hear more about "the boys." The rattle of cups and tongues grew brisk, and the setting sun saw a cheerful company resting in the bright room after the varied labors of the day.

Professor Bhaer was gray now, but robust and genial as ever; for he had the work he loved, and did it so heartily that the whole college felt his beautiful influence. Rob was as much like him as it was possible for a boy to be, and was already called the "young Professor," he so adored study and closely imitated his honored father in all ways.

"Well, heart's dearest, we go to have our boys again, all two, and may rejoice greatly," said Mr. Bhaer, seating himself beside Jo with a beaming face and a handshake of congratulation.

"Oh, Fritz, I'm so delighted about Emil, and if you approve about Franz also. Did you know Ludmilla? Is it a wise match?" asked Mrs. Jo, handing him her cup of tea and drawing closer, as if she welcomed her refuge in joy as well as sorrow.

"It all goes well. I saw the *Mädchen* when I went over to place Franz. A child then, but most sweet and charming. Blumenthal is satisfied, I think, and the boy will be happy. He is too German to be content away from Vaterland, so we shall have him as a link between the new and the old, and that pleases me much."

"And Emil, he is to be second mate next voyage. Isn't that fine? I'm so happy that both *your* boys have done well; you gave up so much for them and their mother. You make light of it, dear, but I never forget it," said Jo, with her hand in his as sentimentally as if she was a girl again and her Fritz had come a-wooing.

He laughed his cheery laugh, and whispered behind her fan, "If I had not come to America for the poor lads, I never should have found my Jo. The hard times are very sweet now, and I bless Gott for all I seemed to lose, because I gained the blessing of my life."

"Spooning! Spooning! Here's an awful flirtation on the sly," cried Teddy, peering over the fan just at that interesting moment, much to his mother's confusion and his father's amusement; for the Professor never was ashamed of the fact that he still considered his wife the dearest woman in the world. Rob promptly ejected his brother from one window, to see him skip in at the other, while Mrs. Jo shut her fan and held it ready to rap her unruly boy's knuckles if he came near her again.

Nat approached in answer to Mr. Bhaer's beckoning tea-spoon, and stood before them with a face full of the respectful affection he felt for the excellent man who had done so much for him.

"I have the letters ready for thee, my son. They are to old

friends of mine in Leipzig, who will befriend thee in that new life. It is well to have them, for thou wilt be heartbroken with *Heimweh* at the first, Nat, and need comforting," said the Professor, giving him several letters.

"Thanks, sir. Yes, I expect to be pretty lonely till I get started, then my music and the hope of getting on will cheer me up," answered Nat, who both longed and dreaded to leave all these friends behind him and make new ones.

He was a man now; but the blue eyes were as honest as ever, the mouth still a little weak, in spite of the carefully cherished moustache over it, and the broad forehead more plainly than ever betrayed the music-loving nature of the youth. Modest, affectionate, and dutiful, Nat was considered a pleasant though not a brilliant success by Mrs. Jo. She loved and trusted him, and was sure he would do his best, but did not expect that he would be great in any way, unless the stimulus of foreign training and self-dependence made him a better artist and a stronger man than now seemed likely.

"I've marked all your things—or rather, Daisy did—and as soon as your books are collected, we can see about the packing," said Mrs. Jo, who was so used to fitting boys off for all quarters of the globe that a trip to the North Pole would not have been too much for her.

Nat grew red at mention of that name—or was it the last glow of the sunset on his rather pale cheek—and his heart beat happily at the thought of the dear girl working N's and B's on his humble socks and handkerchiefs; for Nat adored Daisy, and the cherished dream of his life was to earn a place for himself as a musician and win this angel for his wife. This hope did more for him than the Professor's counsels, Mrs. Jo's care, or Mr. Laurie's generous help. For her sake he worked, waited, and hoped, finding courage and patience in the dream of that happy future when Daisy should make a little home for him and he fiddle a fortune into her lap.

Mrs. Jo knew this; and though he was not exactly the man she would have chosen for her niece, she felt that Nat would always need just the wise and loving care Daisy could give him, and that without it there was danger of his being one of the amiable and aimless men who fail for want of the right pilot to steer them safely through the world. Mrs. Meg decidedly frowned upon the poor boy's love, and would not hear of giving her dear girl to any but the best man to be found on the face of the earth. She was very kind, but as firm as such gentle souls can be; and Nat fled for comfort to Mrs. Jo, who always espoused the interests of her boys heartily. A new set of anxieties was beginning now that the aforesaid boys were growing up, and she foresaw no end of worry as well as amusement in the love affairs already budding in her flock. Mrs. Meg was usually her best ally and adviser, for she loved romances as well now as when a blooming girl herself. But in this case she hardened her heart, and would not hear a word of entreaty. "Nat was not man enough, never would be, no one knew his family, a musician's life was a hard one; Daisy was too young, five or six years hence when time had proved both perhaps. Let us see what absence will do for him." And that was the end of it, for when the maternal Pelican was roused she could be very firm, though for her precious children she would have plucked her last feather and given the last drop of her blood.

Mrs. Jo was thinking of this as she looked at Nat while he talked with her husband about Leipzig, and she resolved to have a clear understanding with him before he went; for she was used to confidences, and talked freely with her boys about the trials and temptations that beset all lives in the beginning, and so often mar them, for want of the right word at the right moment.

This is the first duty of parents, and no false delicacy should keep them from the watchful care, the gentle warning, which makes self-knowledge and self-control the compass and pilot of the young as they leave the safe harbor of home.

"Plato and his disciples approach," announced irreverent

Teddy, as Mr. March came in with several young men and women about him; for the wise old man was universally beloved, and ministered so beautifully to his flock that many of them thanked him all their lives for the help given to both hearts and souls.

Bess went to him at once, for since Marmee died, Grandpapa was her special care, and it was sweet to see the golden head bend over the silver one as she rolled out his easy chair and waited on him with tender alacrity.

"Aesthetic tea always on tap here, sir; will you have a flowing bowl or a bit of ambrosia?" asked Laurie, who was wandering about with a sugar basin in one hand and a plate of cake in the other; for sweetening cups and feeding the hungry was work he loved.

"Neither, thanks. This child has taken care of me." And Mr. March turned to Bess, who sat on one arm of his chair, holding a glass of fresh milk.

"Long may she live to do it, sir, and I be here to see this pretty contradiction of the song that 'youth and age cannot live together!' " answered Laurie, smiling at the pair.

" 'Crabbed age,' Papa—that makes all the difference in the world," said Bess, quickly, for she loved poetry, and read the best.

> "Wouldst thou see fresh roses grow
> In a reverend bed of snow?"

quoted Mr. March, as Josie came and perched on the other arm, looking like a very thorny little rose; for she had been having a hot discussion with Ted, and had got the worst of it.

"Grandpa, must women always obey men and say they are the wisest, just because they are the strongest?" she cried, looking fiercely at her cousin, who came stalking up with a provoking smile on the boyish face that was always very comical atop of that tall figure.

"Well, my dear, that is the old-fashioned belief, and it will take some time to change it. But I think the woman's hour has struck; and it looks to me as if the boys must do their best, for the girls are abreast now, and may reach the goal first," answered Mr. March, surveying with paternal satisfaction the bright faces of the young women, who were among the best students in the college.

"The poor little Atalantas are sadly distracted and delayed by the obstacles thrown in their way—not golden apples, by any means—but I think they will stand a fair chance when they have learned to run better," laughed Uncle Laurie, stroking Josie's breezy hair, which stood up like the fur of an angry kitten.

"Whole barrels of apples won't stop me when *I* start, and a dozen Teds won't trip me up, though they may try. I'll show him that a woman can act as well, if not better, than a man. It *has* been done, and will be again; and I'll never own that *my* brain isn't as good as his, though it may be smaller," cried the excited young person.

"If you shake your head in that violent way, you'll addle what brains you have got; and I'd take care of 'em, if I were you," began teasing Ted.

"What started this civil war?" asked Grandpa, with a gentle emphasis on the adjective, which caused the combatants to calm their ardor a little.

"Why, we were pegging away at the Iliad and came to where Zeus tells Juno not to inquire into his plans or he'll whip her, and Jo was disgusted because Juno meekly hushed up. I said it was all right, and agreed with the old fellow that women didn't know much and ought to obey men," explained Ted, to the great amusement of his hearers.

"Goddesses may do as they like, but those Greek and Trojan women were poor-spirited things if they minded men who couldn't fight their own battles and had to be hustled off by Pallas, and Venus, and Juno, when they were going to get beaten. The idea of two armies stopping and sitting down while a pair of heroes flung stones at one another! I don't think much of your old Homer. Give me Napoleon or Grant for my hero."

Josie's scorn was as funny as if a humming bird scolded at an ostrich, and everyone laughed as she sniffed at the immortal poet and criticized the gods.

"Napoleon's Juno had a nice time, didn't she? That's just the way girls argue—first one way and then the other," jeered Ted.

"Like Johnson's young lady, who was 'not categorical, but all wiggle-waggle,' " added Uncle Laurie, enjoying the battle immensely.

"I was only speaking of them as soldiers. But if you come to the woman side of it, wasn't Grant a kind husband and Mrs. Grant a happy woman? He didn't threaten to whip her if she asked a natural question; and if Napoleon did do wrong about Josephine, he could fight, and didn't want any Minerva to come fussing over him. They *were* a stupid set, from dandified Paris to Achilles sulking in his ships, and I won't change my opinion for all the Hectors and Agamemnons in Greece," said Josie, still unconquered.

"You can fight like a Trojan, that's evident; and we will be the two obedient armies looking on while you and Ted have it out," began Uncle Laurie, assuming the attitude of a warrior leaning on his spear.

"I fear we must give it up, for Pallas is about to descend and carry off our Hector," said Mr. March, smiling, as Jo came to remind her son that suppertime was near.

"We will fight it out later when there are no goddesses to interfere," said Teddy, as he turned away with unusual alacrity, remembering the treat in store.

"Conquered by a muffin, by Jove!" called Josie after him, exulting in an opportunity to use the classical exclamation forbidden to her sex.

But Ted shot a Parthian arrow as he retired in good order by replying, with a highly virtuous expression, "Obedience is a soldier's first duty."

Bent on her woman's privilege of having the last word, Josie
ran after him, but never uttered the scathing speech upon her
lips, for a very brown young man in a blue suit came leaping up
the steps with a cheery "Ahoy! Ahoy! Where is everybody?"

"Emil! Emil!" cried Josie, and in a moment Ted was upon
him, and the late enemies ended their fray in a joyful welcome
to the newcomer.

Muffins were forgotten; and towing their cousin like two fussy
little tugs with a fine merchantman, the children returned to the
parlor, where Emil kissed all the women and shook hands with
all men except his uncle; him he embraced in the good old
German style, to the great delight of the observers.

"Didn't think I could get off today, but found I could, and
steered straight for old Plum. Not a soul there, so I luffed and
bore away for Parnassus, and here is every man Jack of you.
Bless your hearts, how glad I am to see you all!" exclaimed the
sailor boy, beaming at them, as he stood with his legs apart as if
he still felt the rocking deck under his feet.

"You ought to 'shiver your timbers,' not 'bless our hearts,'
Emil; it's not nautical at all. Oh, how nice and shippy and tarry
you do smell!" said Josie, sniffing at him with great enjoyment
of the fresh sea odors he brought with him. This was her favorite cousin, and she was his pet; so she knew that the bulging
pockets of the blue jacket contained treasures for her at least.

"Avast, my hearty, and let me take soundings before you
dive," laughed Emil, understanding her affectionate caresses,
and holding her off with one hand while with the other he
rummaged out sundry foreign little boxes and parcels marked
with different names, and handed them round with appropriate
remarks, which caused much laughter, for Emil was a wag.

"There's a hawser that will hold our little cockboat still about
five minutes," he said, throwing a necklace of pretty pink coral
over Josie's head. "And here's something the mermaids sent to
Undine," he added, handing Bess a string of pearly shells on a
silver chain. "I thought Daisy would like a fiddle, and Nat can

find her a *beau,*" continued the sailor, with a laugh, as he undid a dainty filagree brooch in the shape of a violin.

"I know she will, and I'll take it to her," answered Nat, as he vanished, glad of an errand, and sure that *he* could find Daisy though Emil had missed her.

Emil chuckled, and handed out a quaintly carved bear whose head opened, showing a capacious inkstand. This he presented, with a scrape, to Aunt Jo.

"Knowing your fondness for these fine animals, I brought this one to your pen."

"Very good, Commodore! Try again," said Mrs. Jo, much pleased with her gift, which caused the Professor to prophesy "works of Shakespeare" from its depths, so great would be the inspiration of the beloved bruin.

"As Aunt Meg *will* wear caps, in spite of her youth, I got Ludmilla to get me some bits of lace. Hope you'll like 'em." And out of a soft paper came some filmy things, one of which soon lay like a net of snowflakes on Mrs. Meg's pretty hair.

"I couldn't find anything swell enough for Aunt Amy, because she has everything she wants, so I brought a little picture that always makes me think of her when Bess was a baby." And he handed her an oval ivory locket, on which was painted a golden-haired Madonna with a rosy child folded in her blue mantle.

"How lovely!" cried everyone; and Aunt Amy at once hung it about her neck on the blue ribbon from Bess's hair, charmed with her gift, for it recalled the happiest year of her life.

"Now, I flatter myself I've got just the thing for Nan, neat but not gaudy, a sort of sign you see, and very appropriate for a doctor," said Emil, proudly displaying a pair of lava earrings shaped like little skulls.

"Horrid!" And Bess, who hated ugly things, turned her eyes to her own pretty shells.

"She won't wear earrings," said Josie.

"Well, she'll enjoy punching your ears then. She's never so

happy as when she's overhauling her fellow creatures and going for 'em with a knife," answered Emil, undisturbed. "I've got a lot of plunder for you fellows in my chest, but I knew I should have no peace till my cargo for the girls was unloaded. Now tell me all the news." And, seated on Amy's best marble-topped table, the sailor swung his legs and talked at the rate of ten knots an hour, till Aunt Jo carried them all off to a grand family tea in honor of the Commodore.

CHAPTER 3

JO'S LAST SCRAPE

THE MARCH FAMILY had enjoyed a great many surprises in the course of their varied career, but the greatest of all was when the Ugly Duckling turned out to be, not a swan, but a golden goose, whose literary eggs found such an unexpected market that in ten years Jo's wildest and most cherished dream actually came true. How or why it happened she never clearly understood, but all of a sudden she found herself famous in a small way, and, better still, with a snug little fortune in her pocket to clear away the obstacles of the present and assure the future of her boys.

It began during a bad year when everything went wrong at Plumfield; times were hard, the school dwindled, Jo overworked herself and had a long illness; Laurie and Amy were abroad, and the Bhaers too proud to ask help even of those as near and dear as this generous pair. Confined to her room, Jo got desperate over the state of affairs, till she fell back upon the long-disused pen as the only thing she could do to help fill up the gaps in the income. A book for girls being wanted by a certain publisher, she hastily scribbled a little story describing a few

scenes and adventures in the lives of herself and sisters—
though boys were more in her line—and with very slight hopes
of success sent it out to seek its fortune.

Things always went by contraries with Jo. Her first book, labored over for years, and launched full of the high hopes and
ambitious dreams of youth, floundered on its voyage, though
the wreck continued to float long afterward, to the profit of the
publisher at least. The hastily written story, sent away with no
thought beyond the few dollars it might bring, sailed with a fair
wind and a wise pilot at the helm straight into public favor, and
came home heavily laden with an unexpected cargo of gold and
glory.

A more astonished woman probably never existed than Josephine Bhaer when her little ship came into port with flags flying,
cannon that had been silent before now booming gaily, and,
better than all, many kind faces rejoicing with her, many
friendly hands grasping hers with cordial congratulations. After
that it was plain sailing, and she merely had to load her ships
and send them off on prosperous trips, to bring home stores of
comfort for all she loved and labored for.

The fame she never did quite accept; for it takes very little
fire to make a great deal of smoke nowadays, and notoriety is
not real glory. The fortune she could not doubt, and gratefully
received, though it was not half so large a one as a generous
world reported it to be. The tide having turned continued to
rise, and floated the family comfortably into a snug harbor
where the older members could rest secure from storms, and
whence the younger ones could launch their boats for the voyage of life.

All manner of happiness, peace, and plenty came in those
years to bless the patient waiters, hopeful workers, and devout
believers in the wisdom and justice of Him who sends disappointment, poverty, and sorrow to try the love of human hearts
and make success the sweeter when it comes. The world saw the
prosperity, and kind souls rejoiced over the improved fortunes

of the family; but the success Jo valued most, the happiness that nothing could change or take away, few knew much about.

It was the power of making her mother's last years happy and serene; to see the burden of care laid down forever, the weary hands at rest, the dear face untroubled by any anxiety, and the tender heart free to pour itself out in the wise charity which was its delight. As a girl, Jo's favorite plan had been a room where Marmee could sit in peace and enjoy herself after her hard, heroic life. Now the dream had become a happy fact, and Marmee sat in her pleasant chamber with every comfort and luxury about her, loving daughters to wait on her as infirmities increased, a faithful mate to lean upon, and grandchildren to brighten the twilight of life with their dutiful affection. A very precious time to all, for she rejoiced as only mothers can in the good fortunes of their children. She had lived to reap the harvest she sowed; had seen prayers answered, hopes blossom, good gifts bear fruit, peace and prosperity bless the home she had made; and then, like some brave, patient angel, whose work was done, turned her face heavenward, glad to rest.

This was the sweet and sacred side of the change; but it had its droll and thorny one, as all things have in this curious world of ours. After the first surprise, incredulity, and joy, which came to Jo, with the ingratitude of human nature, she soon tired of renown, and began to resent her loss of liberty. For suddenly the admiring public took possession of her and all her affairs, past, present, and to come. Strangers demanded to look at her, question, advise, warn, congratulate, and drive her out of her wits by well-meant but very wearisome attentions. If she declined to open her heart to them, they reproached her; if she refused to endow pet charities, relieve private wants, or sympathize with every ill and trial known to humanity, she was called hardhearted, selfish, and haughty; if she found it impossible to answer the piles of letters sent her, she was neglectful of her duty to the admiring public; and if she preferred the privacy of

home to the pedestal upon which she was requested to pose,
"the airs of literary people" were freely criticized.

She did her best for the children, they being the public for
whom she wrote, and labored stoutly to supply the demand
always in the mouths of voracious youth—"More stories; more
right away!" Her family objected to this devotion at their ex-
pense, and her health suffered; but for a time she gratefully
offered herself up on the altar of juvenile literature, feeling that
she owed a good deal to the little friends in whose sight she had
found favor after twenty years of effort.

But a time came when her patience gave out; and wearying of
being a lion, she became a bear in nature as in name, and
retiring to her den, growled awfully when ordered out. Her family enjoyed the fun, and had small sympathy with her trials, but
Jo came to consider it the worst scrape of her life; for liberty
had always been her dearest possession, and it seemed to be
fast going from her. Living in a lantern soon loses its charms,
and she was too old, too tired, and too busy to like it. She felt
that she had done all that could reasonably be required of her
when autographs, photographs, and autobiographical sketches
had been sown broadcast over the land; when artists had taken
her home in all its aspects, and reporters had taken her in the
grim one she always assumed on these trying occasions; when a
series of enthusiastic boarding schools had ravaged her grounds
for trophies, and a steady stream of amiable pilgrims had worn
her doorsteps with their respectful feet; when servants left after
a week's trial of the bell that rang all day; when her husband
was forced to guard her at meals, and the boys to cover her
retreat out of back windows on certain occasions when enter-
prising guests walked in unannounced at unfortunate moments.

A sketch of one day may perhaps explain the state of things,
offer some excuse for the unhappy woman, and give a hint to
the autograph fiend now rampant in the land; for it is a true
tale.

"There ought to be a law to protect unfortunate authors,"

said Mrs. Jo one morning soon after Emil's arrival, when the mail brought her an unusually large and varied assortment of letters. "To me it is a more vital subject than international copyright; for time is money, peace is health, and I lose both with no return but less respect for my fellow creatures and a wild desire to fly into the wilderness, since I cannot shut my doors even in free America."

"Lion hunters are awful when in search of their prey. If they could change places for a while it would do them good; and they'd see what bores they were when they 'do themselves the honor of calling to express their admiration of our charming work,' " quoted Ted, with a bow to his parent, now frowning over twelve requests for autographs.

"I have made up my mind on one point," said Mrs. Jo with great firmness. "I will *not* answer this kind of letter. I've sent at least six to this boy, and he probably sells them. This girl writes from a seminary, and if I send her one all the other girls will at once write for more. All begin by saying that they know they intrude, and that I am of course annoyed by these requests; but they venture to ask because I like boys, or they like the books, or it is only one. Emerson and Whittier put these things in the wastepaper basket; and though only a literary nursery maid who provides moral pap for the young, I will follow their illustrious example; for I shall have no time to eat or sleep if I try to satisfy these dear unreasonable children." And Mrs. Jo swept away the entire batch with a sigh of relief.

"I'll open the others and let you eat your breakfast in peace, *liebe Mutter*," said Rob, who often acted as her secretary. "Here's one from the South." And breaking an imposing seal, he read:

MADAM, As it has pleased Heaven to bless your efforts with a large fortune, I feel no hesitation in asking you to supply funds to purchase a new communion service for our

church. To whatever denomination you belong, you will of
course respond with liberality to such a request.

> Respectfully yours,   MRS. X. Y. ZAVIER

"Send a civil refusal, dear. All I have to give must go to feed
and clothe the poor at my gates. That is my thank offering for
success. Go on," answered his mother, with a grateful glance
about her happy home.

"A literary youth of eighteen proposes that you put your
name to a novel he has written; and after the first edition your
name is to be taken off and his put on. There's a cool proposal
for you. I guess you won't agree to that, in spite of your soft-
heartedness towards most of the young scribblers."

"Couldn't be done. Tell him so kindly, and don't let him send
the manuscript. I have seven on hand now, and barely time to
read my own," said Mrs. Jo, pensively fishing a small letter out
of the slop bowl and opening it with care, because the downhill
address suggested that a child wrote it.

"I will answer this myself. A little sick girl wants a book, and
she shall have it, but I can't write sequels to all the rest to please
her. I should never come to an end if I tried to suit these
voracious little Oliver Twists, clamoring for more. What next,
Robin?"

"This is short and sweet."

> DEAR MRS. BHAER, I am now going to give you my opinion
> of your works. I have read them all many times, and call
> them first-rate. Please go ahead.
>
> Your admirer,   BILLY BABCOCK

"Now that is what I like. Billy is a man of sense and a critic
worth having, since he has read my works many times before
expressing his opinion. He asks for no answer, so send my
thanks and regards."

"Here's a lady in England with seven girls, and she wishes to know your views upon education. Also what careers they shall follow—the oldest being twelve. Don't wonder she's worried," laughed Rob.

"I'll try to answer it. But as I have no girls, my opinion isn't worth much and will probably shock her, as I shall tell her to let them run and play and build up good, stout bodies before she talks about careers. They will soon show what they want, if they are let alone, and not all run in the same mold."

"Here's a fellow who wants to know what sort of a girl he shall marry, and if you know of any like those in your stories."

"Give him Nan's address, and see what he'll get," proposed Ted, privately resolving to do it himself if possible.

"This is from a lady who wants you to adopt her child and lend her money to study art abroad for a few years. Better take it, and try your hand at a girl, mother."

"No, thank you, I will keep to my own line of business. What is that blotted one? It looks rather awful, to judge by the ink," asked Mrs. Jo, who beguiled her daily task by trying to guess from the outside what was inside her many letters. This proved to be a poem from an insane admirer, to judge by its incoherent style.

TO J.M.B.

Oh, were I a heliotrope,
  I would play poet,
And blow a breeze of fragrance
  To you; and none should know it.

Your form like the stately elm
  When Phoebus gilds the morning ray;
Your cheeks like the ocean bed
  That blooms a rose in May.

Your words are wise and bright,
  I bequeath them to you a legacy given;

And when your spirit takes its flight,
    May it bloom a flower in heaven.

My tongue in flattering language spoke,
And sweeter silence never broke
In busiest street or loneliest glen.
I take you with the flashes of my pen.

Consider the lilies, how they grow;
    They toil not, yet are fair,
Gems and flowers and Solomon's seal.
    The geranium of the world is J. M. Bhaer.

JAMES

While the boys shouted over this effusion—which is a true
one—their mother read several liberal offers from budding
magazines for her to edit them gratis; one long letter from a
young girl inconsolable because her favorite hero died, and
"would dear Mrs. Bhaer rewrite the tale, and make it end
good?"; another from an irate boy denied an autograph, who
darkly foretold financial ruin and loss of favor if she did not
send him and all other fellows who asked autographs, photographs, and autobiographical sketches; a minister wished to
know her religion; and an undecided maiden asked which of her
two lovers she should marry. These samples will suffice to show
a few of the claims made on a busy woman's time, and make my
readers pardon Mrs. Jo if she did not carefully reply to all.

"That job is done. Now I will dust a bit, and then go to my
work. I'm all behindhand, and serials can't wait, so deny me to
everybody, Mary. I won't see Queen Victoria if she comes today." And Mrs. Bhaer threw down her napkin as if defying all
creation.

"I hope the day will go well with thee, my dearest," answered
her husband, who had been busy with his own voluminous cor-
respondence. "I will dine at college with Professor Plock, who is
to visit us today. The *Jünglings* can lunch on Parnassus; so thou

shalt have a quiet time." And smoothing the worried lines out
of her forehead with his good-bye kiss, the excellent man
marched away, both pockets full of books, an old umbrella in
one hand, and a bag of stones for the geology class in the other.

"If all literary women had such thoughtful angels for husbands, they would live longer and write more. Perhaps that
wouldn't be a blessing to the world though, as most of us write
too much now," said Mrs. Jo, waving her feather duster to her
spouse, who responded with flourishes of the umbrella as he
went down the avenue.

Rob started for school at the same time, looking so much like
him with his books and bag and square shoulders and steady air
that his mother laughed as she turned away, saying heartily,
"Bless both my dear professors, for better creatures never
lived!"

Emil was already gone to his ship in the city; but Ted lingered
to steal the address he wanted, ravage the sugar bowl, and talk
with "Mum," for the two had great larks together.

Mrs. Jo always arranged her own parlor, refilled her vases,
and gave the little touches that left it cool and neat for the day.
Going to draw down the curtain, she beheld an artist sketching
on the lawn, and groaned as she hastily retired to the back
window to shake her duster.

At that moment the bell rang and the sound of wheels was
heard in the road.

"I'll go; Mary lets 'em in." And Ted smoothed his hair as he
made for the hall.

"Can't see anyone. Give me a chance to fly upstairs," whispered Mrs. Jo, preparing to escape. But before she could do so,
a man appeared at the door with a card in his hand. Ted met
him with a stern air, and his mother dodged behind the window
curtains to bide her time to escape.

"I am doing a series of articles for the 'Saturday Tattler,' and
I called to see Mrs. Bhaer the first of all," began the newcomer
in the insinuating tone of his tribe, while his quick eyes were

taking in all they could, experience having taught him to make the most of his time, as his visits were usually short ones.

"Mrs. Bhaer never sees reporters, sir."

"But a few moments will be all I ask," said the man, edging his way further in.

"You can't see her, for she is out," replied Teddy, as a backward glance showed him that his unhappy parent had vanished —through the window, he supposed, as she sometimes did when hard bestead.

"Very sorry. I'll call again. Is this her study? Charming room!" And the intruder fell back on the parlor, bound to see something and bag a fact if he died in the attempt.

"It is not," said Teddy, gently but firmly backing him down the hall, devoutly hoping that his mother had escaped round the corner of the house.

"If you could tell me Mrs. Bhaer's age and birthplace, date of marriage, and number of children, I should be much obliged," continued the unabashed visitor as he tripped over the door-mat.

"She is about sixty, born in Nova Zembla, married just forty years ago today, and has eleven daughters. Anything else, sir?" And Ted's sober face was such a funny contrast to his ridiculous reply that the reporter owned himself routed, and retired laughing just as a lady followed by three beaming girls came up the steps.

"We are all the way from Oshkosh, and couldn't go home without seein' dear Aunt Jo. My girls just admire her works, and lot on gettin' a sight of her. I know it's early; but we are goin' to see Holmes and Longfeller, and the rest of the celebrities, so we ran out here fust thing. Mrs. Erastus Kingsbury Parmalee, of Oshkosh, tell her. We don't mind waitin'; we can look round a spell if she ain't ready to see folks yet."

All this was uttered with such rapidity that Ted could only stand gazing at the buxom damsels, who fixed their six blue eyes upon him so beseechingly that his native gallantry made it impossible to deny them a civil reply at least.

"Mrs. Bhaer is not visible today—out just now, I believe; but you can see the house and grounds if you like," he murmured, falling back as the four pressed in gazing rapturously about them.

"Oh, thank you! Sweet, pretty place I'm sure! That's where she writes, ain't it? Do tell me if that's her picture! Looks just as I imagined her!"

With these remarks the ladies paused before a fine engraving of the Hon. Mrs. Norton, with a pen in her hand and a rapt expression of countenance, likewise a diadem and a pearl necklace.

Keeping his gravity with an effort, Teddy pointed to a very bad portrait of Mrs. Jo, which hung behind the door, and afforded her much amusement, it was so dismal, in spite of a curious effect of light upon the end of the nose and cheeks as red as the chair she sat in.

"This was taken for my mother; but it is not very good," he said, enjoying the struggles of the girls not to look dismayed at the sad difference between the real and the ideal. The youngest, aged twelve, could not conceal her disappointment, and turned away, feeling as so many of us have felt when we discover that our idols are very ordinary men and women.

"I thought she'd be about sixteen and have her hair braided in two tails down her back. I don't care about seeing her now," said the honest child walking off to the hall door, leaving her mother to apologize, and her sisters to declare that the bad portrait was "perfectly lovely, so speaking and poetic, you know, 'specially about the brow."

"Come, girls, we must be goin', if we want to get through today. You can leave your albums and have them sent when Mrs. Bhaer has written a sentiment in 'em. We are a thousand times obliged. Give our best love to your ma, and tell her we are so sorry not to see her."

Just as Mrs. Erastus Kingsbury Parmalee uttered the words her eye fell upon a middle-aged woman in a large checked apron, with a handkerchief tied over her head, busily dusting an end room which looked like a study.

"One peep at her sanctum since she is out," cried the enthusiastic lady, and swept across the hall with her flock before Teddy could warn his mother, whose retreat had been cut off by the artist in front, the reporter at the back part of the house— for he hadn't gone—and the ladies in the hall.

"They've got her!" thought Teddy, in comical dismay. "No use for her to play housemaid since they've seen the portrait."

Mrs. Jo did her best, and being a good actress, would have escaped if the fatal picture had not betrayed her. Mrs. Parmalee paused at the desk, and regardless of the meerschaum that lay there, the man's slippers close by, and a pile of letters directed to "Prof. F. Bhaer," she clasped her hands, exclaiming impressively, "Girls, this is the spot where she wrote those sweet, those moral tales which have thrilled us to the soul! Could I—ah, could I take one morsel of paper, an old pen, a postage stamp even, as a memento of this gifted woman?"

"Yes'm, help yourselves," replied the maid, moving away with a glance at the boy whose eyes were now full of a merriment he could not suppress.

The oldest girl saw it, guessed the truth, and a quick look at the woman in the apron confirmed her suspicion. Touching her mother, she whispered, "Ma, it's Mrs. Bhaer herself. I know it is."

"No? Yes? It is! Well, I do declare, how nice that is!" And hastily pursuing the unhappy woman, who was making for the door, Mrs. Parmalee cried eagerly, "Don't mind us! I know you're busy, but just let me take your hand and then we'll go."

Giving herself up for lost, Mrs. Jo turned and presented her hand like a tea tray, submitting to have it heartily shaken, as the matron said, with somewhat alarming hospitality, "If ever you come to Oshkosh, your feet won't be allowed to touch the pavement, for you'll be borne in the arms of the populace, we shall be so dreadful glad to see you."

Mentally resolving never to visit that effusive town, Jo responded as cordially as she could; and having written her name in the albums, provided each visitor with a memento, and kissed them all round, they at last departed, to call on "Longfeller, Holmes, and the rest"—who were all out, it is devoutly to be hoped.

"You villain, why didn't you give me a chance to whip away? Oh, my dear, what fibs you told that man! I hope we shall be forgiven our sins in this line, but I don't know what *is* to become of us if we don't dodge. So many against one isn't fair play." And Mrs. Jo hung up her apron in the hall closet, with a groan at the trials of her lot.

"More people coming up the avenue! Better dodge while the coast is clear! I'll head them off!" cried Teddy, looking back from the steps, as he was departing to school.

Mrs. Jo flew upstairs, and having locked her door calmly viewed a young ladies' seminary camp on the lawn, and being denied the house, proceed to enjoy themselves by picking the flowers, doing up their hair, eating lunch, and freely expressing their opinion of the place and its possessors before they went.

A few hours of quiet followed, and she was just settling down to a long afternoon of hard work, when Rob came home to tell her that the Young Men's Christian Union would visit the college, and two or three of the fellows whom she knew wanted to pay their respects to her on the way.

"It is going to rain, so they won't come, I daresay; but Father thought you'd like to be ready, in case they do call. You always see the boys, you know, though you harden your heart to the poor girls," said Rob, who had heard from his brother about the morning visitations.

"Boys don't gush, so I can stand it. The last time I let in a party of girls, one fell into my arms and said, 'Darling, love me!'

I wanted to shake her," answered Mrs. Jo, wiping her pen with energy.

"You may be sure the fellows won't do it, but they *will* want autographs, so you'd better be prepared with a few dozen," said Rob, laying out a quire of notepaper, being a hospitable youth and sympathizing with those who admired his mother.

"They can't outdo the girls. At X College I really believe I wrote three hundred during the day I was there, and I left a pile of cards and albums on my table when I came away. It is one of the most absurd and tiresome manias that ever afflicted the world."

Nevertheless Mrs. Jo wrote her name a dozen times, put on her black silk, and resigned herself to the impending call, praying for rain, however, as she returned to her work.

The shower came, and feeling quite secure, she rumpled up her hair, took off her cuffs, and hurried to finish her chapter; for thirty pages a day was her task, and she liked to have it well done before evening. Josie had brought some flowers for the vases, and was just putting the last touches when she saw several umbrellas bobbing down the hill.

"They are coming, Aunty! I see Uncle hurrying across the field to receive them," she called at the stairfoot.

"Keep an eye on them, and let me know when they enter the avenue. It will take but a minute to tidy up and run down," answered Mrs. Jo, scribbling away for dear life, because serials wait for no man, not even the whole Christian Union *en masse.*

"There are more than two or three. I see half a dozen at least," called sister Ann from the hall door. "No! A dozen, I do believe. Aunty, look out! They are all coming! What *shall* we do?" And Josie quailed at the idea of facing the black throng rapidly approaching.

"Mercy on us, there are hundreds! Run and put a tub in the back entry for their umbrellas to drip into. Tell them to go down the hall and leave them, and pile their hats on the table; the tree won't hold them all. No use to get mats. My poor carpets!"

And down went Mrs. Jo to prepare for the invasion, while Josie and the maids flew about dismayed at the prospect of so many muddy boots.

On they came, a long line of umbrellas, with splashed legs and flushed faces underneath; for the gentlemen had been having a good time all over the town, undisturbed by the rain. Professor Bhaer met them at the gate, and was making a little speech of welcome, when Mrs. Jo, touched by their bedraggled state, appeared at the door, beckoning them in. Leaving their host to orate bareheaded in the wet, the young men hastened up the steps, merry, warm, and eager, clutching off their hats as they came, and struggling with their umbrellas, as the order was passed to march in and stack arms.

Tramp, tramp, tramp, down the hall went seventy-five pairs of boots; soon seventy-five umbrellas dripped sociably in the hospitable tub, while their owners swarmed all over the lower part of the house; and seventy-five hearty hands were shaken by the hostess without a murmur, though some were wet, some very warm, and nearly all bore trophies of the day's ramble. One impetuous party flourished a small turtle as he made his compliments; another had a load of sticks cut from noted spots; and all begged for some memento of Plumfield. A pile of cards mysteriously appeared on the table, with a written request for autographs; and despite her morning vow, Mrs. Jo wrote every one, while her husband and boys did the honors of the house.

Josie fled to the back parlor, but was discovered by exploring youths, and mortally insulted by one of them, who innocently inquired if she was Mrs. Bhaer. The reception did not last long, and the end was better than the beginning; for the rain ceased, and a rainbow shone beautifully over them as the good fellows stood upon the lawn singing sweetly for a farewell. A happy omen, that bow of promise arched over the young heads, as if Heaven smiled upon their union, and showed them that above the muddy earth and rainy skies the blessed sun still shone for all.

Three cheers, and then away they went, leaving a pleasant recollection of their visit to amuse the family as they scraped the mud off the carpets with shovels and emptied the tub half-full of water.

"Nice, honest, hardworking fellows, and I don't begrudge my half-hour at all; but I *must* finish, so don't let anyone disturb me till teatime," said Mrs. Jo, leaving Mary to shut up the house; for Papa and the boys had gone off with the guests, and Josie had run home to tell her mother about the fun at Aunt Jo's.

Peace reigned for an hour, then the bell rang, and Mary came giggling up to say, "A queer kind of a lady wants to know if she can catch a grasshopper in the garden."

"A what?" cried Mrs. Jo, dropping her pen with a blot; for of all the odd requests ever made, this was the oddest.

"A grasshopper, ma'am. I said you was busy, and asked what she wanted, and says she, 'I've got grasshoppers from the grounds of several famous folks, and I want one from Plumfield to add to my collection.' Did you ever?" And Mary giggled again at the idea.

"Tell her to take all there are and welcome. I shall be glad to get rid of them; always bouncing in my face and getting in my dress," laughed Mrs. Jo.

Mary retired, to return in a moment nearly speechless with merriment.

"She's much obliged, ma'am, and she'd like an old gown or a pair of stockings of yours to put in a rug she's making. Got a vest of Emerson's, she says, and a pair of Mr. Holmes's trousers, and a dress of Mrs. Stowe's. She must be crazy!"

"Give her that old red shawl, then I shall make a gay show among the great ones in that astonishing rug. Yes, they are all lunatics, these lion hunters; but this seems to be a harmless maniac, for she doesn't take my time and gives me a good laugh," said Mrs. Jo, returning to her work after a glance from the window, which showed her a tall, thin lady in rusty black, skipping wildly to and fro on the lawn in pursuit of the lively insect she wanted.

No more interruptions till the light began to fade, then Mary popped her head in to say a gentleman wished to see Mrs. Bhaer, and wouldn't take no for an answer.

"He must. I shall *not* go down. This has been an awful day, and I won't be disturbed again," replied the harassed authoress, pausing in the midst of the grand *finale* of her chapter.

"I told him so, ma'am; but he walked right in as bold as brass. I guess he's another crazy one, and I declare I'm 'most afraid of him, he's so big and black, and cool as cucumbers, though I will say he's good-looking," added Mary, with a simper; for the stranger had evidently found favor in her sight despite his boldness.

"My day has been ruined, and I *will* have this last half-hour to finish. Tell him to go away; I *won't* go down," cried Mrs. Jo, fiercely.

Mary went; and listening, in spite of herself, her mistress heard first a murmur of voices, then a cry from Mary, and remembering the ways of reporters, also that her maid was both pretty and timid, Mrs. Bhaer flung down her pen and went to the rescue. Descending with her most majestic air she demanded in an awe-inspiring voice, as she paused to survey the somewhat brigandish intruder who seemed to be storming the staircase which Mary was gallantly defending, *"Who* is this person who insists on remaining when I have declined to see him?"

"I'm sure I don't know, ma'am. He won't give no name, and says you'll be sorry if you don't see him," answered Mary, retiring flushed and indignant from her post.

"Won't you be sorry?" asked the stranger, looking up with a pair of black eyes full of laughter, the flash of white teeth through a long beard, and both hands out as he boldly approached the irate lady.

Mrs. Jo gave one keen look, for the voice was familiar; then completed Mary's bewilderment by throwing both arms round the brigand's neck, exclaiming joyfully, "My dearest boy, where did you come from?"

"California, on purpose to see you, Mother Bhaer. Now won't you be sorry if I go away?" answered Dan, with a hearty kiss.

"To think of my ordering you out of the house when I've been longing to see you for a year," laughed Mrs. Jo, as she went down to have a good talk with her returned wanderer, who enjoyed the joke immensely.

CHAPTER 4

DAN

Mrs. Jo often thought that Dan had Indian blood in him, not only because of his love of a wild, wandering life, but his appearance; for as he grew up, this became more striking. At twenty-five he was very tall, with sinewy limbs, a keen, dark face, and the alert look of one whose senses were all alive; rough in manner, full of energy, quick with word and blow, eyes full of the old fire, always watchful as if used to keep guard, and a general air of vigor and freshness very charming to those who knew the dangers and delights of his adventurous life. He was looking his best as he sat talking with "Mother Bhaer," one strong brown hand in hers, and a world of affection in his voice as he said, "Forget old friends! How could I forget the only home I ever knew? Why, I was in such a hurry to come and tell my good luck that I didn't stop to fix up, you see; though I knew you'd think I looked more like a wild buffalo than ever," with a shake of his shaggy black head, a tug at his beard, and a laugh that made the room ring.

"I like it; I always had a fancy for banditti—and you look just like one. Mary, being a newcomer, was frightened at your looks and manners. Josie won't know you, but Ted will recognize his Danny in spite of the big beard and flowing mane. They will all be here soon to welcome you; so before they come tell me more about yourself. Why, Dan, dear! It's nearly two years since you were here! Has it gone well with you?" asked Mrs. Jo, who had been listening with maternal interest to his account of life in California, and the unexpected success of a small investment he had made.

"First-rate! I don't care for the money, you know. I only want a trifle to pay my way—rather earn as I go, and not be bothered with the care of a lot. It's the fun of the thing coming to me, and my being able to give away, that I like. No use to lay up; I shan't live to be old and need it—my sort never do," said Dan, looking as if his little fortune rather oppressed him.

"But if you marry and settle somewhere, as I hope you will, you must have something to begin with, my son. So be prudent and invest your money; don't give it away, for rainy days come to all of us, and dependence would be very hard for you to bear," answered Mrs. Jo with a sage air, though she liked to see that the money-making fever had not seized her lucky boy yet.

Dan shook his head, and glanced about the room as if he already found it rather confined and longed for all out-of-doors again.

"Who would marry a jack-o'-lantern like me? Women like a steady-going man; I shall never be that."

"My dear boy, when I was a girl I liked just such adventurous fellows as you are. Anything fresh and daring, free and romantic, is always attractive to us womenfolk. Don't be discouraged. You'll find an anchor some day, and be content to take shorter voyages and bring home a good cargo."

"What should you say if I brought you an Indian squaw some day?" asked Dan, with a glimmer of mischief in the eyes that rested on a marble bust of Galatea gleaming white and lovely in the corner.

"Welcome her heartily, if she was a good one. Is there a

prospect of it?" and Mrs. Jo peered at him with the interest which even literary ladies take in love affairs.

"Not at present, thank you. I'm too busy 'to gallivant,' as Ted calls it. How is the boy?" asked Dan, skillfully turning the conversation, as if he had had enough of sentiment.

Mrs. Jo was off at once, and expatiated upon the talents and virtues of her sons till they came bursting in and fell upon Dan like two affectionate young bears, finding a vent for their joyful emotions in a sort of friendly wrestling match, in which both got worsted, of course, for the hunter soon settled them. The Professor followed, and tongues went like mill clappers while Mary lighted up and cook devoted herself to an unusually good supper, instinctively divining that this guest was a welcome one.

After tea Dan was walking up and down the long rooms as he talked, with occasional trips into the hall for a fresher breath of air, his lungs seeming to need more than those of civilized people. In one of these trips he saw a white figure framed in the dark doorway, and paused to look at it. Bess paused also, not recognizing her old friend, and quite unconscious of the pretty picture she made standing, tall and slender, against the soft gloom of the summer night, with her golden hair like a halo round her head, and the ends of a white shawl blown out like wings by the cool wind sweeping through the hall.

"Is it Dan?" she asked, coming in with a gracious smile and an outstretched hand.

"Looks like it; but I didn't know *you,* Princess. I thought it was a spirit," answered Dan, looking down at her with a curious softness and wonder in his face.

"I've grown very much, but two years have changed you entirely." And Bess looked up with girlish pleasure at the picturesque figure before her—for it was a decided contrast to the well-dressed people about her.

Before they could say more, Josie rushed in, and, forgetful of the newly acquired dignity of her teens, let Dan catch her up and kiss her like a child. Not till he set her down did he discover that she also was changed, and exclaimed in comic dismay, "Hallo! Why, you are growing up too! What am I going to do, with no young one to play with? Here's Ted going it like a beanstalk, and Bess a young lady, and even you, my mustard seed, letting down your frocks and putting on airs."

The girls laughed, and Josie blushed as she stared at the tall man, conscious that she had leaped before she looked. They made a pretty contrast, these two young cousins—one as fair as a lily, the other a little wild rose. And Dan gave a nod of satisfaction as he surveyed them; for he had seen many bonny girls in his travels, and was glad that these old friends were blooming so beautifully.

"Here! We can't allow any monopoly of Dan!" called Mrs. Jo. "Bring him back and keep an eye on him, or he will be slipping off for another little run of a year or two before we have half seen him."

Led by these agreeable captors, Dan returned to the parlor to receive a scolding from Josie for getting ahead of all the other boys and looking like a man first.

"Emil is older, but he's only a boy, and dances jigs and sings sailor songs just as he used to. You look about thirty, and as big and black as a villain in a play. Oh, I've got a splendid idea! You are just the thing for Arbaces in 'The Last Days of Pompeii.' We want to act it; have the lion and the gladiators and the eruption. Tom and Ted are going to shower bushels of ashes down and roll barrels of stones about. We wanted a dark man for the Egyptian, and you will be gorgeous in red and white shawls. Won't he, Aunt Jo?"

This deluge of words made Dan clap his hands over his ears; and before Mrs. Bhaer could answer her impetuous niece the Laurences, with Meg and her family, arrived, soon followed by Tom and Nan, and all sat down to listen to Dan's adventures— told in a brief yet effective manner, as the varying expressions of interest, wonder, merriment, and suspense painted on the circle of faces round him plainly showed. The boys all wanted to start at once for California and make fortunes; the girls could hardly wait for the curious and pretty things he had picked up for them in his travels; while the elders rejoiced heartily over the energy and good prospects of their wild boy.

"Of course you will want to go back for another stroke of luck; and I hope you will have it. But speculation is a dangerous game, and you may lose all you've won," said Mr. Laurie, who had enjoyed the stirring tale as much as any of the boys, and would have liked to rough it with Dan as well as they.

"I've had enough of it, for a while at least; too much like gambling. The excitement is all I care for, and it isn't good for me. I have a notion to try farming out West. It's grand on a large scale; and I feel as if steady work would be rather jolly after loafing round so long. I can make a beginning, and you can send me your black sheep to stock my place with. I tried sheep farming in Australia, and know something about black ones, anyway."

A laugh chased away the sober look in Dan's face as he ended; and those who knew him best guessed that he had learned a lesson there in San Francisco, and dared not try again.

"That is a capital idea, Dan!" cried Mrs. Jo, seeing great hope in this desire to fix himself somewhere and help others. "We shall know where you are, and can go and see you, and not have half the world between us. I'll send my Ted for a visit. He's such a restless spirit, it would do him good. With you he would be safe while he worked off his surplus energies and learned a wholesome business."

"I'll use the 'shubble and de hoe' like a good one, if I get a chance out there; but the Speranza mines sound rather jollier," said Ted, examining the samples of ore Dan had brought for the Professor.

"You go and start a new town, and when we are ready to swarm we will come out and settle there. You will want a newspaper very soon, and I like the idea of running one myself much

better than grinding away as I do now," observed Demi, panting
to distinguish himself in the journalistic line.

"We could easily plant a new college there. These sturdy
Westerners are hungry for learning, and very quick to see and
choose the best," added ever-young Mr. March, beholding with
his prophetic eye many duplicates of their own flourishing establishment springing up in the wide West.

"Go on, Dan. It is a fine plan, and we will back you up. I
shouldn't mind investing in a few prairies and cowboys myself,"
said Mr. Laurie, always ready to help the lads to help themselves, both by his cheery words and ever-open purse.

"A little money sort of ballasts a fellow, and investing it in
land anchors him—for a while, at least. I'd like to see what I can
do, but I thought I'd consult you before I decided. Have my
doubts about its suiting me for many years; but I can cut loose
when I'm tired," answered Dan, both touched and pleased at
the eager interest of these friends in his plans.

"I know you *won't* like it. After having the whole world to
roam over, one farm will seem dreadfully small and stupid,"
said Josie, who much preferred the romance of the wandering
life which brought her thrilling tales and pretty things at each
return.

"Is there any art out there?" asked Bess, thinking what a
good study in black and white Dan would make as he stood
talking, half turned from the light.

"Plenty of nature, dear, and that is better. You will find
splendid animals to model, and scenery such as you never saw
in Europe to paint. Even prosaic pumpkins are grand out there.
You can play 'Cinderella' in one of them, Josie, when you open
your theater in Dansville," said Mr. Laurie, anxious that no cold
water should be thrown on the new plan.

Stagestruck Josie was caught at once, and being promised all
the tragic parts on the yet unbuilt stage, she felt a deep interest
in the project, and begged Dan to lose no time in beginning his
experiment. Bess also confessed that studies from nature would

be good for her, and wild scenery improve her taste, which
might grow over-nice if only the delicate and beautiful were set
before her.

"I speak for the practice of the new town," said Nan, always
eager for fresh enterprises. "I shall be ready by the time you get
well started—towns grow so fast out there."

"Dan isn't going to allow any woman under forty in his place.
He doesn't like them, 'specially young and pretty ones," put in
Tom, who was raging with jealousy, because he read admiration
for Nan in Dan's eyes.

"That won't affect me, because doctors are exceptions to all
rules. There won't be much sickness in Dansville, everyone will
lead such active, wholesome lives, and only energetic young
people will go there. But accidents will be frequent, owing to
wild cattle, fast riding, Indian scrimmages, and the recklessness
of Western life. That will just suit me. I long for broken bones,
surgery is *so* interesting, and I get so little here," answered Nan,
yearning to put out her shingle and begin.

"I'll have you, Doctor, and be glad of such a good sample of
what we can do in the East. Peg away, and I'll send for you as
soon as I have a roof to cover you. I'll scalp a few red fellows or
smash up a dozen or so of cowboys for your special benefit,"
laughed Dan, well pleased with the energy and fine physique
which made Nan a conspicuous figure among other girls.

"Thanks. I'll come. Would you just let me feel your arm?
Splendid biceps! Now, boys, see here: *this* is what I call muscle."
And Nan delivered a short lecture with Dan's sinewy arm to
illustrate it.

Tom retired to the alcove and glowered at the stars, while he
swung his own right arm with a vigor suggestive of knocking
someone down.

"Make Tom sexton; he'll enjoy burying the patients Nan kills.
He's trying to get up the glum expression proper to the business. Don't forget him, Dan," said Ted, directing attention to
the blighted being in the corner.

But Tom never sulked long, and came out from his brief eclipse with the cheerful proposition, "Look here, we'll get the city to ship out to Dansville all the cases of yellow fever, small-pox, and cholera that arrive; then Nan will be happy, and her mistakes won't matter much with emigrants and convicts."

"I should advise settling near Jacksonville, or some such city, that you might enjoy the society of cultivated persons. The Plato Club is there, and a most ardent thirst for philosophy. Everything from the East is welcomed hospitably, and new enterprises would flourish in such kindly soil," observed Mr. March, mildly offering a suggestion, as he sat among the elders enjoying the lively scene.

The idea of Dan studying Plato was very funny; but no one except naughty Ted smiled, and Dan made haste to unfold another plan seething in that active brain of his.

"I'm not sure the farming will succeed, and have a strong leaning toward my old friends the Montana Indians. They are a peaceful tribe, and need help awfully; hundreds have died of starvation because they don't get their share. The Sioux are fighters, thirty thousand strong, so government fears 'em, and gives 'em all they want. I call that a damned shame!" Dan stopped short as the oath slipped out, but his eyes flashed, and he went on quickly, "It *is* just that, and I won't beg pardon. If I'd had any money when I was there I'd have given every cent to those poor devils, cheated out of everything, and waiting patiently, after being driven from their own land to places where nothing will grow. Now, honest agents could do much, and I've a feeling that I ought to go and lend a hand. I know their lingo, and I like 'em. I've got a few thousands, and I ain't sure I have any right to spend it on myself and settle down to enjoy it. Hey?"

Dan looked very manly and earnest as he faced his friends, flushed and excited by the energy of his words; and all felt that little thrill of sympathy which links hearts together by the tie of pity for the wronged.

"Do it, do it!" cried Mrs. Jo, fired at once; for misfortune was much more interesting to her than good luck.

"Do it, do it!" echoed Ted, applauding as if at a play, "and take me along to help. I'm just raging to get among those fine fellows and hunt."

"Let us hear more and see if it is wise," said Mr. Laurie, privately resolving to people his as yet unbought prairies with Montana Indians, and increase his donations to the society that sent missionaries to this much-wronged people.

Dan plunged at once into the history of what he saw among the Dakotas and other tribes in the Northwest, telling of their wrongs, patience, and courage as if they were his brothers.

"They call me Dan Fire Cloud, because my rifle was the best they ever saw. And Black Hawk was as good a friend as a fellow would want; saved my life more than once, and taught me just what will be useful if I go back. They are down on their luck, now, and I'd like to pay my debts."

By this time everyone was interested, and Dansville began to lose its charms. But prudent Mr. Bhaer suggested that one honest agent among many could not do much, and noble as the effort would be, it was wiser to think over the matter carefully, get influence and authority from the right quarters, and meantime look at lands before deciding.

"Well, I will. I'm going to take a run to Kansas and see how that promises. Met a fellow in 'Frisco who'd been there, and he spoke well of it. The fact is, there's so much to be done *everywhere* that I don't know where to catch on, and half wish I hadn't any money," answered Dan, knitting his brows in the perplexity all kind souls feel when anxious to help at the great task of the world's charity.

"I'll keep it for you till you decide. You are such an impetuous lad you'll give it to the first beggar that gets hold of you. I'll turn it over while you are prospecting, and hand it back when you are ready to invest, shall I?" asked Mr. Laurie, who had learned wisdom since the days of his own extravagant youth.

"Thanky, sir, I'd be glad to get rid of it. You just hold on till I say the word; and if anything happens to me this time, keep it to help some other scamp as you helped me. This is my will, and you all witness it. Now I feel better." And Dan squared his shoulders as if relieved of a burden, after handing over the belt in which he carried his little fortune.

No one dreamed how much was to happen before Dan came to take his money back, nor how nearly that act *was* his last will and testament; and while Mr. Laurie was explaining how he would invest it, a cheery voice was heard singing—

> "Oh, Peggy was a jolly lass,
>   Ye heave ho, boys, ye heave ho!
> She never grudged her Jack a glass,
>   Ye heave ho, boys, ye heave ho!
> And when he sailed the raging main,
> She faithful was unto her swain,
>   Ye heave ho, boys, ye heave ho!"

Emil always announced his arrival in that fashion, and in a moment he came hurrying in with Nat, who had been giving lessons in town all day. It was good to see the latter beam at his friend as he nearly shook his hand off; better still to see how Dan gratefully remembered all he owed Nat, and tried to pay the debt in his rough way; and best of all to hear the two travelers compare notes and reel off yarns to dazzle the landlubbers and homekeepers.

After this addition the house would not contain the gay youngsters, so they migrated to the piazza and settled on the steps, like a flock of night-loving birds. Mr. March and the Professor retired to the study, Meg and Amy went to look after the little refection of fruit and cake which was to come, and Mrs. Jo and Mr. Laurie sat in the long window listening to the chat that went on outside.

"There they are, the flower of our flock!" she said, pointing to the group before them. "The others are dead or scattered, but these seven boys and four girls are my especial comfort and pride. Counting Alice Heath, my dozen is made up, and my hands are full trying to guide these young lives as far as human skill can do it."

"When we remember how different they are, from what some of them came, and the home influences about others, I think we may feel pretty well satisfied so far," answered Mr. Laurie soberly, as his eyes rested on one bright head among the black and brown ones, for the young moon shone alike on all.

"I don't worry about the girls. Meg sees to them, and is so wise and patient and tender they can't help doing well; but my boys are more care every year, and seem to drift farther away from me each time they go," sighed Mrs. Jo. "They *will* grow up, and I can only hold them by one little thread, which may snap at any time, as it has with Jack and Ned. Dolly and George still like to come back, and I can say my word to them; and dear old Franz is too true ever to forget his own. But the three who are soon going out into the world again I can't help worrying about. Emil's good heart will keep him straight, I hope, and

'A sweet little cherub sits up aloft,
To look out for the life of poor Jack.'

Nat is to make his first flight, and he's weak in spite of your strengthening influence; and Dan is still untamed. I fear it will take some hard lesson to do that."

"He's a fine fellow, Jo, and I almost regret this farming project. A little polish would make a gentleman of him, and who knows what he might become here among us," answered Mr. Laurie, leaning over Mrs. Bhaer's chair, just as he used to do years ago when they had mischievous secrets together.

"It wouldn't be safe, Teddy. Work and the free life he loves

will make a good man of him, and that is better than any
amount of polish, with the dangers an easy life in a city would
bring him. We can't change his nature—only help it to develop
in the right direction. The old impulses are there, and must be
controlled, or he will go wrong. I see that; but his love for us is a
safeguard, and we must keep a hold on him till he is older or
has a stronger tie to help him."

Mrs. Jo spoke earnestly, for, knowing Dan better than anyone
else, she saw that her colt was not thoroughly broken yet, and
feared while she hoped, knowing that life would always be hard
for one like him. She was sure that before he went away again,
in some quiet moment he would give her a glimpse of his inner
self, and then she could say the word of warning or encouragement that he needed. So she bided her time, studying him
meanwhile, glad to see all that was promising, and quick to
detect the harm the world was doing him. She was very anxious
to make a success of her "firebrand" because others predicted a
failure; but having learned that people cannot be molded like
clay, she contented herself with the hope that this neglected boy
might become a good man, and asked no more. Even that was
much to expect, so full was he of wayward impulses, strong
passions, and the lawless nature born in him. Nothing held him
but the one affection of his life—the memory of Plumfield, the
fear of disappointing these faithful friends, the pride, stronger
than principle, that made him want to keep the regard of the
mates who always had admired and loved him in spite of all his
faults.

"Don't fret, old dear; Emil is one of the happy-go-lucky sort
who always fall on their legs. I'll see to Nat, and Dan is in a
good way now. Let him take a look at Kansas, and if the farm
plan loses its charm, he can fall back on poor Lo, and really do
good out there. He's unusually fitted for that peculiar task, and
I hope he'll decide to do it. Fighting oppressors and befriending
the oppressed will keep those dangerous energies of his busy,

and the life will suit him better than sheepfolds and wheatfields."

"I hope so. What is that?" and Mrs. Jo leaned forward to listen, as exclamations from Ted and Josie caught her ear.

"A mustang! A real, live one, and we can ride it. Dan, you are a first class trump!" cried the boy.

"A whole Indian dress for me! Now I can play Namioka, if the boys act 'Metamora,' " added Josie, clapping her hands.

"A buffalo's head for Bess! Good gracious, Dan, why did you bring such a horrid thing as that to her?" asked Nan.

"Though it would do her good to model something strong and natural. She'll never amount to anything if she keeps on making namby-pamby gods and pet kittens," answered irreverent Dan, remembering that when he was last here Bess was vibrating distractedly between a head of Apollo and her Persian cat as models.

"Thank you. I'll try it, and if I fail we can put the buffalo up in the hall to remind us of you," said Bess, indignant at the insult offered the gods of her idolatry, but too well bred to show it except in her voice, which was as sweet and as cold as ice cream.

"I suppose you won't come out to see our new settlement when the rest do? Too rough for you?" asked Dan, trying to assume the deferential air all the boys used when addressing their Princess.

"I am going to Rome to study for years. All the beauty and art of the world is there, and a lifetime isn't long enough to enjoy it," answered Bess.

"Rome is a moldy old tomb compared to the 'Garden of the gods' and my magnificent Rockies. I don't care a hang for art; nature is as much as I can stand, and I guess I could show you things that would knock your old masters higher than kites. Better come, and while Josie rides the horses you can model 'em. If a drove of a hundred or so of wild ones can't show you beauty, I'll give up," cried Dan, waxing enthusiastic over the

wild grace and vigor which he could enjoy but had no power to
describe.

"I'll come someday with Papa, and see if they are better than
the horses of St. Mark and those on Capitol Hill. Please don't
abuse my gods, and I will try to like yours," said Bess, beginning
to think the West might be worth seeing, though no Raphael or
Angelo had yet appeared there.

"That's a bargain! I do think people ought to see their own
country before they go scooting off to foreign parts, as if the
new world wasn't worth discovering," began Dan, ready to bury
the hatchet.

"It has some advantages, but not all. The women of England
can vote, and we can't. I'm ashamed of America that she isn't
ahead in *all* good things," cried Nan, who held advanced views
on all reforms, and was anxious about her rights, having had to
fight for some of them.

"Oh, please don't begin on that. People always quarrel over
that question, and call names, and never agree. Do let us be
quiet and happy tonight," pleaded Daisy, who hated discussion
as much as Nan loved it.

"You shall vote as much as you like in our new town, Nan; be
mayor and aldermen, and run the whole concern. It's going to
be as free as air, or I can't live in it," said Dan, adding, with a
laugh, "I see Mrs. Giddy-gaddy and Mrs. Shakespeare Smith
don't agree any better than they used to."

"If everyone agreed, we should never get on. Daisy is a dear,
but inclined to be an old fogey; so I stir her up; and next fall she
will go and vote with me. Demi will escort us to do the one
thing we *are* allowed to do as yet."

"Will you take 'em, Deacon?" asked Dan, using the old name
as if he liked it. "It works capitally in Wyoming."

"I shall be proud to do it. Mother and the aunts go every
year, and Daisy will come with me. She is my better half still;
and I don't mean to leave her behind in anything," said Demi,
with an arm round his sister of whom he was fonder than ever.

Dan looked at them wistfully, thinking how sweet it must be to have such a tie; and his lonely youth seemed sadder than ever as he recalled its struggles. A gusty sigh from Tom made sentiment impossible, as he said pensively, "I always wanted to be a twin. It's so sociable and so cozy to have someone glad to lean on a fellow and comfort him, if other girls are cruel."

As Tom's unrequited passion was the standing joke of the family, this allusion produced a laugh, which Nan increased by whipping out a bottle of *Nux,* saying, with her professional air, "I knew you ate too much lobster for tea. Take four pellets, and your dyspepsia will be all right. Tom always sighs and is silly when he's overeaten."

"I'll take 'em. These are the only sweet things you ever give me." And Tom gloomily crunched his dose.

" 'Who can minister to a mind diseased, or pluck out a rooted sorrow?' " quoted Josie tragically from her perch on the railing.

"Come with me, Tommy, and I'll make a man of you. Drop your pills and powders, and cavort round the world a spell, and you'll soon forget you've got a heart, or a stomach either," said Dan, offering his one panacea for all ills.

"Ship with me, Tom. A good fit of seasickness will set you up, and a stiff northeaster blow your blue devils away. Come along as surgeon—easy berth, and no end of larks.

"And if your Nancy frowns, my lad,
  And scorns a jacket blue,
 Just hist your sails for other ports,
  And find a maid more true."

—added Emil, who had a fragment of song to cheer every care and sorrow, and freely offered them to his friends.

"Perhaps I'll think of it when I've got my diploma. I'm not going to grind three mortal years and have nothing to show for it. Till then—"

"I'll never desert Mrs. Micawber," interrupted Teddy, with a gurgling sob.

Tom immediately rolled him off the step into the wet grass below; and by the time this slight skirmish was over, the jingle of teaspoons suggested refreshments of a more agreeable sort. In former times the little girls waited on the boys, to save confusion; now the young men flew to serve the ladies, young and old; and that slight fact showed plainly how the tables were turned by time. And what a pleasant arrangement it was! Even Josie sat still, and let Emil bring her berries, enjoying her young ladyhood, till Ted stole her cake, when she forgot manners, and chastised him with a rap on the knuckles. As guest of honor, Dan was only allowed to wait on Bess, who still held the highest place in this small world. Tom carefully selected the best of everything for Nan, to be crushed by the remark, "I never eat at this hour; and you will have nightmares if *you* do."

So, dutifully curbing the pangs of hunger, he gave the plate to Daisy, and chewed rose leaves for his supper.

When a surprising quantity of wholesome nourishment had been consumed, someone said, "Let's sing!" and a tuneful hour followed. Nat fiddled, Demi piped, Dan strummed the old banjo, and Emil warbled a doleful ballad about the wreck of the "Bounding Betsey"; then everybody joined in the old songs till there was very decidedly "music in the air"; and passersby said, as they listened smiling, "Old Plum is gay tonight!"

When all had gone Dan lingered on the piazza, enjoying the balmy wind that blew up from the hayfields, and brought the breath of flowers from Parnassus; and as he leaned there romantically in the moonlight, Mrs. Jo came to shut the door.

"Dreaming dreams, Dan?" she asked, thinking the tender moment might have come. Imagine the shock when, instead of some interesting confidence or affectionate word, Dan swung round, saying bluntly, "I was wishing I could smoke."

Mrs. Jo laughed at the downfall of her hopes, and answered kindly, "You may, in your room, but don't set the house afire."

Perhaps Dan saw a little disappointment in her face, or the memory of the sequel of that boyish frolic touched his heart; for he stooped and kissed her, saying in a whisper, "Good night, Mother." And Mrs. Jo was half satisfied.

CHAPTER 5

VACATION

EVERYONE was glad of a holiday next morning and all lingered over the breakfast table, till Mrs. Jo suddenly exclaimed, "Why, there's a dog!" And on the threshold of the door appeared a great deerhound standing motionless, with his eyes fixed on Dan.

"Hullo, old boy! Couldn't you wait till I came for you? Have you cut away on the sly? Own up now, and take your whipping like a man," said Dan, rising to meet the dog, who reared on his hind legs to look his master in the face and bark as if uttering an indignant denial of any disobedience.

"All right; Don never lies." And Dan gave the tall beast a hug, adding as he glanced out of the window, where a man and horse were seen approaching, "I left my plunder at the hotel over night, not knowing how I should find you. Come out and see Octoo, my mustang. She's a beauty." And Dan was off, with the family streaming after him, to welcome the newcomer.

They found her preparing to go up the steps in her eagerness to reach her master, to the great dismay of the man, who was holding her back.

"Let her come," called Dan. "She climbs like a cat and jumps like a deer. Well, my girl, do you want a gallop?" he asked, as the pretty creature clattered up to him and whinnied with pleasure as he rubbed her nose and slapped her glossy flank.

"That's what I call a horse worth having," said Ted, full of admiration and delight; for he was to have the care of her during Dan's absence.

"What intelligent eyes! She looks as if she would speak," said Mrs. Jo.

"She talks like a human in her way. Very little that *she* don't know. Hey, old lass?" and Dan laid his cheek to hers as if the little black mare was very dear to him.

"What does 'Octoo' mean?" asked Rob.

"Lightning. She deserves it, as you'll see. Black Hawk gave her to me for my rifle, and we've had high times together out yonder. She's saved my life more than once. Do you see that scar?"

Dan pointed to a small one, half hidden by the long mane; and standing with his arm about Octoo's neck, he told the story of it.

"Black Hawk and I were after buffalo one time, but didn't find 'em as soon as we expected; so our food gave out, and there we were a hundred miles from Red Deer River, where our camp was. I thought we were done for, but my brave pal says, 'Now I'll show you how we can live till we find the herds.' We were unsaddling for the night by a little pond; there wasn't a living creature in sight anywhere, not even a bird, and we could see for miles over the prairies. What do you think we did?" And Dan looked into the faces round him.

"Ate worms, like the Australian fellows," said Rob.

"Boiled grass or leaves," added Mrs. Jo.

"Perhaps filled the stomach with clay, as we read of savages doing?" suggested Mr. Bhaer.

"Killed one of the horses," cried Ted, eager for bloodshed of some sort.

"No; but we bled one of them. See, just here; filled a tin cup, put some wild sage leaves in it, with water, and heated it over a fire of sticks. It was good, and we slept well."

"I guess Octoo didn't." And Josie patted the animal, with a face full of sympathy.

"Never minded it a bit. Black Hawk said we could live on the horses several days and still travel before they felt it. But by another morning we found the buffalo, and I shot the one whose head is in my box, ready to hang up and scare brats into fits. He's a fierce old fellow, you bet."

"What is this strap for?" asked Ted, who was busily examining the Indian saddle, the single rein and snaffle, with lariat, and round the neck the leather band he spoke of.

"We hold onto that when we lie along the horse's flank farthest from the enemy, and fire under the neck as we gallop round and round. I'll show you." And springing into the saddle, Dan was off down the steps, tearing over the lawn at a great pace, sometimes on Octoo's back, sometimes half hidden as he hung by stirrup and strap, and sometimes off altogether, running beside her as she loped along, enjoying the fun immensely; while Don raced after, in a canine rapture at being free again and with his mates.

It was a fine sight—the three wild things at play, so full of vigor, grace, and freedom, that for the moment the smooth lawn seemed a prairie; and the spectators felt as if this glimpse of another life made their own seem rather tame and colorless.

"That is better than a circus!" cried Mrs. Jo, wishing she were a girl again, that she might take a gallop on this chained lightning of a horse. "I foresee that Nan will have her hands full setting bones, for Ted will break every one of his trying to rival Dan."

"A few falls will not harm, and this new care and pleasure will be good for him in all ways. But I fear Dan will never follow a plow after riding a Pegasus like that," answered Mr. Bhaer, as the black mare leaped the gate and came flying up the avenue, to stop at a word and stand quivering with excitement, while Dan swung himself off and looked up for applause.

He received plenty of it, and seemed more pleased for his pet's sake than for his own. Ted clamored for a lesson at once, and was soon at ease in the queer saddle, finding Octoo gentle as a lamb, as he trotted away to show off at college. Bess came hastening down the hill, having seen the race from afar; and all collected on the piazza while Dan "yanked" the cover off the big box the express had "dumped" before the door—to borrow his own words.

Dan usually traveled in light marching order, and hated to have more luggage than he could carry in his well-worn valise. But now that he had a little money of his own, he had cumbered himself with a collection of trophies won by his bow and spear, and brought them home to bestow upon his friends.

"We shall be devoured with moths," thought Mrs. Jo, as the shaggy head appeared, followed by a wolfskin rug for her feet, a bearskin ditto for the Professor's study, and Indian garments bedecked with foxes' tails for the boys.

All nice and warm for a July day, but received with delight nevertheless. Ted and Josie immediately "dressed up," learned the war-whoop, and proceeded to astonish their friends by a series of skirmishes about the house and grounds, with tomahawks and bows and arrows, till weariness produced a lull. Gay birds' wings, plumy pampas grass, strings of wampum, and pretty work in beads, bark, and feathers, pleased the girls. Minerals, arrowheads, and rude sketches interested the Professor; and when the box was empty, Dan gave Mr. Laurie, as his gift, several plaintive Indian songs written on birchbark.

"We only want a tent over us to be quite perfect. I feel as if I ought to give you parched corn and dried meat for dinner, my braves. Nobody will want lamb and green peas after this splendid powwow," said Mrs. Jo, surveying the picturesque confusion of the long hall, where people lay about on the rugs, all more or less bedecked with feathers, moccasins, or beads.

"Moose noses, buffalo tongues, bear steaks, and roasted marrowbones would be the thing, but I don't mind a change; so bring on your baa-baa and green meat," answered Dan from the box, where he sat in state like a chief among his tribe, with the great hound at his feet.

The girls began to clear up, but made little headway; for everything they touched had a story, and all were thrilling, comical, or wild; so they found it hard to settle to their work, till Dan was carried off by Mr. Laurie.

This was the beginning of the summer holiday, and it was curious to see what a pleasant little stir Dan's and Emil's coming made in the quiet life of the studious community; for they seemed to bring a fresh breeze with them that enlivened everyone. Many of the collegians remained during vacation; and Plumfield and Parnassus did their best to make these days pleasant for them, since most came from distant states, were poor, and had few opportunities but this for culture or amusement. Emil was hail-fellow-well-met with men and maids, and went rollicking about in true sailor fashion; but Dan stood rather in awe of the "fair girl-graduates," and was silent when among them, eyeing them as an eagle might a flock of doves. He got on better with the young men, and was their hero at once. Their admiration for his manly accomplishments did him good; because he felt his educational defects keenly, and often wondered if he could find anything in books to satisfy him as thoroughly as did the lessons he was learning from Nature's splendidly illustrated volume. In spite of his silence, the girls found out his good qualities, and regarded "the Spaniard," as they named him, with great favor; for his black eyes were more eloquent than his tongue, and the kind creatures tried to show their friendly interest in many charming ways.

He saw this, and endeavored to be worthy of it—curbing his free speech, toning down his rough manners, and watching the effect of all he said and did, anxious to make a good impression. The social atmosphere warmed his lonely heart, the culture excited him to do his best, and the changes which had taken place during his absence, both in himself and others, made the old home seem like a new world. After the life in California, it was sweet and restful to be here, with these familiar faces round him, helping him to forget much that he regretted, and to resolve to deserve more entirely the confidence of these good fellows, the respect of these innocent girls.

So there was riding, rowing, and picnicking by day, music, dancing, and plays by night; and everyone said there had not been so gay a vacation for years. Bess kept her promise, and let the dust gather on her beloved clay while she went pleasuring with her mates or studied music with her father, who rejoiced over the fresh roses in her cheeks and the laughter which chased away the dreamy look she used to wear. Josie quarreled less with Ted; for Dan had a way of looking at her which quelled her instantly, and had almost as good an effect upon her rebellious cousin. But Octoo did even more for the lively youth, who found that her charms entirely eclipsed those of the bicycle which had been his heart's delight before. Early and late he rode this untiring beast, and began to gain flesh—to the great joy of his mother, who feared that her beanstalk was growing too fast for health.

Demi, finding business dull, solaced his leisure by photographing everybody he could induce to sit or stand to him, producing some excellent pictures among many failures; for he had a pretty taste in grouping, and endless patience. He might be said to view the world through the lens of his camera, and seemed to enjoy himself very much squinting at his fellow beings from under a bit of black cambric. Dan was a treasure to him; for he took well, and willingly posed in his Mexican costume, with horse and hound, and all wanted copies of these effective photographs.

Bess, also, was a favorite sitter; and Demi received a prize at the Amateur Photographic Exposition for one of his cousin with all her pretty hair about her face, which rose from the cloud of white lace draping the shoulders. These were freely handed round by the proud artist; and one copy had a tender little history yet to be told.

Nat was snatching every minute he could get with Daisy before the long parting; and Mrs. Meg relented somewhat, feeling sure that absence would quite cure this unfortunate fancy. Daisy said little; but her gentle face was sad when she was alone, and a few quiet tears dropped on the handkerchiefs she marked so daintily with her own hair. She was sure Nat would *not* forget her; and life looked rather forlorn without the dear fellow who had been her friend since the days of patty pans and confidences in the willow tree. She was an old-fashioned daughter, dutiful and docile, with such love and reverence for her mother that her will was law; and if love was forbidden, friendship must suffice. So she kept her little sorrow to herself, smiled cheerfully at Nat, and made his last days of home life very happy with every comfort and pleasure she could give, from sensible advice and sweet words to a well-filled workbag for his bachelor establishment and a box of goodies for the voyage.

Tom and Nan took all the time they could spare from their studies to enjoy high jinks at Plumfield with their old friends; for Emil's next voyage was to be a long one, Nat's absence was uncertain, and no one ever knew when Dan would turn up again. They all seemed to feel that life was beginning to grow serious; and even while they enjoyed those lovely summer days together they were conscious that they were children no longer, and often in the pauses of their fun talked soberly of their plans and hopes, as if anxious to know and help one another before they drifted further apart on their different ways.

A few weeks were all they had; then the "Brenda" was ready, Nat was to sail from New York, and Dan went along to see him off; for his own plans fermented in his head, and he was eager to be up and doing. A farewell dance was given on Parnassus in honor of the travelers, and all turned out in their best array and gayest spirits. George and Dolly came with the latest Harvard airs and graces, radiant to behold, in dress suits and "crushed hats," as Josie called the especial pride and joy of their boyish souls. Jack and Ned sent regrets and best wishes, and no one mourned their absence; for they were among what Mrs. Jo called her failures. Poor Tom got into trouble, as usual, by deluging his head with some highly scented preparation in the vain hope of making his tight curls lie flat and smooth, as was the style. Unhappily, his rebellious crop only kinked the closer, and the odor of many barber shops clung to him in spite of his frantic efforts to banish it. Nan wouldn't allow him near her, and flapped her fan vigorously whenever he was in sight, which cut him to the heart, and made him feel like the Peri shut out from Paradise. Of course his mates jeered at him, and nothing but the unquenchable jollity of his nature kept him from despair.

Emil was resplendent in his new uniform, and danced with an abandon which only sailors know. His pumps seemed to be everywhere, and his partners soon lost breath trying to keep up with him; but the girls all declared he steered like an angel, and in spite of his pace no collisions took place; so he was happy, and found no lack of damsels to ship with him.

Having no dress suit, Dan had been coaxed to wear his Mexican costume, and feeling at ease in the many-buttoned trousers, loose jacket, and gay sash, flung his *serape* over his shoulder with a flourish and looked his best, doing great execution with his long spurs, as he taught Josie strange steps or rolled his black eyes admiringly after certain blonde damsels whom he dared not address.

The mammas sat in the alcove, supplying pins, smiles, and kindly words to all, especially the awkward youths new to such scenes, and the bashful girls conscious of faded muslins and cleaned gloves. It was pleasant to see stately Mrs. Amy promenade on the arm of a tall country boy with thick boots and a big forehead, or Mrs. Jo dance like a girl with a shy fellow whose arms went like pump handles, and whose face was scarlet with

confusion and pride at the honor of treading on the toes of the
president's wife. Mrs. Meg always had room on her sofa for two
or three girls, and Mr. Laurie devoted himself to these plain,
poorly dressed damsels with a kindly grace that won their hearts
and made them happy. The good Professor circulated like refreshments, and his cheerful face shone on all alike, while Mr.
March discussed Greek comedy in the study with such serious
gentlemen as never unbent their mighty minds to frivolous joys.

The long music room, parlor, hall, and piazza were full of
white-gowned maidens with attendant shadows; the air was full
of lively voices, and hearts and feet went lightly together as the
home band played vigorously, and the friendly moon did her
best to add enchantment to the scene.

"Pin me up, Meg; that dear Dunbar boy has nearly rent me
'in sunder,' as Mr. Peggotty would say. But didn't he enjoy himself, bumping against his fellow men and swinging me round
like a mop? On these occasions I find that I'm not as young as I
was, nor as light of foot. In ten years more we shall be
mealbags, sister; so be resigned." And Mrs. Jo subsided into a
corner, much disheveled by her benevolent exertions.

"I know *I* shall be stout; but you won't keep still long enough
to get much flesh on your bones, dear; and Amy will always
keep her lovely figure. She looks about eighteen tonight, in her
white gown and roses," answered Meg, busily pinning up one
sister's torn frills, while her eyes fondly followed the other's
graceful movements; for Meg still adored Amy in the old
fashion.

It was one of the family jokes that Jo was getting fat, and she
kept it up, though as yet she had only acquired a matronly
outline, which was very becoming. They were laughing over the
impending double chins, when Mr. Laurie came off duty for a
moment.

"Repairing damages as usual, Jo? You never could take a
little gentle exercise without returning in rags. Come and have a
quiet stroll with me and cool off before supper. I've a series of

pretty tableaux to show you while Meg listens to the raptures of lisping Miss Carr, whom I made happy by giving her Demi for a partner."

As he spoke, Laurie led Jo to the music room, nearly empty now after a dance which sent the young people into garden and hall. Passing before the first of the four long windows that opened on a very wide piazza, he pointed to a group outside, saying, "The name of this is 'Jack Ashore.' "

A pair of long, blue legs, ending in very neat pumps, hung from the veranda roof among the vines; and roses, gathered by unseen hands, evidently appertaining to aforesaid legs, were being dropped into the laps of several girls perched like a flock of white birds on the railing below; while a manly voice "fell like a falling star," as it sung this pensive ditty to a most appreciative audience:

MARY'S DREAM

"The moon had climbed the eastern hill
　　Which rises o'er the sands of Dee,
And from its highest summit shed
　　A silver light on tower and tree,
When Mary laid her down to sleep
　　(Her thoughts on Sandy far at sea);
When soft and low a voice was heard,
　　Saying, 'Mary, weep no more for me.'

"She from her pillow gently raised
　　Her head, to see who there might be,
And saw young Sandy, shivering, stand
　　With visage pale and hollow e'e.
'O Mary dear, cold is my clay;
　　It lies beneath the stormy sea;
Far, far from thee, I sleep in death.
　　Dear Mary, weep no more for me.

" 'Three stormy nights and stormy days
    We tossed upon the raging main.
And long we strove our bark to save;
    But all our striving was in vain.
E'en then, when terror chilled my blood,
    My heart was filled with love of thee.
The storm is past, and I'm at rest;
    So, Mary, weep no more for me.

" 'O maiden dear, yourself prepare;
    We soon shall meet upon that shore
Where love is free from doubt and care,
    And you and I shall part no more.'
Loud crew the cock, the shadow fled;
    No more her Sandy did she see;
But soft the passing spirit said,
    'Sweet Mary, weep no more for me.' "

"The constant jollity of that boy is worth a fortune to him. He'll never sink with such a buoyant spirit to keep him afloat through life," said Mrs. Jo, as the roses were tossed back with much applause when the song ended.

"Not he. And it's a blessing to be grateful for, isn't it? We moody people know its worth. Glad you like my first tableau. Come and see number two. Hope it isn't spoilt; it was very pretty just now. This is 'Othello telling his adventures to Desdemona.' "

The second window framed a very picturesque group of three. Mr. March in an armchair, with Bess on a cushion at his feet, was listening to Dan, who, leaning against a pillar, was talking with unusual animation. The old man was in shadow, but little Desdemona was looking up with the moonlight full upon her into young Othello's face, quite absorbed in the story he was telling so well. The gay drapery over Dan's shoulder, his dark coloring, and the gesture of his arm made the picture very striking, and both spectators enjoyed it with silent pleasure, till Mrs. Jo said in a quick whisper, "I'm glad he's going away. He's too picturesque to have here among so many romantic girls. Afraid his 'grand, gloomy, and peculiar' style will be too much for our simple maids."

"No danger. Dan is in the rough as yet, and always will be, I fancy, though he is improving in many ways. How well Queenie looks in that soft light!"

"Dear little Goldilocks looks well everywhere." And with a backward glance full of pride and fondness, Mrs. Jo went on. But that scene returned to her long afterward and her own prophetic words also.

Number three was a tragical tableau at first sight; and Mr. Laurie stifled a laugh as he whispered "The Wounded Knight," pointing to Tom with his head enveloped in a large handkerchief, as he knelt before Nan, who was extracting a thorn or splinter from the palm of his hand with great skill, to judge from the patient's blissful expression of countenance.

"Do I hurt you?" she asked, turning the hand to the moonlight for a better view.

"Not a bit. Dig away. I like it," answered Tom, regardless of his aching knees and the damage done his best trousers.

"I won't keep you long."

"Hours, if you please. Never so happy as here."

Quite unmoved by this tender remark, Nan put on a pair of large, round-eyed glasses, saying in a matter-of-fact tone, "Now I see it. Only a splinter, and there it is."

"My hand is bleeding. Won't you bind it up?" asked Tom, wishing to prolong the situation.

"Nonsense. Suck it. Only take care of it tomorrow if you dissect. Don't want any more blood poisoning."

"That was the only time you were kind to me. Wish I'd lost my arm."

"I wish you'd lost your head; it smells more like turpentine and kerosene than ever. Do take a run in the garden and air it."

Fearing to betray themselves by laughter, the watchers went on, leaving the Knight to rush away in despair, and the Lady to bury her nose in the cup of a tall lily for refreshment.

"Poor Tom, his fate is a hard one, and he's wasting his time! Do advise him to quit philandering, and go to work, Jo."

"I have, Teddy, often; but it will take some great shock to make that boy wise. I wait with interest to see what it will be. Bless me! What is all this?"

She might well ask; for on a rustic stool stood Ted trying to pose on one foot, with the other extended, and both hands waving in the air. Josie, with several young mates, was watching his contortions with deep interest as they talked about "little wings," "gilded wire twisted," and a "cunning skullcap."

"This might be called 'Mercury Trying to Fly,' " said Mr. Laurie, as they peeped through the lace curtains.

"Bless the long legs of that boy! How does he expect to manage them? They are planning for the Owlsdark Marbles, and a nice muddle they will make of my gods and goddesses with no one to show them how," answered Mrs. Jo, enjoying this scene immensely.

"Now, he's got it!" "That's perfectly splendid!" "See how long you can keep so!" cried the girls, as Ted managed to maintain his equilibrium a moment by resting one toe on the trellis. Unfortunately this brought all his weight on the other foot; the straw seat of the stool gave way, and the flying Mercury came down with a crash, amid shrieks of laughter from the girls. Being accustomed to ground and lofty tumbling, he quickly recovered himself, and hopped gaily about, with one leg through the stool as he improvised a classic jig.

"Thanks, for four nice little pictures. You have given me an idea, and I think some time we will get up regular tableaux of this sort and march our company round a set of dissolving views. New and striking; I'll propose it to our manager and give you all the glory," said Mrs. Jo, as they strolled toward the room whence came the clash of glass and china, and glimpses of agitated black coats.

Let us follow the example of our old friends and stroll about among the young people, eavesdropping, so gathering up various little threads to help in the weaving of the story. George and Dolly were at supper, and having served the ladies in their care stood in a corner absorbing nourishment of all kinds with a vain attempt to conceal hearty appetites under an air of elegant indifference.

"Good spread, this; Laurence does things in style. First-rate coffee, but no wine, and that's a mistake," said Stuffy, who still deserved his name, and was a stout youth with a heavy eye and bilious complexion.

"Bad for boys, he says. Jove! Wish he could see us at some of our wines. Don't we just 'splice the main brace' as Emil says," answered Dolly, the dandy, carefully spreading a napkin over the glossy expanse of shirtfront whereon a diamond stud shone like a lone star. His stutter was nearly outgrown; but he, as well as George, spoke in the tone of condescension, which, with the *blasé* airs they assumed, made a very funny contrast to their youthful faces and foolish remarks. Good-hearted little fellows both, but top-heavy with the pride of being Sophs and the freedom that college life gave them.

"Little Jo is getting to be a deuced pretty girl, isn't she?" said George, with a long sigh of satisfaction as his first mouthful of ice went slowly down his throat.

"H'm—well, fairish. The Princess is rather more to my taste. I like 'em blonde and queenly and elegant, don't you know."

"Yes, Jo *is* too lively; might as well dance with a grasshopper. I've tried her, and she's one too many for me. Miss Perry is a nice, easy-going girl. Got her for the german."

"You'll never be a dancing man. Too lazy. Now I'll undertake to steer any girl and dance down any fellow you please. Dancing's my forte." And Dolly glanced from his trim feet to his flashing gem with the defiant air of a young turkey cock on parade.

"Miss Grey is looking for you. Wants more grub. Just see if Miss Nelson's plate is empty, there's a good fellow. Can't eat ice in a hurry." And George remained in his safe corner, while Dolly struggled through the crowd to do his duty, coming back in a fume, with a splash of salad dressing on his coat cuff.

"Confound these country chaps! They go blundering round like so many dorbugs, and make a deuce of a mess. Better stick to books and not try to be society man. Can't do it. Beastly stain. Give it a rub, and let me bolt a mouthful, I'm starved. Never saw girls eat such a lot. It proves that they ought not to study so much. Never liked co-ed," growled Dolly, much ruffled in spirit.

"So they do. 'Tisn't ladylike. Ought to be satisfied with an ice and a bit of cake, and eat it prettily. Don't like to see a girl feed. We hard-working men need it, and, by Jove, I mean to get some more of that meringue if it's not all gone. Here, waiter! Bring along that dish over there, and be lively," commanded Stuffy, poking a young man in a rather shabby dress suit, who was passing with a tray of glasses.

His order was obeyed promptly; but George's appetite was taken away the next moment by Dolly's exclaiming, as he looked up from his damaged coat, with a scandalized face, "You've put your foot in it now, old boy! That's Morton, Mr. Bhaer's crack man. Knows everything, no end of a 'dig,' and bound to carry off all the honors. You won't hear the last of it in a hurry." And Dolly laughed so heartily that a spoonful of ice flew upon the head of a lady sitting below him, and got *him* into a scrape also.

Leaving them to their despair, let us listen to the whispered chat of two girls comfortably seated in a recess waiting till their escorts were fed.

"I do think the Laurences give lovely parties. Don't you enjoy them?" asked the younger, looking about her with the eager air of one unused to this sort of pleasure.

"Very much, only I never feel as if I was dressed right. My things seemed elegant at home, and I thought I'd be *over* over-dressed if anything; but I look countrified and dowdy here. No time or money to change now, even if I knew how to do it," answered the other, glancing anxiously at her bright pink silk gown, trimmed with cheap lace.

"You must get Mrs. Brooke to tell you how to fix your things. She was very kind to me. I had a green silk, and it looked so cheap and horrid by the side of the nice dresses here I felt regularly unhappy about it, and asked her how much a dress like one Mrs. Laurence had would cost. That looked so simple and elegant I thought it wouldn't be costly; but it was India mull and Valenciennes lace, so of course I couldn't have it. Then Mrs. Brooke said, 'Get some muslin to cover the green silk, and wear hops or some white flowers, instead of pink, in your hair, and you will have a pretty suit.' Isn't it lovely and becoming?" And Miss Burton surveyed herself with girlish satisfaction; for a little taste had softened the harsh green, and hop-bells became her red hair better than roses.

"It's sweet: I've been admiring it. I'll do mine so and ask about my purple one. Mrs. Brooke has helped me to get rid of my headaches, and Mary Clay's dyspepsia is all gone since she gave up coffee and hot bread."

"Mrs. Laurence advised me to walk and run and use the gymnasium to cure my round shoulders and open my chest, and I'm a much better figure than I was."

"Did you know that Mr. Laurence pays all Amelia Merrill's bills? Her father failed, and she was heartbroken at having to leave college; but that splendid man just stepped in and made it all right."

"Yes, and Professor Bhaer has several of the boys down at his house evenings to help them along so they can keep up with the rest; and Mrs. Bhaer took care of Charles Mackay herself when he had a fever last year. I do think they are the best and kindest people in the world."

"So do I, and my time here will be the happiest and most useful years of my life."

And both girls forgot their gowns and their suppers for a moment to look with grateful, affectionate eyes at the friends who tried to care for bodies and for souls as well as minds.

Now come to a lively party supping on the stairs, girls like foam at the top, and a substratum of youths below, where the heaviest particles always settle. Emil, who never sat if he could climb or perch, adorned the newel post; Tom, Nat, Demi, and Dan were camped on the steps, eating busily, as their ladies were well served and they had earned a moment's rest, which they enjoyed with their eyes fixed on the pleasing prospect above them.

"I'm so sorry the boys are going. It will be dreadfully dull without them. Now they have stopped teasing and are polite, I really enjoy them," said Nan, who felt unusually gracious tonight as Tom's mishap kept him from annoying her.

"So do I. And Bess was mourning about it today, though as a general thing she doesn't like boys unless they are models of elegance. She has been doing Dan's head, and it is not quite finished. I never saw her so interested in any work, and it's very well done. He is so striking and big he always makes me think of the Dying Gladiator or some of those antique creatures. There's Bess now. Dear child, how sweet she looks tonight!" answered Daisy, waving her hand as the Princess went by with Grandpa on her arm.

"I never thought he would turn out so well. Don't you remember how we used to call him 'the bad boy,' and be sure he would become a pirate or something awful because he glared at us and swore sometimes? Now he is the handsomest of all the boys, and very entertaining with his stories and plans. I like him very much; he's so big and strong and independent. I'm tired of mollycoddles and bookworms," said Nan, in her decided way.

"Not handsomer than Nat!" cried loyal Daisy, contrasting two faces below, one unusually gay, the other sentimentally sober even in the act of munching cake. "I like Dan, and am glad he is doing well; but he tires me, and I'm still a little afraid of him. Quiet people suit me best."

"Life is a fight, and I like a good soldier. Boys take things too easily, don't see how serious it all is and go to work in earnest. Look at that absurd Tom, wasting his time and making an object of himself just because he can't have what he wants, like a baby crying for the moon. I've no patience with such nonsense," scolded Nan, looking down at the jovial Thomas, who was playfully putting macaroons in Emil's shoes, and trying to beguile his exile as best he could.

"Most girls would be touched by such fidelity. I think it's beautiful," said Daisy behind her fan; for other girls sat just below.

"You are a sentimental goose and not a judge. Nat will be twice the man when he comes back after his trip. I wish Tom was going with him. My idea is that if we girls have any influence we should use it for the good of these boys, and not pamper them up, making slaves of ourselves and tyrants of them. Let them prove what they can do and be before they ask anything of us, and give us a chance to do the same. Then we know where we are, and shall not make mistakes to mourn over all our lives."

"Hear, hear!" cried Alice Heath, who was a girl after Nan's own heart, and had chosen a career, like a brave and sensible young woman. "Only give us a chance, and have patience till we can do our best. Now we are expected to be as wise as men who have had generations of all the help there is, and we scarcely anything. Let us have equal opportunities, and in a few generations we will see what the judgment is. I like justice, and we get very little of it."

"Still shouting the battle cry of freedom?" asked Demi, peering through the banisters at this moment. "Up with your flag!

I'll stand by and lend a hand if you want it. With you and Nan to lead the van, I think you won't need much help."

"You are a great comfort, Demi, and I'll call on you in all emergencies; for you are an honest boy, and don't forget that you owe much to your mother and your sisters and your aunts," continued Nan. "I do like men who come out frankly and own that they are *not* gods. How can *we* think them so when such awful mistakes are being made all the time by these great creatures? See them sick, as I do, then you know them."

"Don't hit us when we are down; be merciful, and set us up to bless and believe in you evermore," pleaded Demi from behind the bars.

"We'll be kind to you if you will be just to us. I don't say generous, only just. I went to a suffrage debate in the Legislature last winter; and of all the feeble, vulgar twaddle I ever heard, that was the worst; and those men were *our* representatives. I blushed for them, and their wives and mothers. I want an intelligent man to represent *me,* if I can't do it myself, not a fool."

"Nan is on the stump. Now we shall catch it," cried Tom, putting up an umbrella to shield his unhappy head; for Nan's earnest voice was audible, and her indignant eye happened to rest on him as she spoke.

"Go on, go on! I'll take notes, and put in 'great applause' liberally," added Demi, producing his ball book and pencil, with his Jenkins air.

Daisy pinched his nose through the bars, and the meeting was rather tumultuous for a moment, for Emil called, "Avast, avast, here's a squall to wind'ard"; Tom applauded wildly; Dan looked up as if the prospect of a fight, even with words, pleased him, and Nat went to support Demi, as his position seemed to be a good one. At this crisis, when everyone laughed and talked at once, Bess came floating through the upper hall and looked down like an angel of peace upon the noisy group below, as she asked, with wondering eyes and smiling lips, "What is it?"

"An indignation meeting. Nan and Alice are on a rampage, and we are at the bar to be tried for our lives. Will Your Highness preside and judge between us?" answered Demi, as a lull at once took place; for no one rioted in the presence of the Princess.

"I'm not wise enough. I'll sit here and listen. Please go on." And Bess took her place above them all as cool and calm as a little statue of Justice, with fan and nosegay in place of sword and scales.

"Now, ladies, free your minds, only spare us till morning; for we've got a german to dance as soon as everyone is fed, and Parnassus expects every man to do his duty. Mrs. President Giddy-gaddy has the floor," said Demi, who liked this sort of fun better than the very mild sort of flirtation which was allowed at Plumfield, for the simple reason that it could not be entirely banished, and is a part of all education, co- or otherwise.

"I have only one thing to say, and it is this," began Nan, soberly, though her eyes sparkled with a mixture of fun and earnestness. "I want to ask every boy of you what you really think on this subject. Dan and Emil have seen the world and ought to know their own minds. Tom and Nat have had fine examples before them for years. Demi is ours and we are proud of him. So is Rob. Ted is a weathercock, and Dolly and George of course are fogies in spite of the Annex, and girls at Girton going ahead of the men. Commodore, are you ready for the question?"

"Ay, ay, skipper."

"Do you believe in Woman's Suffrage?"

"Bless your pretty figger-head! I do, and I'll ship a crew of girls any time you say so. Aren't they worse than a press-gang to carry a fellow out of his moorings? Don't we all need one as pilot to steer us safe to port? And why shouldn't they share our mess afloat and ashore since we are sure to be wrecked without 'em?"

"Good for you, Emil! Nan will take you for first mate after that handsome speech," said Demi, as the girls applauded, and Tom glowered.

"Now, Dan, you love liberty so well yourself, are you willing we should have it?"

"All you can get, and I'll fight any man who's mean enough to say you don't deserve it."

This brief and forcible reply delighted the energetic President, and she beamed upon the member from California, as she said briskly, "Nat wouldn't dare to say he was on the other side even if he were, but I hope he has made up his mind to pipe for us, at least when we take the field, and not be one of those who wait till the battle is won, and then beat the drums and share the glory."

Mrs. Giddy-gaddy's doubts were most effectually removed, and her sharp speech regretted, as Nat looked up blushing, but with a new sort of manliness in face and manner, saying, in a tone that touched them all, "I should be the most ungrateful fellow alive if I did not love, honor, and serve women with all my heart and might, for to them I owe everything I am or ever shall be."

Daisy clapped her hands, and Bess threw her bouquet into Nat's lap, while the other girls waved their fans, well pleased; for real feeling made his little speech eloquent.

"Thomas B. Bangs, come into court and tell the truth, the whole truth, and nothing but the truth, if you can," commanded Nan, with a rap to call the meeting to order.

Tom shut the umbrella, and standing up raised his hand, saying solemnly, "I believe in suffrage of *all* kinds. I adore *all* women, and will die for them at any moment if it will help the cause."

"Living and working for it is harder, and therefore more honorable. Men are always ready to die for us, but not to make our lives worth having. Cheap sentiment and bad logic. You will pass, Tom, only don't twaddle. Now, having taken the sense of the meeting we will adjourn, as the hour for festive gymnastics has arrived. I am glad to see that old Plum has given six true men to the world, and hope they will continue to be stanch to her and the principles she has taught them, wherever they may go. Now, girls, don't sit in drafts, and, boys, beware of ice water when you are warm."

With this characteristic close Nan retired from office, and the girls went to enjoy one of the few rights allowed them.

CHAPTER 6

LAST WORDS

THE NEXT DAY was Sunday, and a goodly troop of young and old set forth to church—some driving, some walking, all enjoying the lovely weather and the happy quietude which comes to refresh us when the work and worry of the week are over. Daisy had a headache; and Aunt Jo remained at home to keep her company, knowing very well that the worst ache was in the tender heart struggling dutifully against the love that grew stronger as the parting drew nearer.

"Daisy knows my wishes, and I trust her. You must keep an eye on Nat, and let him clearly understand that there is to be no 'lovering,' or I shall forbid the letter writing. I hate to seem cruel, but it is too soon for my dear girl to bind herself in any way," said Mrs. Meg, as she rustled about in her best gray silk, while waiting for Demi, who always escorted his pious mother to church as a peace offering for crossing her wishes in other things.

"I will, dear; I'm lying in wait for all three boys today, like an old spider; and I will have a good talk with each. They know I understand them, and they always open their hearts sooner or

91

later. You look like a nice, plump little Quakeress, Meg; and no one will believe that big boy is your son," added Mrs. Jo, as Demi came in shining with Sunday neatness, from his well-blacked boots to his smooth brown head.

"You flatter me, to soften my heart toward *your* boy. I know your ways, Jo, and I don't give in. Be firm, and spare me a scene by and by. As for John, as long as he is satisfied with his old mother, I don't care what people think," answered Mrs. Meg, accepting with a smile the little posy of sweet peas and mignon-ette Demi brought her.

Then, having buttoned her dove-colored gloves with care, she took her son's arm and went proudly away to the carriage, where Amy and Bess waited, while Jo called after them, just as Marmee used to do, "Girls, *have* you got nice pocket-handker-chiefs?" They all smiled at the familiar words, and three white banners waved as they drove away, leaving the spider to watch for her first fly. She did not wait long. Daisy was lying down with a wet cheek on the little hymnbook out of which she and Nat used to sing together; so Mrs. Jo strolled about the lawn, look-ing very like a wandering mushroom with her large buff um-brella.

Dan had gone for a ten-mile stroll; and Nat was supposed to have accompanied him, but presently came sneaking back, un-able to tear himself away from the Dovecote or lose a moment of nearness to his idol that last day. Mrs. Jo saw him at once, and beckoned him to a rustic seat under the old elm, where they could have their confidences undisturbed, and both keep an eye on a certain white-curtained window, half hidden in vines.

"Nice and cool here. I'm not up to one of Dan's tramps today —it's so warm, and he goes so like a steam-engine. He headed for the swamp where his pet snakes used to live, and I begged to be excused," said Nat, fanning himself with his straw hat, though the day was not oppressive.

"I'm glad you did. Sit and rest with me, and have one of our good old talks. We've both been so busy lately, I feel as if I didn't half know your plans; and I want to," answered Mrs. Jo, feeling sure that though they might start with Leipzig they would bring up at Plumfield.

"You are very kind, and there's nothing I'd like better. I don't realize I'm going so far—suppose I sha'n't till I get afloat. It's a splendid start, and I don't know how I can ever thank Mr. Laurie for all he's done, or you either," added Nat, with a break in his voice; for he was a tender-hearted fellow, and never forgot a kindness.

"You can thank us beautifully by being and doing all we hope and expect of you, my dear. In the new life you are going to there will be a thousand trials and temptations, and only your own wit and wisdom to rely on. That will be the time to test the principles we have tried to give you, and see how firm they are. Of course you will make mistakes—we all do; but don't let go of your conscience and drift along blindly. Watch and pray, dear Nat; and while your hand gains skill, let head grow wiser, and keep heart as innocent and warm as it is now."

"I'll try, Mother Bhaer, my very best to be a credit to you. I know I shall improve in my music—can't help it there; but I never shall be very wise, I'm afraid. As for my heart, you know I leave it behind me in good keeping."

As he spoke, Nat's eyes were fixed on the window with a look of love and longing that made his quiet face both manly and sad —plainly showing how strong a hold this boyish affection had upon him.

"I want to speak of that; and I know you will forgive what seems hard, because I do most heartily sympathize with you," said Mrs. Jo, glad to have her say.

"Yes, do talk about Daisy! I think of nothing but leaving and losing her. I have no hope—I suppose it is too much to ask; only I can't help loving her, wherever I am!" cried Nat, with a mixture of defiance and despair in his face that rather startled Mrs. Jo.

"Listen to me and I'll try to give you both comfort and good advice. We all know that Daisy is fond of you, but her mother objects, and being a good girl she tries to obey. Young people think they never can change, but they do in the most wonderful manner, and very few die of broken hearts." Mrs. Jo smiled as she remembered another boy whom she had once tried to comfort, and then went soberly on while Nat listened as if his fate hung upon her lips.

"One of two things will happen. You will find someone else to love, or, better still, be so busy and happy in your music that you will be willing to wait for time to settle the matter for you both. Daisy will perhaps forget when you are gone, and be glad you are only friends. At any rate it is much wiser to have no promises made; then both are free, and in a year or two may meet to laugh over the little romance nipped in the bud."

"Do you honestly think that?" asked Nat, looking at her so keenly that the truth had to come; for all his heart was in those frank blue eyes of his.

"No, I don't!" answered Mrs. Jo.

"Then if you were in my place, what would you do?" he added, with a tone of command never heard in his gentle voice before.

"Bless me! The boy is in dead earnest, and I shall forget prudence in sympathy I'm afraid," thought Mrs. Jo, surprised and pleased by the unexpected manliness Nat showed.

"I'll tell you what I should do. I'd say to myself, 'I'll prove that my love is strong and faithful, and make Daisy's mother proud to give her to me by being not only a good musician but an excellent man, and so command respect and confidence. This I will try for; and if I fail, I shall be the better for the effort, and find comfort in the thought that I did my best for her sake.'"

"That is what I meant to do. But I wanted a word of hope to give me courage," cried Nat, firing up as if the smouldering spark was set ablaze by a breath of encouragement. "Other fellows, poorer and stupider than I, have done great things and come to honor. Why may not I, though I'm nothing now? I know Mrs. Brooke remembers what I came from, but my father was *honest* though everything went wrong; and I have nothing to be ashamed of though I *was* a charity boy. I never will be ashamed of my people or myself, and I'll make other folks respect me if I can."

"Good! That's the right spirit, Nat. Hold to it and make yourself a man. No one will be quicker to see and admire the brave work than my sister Meg. She does not despise your poverty or your past; but mothers are very tender over their daughters, and we Marches, though we have been poor, *are,* I confess, a little proud of our good family. We don't care for money; but a long line of virtuous ancestors *is* something to desire and to be proud of."

"Well, the Blakes are a good lot. I looked 'em up, and not one was ever in prison, hanged, or disgraced in any way. We used to be rich and honored years ago, but we've died out and got poor, and father was a street musician rather than beg; and I'll be one again before I'll do the mean things some men do and pass muster."

Nat was so excited that Mrs. Jo indulged in a laugh to calm him, and both went on more quietly.

"I told my sister all that and it pleased her. I am sure if you do well these next few years that she will relent and all be happily settled, unless that wonderful change, which you don't believe possible, should occur. Now, cheer up; don't be lackadaisical and blue. Say good-bye cheerfully and bravely, show a manly front, and leave a pleasant memory behind you. We all wish you well and hope much for you. Don't disappoint but surprise us by your success in all ways. Write to me every week and I'll send a good, gossipy answer. Be careful what you write to Daisy; don't gush or wail, for sister Meg will see the letters; and you can help your cause very much by sending sensible, cheery accounts of your life to us all."

"I will. I will. It looks brighter and better already, and I won't lose my one comfort by any fault of my own. Thank you so much, Mother Bhaer, for taking my side. I felt so ungrateful and mean and crushed when I thought you all considered me a sneak, who had no business to love such a precious girl as Daisy. No one said anything, but I knew how you felt, and that Mr. Laurie sent me off partly to get me out of the way. Oh, dear, life is pretty tough sometimes, isn't it?" And Nat took his head in both hands as if it ached with the confusion of hopes and fears, passions and plans that proved boyhood was past and manhood begun.

"Very tough, but it is that very struggle with obstacles which does us good. Things have been made easy for you in many ways, but no one can do everything. You must paddle your own canoe now, and learn to avoid the rapids and steer straight to the port you want to reach. I don't know just what your temptations will be, for you have no bad habits and seem to love music so well, nothing can lure you from it. I only hope you won't work too hard."

"I feel as if I *could* work like a horse, I'm so eager to get on; but I'll take care. Can't waste time being sick, and you've given me doses enough to keep me all right, I guess." Nat laughed as he remembered the book of directions Mrs. Jo had written for him to consult on all occasions.

She immediately added some verbal ones on the subject of foreign messes, and having mounted one of her pet hobbies, was on full gallop when Emil was seen strolling about on the roof of the old house, that being his favorite promenade; for there he could fancy himself walking the deck, with only blue sky and fresh air about him.

"I want a word with the Commodore, and up there we shall be nice and quiet. Go and play to Daisy; it will put her to sleep and do you both good. Sit in the porch so I can keep an eye on you as I promised." And with a motherly pat on the shoulder, Mrs. Jo left Nat to his delightful task and briskly ascended to the housetop, not up the trellis as of old but by means of the stairs inside.

Emerging on the platform she found Emil cutting his initials afresh in the woodwork and singing "Pull for the Shore" like the tuneful mariner he was.

"Come aboard and make yourself at home, Aunty," he said, with a playful salute. "I'm just leaving a P.P.C. in the old place, so when you fly up here for refuge, you'll remember me."

"Ah, my dear, I'm not likely to forget you. It doesn't need E.B.H. cut on all the trees and railings to remind me of my sailor boy." And Mrs. Jo took the seat nearest the blue figure astride the balustrade, not quite sure how to begin the little sermon she wanted to preach.

"Well, you don't pipe your eye and look squally when I sheer off as you used to, and that's a comfort. I like to leave port in fair weather and have a jolly send-off all round. Specially this time, for it will be a year or more before we drop anchor here again," answered Emil pushing his cap back, and glancing about him as if he loved old Plum and would be sorry never to see it anymore.

"You have salt water enough without my adding to it. I'm getting to be quite a Spartan mother, and send my sons to battle with no wailing, only the command, 'With your shield or on it,' " said Mrs. Jo, cheerfully, adding after a pause, "I often wish I could go too, and some day I will, when you are captain and have a ship of your own—as I've no doubt you will before long with Uncle Herman to push you on."

"When I do I'll christen her the 'Jolly Jo' and take you as first mate. It would be regular larks to have you aboard, and I'd be a proud man to carry you round the world you've wanted to see so long and never could," answered Emil, caught at once by this splendid vision.

"I'll make my first voyage with you and enjoy myself immensely in spite of seasickness and all the stormy winds that blow. I've always thought I'd like to see a wreck, a nice safe one with all saved after great danger and heroic deeds, while we clung like Mr. Pillicoddy to maintop jibs and lee scuppers."

"No wrecks yet, ma'am, but we'll try to accommodate customers. Captain says I'm a lucky dog and bring fair weather, so we'll save the dirty weather for you if you want it," laughed Emil, digging away at the ship in full sail which he was adding to his design.

"Thanks, I hope you will. This long voyage will give you new experiences, and being an officer, you will have new duties and responsibilities. Are you ready for them? You take everything so gaily, I've been wondering if you realized that now you will have not only to obey but to command also, and power is a dangerous thing. Be careful that you don't abuse it or let it make a tyrant of you."

"Right you are, ma'am. I've seen plenty of that, and have got my bearings pretty well, I guess. I sha'n't have very wide swing with Peters over me, but I'll see that the boys don't get abused when he's bowsed up his jib. No right to speak before, but now I won't stand it."

"That sounds mysteriously awful. Could I ask what nautical torture 'bowsing jibs' is?" asked Mrs. Jo, in a tone of deep interest.

"Getting drunk. Peters can hold more grog than any man I ever saw; he keeps right side up, but is as savage as a norther, and makes things lively all round. I've seen him knock a fellow down with a belaying pin, and couldn't lend a hand. Better luck now, I hope." And Emil frowned as if he already trod the quarter-deck, lord of all he surveyed.

"Don't get into trouble, for even Uncle Herman's favor won't cover insubordination, you know. You have proved yourself a good sailor; now be a good officer, which is a harder thing, I fancy. It takes a fine character to rule justly and kindly; you will have to put by your boyish ways and remember your dignity. That will be excellent training for you, Emil, and sober you down a bit. No more skylarking except here, so mind your ways and do honor to your buttons," said Mrs. Jo, tapping one of the very bright brass ones that ornamented the new suit Emil was so proud of.

"I'll do my best. I know my time for skrim-shander (chaff) is over, and I must steer a straighter course; but don't you fear, Jack ashore is a very different craft from what he is with blue water under his keel. I had a long talk with Uncle last night and got my orders; I won't forget 'em nor all I owe him. As for you, I'll name my first ship as I say, and have your bust for the figurehead, see if I don't." And Emil gave his aunt a hearty kiss to seal the vow, which proceeding much amused Nat, playing softly in the porch of the Dovecote.

"You do me proud, Captain. But, dear, I want to say one thing and then I'm done, for you don't need much advice of mine after my good man has spoken. I read somewhere that every inch of rope used in the British Navy has a strand of red in it, so that wherever a bit of it is found it is known. That is the text of my little sermon to you. Virtue, which means honor, honesty, courage, and all that makes character, is the red thread that marks a good man wherever he is. Keep that always and everywhere, so that even if wrecked by misfortune, that sign shall still be found and recognized. Yours is a rough life, and your mates not all we could wish, but you can be a gentleman in the true sense of the word; and no matter what happens to your body, keep your soul clean, your heart true to those who love you, and do your duty to the end."

As she spoke Emil had risen and stood listening with his cap off and a grave, bright look as if taking orders from a superior officer; when she ended, he answered briefly but heartily, "Please God, I will!"

"That's all. I have little fear for you, but one never knows when or how the weak moment may come, and sometimes a chance word helps us, as so many my dear mother spoke come back to me now for my own comfort and the guidance of my boys," said Mrs. Jo, rising; for the word had been said and no more were needed.

"I've stored 'em up and know where to find 'em when wanted. Often and often in my watch I've seen old Plum, and heard you and Uncle talking so plainly, I'd have sworn I was here. It *is* a rough life, Aunty, but a wholesome one if a fellow loves it as I do, and has an anchor to windward as I have. Don't worry about me, and I'll come home next year with a chest of tea that will cheer your heart and give you ideas enough for a dozen novels. Going below? All right, steady in the gangway! I'll be along by the time you've got out the cake box. Last chance for a good old lunch ashore."

Mrs. Jo descended laughing, and Emil finished his ship, whistling cheerfully, neither dreaming when and where this little chat on the housetop would return to the memory of one of them.

Dan was harder to catch, and not until evening did a quiet moment come in that busy family; then, while the rest were roaming about, Mrs. Jo sat down to read in the study, and presently Dan looked in at the window.

"Come and rest after your long tramp; you must be tired," she called, with an inviting nod toward the big sofa where so many boys had reposed—as much as that active animal ever does.

"Afraid I shall disturb you." But Dan looked as if he wanted to stay his restless feet somewhere.

"Not a bit; I'm always ready to talk, shouldn't be a woman if I were not," laughed Mrs. Jo, as Dan swung himself in and sat down with an air of contentment very pleasant to see.

"Last day is over, yet somehow I don't seem to hanker to be off. Generally, I'm rather anxious to cut loose after a short stop. Odd, ain't it?" asked Dan, gravely picking grass and leaves out of his hair and beard, for he had been lying on the grass, thinking many thoughts in the quiet summer night.

"Not at all. You are beginning to get civilized. It's a good sign, and I'm glad to see it," answered Mrs. Jo, promptly. "You've had your swing, and want a change. Hope the farming will give it to you, though helping the Indians pleases me more —it is so much better to work for others than for one's self alone."

"So 'tis," assented Dan, heartily. "I seem to want to root somewhere and have folks of my own to take care of. Tired of my own company, I suppose, now I've seen so much better. I'm a rough, ignorant lot, and I've been thinking maybe I've missed it loafing round creation, instead of going in for education as the other chaps did. Hey?"

He looked anxiously at Mrs. Jo; and she tried to hide the surprise this new outburst caused her; for till now Dan had scorned books and gloried in his freedom.

"No. I don't think so in your case. So far I'm sure the free life was best. Now that you are a man you can control that lawless nature better, but as a boy only great activity and much adventure could keep you out of mischief. Time is taming my colt, you see, and I shall yet be proud of him, whether he makes a pack-horse of himself to carry help to the starving or goes to plowing as Pegasus did."

Dan liked the comparison, and smiled as he lounged in the sofa corner, with the new thoughtfulness in his eyes.

"Glad you think so. The fact is it's going to take a heap of taming to make me go well in harness anywhere. I want to, and I try now and then, but always kick over the traces and run away. No lives lost yet; but I shouldn't wonder if there was some time, and a general smash-up."

"Why, Dan, did you have any dangerous adventures during this last absence? I fancied so, but didn't ask before, knowing you'd tell me if I could help in any way. Can I?" And Mrs. Jo looked anxiously at him; for a sudden lowering expression had come into his face, and he leaned forward as if to hide it.

"Nothing very bad; but 'Frisco isn't just a heaven on earth, you know, and it's harder to be a saint there than here," he

answered slowly. Then, as if he had made up his mind to
" 'fess," as the children used to say, he sat up, and added rapidly, in a half-defiant, half-shamefaced way, "I tried gambling,
and it wasn't good for me."

"Was that how you made your money?"

"Not a penny of it! That's all honest, if speculation isn't a
bigger sort of gambling. I won a lot, but I lost or gave it away,
and cut the whole concern before it got the better of me."

"Thank heaven for that! Don't try it again; it may have the
terrible fascination for you it has for so many. Keep to your
mountains and prairies, and shun cities, if these things tempt
you, Dan. Better lose your life than your soul, and one such
passion leads to worse sins, as you know better than I."

Dan nodded, and seeing how troubled she was, said, in a
lighter tone, though still the shadow of that past experience
remained, "Don't be scared; I'm all right now; and a burnt dog
dreads the fire. I don't drink, or do the things you dread; don't
care for 'em; but I get excited, and then this devilish temper of
mine is more than I can manage. Fighting a moose or a buffalo
is all right; but when you pitch into a man, no matter how great
a scamp he is, you've got to look out. I shall kill someone someday; that's all I'm afraid of. I do hate a sneak!" And Dan
brought his fist down on the table with a blow that made the
lamp totter and the books skip.

"That always was your trial, Dan, and I can sympathize with
you, for I've been trying to govern my own temper all my life,
and haven't learnt yet," said Mrs. Jo, with a sigh. "For heaven's
sake, guard your demon well, and don't let a moment's fury ruin
all your life. As I said to Nat, watch and pray, my dear boy.
There is no other help or hope for human weakness but God's
love and patience."

Tears were in Mrs. Jo's eyes as she spoke, for she felt this
deeply, and knew how hard a task it is to rule these bosom sins
of ours. Dan looked touched, also uncomfortable, as he always
did when religion of any sort was mentioned, though he had a

simple creed of his own, and tried to live up to it in his blind way.

"I don't do much praying; don't seem to come handy to me; but I can watch like a redskin, only it's easier to mount guard over a lurking grizzly than my own cursed temper. It's that I'm afraid of, if I settle down. I can get on with wild beasts first-rate; but men rile me awfully, and I can't take it out in a free fight, as I can with a bear or a wolf. Guess I'd better head for the Rockies, and stay there a spell longer—till I'm tame enough for decent folks, if I ever am." And Dan leaned his rough head on his hands in a despondent attitude.

"Try my sort of help, and don't give up. Read more, study a little, and try to meet a better class of people, who won't 'rile,' but soothe and strengthen you. *We* don't make you savage, I'm sure; for you have been as meek as a lamb, and made us very happy."

"Glad of it; but I've felt like a hawk in a henhouse all the same, and wanted to pounce and tear more than once. Not so much as I used, though," added Dan, after a short laugh at Mrs. Jo's surprised face. "I'll try your plan, and keep good company this bout if I can; but a man can't pick and choose, knocking about as I do."

"Yes, you can this time, for you are going on a peaceful errand and can keep clear of temptation if you try. Take some books and read. That's an immense help, and books are always good company if you have the right sort. Let me pick out some for you." And Mrs. Jo made a beeline to the well-laden shelves, which were the joy of her heart and the comfort of her life.

"Give me travels and stories, please; don't want any pious works, can't seem to relish 'em, and won't pretend I do," said Dan, following to look over her head with small favor at the long lines of well-worn volumes.

Mrs. Jo turned short round, and putting a hand on either broad shoulder, looked him in the eye, saying soberly, "Now, Dan, see here. Never sneer at good things or pretend to be worse than you are. Don't let false shame make you neglect the religion without which no man can live. You needn't talk about it if you don't like, but don't shut your heart to it in whatever shape it comes. Nature is your God now; she has done much for you; let her do more, and lead you to know and love a wiser and more tender teacher, friend, and comforter than she can ever be. That is your only hope. Don't throw it away, and waste time, for sooner or later you will feel the need of Him, and He will come to you and hold you up when all other help fails."

Dan stood motionless, and let her read in his softened eyes the dumb desire that lived in his heart, though he had no words to tell it, and only permitted her to catch a glimpse of the divine spark which smoulders or burns clearly in every human soul. He did not speak; and glad to be spared some answer which should belie his real feeling, Mrs. Jo hastened to say, with her most motherly smile, "I saw in your room the little Bible I gave you long ago; it was well worn *outside,* but fresh within, as if not much read. Will you promise me to read a little once a week, dear, for my sake? Sunday is a quiet day everywhere, and this book is never old nor out of place. Begin with the stories you used to love when I told them to you boys. David was your favorite, you remember? Read him again; he'll suit you even better now, and you'll find his sins and repentance useful reading till you come to the life and work of a diviner example than he. You will do it, for love of Mother Bhaer, who always loved her 'firebrand' and hoped to save him?"

"I will," answered Dan, with the sudden brightening of face that was like a sunburst through a cloud, full of promise though so short-lived and rare.

Mrs. Jo turned at once to the books and began to talk of them, knowing well that Dan would not bear anymore just then. He seemed relieved, for it was always hard for him to show his inner self, and he took pride in hiding it as an Indian does in concealing pain or fear.

"Hullo, here's old Sintram! I remember him; used to like him and his tantrums, and read about 'em to Ted. There he is riding ahead with Death and the Devil alongside."

As Dan looked at the little picture of the young man with horse and hound going bravely up the rocky defile, accompanied by the companions who ride beside most men through this world, a curious impulse made Mrs. Jo say quickly, "That's you, Dan, just you at this time! Danger and sin are near you in the life you lead; moods and passions torment you; the bad father left you to fight alone, and the wild spirit drives you to wander up and down the world looking for peace and self-control. Even the horse and hound are there, your Octoo and Don, faithful friends, unscared by the strange mates that go with you. You have not got the armor yet, but I'm trying to show you where to find it. You remember the mother Sintram loved and longed to find, and did find when his battle was bravely fought, his reward well earned? You can recollect *your* mother; and I have always felt that all the good qualities you possess come from her. Act out the beautiful old story in this as in the other parts, and try to give her back a son to be proud of."

Quite carried away by the likeness of the quaint tale to Dan's life and needs, Mrs. Jo went on pointing to the various pictures which illustrated it, and when she looked up was surprised to see how struck and interested he seemed to be. Like all people of his temperament he was very impressionable, and his life among hunters and Indians had made him superstitious; he believed in dreams, liked weird tales, and whatever appealed to the eye or mind vividly impressed him more than the wisest words. The story of poor, tormented Sintram came back clearly as he looked and listened, symbolizing his secret trials even more truly than Mrs. Jo knew; and just at that moment this had an effect upon him that never was forgotten. But all he said was, "Small chance of that. I don't take much stock in the idea of meeting folks in heaven. Guess Mother won't remember the poor little brat she left so long ago. Why should she?"

"Because true mothers never forget their children; and I

know *she* was one, from the fact that she ran away from the cruel husband, to save her little son from bad influences. Had she lived, life would have been happier for you, with this tender friend to help and comfort you. Never forget that she risked everything for your sake, and don't let it be in vain."

Mrs. Jo spoke very earnestly, knowing that this was the one sweet memory of Dan's early life, and glad to have recalled it at this moment; for suddenly a great tear splashed down on the page where Sintram kneels at his mother's feet, wounded, but victorious over sin and death. She looked up, well pleased to have touched Dan to the heart's core, as that drop proved; but a sweep of the arm brushed away the telltale, and his beard hid the mate to it, as he shut the book, saying with a suppressed quiver in his strong voice, "I'll keep this, if nobody wants it. I'll read it over, and maybe it will do me good. I'd like to meet her anywhere, but don't believe I ever shall."

"Keep it and welcome. My mother gave it to me; and when you read it try to believe that neither of your mothers will ever forget you."

Mrs. Jo gave the book with a caress; and simply saying, "Thanks. Good night," Dan thrust it into his pocket, and walked straight away to the river to recover from this unwonted mood of tenderness and confidence.

Next day the travelers were off. All were in good spirits, and a cloud of handkerchiefs whitened the air as they drove away in the old 'bus, waving their hats to everyone and kissing their hands, especially to Mother Bhaer, who said in her prophetic tone as she wiped her eyes, when the familiar rumble died away, "I have a feeling that something is going to happen to some of them, and they will never come back to me, or come back changed. Well, I can only say, 'God be with my boys!' "

And He was.

CHAPTER 7

THE LION AND THE LAMB

WHEN THE BOYS were gone a lull fell upon Plumfield, and the family scattered to various places for brief outings, as August had come and all felt the need of change. The Professor took Mrs. Jo to the mountains. The Laurences were at the seashore, and there Meg's family and the Bhaer boys took turns to visit, as someone must always be at home to keep things in order.

Mrs. Meg, with Daisy, was in office when the events occurred which we are about to relate. Rob and Ted were just up from Rocky Nook, and Nan was passing a week with her friend as the only relaxation she allowed herself. Demi was off on a run with Tom, so Rob was man of the house, with old Silas as general overseer. The sea air seemed to have gone to Ted's head, for he was unusually freakish, and led his gentle aunt and poor Rob a life of it with his pranks. Octoo was worn out with the wild rides he took, and Don openly rebelled when ordered to leap and show off his accomplishments; while the girls at college were both amused and worried by the ghosts who haunted the grounds at night, the unearthly melodies that disturbed their studious hours, and the hairsbreadth escapes of this restless boy

107

by flood and field and fire. Something happened at length which effectually sobered Ted and made a lasting impression on both the boys; for sudden danger and a haunting fear turned the Lion into a lamb and the Lamb into a lion, as far as courage went.

On the first of September—the boys never forgot the date— after a pleasant tramp and good luck with their fishing, the brothers were lounging in the barn; for Daisy had company, and the lads kept out of the way.

"I tell you what it is, Bobby, that dog is sick. He won't play, nor eat, nor drink, and acts queerly. Dan will kill us if anything happens to him," said Ted, looking at Don, who lay near his kennel resting a moment after one of the restless wanderings which kept him vibrating between the door of Dan's room and the shady corner of the yard, where his master had settled him with an old cap to guard till he came back.

"It's the hot weather, perhaps. But I sometimes think he's pining for Dan. Dogs do, you know, and the poor fellow has been low in his mind ever since the boys went. Maybe something has happened to Dan. Don howled last night and can't rest. I've heard of such things," answered Rob, thoughtfully.

"Pooh! He can't know. He's cross. I'll stir him up and take him for a run. Always makes me feel better. Hi, boy! Wake up and be jolly." And Ted snapped his fingers at the dog, who only looked at him with grim indifference.

"Better let him alone. If he isn't right tomorrow, we'll take him to Dr. Watkins and see what he says." And Rob went on watching the swallows as he lay in the hay polishing up some Latin verses he had made.

The spirit of perversity entered into Ted, and merely because he was told not to tease Don he went on doing it, pretending that it was for the dog's good. Don took no heed of his pats, commands, reproaches, or insults, till Ted's patience gave out; and seeing a convenient switch nearby he could not resist the temptation to conquer the great hound by force, since gentleness failed to win obedience. He had the wisdom to chain Don up first, for a blow from any hand but his master's made him savage, and Ted had more than once tried the experiment, as the dog remembered. This indignity roused Don and he sat up with a growl. Rob heard it, and seeing Ted raise the switch, ran to interfere, exclaiming, "Don't touch him! Dan forbade it! Leave the poor thing in peace. I won't allow it."

Rob seldom commanded, but when he did Master Ted had to give in. His temper was up, and Rob's masterful tone made it impossible to resist one cut at the rebellious dog before he submitted. Only a single blow, but it was a costly one, for as it fell, the dog sprung at Ted with a snarl, and Rob, rushing between the two, felt the sharp teeth pierce his leg. A word made Don let go and drop remorsefully at Rob's feet, for he loved him and was evidently sorry to have hurt his friend by mistake. With a forgiving pat Rob left him, to limp to the barn followed by Ted, whose wrath was changed to shame and sorrow when he saw the red drops on Rob's sock and the little wounds in his leg.

"I'm awfully sorry. Why *did* you get in the way? Here, wash it up, and I'll get a rag to tie on it," he said, quickly filling a sponge with water and pulling out a very demoralized handkerchief.

Rob usually made light of his own mishaps and was over ready to forgive if others were to blame; but now he sat quite still, looking at the purple marks with such a strange expression on his white face that Ted was troubled, though he added with a laugh, "Why, you're not afraid of a little dog like that, are you, Bobby?"

"I am afraid of hydrophobia. But if Don *is* mad I'd rather be the one to have it," answered Rob, with a smile and a shiver.

At that dreadful word Ted turned whiter than his brother, and, dropping sponge and handkerchief, stared at him with a frightened face, whispering in a tone of despair, "Oh, Rob, don't say it! What shall we do, what *shall* we do?"

"Call Nan. She will know. Don't scare Aunty, or tell a soul

but Nan. She's on the back piazza. Get her out here as quick as
you can. I'll wash it till she comes. Maybe it's nothing; don't
look so staggered, Ted. I only thought it might be, as Don is
queer."

Rob tried to speak bravely, but Ted's long legs felt strangely
weak as he hurried away, and it was lucky he met no one, for his
face would have betrayed him. Nan was swinging luxuriously in
a hammock, amusing herself with a lively treatise on croup,
when an agitated boy suddenly clutched her, whispering, as he
nearly pulled her overboard, "Come to Rob in the barn! Don's
mad and he's bitten him, and we don't know what to do! It's all
my fault! No one must know. Oh, do be quick!"

Nan was on her feet at once, startled, but with her wits about
her, and both were off without more words as they dodged
round the house where unconscious Daisy chatted with her
friends in the parlor and Aunt Meg peacefully took her afternoon nap upstairs.

Rob had braced up, and was as calm and steady as ever when
they found him in the harness room, whither he had wisely
retired, to escape observation. The story was soon told, and
after a look at Don, now in his kennel, sad and surly, Nan said
slowly, with her eye on the full water pan, "Rob, there is one
thing to do for the sake of safety, and it must be done at once.
We can't wait to see if Don is—sick—or to go for a doctor. I *can*
do it, and I *will;* but it is very painful, and I hate to hurt you,
dear."

A most unprofessional quiver got into Nan's voice as she
spoke, and her keen eyes dimmed as she looked at the two
anxious young faces turned so confidingly to her for help.

"I know, burn it. Well, do it, please. I can bear it. But Ted
better go away," said Rob, with a firm setting of his lips, and a
nod at his afflicted brother.

"I won't stir! I can stand it if he can, only it ought to be me!"
cried Ted, with a desperate effort not to cry, so full of grief and

fear and shame was he that it seemed as if he couldn't bear it like a man.

"He'd better stay and help; do him good," answered Nan, sternly, because her heart was faint within her, knowing as she did all that might be in store for both poor boys. "Keep quiet. I'll be back in a minute," she added, going toward the house, while her quick mind hastily planned what was best to be done.

It was ironing day, and a hot fire still burned in the empty kitchen, for the maids were upstairs resting. Nan put a slender poker to heat, and as she sat waiting for it, covered her face with her hands, asking help in this sudden need, strength, courage, and wisdom; for there was no one else to call upon, and young as she was, she knew what was to be done if she only had the nerve to do it. Any other patient would have been calmly interesting, but dear, good Robin, his father's pride, his mother's comfort, everyone's favorite and friend, that he should be in danger was very terrible. And a few hot tears dropped on the well-scoured table as Nan tried to calm her trouble by remembering how very likely it was to be all a mistake, a natural but vain alarm.

"I must make light of it or the boys will break down, and then there will be a panic. Why afflict and frighten everyone when all is in doubt? I won't. I'll take Rob to Dr. Morrison at once, and have the dog man to see Don. Then, having done all we can, we will either laugh at our scare—if it is one—or be ready for whatever comes. Now for my poor boy."

Armed with the red-hot poker, a pitcher of ice water, and several handkerchiefs from the clotheshorse, Nan went back to the barn, ready to do her best in this her most serious "emergency case." The boys sat like statues, one of despair, the other of resignation; and it took all Nan's boasted nerve to do her work quickly and well.

"Now, Rob, only a minute, then we are safe. Stand by, Ted; he may be a bit faintish."

Rob shut his eyes, clinched his hands, and sat like a hero. Ted

knelt behind him, white as a sheet, and as weak as a girl; for the
pangs of remorse were rending him, and his heart failed at the
thought of all this pain because of his willfulness. It was all over
in a moment, with only one little groan; but when Nan looked
to her assistant to hand the water, poor Ted needed it the most,
for he had fainted away, and lay on the floor in a pathetic heap
of arms and legs.

Rob laughed, and, cheered by that unexpected sound, Nan
bound up the wound with hands that never trembled, though
great drops stood on her forehead, and she shared the water
with patient number one before she turned to patient number
two. Ted was much ashamed, and quite broken in spirit, when
he found how he had failed at the critical moment, and begged
them not to tell, as he really could not help it; then by way of
finishing his utter humiliation, a burst of hysterical tears disgraced his manly soul, and did him a world of good.

"Never mind, never mind, we are all right now, and no one
need be the wiser," said Nan, briskly, as poor Ted hiccoughed
on Rob's shoulder, laughing and crying in the most tempestuous
manner, while his brother soothed him, and the young doctor
fanned both with Silas's old straw hat.

"Now, boys, listen to me and remember what I say. We won't
alarm anyone *yet,* for I've made up my mind our scare is all
nonsense. Don was out lapping the water as I came by, and I
don't believe he's mad anymore than I am. Still, to ease our
minds and compose our spirits, and get our guilty faces out of
sight for a while, I think we had better drive in town to my old
Dr. Morrison, and let him just take a look at my work, and give
us some quieting little dose; for we are all rather shaken by this
flurry. Sit still, Rob, and Ted, you harness up while I run and get
my hat and tell Aunty to excuse me to Daisy. I don't know those
Penniman girls, and she will be glad of our room at tea, and
we'll have a cozy bite at my house, and come home as gay as
larks."

Nan talked on as a vent for the hidden emotions which

professional pride would not allow her to show, and the boys approved her plan at once; for action is always easier than quiet waiting. Ted went staggering away to wash his face at the pump, and rub some color into his cheeks before he harnessed the horse. Rob lay tranquilly on the hay, looking up at the swallows again as he lived through some very memorable moments. Boy as he was, the thought of death coming suddenly to him, and in this way, might well make him sober; for it is a very solemn thing to be arrested in the midst of busy life by the possibility of the great change. There were no sins to be repented of, few faults, and many happy, dutiful years to remember with infinite comfort. So Rob had no fears to daunt him, no regrets to sadden, and, best of all, a very strong and simple piety to sustain and cheer him.

"Mein Vater," was his first thought; for Rob was very near the Professor's heart, and the loss of his eldest would have been a bitter blow. These words, whispered with a tremble of the lips that had been so firm when the hot iron burned, recalled that other Father who is always near, always tender and helpful. And, folding his hands, Rob said the heartiest little prayer he ever prayed, there on the hay, to the soft twitter of the brooding birds. It did him good. And wisely laying all his fear and doubt and trouble in God's hand, the boy felt ready for whatever was to come, and from that hour kept steadily before him the one duty that was plain—to be brave and cheerful, keep silent, and hope for the best.

Nan stole her hat, and left a note on Daisy's pincushion, saying she had taken the boys to drive, and all would be out of the way till after tea. Then she hurried back and found her patients much better, the one for work, the other for rest. In they got, and putting Rob on the back seat with his leg up, drove away, looking as gay and carefree as if nothing had happened.

Dr. Morrison made light of the affair, but told Nan she had done right; and as the much-relieved lads went downstairs, he

added in a whisper, "Send the dog off for a while, and keep
your eye on the boy. Don't let him know it, and report to me if
anything seems wrong. One never knows in these cases. No
harm to be careful."

Nan nodded, and feeling much relieved now that the responsibility was off her shoulders, took the lads to Dr. Watkins, who
promised to come out later and examine Don. A merry tea at
Nan's house, which was kept open for her all summer, did them
good, and by the time they got home in the cool of the evening
no sign of the panic remained but Ted's heavy eyes, and a slight
limp when Rob walked. As the guests were still chattering on
the front piazza they retired to the back, and Ted soothed his
remorseful soul by swinging Rob in the hammock, while Nan
told stories till the dog man arrived.

He said Don was a little under the weather, but no more mad
than the gray kitten that purred round his legs while the exami-
nation went on.

"He wants his master, and feels the heat. Fed too well, perhaps. I'll keep him a few weeks and send him home all right,"
said Dr. Watkins, as Don laid his great head in his hand, and
kept his intelligent eyes on his face, evidently feeling that this
man understood his trials, and knew what to do for him.

So Don departed without a murmur, and our three conspira-
tors took counsel together how to spare the family all anxiety,
and give Rob the rest his leg demanded. Fortunately, he always
spent many hours in his little study, so he could lie on the sofa
with a book in his hand as long as he liked, without exciting any
remark. Being of a quiet temperament, he did not worry himself
or Nan with useless fears, but believed what was told him, and
dismissing all dark possibilities, went cheerfully on his way, soon
recovering from the shock of what he called "our scare."

But excitable Ted was harder to manage, and it took all Nan's
wit and wisdom to keep him from betraying the secret; for it
was best to say nothing and spare all discussion of the subject
for Rob's sake. Ted's remorse preyed upon him, and having no

"Mum" to confide in, he was very miserable. By day he devoted himself to Rob, waiting on him, talking to him, gazing anxiously at him, and worrying the good fellow very much; though he wouldn't own it, since Ted found comfort in it. But at night, when all was quiet, Ted's lively imagination and heavy heart got the better of him, and kept him awake, or set him walking in his sleep. Nan had her eye on him, and more than once administered a little dose to give him rest, read to him, scolded him, and when she caught him haunting the house in the watches of the night, threatened to lock him up if he did not stay in his bed.

This wore off after a while, but a change came over the freakish boy, and everyone observed it, even before his mother returned to ask what they had done to quench the Lion's spirits. He was gay, but not so heedless; and often when the old willfulness beset him, he would check it sharply, look at Rob, and give up, or stalk away to have his sulk out alone. He no longer made fun of his brother's old-fashioned ways and bookish tastes, but treated him with a new and very marked respect, which touched and pleased modest Rob, and much amazed all observers. It seemed as if he felt that he owed him reparation for the foolish act that might have cost him his life. And love being stronger than will, Ted forgot his pride, and paid his debt like an honest boy.

"I don't understand it," said Mrs. Jo, after a week of home life, much impressed by the good behavior of her younger son. "Ted is such a saint, I'm afraid we are going to lose him. Is it Meg's sweet influence, or Daisy's fine cooking, or the pellets I catch Nan giving him on the sly? Some witchcraft has been at work during my absence, and this will-o'-the-wisp is so amiable, quiet, and obedient, I don't know him."

"He is growing up, heart's dearest, and being a precocious plant, he begins to bloom early. I also see a change in my Robchen. He is more manly and serious than ever, and is seldom far from me, as if his love for the old papa was growing with his growth. Our boys will often surprise us in this way, Jo, and we can only rejoice over them and leave them to become what Gott pleases."

As the Professor spoke, his eyes rested proudly on the brothers, who came walking up the steps together, Ted's arm over Rob's shoulder as he listened attentively to some geological remarks Rob was making on a stone he held. Usually, Ted made fun of such tastes, and loved to lay boulders in the student's path, put brickbats under his pillow, gravel in his shoes, or send parcels of dirt by express to "Prof. R. M. Bhaer." Lately, he had treated Rob's hobbies respectfully, and had begun to appreciate the good qualities of this quiet brother whom he had always loved but rather undervalued, till his courage under fire won Ted's admiration, and made it impossible to forget a fault, the consequences of which might have been so terrible. The leg was still lame, though doing well, and Ted was always offering an arm as support, gazing anxiously at his brother, and trying to guess his wants; for regret was still keen in Ted's soul, and Rob's forgiveness only made it deeper. A fortunate slip on the stairs gave Rob an excuse for limping, and no one but Nan and Ted saw the wound; so the secret was safe up to this time.

"We are talking about you, my lads. Come in and tell us what good fairy has been at work while we were gone. Or is it because absence sharpens our eyes, that we find such pleasant changes when we come back?" said Mrs. Jo, patting the sofa on either side, while the Professor forgot his piles of letters to admire the pleasing prospect of his wife in a bower of arms, as the boys sat down beside her, smiling affectionately, but feeling a little guilty; for till now "Mum" and "Vater" knew every event in their boyish lives.

"Oh, it's only because Bobby and I have been alone so much; we are sort of twins. I stir him up a bit, and he steadies me a great deal. You and Father do the same, you know. Nice plan. I like it." And Ted felt that he had settled the matter capitally.

"Mother won't thank you for comparing yourself to her, Ted.

I'm flattered at being like father in any way. I try to be," answered Rob, as they laughed at Ted's compliment.

"I do thank him, for it's true. And if you, Robin, do half as much for your brother as Papa has for me, your life won't be a failure," said Mrs. Jo, heartily. "I'm very glad to see you helping one another. It's the right way, and we can't begin too soon to try to understand the needs, virtues, and failings of those nearest us. Love should not make us blind to faults, nor familiarity make us too ready to blame the shortcomings we see. So work away, my sonnies, and give us more surprises of this sort as often as you like."

"The liebe Mutter has said all. I too am well pleased at the friendly brother-warmth I find. It is good for everyone; long may it last!" and Professor Bhaer nodded at the boys, who looked gratified, but rather at a loss how to respond to these flattering remarks.

Rob wisely kept still, fearing to say too much; but Ted burst out, finding it impossible to help telling something, "The fact is I've been finding out what a brave, good chap Bobby is, and I'm trying to make up for all the bother I've been to him. I knew he was awfully wise, but I thought him rather soft, because he liked books better than larks, and was always fussing about his conscience. But I begin to see that it isn't the fellows who talk loudest and show off best that are the manliest. No, sir! Quiet old Bob is a hero and a trump, and I'm proud of him; so would you be if you knew all about it."

Here a look from Rob brought Ted up with a round turn; he stopped short, grew red, and clapped his hand on his mouth in dismay.

"Well, are we not to 'know all about it?'" asked Mrs. Jo, quickly; for her sharp eye saw signs of danger and her maternal heart felt that something had come between her and her sons. "Boys," she went on solemnly, "I suspect that the change we talk about is not altogether the effect of growing up, as we say. It strikes me that Ted has been in mischief and Rob has got him

out of some scrape; hence the lovely mood of my bad boy and
the sober one of my conscientious son, who never hides anything from his mother."

Rob was as red as Ted now, but after a moment's hesitation
he looked up and answered with an air of relief, "Yes, Mother,
that's it; but it's all over and no harm done, and I think we'd
better let it be, for a while at least. I did feel guilty to keep
anything from you, but now you know so much I shall not worry
and you needn't either. Ted's sorry, I don't mind, and it has
done us both good."

Mrs. Jo looked at Ted, who winked hard but bore the look
like a man; then she turned to Rob, who smiled at her so cheerfully that she felt reassured; but something in his face struck
her, and she saw what it was that made him seem older, graver,
yet more lovable than ever. It was the look pain of mind, as well
as body, brings, and the patience of a sweet submission to some
inevitable trial. Like a flash she guessed that some danger had
been near her boy, and the glances she had caught between the
two lads and Nan confirmed her fears.

"Rob, dear, you have been ill, hurt, or seriously troubled by
Ted? Tell me at once. I will not have any secrets now. Boys
sometimes suffer all their lives from neglected accidents or
carelessness. Fritz, make them speak out!"

Mr. Bhaer put down his papers and came to stand before
them, saying in a tone that quieted Mrs. Jo, and gave the boys
courage, "My sons, give us the truth. We can bear it. Do not
hold it back to spare us. Ted knows we forgive much because we
love him, so be frank, all two."

Ted instantly dived among the sofa pillows and kept there,
with only a pair of scarlet ears visible, while Rob in a few words
told the little story, truthfully, but as gently as he could, hastening to add the comfortable assurance that Don was *not* mad, the
wound nearly well, and no danger would ever come of it.

But Mrs. Jo grew so pale he had to put his arms about her,
and his father turned and walked away, exclaiming, "Ach Him-

mel!" in a tone of such mingled pain, relief, and gratitude, that Ted pulled an extra pillow over his head to smother the sound. They were all right in a minute; but such news is always a shock, even if the peril is past, and Mrs. Jo hugged her boy close till his father came and took him away, saying with a strong shake of both hands and a quiver in his voice, "To be in danger of one's life tries a man's mettle, and you bear it well, but I cannot spare my good boy yet. Thank Gott, we keep him safe!"

A smothered sound, between a choke and a groan, came from under the pillows, and the writhing of Ted's long legs so plainly expressed despair that his mother relented toward him, and burrowing till she found a tousled yellow head, pulled it out and smoothed it, exclaiming with an irrepressible laugh, though her cheeks were wet with tears, "Come and be forgiven, poor sinner! I know you have suffered enough, and I won't say a word; only if harm *had* come to Rob you would have made me more miserable than yourself. Oh, Teddy, Teddy, do try to cure that willful spirit of yours before it is too late!"

"Oh, Mum, I do try! I never can forget this—I hope it's cured me; if it hasn't, I am afraid I ain't worth saving," answered Ted, pulling his own hair as the only way of expressing his deep remorse.

"Yes, you are, my dear; I felt just so at fifteen when Amy was nearly drowned, and Marmee helped me as I'll help you. Come to me, Teddy, when the evil one gets hold of you, and together we'll rout him. Ah, me! I've had many a tussle with that old Apollyon, and often got worsted, but not always. Come under my shield, and we'll fight till we win."

No one spoke for a minute as Ted and his mother laughed and cried in one handkerchief, and Rob stood with his father's arm round him so happy that all was told and forgiven, though never to be forgotten; for such experiences do one good and knit hearts that love more closely together.

Presently Ted rose straight up and going to his father, said bravely and humbly, "I ought to be punished. Please do it; but first say you forgive me, as Rob does."

"Always that, mein sohn, seventy times seven, if need be, else I am not worthy the name you give me. The punishment has come; I can give no greater. Let it not be in vain. It will not with the help of the Mother and the All Father. Room here for both, always!"

The good Professor opened his arms and embraced his boys like a true German, not ashamed to express by gesture or by word the fatherly emotions an American would have compressed into a slap on the shoulder and a brief "All right."

Mrs. Jo sat and enjoyed the prospect like a romantic soul as she was, and then they had a quiet talk together, saying freely all that was in their hearts and finding much comfort in the confidence which comes when love casts out fear. It was agreed that nothing be said except to Nan, who was to be thanked and rewarded for her courage, discretion, and fidelity.

"I always knew that girl had the making of a fine woman in her, and this proves it. No panics and shrieks and faintings and fuss, but calm sense and energetic skill. Dear child, what can I give or do to show my gratitude?" said Mrs. Jo, enthusiastically.

"Make Tom clear out and leave her in peace," suggested Ted, almost himself again, though a pensive haze still partially obscured his native gaiety.

"Yes, do! He frets her like a mosquito. She forbade him to come out here while she stayed, and packed him off with Demi. I like old Tom, but he is a regular noodle about Nan," added Rob, as he went away to help his father with the accumulated letters.

"I'll do it!" said Mrs. Jo, decidedly. "That girl's career shall *not* be hampered by a foolish boy's fancy. In a moment of weariness she may give in, and then it's all over. Wiser women have done so and regretted it all their lives. Nan shall earn her place first, and prove that she can fill it; then she may marry if she likes, and can find a man worthy of her."

But Mrs. Jo's help was not needed; for love and gratitude can work miracles, and when youth, beauty, accident, and photography are added, success is sure, as was proved in the case of the unsuspecting but too susceptible Thomas.

CHAPTER 8

JOSIE PLAYS MERMAID

WHILE THE young Bhaers were having serious experiences at home, Josie was enjoying herself immensely at Rocky Nook; for the Laurences knew how to make summer idleness both charming and wholesome. Bess was very fond of her little cousin; Mrs. Amy felt that whether her niece was an actress or not she *must* be a gentlewoman, and gave her the social training which marks the well-bred woman everywhere; while Uncle Laurie was never happier than when rowing, riding, playing, or lounging with two gay girls beside him. Josie bloomed like a wildflower in this free life; Bess grew rosy, brisk, and merry; and both were great favorites with the neighbors, whose villas were by the shore or perched on the cliffs along the pretty bay.

One crumpled rose leaf disturbed Josie's peace, one baffled wish filled her with a longing which became a mania, and kept her as restless and watchful as a detective with a case to "work up." Miss Cameron, the great actress, had hired one of the villas and retired thither to rest and "create" a new part for next season. She saw no one but a friend or two, had a private beach, and was invisible except during her daily drive, or when the opera glasses of curious gazers were fixed on a blue figure disporting itself in the sea. The Laurences knew her, but respected her privacy, and after a call left her in peace till she expressed a wish for society—a courtesy which she remembered and repaid later, as we shall see.

But Josie was like a thirsty fly buzzing about a sealed honeypot, for this nearness to her idol was both delightful and maddening. She pined to see, hear, talk with, and study this great and happy woman who could thrill thousands by her art, and win friends by her virtue, benevolence, and beauty. This was the sort of actress the girl meant to be, and few could object if the gift was really hers; for the stage needs just such women to purify and elevate the profession which should teach as well as amuse. If kindly Miss Cameron had known what passionate love and longing burned in the bosom of the little girl whom she idly observed skipping over the rocks, splashing about the beach, or galloping past her gate on a Shetland pony, she would have made her happy by a look or a word. But being tired with her winter's work and busy with her new part, the lady took no more notice of this young neighbor than of the seagulls in the bay or the daisies dancing in the fields. Nosegays left on her doorstep, serenades under her garden wall, and the fixed stare of admiring eyes were such familiar things that she scarcely minded them; and Josie grew desperate when all her little attempts failed.

"I might climb that pine tree and tumble off on her piazza roof, or get Sheltie to throw me just at her gate and be taken in fainting. It's no use to try to drown myself when she is bathing. I can't sink, and she'd only send a man to pull me out. What can I do? I *will* see her and tell her my hopes and make her say I can act some day. Mamma would believe *her,* and if—oh, if she only *would* let me study with her, what perfect joy that would be!"

Josie made these remarks one afternoon as she and Bess prepared for a swim, a fishing party having prevented their morning bath.

"You must bide your time, dear, and not be so impatient. Papa promised to give you a chance before the season is over, and he always manages things nicely. That will be better than any queer prank of yours," answered Bess, tying her pretty hair in a white net to match her suit, while Josie made a little lobster of herself in scarlet.

"I hate to wait, but I suppose I must. Hope she will bathe this afternoon, though it is low tide. She told Uncle she should have to go in then because in the morning people stared so and went on her beach. Come and have a good dive from the big rock. No one round but nurses and babies, so we can romp and splash as much as we like."

Away they went to have a fine time, for the little bay was free from other bathers, and the babies greatly admired their aquatic gymnastics, both being expert swimmers.

As they sat dripping on the big rock Josie suddenly gave a clutch that nearly sent Bess overboard, as she cried excitedly, "There she is! Look—coming to bathe. How splendid! Oh, if she only would drown a little and let me save her! Or even get her toe nipped by a crab—anything so I could go and speak!"

"Don't seem to look. She comes to be quiet and enjoy herself. Pretend we don't see her, that's only civil," answered Bess, affecting to be absorbed in a white-winged yacht going by.

"Let's carelessly float that way as if going for seaweed on the rocks. She can't mind if we are flat on our backs, with only our noses out. Then when we can't help seeing her, we'll swim back as if anxious to retire. That will impress her, and she may call to thank the very polite young ladies who respect her wishes," proposed Josie, whose lively fancy was always planning dramatic situations.

Just as they were going to slip from their rock, as if Fate relented at last, Miss Cameron was seen to beckon wildly as she stood waist-deep in the water, looking down. She called to her maid, who seemed searching along the beach for something, and not finding what she sought, waved a towel toward the girls as if summoning them to help her.

"Run, fly! She wants us, she wants us!" cried Josie, tumbling into the water like a very energetic turtle, and swimming away in her best style toward this long-desired haven of joy. Bess followed more slowly, and both came panting and smiling up to Miss Cameron, who never lifted her eyes, but said in that wonderful voice of hers, "I've dropped a bracelet. I see it, but can't get it. Will the little boy find me a long stick? I'll keep my eye on it, so the water shall not wash it away."

"I'll dive for it with pleasure, but I'm not a boy," answered Josie, laughing as she shook the curly head which at a distance had deceived the lady.

"I beg your pardon. Dive away, child. The sand is covering it fast. I value it very much. Never forgot to take it off before."

"I'll get it!" And down went Josie, to come up with a handful of pebbles, but no bracelet.

"It's gone. Never mind—my fault," said Miss Cameron, disappointed, but amused at the girl's dismay as she shook the water out of her eyes and gasped bravely, "No, it isn't. I'll have it, if I stay down all night!" and with one long breath Josie dived again, leaving nothing but a pair of agitated feet to be seen.

"I'm afraid she will hurt herself," said Miss Cameron, looking at Bess, whom she recognized by her likeness to her mother.

"Oh, no. Josie is a little fish. She likes it;" and Bess smiled happily at this wonderful granting of her cousin's desire.

"You are Mr. Laurence's daughter, I think? How d'ye do, dear? Tell Papa I'm coming to see him soon. Too tired before. Quite savage. Better now. Ah! Here's our pearl of divers. What luck?" she asked, as the heels went down and a dripping head came up.

Josie could only choke and splutter at first, being half strangled; but though her hands had failed again, her courage had not; and with a resolute shake of her wet hair, a bright look at the tall lady, and a series of puffs to fill her lungs, she said calmly, " 'Never give up' is my motto. I'm going to get it, if I go to Liverpool for it! Now, then!" And down went the mermaid quite out of sight this time, groping like a real lobster at the bottom of the sea.

"Plucky little girl! I like that. Who is she?" asked the lady, sitting down on a half-covered stone to watch her diver, since the bracelet was lost sight of.

Bess told her, adding, with the persuasive smile of her father, "Josie longs to be an actress and has waited for a month to see you. This is a great happiness for her."

"Bless the child! Why didn't she come and call? I'd have let her in, though usually I avoid stage-struck girls as I do reporters," laughed Miss Cameron.

There was no time for more. A brown hand, grasping the bracelet, rose out of the sea, followed by a purple face as Josie came up so blind and dizzy she could only cling to Bess, half drowned but triumphant.

Miss Cameron drew her to the rock where she sat, and pushing the hair out of her eyes, revived her with a hearty "Bravo! Bravo!" which assured the girl that her first act was a hit. Josie had often imagined her meeting with the great actress—the dignity and grace with which she would enter and tell her ambitious hopes, the effective dress she would wear, the witty things she would say, the deep impression her budding genius would make. But never in her wildest moments had she imagined an interview like this. Scarlet, sandy, streaming, and speechless she leaned against the illustrious shoulder, looking like a beatified seal as she blinked and wheezed till she could smile joyfully and exclaim proudly, "I did get it! I'm so glad!"

"Now get your breath, my dear; then I shall be glad also. It was very nice of you to take all that trouble for me. How shall I thank you?" asked the lady, looking at her with the beautiful eyes that could say so many things without words.

Josie clasped her hands with a wet spat which rather destroyed the effect of the gesture, and answered in a beseeching tone that would have softened a far harder heart than Miss Cameron's, "Let me come and see you once—only once! I want you to tell me if I can act; you will know. I'll abide by what you say; and if you think I can—by and by, when I've studied very hard—I shall be the happiest girl in the world. May I?"

"Yes. Come tomorrow at eleven. We'll have a good talk; you shall show me what you can do, and I'll give you my opinion. But you won't like it."

"I will, no matter if you tell me I'm a fool. I want it settled; so does Mamma. I'll take it bravely if you say no; and if you say yes, I'll never give up till I've done my best—as you did."

"Ah, my child, it's a weary road, and there are plenty of thorns among the roses when you've won them. I think you have the courage, and this proves that you have perseverance. Perhaps you'll do. Come, and we'll see."

Miss Cameron touched the bracelet as she spoke, and smiled so kindly that impetuous Josie wanted to kiss her; but wisely refrained, though her eyes were wet with softer water than any in the sea as she thanked her.

"We are keeping Miss Cameron from her bath, and the tide is going out. Come, Josie," said thoughtful Bess, fearing to outstay their welcome.

"Run over the beach and get warm. Thank you very much, little mermaid. Tell Papa to bring his daughter to see me any time. Good-bye." And with a wave of her hand the tragedy queen dismissed her court, but remained on her weedy throne watching the two lithe figures race over the sand with twinkling feet till they were out of sight. Then, as she calmly bobbed up and down in the water, she said to herself, "The child has a good stage face, vivid, mobile; fine eyes, abandon, pluck, will. Perhaps she'll do. Good stock—talent in the family. We shall see."

Of course Josie never slept a wink, and was in a fever of joyful excitement next day. Uncle Laurie enjoyed the episode very much, and Aunt Amy looked out her most becoming white

dress for the grand occasion; Bess lent her most artistic hat, and
Josie ranged the wood and marsh for a bouquet of wild roses,
sweet white azalea, ferns, and graceful grasses, as the offering
of a very grateful heart.

At ten she solemnly arrayed herself, and then sat looking at
her neat gloves and buckled shoes till it was time to go, growing
pale and sober with the thought that her fate was soon to be
decided; for, like all young people, she was sure that her whole
life could be settled by one human creature, quite forgetting
how wonderfully Providence trains us by disappointment, surprises us with unexpected success, and turns our seeming trials
into blessing.

"I will go alone: we shall be freer so. Oh, Bess, pray that she
may tell me rightly! So much depends on that! Don't laugh,
Uncle! It *is* a very serious moment for me. Miss Cameron
knows that, and will tell you so. Kiss me, Aunt Amy, since
Mamma isn't here. If you say I look nice, I'm quite satisfied.
Good-bye." And with a wave of the hand as much like her
model's as she could make it, Josie departed, looking very
pretty and feeling very tragical.

Sure now of admittance, she boldly rung at the door which
excluded so many, and being ushered into a shady parlor,
feasted her eyes upon several fine portraits of great actors while
she waited. She had read about most of them, and knew their
trials and triumphs so well that she soon forgot herself, and
tried to imitate Mrs. Siddons as Lady Macbeth, looking up at
the engraving as she held her nosegay like the candle in the
sleepwalking scene, and knit her youthful brows distressfully
while murmuring the speech of the haunted queen. So busy was
she that Miss Cameron watched her for several minutes unseen,
then startled her by suddenly sweeping in with the words upon
her lips, the look upon her face, which made that one of her
greatest scenes.

"I never can do it like that; but I'll keep trying, if you say I may," cried Josie, forgetting her manners in the intense interest of the moment.

"Show me what you *can* do," answered the actress, wisely plunging into the middle of things at once, well knowing that no common chat would satisfy this very earnest little person.

"First let me give you these. I thought you'd like wild things better than hothouse flowers; and I loved to bring them, as I'd no other way to thank you for your great kindness to me," said Josie, offering her nosegay with a simple warmth that was very sweet.

"I do love them best, and keep my room full of the posies some good fairy hangs on my gate. Upon my word, I think I've found the fairy out—these are so like," she added quickly, as her eye went from the flowers in her hand to others that stood near by, arranged with the same taste.

Josie's blush and smile betrayed her before she said, with a look full of girlish adoration and humility, "I couldn't help it; I admire you so much. I know it was a liberty, but as I couldn't get in myself, I loved to think my roses pleased you."

Something about the child and her little offering touched the woman, and drawing Josie to her, she said, with no trace of actress in face or voice, "They did please me, dear, and so do you. I'm tired of praise; and love is very sweet, when it is simple and sincere like this."

Josie remembered to have heard, among many other stories, that Miss Cameron lost her lover years ago, and since had lived only for art. Now she felt that this might have been true; and pity for the splendid, lonely life made her face very eloquent, as well as grateful. Then, as if anxious to forget the past, her new friend said, in the commanding way that seemed natural to her, "Let me see what you can do. Juliet, of course. All begin with that. Poor soul, how she is murdered!"

Now, Josie *had* intended to begin with Romeo's much-enduring sweetheart, and follow her up with Bianca, Pauline, and several of the favorite idols of stage-struck girls; but being a

shrewd little person, she suddenly saw the wisdom of Uncle
Laurie's advice, and resolved to follow it. So instead of the rant
Miss Cameron expected, Josie gave poor Ophelia's mad scene,
and gave it very well, having been trained by the college professor of elocution and done it many times. She was too young, of
course; but the white gown, the loose hair, the real flowers she
scattered over the imaginary grave, added to the illusion; and
she sang the songs sweetly, dropped her pathetic courtesies, and
vanished behind the curtain that divided the rooms with a backward look that surprised her critical auditor into a quick gesture
of applause. Cheered by that welcome sound, Josie ran back as
a little hoyden in one of the farces she had often acted, telling a
story full of fun and naughtiness at first, but ending with a sob
of repentance and an earnest prayer for pardon.

"Very good! Try again. Better than I expected," called the
voice of the oracle.

Josie tried Portia's speech, and recited very well, giving due
emphasis to each fine sentence. Then, unable to refrain from
what she considered her greatest effort, she burst into Juliet's
balcony scene, ending with the poison and the tomb. She felt
sure that she surpassed herself, and waited for applause. A ringing laugh made her tingle with indignation and disappointment,
as she went to stand before Miss Cameron, saying in a tone of
polite surprise, "I have been told that I did it *very well.* I'm sorry
you don't think so."

"My dear, it's very bad. How can it help being so? What can a
child like you know of love and fear and death? Don't try it yet.
Leave tragedy alone till you are ready for it."

"But you clapped Ophelia."

"Yes, that was very pretty. Any clever girl can do it effectively. But the real meaning of Shakespeare is far above you yet,
child. The comedy bit was best. There you showed real talent. It
was both comic and pathetic. That's art. Don't lose it. The Portia was good declamation. Go on with that sort of thing; it trains

the voice—teaches shades of expression. You've a good voice and natural grace—great helps both, hard to acquire."

"Well, I'm glad I've got something," sighed Josie, sitting meekly on a stool, much crestfallen, but not daunted yet, and bound to have her say out.

"My dear little girl, I told you that you would not like what I should say to you; yet I must be honest, if I would really help you. I've had to do it for many like you; and most of them have never forgiven me, though my words have proved true, and they are what I advised them to be—good wives and happy mothers in quiet homes. A few have kept on, and done fairly well. One you will hear of soon, I think; for she has talent, indomitable patience, and mind as well as beauty. You are too young to show to which class you belong. Geniuses are very rare, and even at fifteen seldom give much promise of future power."

"Oh, I don't think I'm a genius!" cried Josie, growing calm and sober as she listened to the melodious voice and looked into the expressive face that filled her with confidence, so strong, sincere, and kindly was it. "I only want to find out if I have talent enough to go on, and after years of study be able to act well in any of the good plays people never tire of seeing. I don't expect to be a Mrs. Siddons or a Miss Cameron, much as I long to be; but it *does* seem as if I had something in me which can't come out in any way but this. When I act I'm perfectly happy. I seem to live, to be in my own world, and each new part is a new friend. I love Shakespeare, and am never tired of his splendid people. Of course I don't understand it all; but it's like being alone at night with the mountains and the stars, solemn and grand, and I try to imagine how it will look when the sun comes up, and all is glorious and clear to me. I can't see, but I feel the beauty, and long to express it."

As she spoke with the most perfect self-forgetfulness Josie was pale with excitement, her eyes shone, her lips trembled, and all her little soul seemed trying to put into words the emotions that filled it to overflowing. Miss Cameron understood, felt that this was something more than a girlish whim; and when she answered there was a new tone of sympathy in her voice, a new interest in her face, though she wisely refrained from saying all she thought, well knowing what splendid dreams young people build upon a word, and how bitter is the pain when the bright bubbles burst.

"If you feel this, I can give you no better advice than to go on loving and studying our great master," she said slowly; but Josie caught the changed tone, and felt, with a thrill of joy, that her new friend was speaking to her now as to a comrade. "It is an education in itself, and a lifetime is not long enough to teach you all his secrets. But there is much to do before you can hope to echo his words. Have you the patience, courage, strength, to begin at the beginning, and slowly, painfully, lay the foundation for future work? Fame is a pearl many dive for and only a few bring up. Even when they do, it is not perfect, and they sigh for more, and lose better things in struggling for them."

The last words seemed spoken more to herself than to her hearer, but Josie answered quickly, with a smile and an expressive gesture, "I got the bracelet in spite of all the bitter water in my eyes."

"You did! I don't forget it. A good omen. We will accept it."

Miss Cameron answered the smile with one that was like sunshine to the girl, and stretched her white hand as if taking some invisible gift. Then added in a different tone, watching the effect of her words on the expressive face before her, "Now you will be disappointed, for instead of telling you to come and study with me, or go and act in some second-rate theater at once, I advise you to go back to school and finish your education. That is the first step, for all accomplishments are needed, and a single talent makes a very imperfect character. Cultivate mind and body, heart and soul, and make yourself an intelligent, graceful, beautiful, and healthy girl. Then, at eighteen or twenty, go into training and try your powers. Better start for the battle with your arms in order, and save the hard lesson which

comes when we rush on too soon. Now and then genius carries
all before it, but not often. We have to climb slowly, with many
slips and falls. Can you wait as well as work?"

"I will!"

"We shall see. It would be pleasant to me to know that when
I quit the stage I leave behind me a well-trained, faithful, gifted
comrade to more than fill my place, and carry on what I have
much at heart—the purification of the stage. Perhaps you are
she; but remember, mere beauty and rich costumes do not
make an actress, nor are the efforts of a clever little girl to play
great characters real art. It is all dazzle and sham, and a disgrace and disappointment now. Why will the public be satisfied
with opera-bouffe, or the trash called society plays, when a
world of truth and beauty, poetry and pathos, lies waiting to be
interpreted and enjoyed?"

Miss Cameron had forgotten to whom she spoke, and walked
to and fro, full of the noble regret all cultivated people feel at
the low state of the stage nowadays.

"That's what Uncle Laurie says; and he and Aunt Jo try to
plan plays about true and lovely things—simple domestic scenes
that touch people's hearts, and make them laugh and cry and
feel better. Uncle says that sort is my style, and I must not think
of tragedy. But it's so much nicer to sweep about in crowns and
velvet trains than to wear everyday clothes, and just be myself,
though it is so easy."

"Yet that is high art, child, and what we need for a time till
we are ready for the masters. Cultivate that talent of yours. It is
a special gift, this power to bring tears and smiles, and a sweeter
task to touch the heart than to freeze the blood or fire the
imagination. Tell your uncle he is right, and ask your aunt to try
a play for you. I'll come and see it when you are ready."

"Will you? Oh! Will you? We are going to have some at
Christmas, with a nice part for me. A simple little thing, but I
can do it, and should be so proud, so happy, to have you there."

Josie rose as she spoke, for a glance at the clock showed her

that her call was a long one; and hard as it was to end this
momentous interview, she felt that she must go. Catching up
her hat she went to Miss Cameron, who stood looking at her so
keenly that she felt as transparent as a pane of glass, and
colored prettily as she looked up, saying with a grateful little
tremor in her voice, "I can never thank you for this hour and all
you have told me. I shall do just what you advise, and Mamma
will be very glad to see me settled at my books again. I can study
now with all my heart, because it is to help me on; and I won't
hope too much, but work and wait, and try to please you, as the
only way to pay my debt."

"That reminds me that I have not paid mine. Little friend,
wear this for my sake. It is fit for a mermaid, and will remind
you of your first dive. May the next bring up a better jewel, and
leave no bitter water on your lips!"

As she spoke, Miss Cameron took from the lace at her throat
a pretty pin of aquamarine, and fastened it like an order on
Josie's proud bosom; then lifting the happy little face, she
kissed it very tenderly, and watched it go smiling away with eyes
that seemed to see into a future full of the trials and the triumphs which she knew so well.

Bess expected to see Josie come flying in, all raptures and
excitement, or drowned in tears of disappointment, but was surprised at the expression of calm content and resolution which
she wore. Pride and satisfaction, and a new feeling of responsibility both sobered and sustained her, and she felt that any
amount of dry study and long waiting would be bearable, if in
the glorious future she could be an honor to her profession and
a comrade to the new friend whom she already adored with
girlish ardor.

She told her little story to a deeply interested audience, and
all felt that Miss Cameron's advice was good. Mrs. Amy was
relieved at the prospect of delay; for she did not want her niece
to be an actress, and hoped the fancy would die out.

Uncle Laurie was full of charming plans and prophecies, and

wrote one of his most delightful notes to thank their neighbor
for her kindness; while Bess, who loved art of all kinds, fully
sympathized with her cousin's ambitious hopes, only wondering
why she preferred to act out her visions rather than embody
them in marble.

That first interview was not the last; for Miss Cameron was
really interested, and had several memorable conversations with
the Laurences, while the girls sat by, drinking in every word
with the delight all artists feel in their own beautiful world, and
learning to see how sacred good gifts are, how powerful, and
how faithfully they should be used for high ends, each in its own
place helping to educate, refine, and refresh.

Josie wrote reams to her mother; and when the visit ended
rejoiced her heart by bringing her a somewhat changed little
daughter, who fell to work at the once-detested books with a
patient energy which surprised and pleased everyone. The right
string had been touched, and even French exercises and piano
practice became endurable, since accomplishments would be
useful by and by; dress, manners, and habits were all interesting
now, because "mind and body, heart and soul, must be cultivated," and while training to become an "intelligent, graceful,
healthy girl," little Josie was unconsciously fitting herself to play
her part well on whatever stage the great Manager might prepare for her.

CHAPTER 9

THE WORM TURNS

Two VERY superior bicycles went twinkling up the road to Plumfield one September afternoon, bearing two brown and dusty riders evidently returning from a successful run, for though their legs might be a trifle weary, their faces beamed as they surveyed the world from their lofty perches with the air of calm content all wheelmen wear *after* they have learned to ride; before that happy period anguish of mind and body is the chief expression of the manly countenance.

"Go ahead and report, Tom; I'm due here. See you later," said Demi, swinging himself down at the door of the Dovecote.

"Don't peach, there's a good fellow. Let me have it out with Mother Bhaer first," returned Tom, wheeling in at the gate with a heavy sigh.

Demi laughed, and his comrade went slowly up the avenue, devoutly hoping that the coast was clear; for he was the bearer of tidings which would, he thought, convulse the entire family with astonishment and dismay.

To his great joy Mrs. Jo was discovered alone in a grove of proof sheets, which she dropped, to greet the returning

137

wanderer cordially. But after the first glance she saw that
something was the matter, recent events having made her unusually sharp-eyed and suspicious.

"What is it now, Tom?" she asked, as he subsided into an
easy chair with a curious expression of mingled fear, shame,
amusement, and distress in his brick red countenance.

"I'm in an awful scrape, ma'am."

"Of course; I'm always prepared for scrapes when you appear. What is it? Run over some old lady who is going to law
about it?" asked Mrs. Jo, cheerfully.

"Worse than that," groaned Tom.

"Not poisoned some trusting soul who asked you to pre-
scribe, I hope?"

"Worse than that."

"You haven't let Demi catch any horrid thing and left him
behind, have you?"

"Worse even than that."

"I give it up. Tell me quick; I hate to wait for bad news."

Having got his listener sufficiently excited, Tom launched his
thunderbolt in one brief sentence, and fell back to watch the
effect.

"I'm engaged."

Mrs. Jo's proof sheets flew wildly about as she clasped her
hands, exclaiming in dismay, "If Nan has yielded, I'll never forgive her!"

"She hasn't; it's another girl."

Tom's face was so funny as he said the words, that it was
impossible to help laughing; for he looked both sheepish and
pleased, besides very much perplexed and worried.

"I'm glad, *very* glad indeed! Don't care who it is; and I hope
you'll be married soon. Now tell me all about it," commanded
Mrs. Jo, so much relieved that she felt ready for anything.

"What will Nan say?" demanded Tom, rather taken aback at
this view of his predicament.

"She will be rejoiced to get rid of the mosquito who has

plagued her so long. Don't worry about Nan. Who is this 'other girl'?"

"Demi hasn't written about her?"

"Only something about your upsetting a Miss West down at Quitno; I thought that was scrape enough."

"That was only the beginning of a series of scrapes. Just my luck! Of course after sousing the poor girl I had to be attentive to her, hadn't I? Everyone seemed to think so, and I couldn't get away, and so I was lost before I knew it. It's all Demi's fault; he *would* stay there and fuss with his old photos, because the views were good and all the girls wanted to be taken. Look at these, will you, ma'am? That's the way we spent our time when we weren't playing tennis." And Tom pulled a handful of pictures from his pocket, displaying several in which he was conspicuous, either holding a sun umbrella over a very pretty young lady on the rocks, reposing at her feet in the grass, or perched on a piazza railing with other couples in seaside costumes and effective attitudes.

"This is *she* of course?" asked Mrs. Jo, pointing to the much-ruffled damsel with the jaunty hat, coquettish shoes, and racquet in her hand.

"That's Dora. Isn't she lovely?" cried Tom, forgetting his tribulations for a moment and speaking with lover-like ardor.

"Very nice little person to look at. Hope she is not a Dickens Dora? That curly crop looks like it."

"Not a bit; she's very smart; can keep house, and sew, and do lots of things, I assure you, ma'am. All the girls like her, and she's sweet-tempered and jolly, and sings like a bird, and dances beautifully, and loves books. Thinks yours are splendid, and made me talk about you no end."

"That last sentence is to flatter me and win my help to get you out of the scrape. Tell me first how you got in." And Mrs. Jo settled herself to listen with interest, never tired of boys' affairs.

Tom gave his head a rousing rub all over to clear his wits, and plunged into his story with a will.

"Well, we've met before, but I didn't know she was there. Demi wanted to see a fellow, so we went, and finding it nice and cool rested over Sunday. Found some pleasant people and went out rowing; I had Dora, and came to grief on a confounded rock. She could swim, no harm done, only the scare and the spoilt gown. She took it well, and we got friendly at once— couldn't help it, scrambling into that beast of a boat while the rest laughed at us. Of course we had to stay another day to see that Dora was all right. Demi wanted to. Alice Heath is down there and two other girls from our college, so we sort of lingered along, and Demi kept taking pictures, and we danced, and got into a tennis tournament; and that was as good exercise as wheeling, we thought. Fact is, tennis is a dangerous game, ma'am. A great deal of courting goes on in those courts, and we fellows find that sort of 'serving' mighty agreeable, don't you know?"

"Not much tennis in my day, but I understand perfectly," said Mrs. Jo, enjoying it all as much as Tom did.

"Upon my word, I hadn't the least idea of being serious," he continued slowly, as if this part of his tale was hard to tell, "but everyone else spooned, so I did. Dora seemed to like it and expect it, and of course I was glad to be agreeable. *She* thought I amounted to something, though Nan does not, and it was pleasant to be appreciated after years of snubbing. Yes, it was right down jolly to have a sweet girl smile at you all day, and blush prettily when you said a neat thing to her, and look glad when you came, sorry when you left, and admire all you did, and make you feel like a man and act your best. That's the sort of treatment a fellow enjoys and ought to get if he behaves himself; not frowns and cold shoulders year in and year out, and made to look like a fool when he means well, and is faithful, and has loved a girl ever since he was a boy. No, by Jove, it's not fair, and I won't stand it!"

Tom waxed warm and eloquent as he thought over his wrongs, and bounced up to march about the room, wagging his head and trying to feel aggrieved as usual, but surprised to find that his heart did not ache a bit.

"I wouldn't. Drop the old fancy—for it was nothing more—and take up the new one, if it is genuine. But how came you to propose, Tom, as you must have done to be engaged?" asked Mrs. Jo, impatient for the crisis of the tale.

"Oh, that was an accident. I didn't mean it at all; the donkey did it, and I couldn't get out of the scrape without hurting Dora's feelings, you see," began Tom, seeing that the fatal moment had come.

"So there were two donkeys in it, were there?" said Mrs. Jo, foreseeing fun of some sort.

"Don't laugh! It sounds funny, I know; but it might have been awful," answered Tom, darkly, though a twinkle of the eye showed that his love trials did not quite blind him to the comic side of the adventure. "The girls admired our new wheels, and of course we liked to show off. Took 'em to ride, and had larks generally. Well, one day Dora was on behind, and we were going nicely along a good bit of road, when a ridiculous old donkey got right across the way. I thought he'd move, but he didn't, so I gave him a kick; he kicked back, and over we went in a heap, donkey and all. Such a mess! I thought only of Dora, and she had hysterics; at least, she laughed till she cried, and that beast brayed, and I lost my head. Any fellow would, with a poor girl gasping in the road, and he wiping her tears and begging pardon, not knowing whether her bones were broken or not. I called her my darling, and went on like a fool in my flurry, till she grew calmer, and said, with such a look, 'I forgive you, Tom. Pick me up, and let us go on again.'

"Wasn't that sweet now, after I'd upset her for the second time? It touched me to the heart; and I said I'd like to go on forever with such an angel to steer for, and—well, I don't know *what* I did say; but you might have knocked me down with a feather when she put her arm round my neck and whispered, 'Tom, dear, with you I'm not afraid of any lions in the path.' She

might have said *donkeys;* but she was in earnest, and she spared
my feelings. Very nice of the dear girl; but there I am with two
sweethearts on my hands, and in a deuce of a scrape."

Finding it impossible to contain herself another moment,
Mrs. Jo laughed till the tears ran down her cheeks at this characteristic episode; and after one reproachful look, which only
added to her merriment, Tom burst into a jolly roar that made
the room ring.

"Tommy Bangs! Tommy Bangs! Who but you could ever get
into such a catastrophe?" said Mrs. Jo, when she recovered her
breath.

"Isn't it a muddle all round, and won't everyone chaff me to
death about it? I shall have to quit old Plum for a while," answered Tom, as he mopped his face, trying to realize the full
danger of his position.

"No, indeed; I'll stand by you, for I think it the best joke of
the season. But tell me how things ended. Is it really serious, or
only a summer flirtation? I don't approve of them, but boys and
girls will play with edged tools and cut their fingers."

"Well, Dora considers herself engaged, and wrote to her people at once. I couldn't say a word when she took it all in solemn
earnest and seemed so happy. She's only seventeen, never liked
anyone before, and is sure all will be right; as her father knows
mine, and we are both well off. I was so staggered that I said,
'Why, you can't love me *really* when we know so little of one
another?' But she answered right out of her tender little heart,
'Yes, I do, dearly, Tom; you are so gay and kind and honest, I
couldn't help it.' Now, after that what *could* I do but go ahead
and make her happy while I stayed, and trust to luck to
straighten the snarl out afterward?"

"A truly Tomian way of taking things easy. I hope you told
your father at once."

"Oh, yes, I wrote right off and broke it to him in three lines. I
said, 'Dear Father, I'm engaged to Dora West, and I hope she
will suit the family. She suits me tiptop. Yours ever, Tom.' He

was all right, never liked Nan, you know; but Dora will suit him down to the ground." And Tom looked entirely satisfied with his own tact and taste.

"What did Demi say to this rapid and funny lovemaking? Wasn't he scandalized?" asked Mrs. Jo, trying not to laugh again as she thought of the unromantic spectacle of donkey, bicycle, boy, and girl all in the dust together.

"Not a bit. He was immensely interested and very kind; talked to me like a father; said it was a good thing to steady a fellow, only I must be honest with her and myself and not trifle a moment. Demi is a regular Solomon, especially when he is in the same boat," answered Tom, looking wise.

"You don't mean—?" gasped Mrs. Jo, in sudden alarm at the bare idea of more love affairs just yet.

"Yes, I do, please ma'am; it's a regular sell all the way through, and I owe Demi one for taking me into temptation blindfold. He *said* he went to Quitno to see Fred Wallace, but he never saw the fellow. How could he, when Wallace was off in his yacht all the time we were there? Alice was the real attraction, and I was left to my fate, while they went maundering round with that old camera. There were three donkeys in this affair, and I'm not the worst one, though I shall have to bear the laugh. Demi will look innocent and sober, and no one will say a word to him."

"The midsummer madness has broken out, and no one knows who will be stricken next. Well, leave Demi to his mother, and let us see what you are going to do, Tom."

"I don't know exactly; it's awkward to be in love with two girls at once. What do you advise?"

"A common-sense view of the case, by all means. Dora loves you and thinks you love her. Nan does not care for you, and you only care for her as a friend, though you have tried to do more. It is my opinion, Tom, that you love Dora, or are on the way to it; for in all these years I've never seen you look or speak about Nan as you do about Dora. Opposition has made you obstinately cling to her till accident has shown you a more attractive girl. Now, I think you had better take the old love for a friend, the new one for a sweetheart, and in due time, if the sentiment is genuine, marry her."

If Mrs. Jo had any doubts about the matter, Tom's face would have proved the truth of her opinion; for his eyes shone, his lips smiled, and in spite of dust and sunburn a new expression of happiness quite glorified him as he stood silent for a moment, trying to understand the beautiful miracle which real love works when it comes to a young man's heart.

"The fact is I meant to make Nan jealous, for she knows Dora, and I was sure would hear of our doings. I was tired of being walked on, and I thought I'd try to break away and not be a bore and a laughingstock anymore," he said slowly, as if it relieved him to pour out his doubts and woes and hopes and joys to this old friend. "I was regularly astonished to find it so easy and so pleasant. I didn't mean to do any harm, but drifted along beautifully, and told Demi to mention things in his letters to Daisy, so Nan might know. Then I forgot Nan altogether, and saw, heard, felt, cared for no one but Dora, till the donkey— bless his old heart!—pitched her into my arms and I found she loved me. Upon my soul, I don't see why she should! I'm not half good enough."

"Every honest man feels that when an innocent girl puts her hand in his. Make yourself worthy of her, for she isn't an angel but a woman with faults of her own for you to bear and forgive, and you must help one another," said Mrs. Jo, trying to realize that this sober youth was her scapegrace Tommy.

"What troubles me is that I didn't mean it when I began, and was going to use the dear girl as an instrument of torture for Nan. It wasn't right, and I don't deserve to be so happy. If all my scrapes ended as well as this, what a state of bliss I should be in!" and Tom beamed again at the rapturous prospect.

"My dear boy, it is not a scrape, but a very sweet experience suddenly dawning upon you," answered Mrs. Jo, speaking very soberly; for she saw he was in earnest. "Enjoy it wisely and be worthy of it, for it is a serious thing to accept a girl's love and trust, and let her look up to you for tenderness and truth in return. Don't let little Dora look in vain, but be a man in all things for her sake, and make this affection a blessing to you both."

"I'll try. Yes, I do love her, only I can't believe it just yet. Wish you knew her. Dear little soul, I long to see her already! She cried when we parted last night, and I hated to go." Tom's hand went to his cheek as if he still felt the rosy little seal Dora had set upon his promise not to forget her, and for the first time in his happy-go-lucky life Tommy Bangs understood the difference between sentiment and sentimentality. The feeling recalled Nan, for he had never known that tender thrill when thinking of her, and the old friendship seemed rather a prosaic affair beside this delightful mingling of romance, surprise, love, and fun.

"I declare, I feel as if a weight was off me, but what the dickens *will* Nan say when she knows it!" he exclaimed with a chuckle.

"Knows what?" asked a clear voice that made both start and turn, for there was Nan calmly surveying them from the doorway.

Anxious to put Tom out of suspense and to see how Nan would take the news, Mrs. Jo answered quickly, "Tom's engagement to Dora West."

"Really?" and Nan looked so surprised that Mrs. Jo was afraid she might be fonder of her old playmate than she knew; but her next words set the fear at rest, and made everything comfortable and merry at once.

"I knew my prescription would work wonders if he only took it long enough. Dear old Tom, I'm so glad. Bless you! Bless you!" And she shook both his hands with hearty affection.

"It was an accident, Nan. I didn't mean to, but I'm always

getting into messes, and I couldn't seem to get out of this in any other way. Mother Bhaer will tell you about it. I must go and make myself tidy. Going to tea with Demi. See you later."

Stammering, blushing, and looking both sheepish and gratified, Tom suddenly bolted, leaving the elder lady to enlighten the younger at length, and have another laugh over this new sort of courtship, which might well be called accidental. Nan was deeply interested, for she knew Dora, thought her a nice little thing, and predicted that in time she would make Tom an excellent wife, since she admired and "appreciated" him so much.

"I shall miss him of course, but it will be a relief to me and better for him; dangling is so bad for a boy. Now he will go into business with his father and do well, and everyone be happy. I shall give Dora an elegant family medicine chest for a wedding present, and teach her how to use it. Tom can't be trusted, and is no more fit for the profession than Silas."

The latter part of this speech relieved Mrs. Jo's mind, for Nan had looked about her as if she had lost something valuable when she began; but the medicine chest seemed to cheer her, and the thought of Tom in a *safe* profession was evidently a great comfort.

"The worm has turned at last, Nan, and your bondman is free. Let him go, and give your whole mind to your work; for *you* are fitted for the profession, and will be an honor to it by and by," she said, approvingly.

"I hope so. That reminds me—measles are in the village, and you had better tell the girls not to call where there are children. It would be bad to have a run of them just as term begins. Now I'm off to Daisy. Wonder what she will say to Tom. Isn't he great fun?" And Nan departed, laughing over the joke with such genuine satisfaction that it was evident no sentimental regrets disturbed her "maiden meditation, fancy-free."

"I shall have my eye on Demi, but won't say a word. Meg

likes to manage her children in her own way, and a very good
way it is. But the dear Pelican will be somewhat ruffled if her
boy has caught the epidemic which seems to have broken out
among us this summer."

Mrs. Jo did not mean the measles, but that more serious
malady called love, which is apt to ravage communities, spring
and autumn, when winter gaiety and summer idleness produce
whole bouquets of engagements, and set young people to pair-
ing off like the birds. Franz began it, Nat was a chronic and Tom
a sudden case; Demi seemed to have the symptoms; and worst
of all, her own Ted had only the day before calmly said to her,
"Mum, I think I should be happier if I had a sweetheart, like
the other boys." If her cherished son had asked her for dyna-
mite to play with, she would hardly have been more startled, or
have more decidedly refused the absurd request.

"Well, Barry Morgan said I ought to have one and offered to
pick me out a nice one among our set. I asked Josie first, and
she hooted at the idea, so I thought I'd let Barry look round.
You say it steadies a fellow, and I want to be steady," explained
Ted in a serious tone, which would have convulsed his parent at
any other time.

"Good lack! What are we coming to in this fast age when
babes and boys make such demands and want to play with one
of the most sacred things in life?" exclaimed Mrs. Jo, and having in a few words set the matter in its true light, sent her son
away to wholesome baseball and Octoo for a safe sweetheart.

Now, here was Tom's bombshell to explode in their midst,
carrying widespread destruction, perhaps; for though one swal-
low does not make a summer, one engagement is apt to make
several, and her boys were, most of them, at the inflammable
age when a spark ignites the flame, which soon flickers and dies
out, or burns warm and clear for life. Nothing could be done
about it but to help them make wise choices, and be worthy of
good mates. But of all the lessons Mrs. Jo had tried to teach her
boys, this great one was the hardest; for love is apt to make

lunatics of even saints and sages, so young people cannot be expected to escape the delusions, disappointments, and mistakes, as well as the delights, of this sweet madness.

"I suppose it is inevitable, since we live in America, so I won't borrow trouble, but hope that some of the new ideas of education will produce a few hearty, happy, capable, and intelligent girls for my lads. Lucky for me that I haven't the whole twelve on my hands. I should lose my wits if I had, for I foresee complications and troubles ahead worse than Tom's boats, bicycles, donkeys and Doras," meditated Mrs. Jo, as she went back to her neglected proof sheets.

Tom was quite satisfied with the tremendous effect his engagement produced in the little community at Plumfield. "It was paralyzing," as Demi said; and astonishment left most of Tom's mates little breath for chaff. That he, the faithful one, should turn from the idol to strange goddesses, was a shock to the romantic and a warning to the susceptible. It was comical to see the airs our Thomas put on; for the most ludicrous parts of the affair were kindly buried in oblivion by the few who knew them, and Tom burst forth as a full-blown hero who had rescued the maiden from a watery grave, and won her gratitude and love by his daring deed. Dora kept the secret, and enjoyed the fun when she came to see Mother Bhaer and pay her respects to the family generally. Everyone liked her at once, for she was a gay and winning little soul; fresh, frank, and so happy, it was beautiful to see her innocent pride in Tom, who was a new boy, or man rather; for with this change in his life a great change took place in him. Jolly he would always be, and impulsive, but he tried to become all that Dora believed him, and his best side came uppermost for everyday wear. It was surprising to see how many good traits Tom had; and his efforts to preserve the manly dignity becoming to his proud position as an engaged man was very comical. So was the entire change from his former abasement and devotion to Nan to a somewhat lordly air with his little betrothed; for Dora made an idol of him, and resented the idea of a fault or a flaw in her Tom. This new state of things suited both, and the once blighted being bloomed finely in the warm atmosphere of appreciation, love, and confidence. He was very fond of the dear girl, but meant to be a slave no longer, and enjoyed his freedom immensely, quite unconscious that the great tyrant of the world had got hold of him for life.

To his father's satisfaction he gave up his medical studies, and prepared to go into business with the old gentleman, who was a flourishing merchant, ready now to make the way smooth and smile upon his marriage with Mr. West's well-endowed daughter. The only thorn in Tom's bed of roses was Nan's placid interest in his affairs, and evident relief at his disloyalty. He did not want her to suffer, but a decent amount of regret at the loss of such a lover would have gratified him; a slight melancholy, a word of reproach, a glance of envy as he passed with adoring Dora on his arm, seemed but the fitting tribute to such years of faithful service and sincere affection. But Nan regarded him with a maternal sort of air that nettled him very much, and patted Dora's curly head with a worldly-wise air worthy of the withered spinster, Julia Mills, in "David Copperfield."

It took some time to get the old and the new emotions comfortably adjusted, but Mrs. Jo helped him, and Mr. Laurie gave him some wise advice upon the astonishing gymnastic feats the human heart can perform, and be all the better for it if it only held fast to the balancing pole of truth and common sense. At last our Tommy got his bearings, and as autumn came on Plumfield saw but little of him; for his new lodestar was in the city, and business kept him hard at work. He was evidently in his right place now, and soon throve finely, to his father's great contentment; for his jovial presence pervaded the once quiet office like a gale of fresh wind, and his lively wits found managing men and affairs much more congenial employment than studying disease, or playing unseemly pranks with skeletons.

Here we will leave him for a time and turn to the more serious adventures of his mates, though this engagement, so merrily made, was the anchor which kept our mercurial Tom happy, and made a man of him.

CHAPTER 10

DEMI SETTLES

"MOTHER, CAN I have a little serious conversation with you?" asked Demi one evening, as they sat together enjoying the first fire of the season, while Daisy wrote letters upstairs and Josie was studying in the little library close by.

"Certainly, dear. No bad news, I hope?" and Mrs. Meg looked up from her sewing with a mixture of pleasure and anxiety in her motherly face; for she dearly loved a good talk with her son, and knew that he always had something worth telling.

"It will be good news to you, I think," answered Demi, smiling as he threw away his paper and went to sit beside her on the little sofa which just held two.

"Let me hear it, then, at once."

"I know you don't like the reporting, and will be glad to hear that I have given it up."

"I am very glad! It is too uncertain a business, and there is no prospect of getting on for a long time. I want you settled in some good place where you can stay, and in time make money. I wish you liked a profession; but as you don't any clean, well-established business will do."

"What do you say to a railroad office?"

"I don't like it. A noisy, hurried kind of place, I know, with all sorts of rough men about. I hope it isn't that, dear?"

"I could have it; but does bookkeeping in a wholesale leather business please you better?"

"No. You'll get round-shouldered writing at a tall desk; and they say, once a bookkeeper always a bookkeeper."

"How does a traveling agent suit your views?"

"Not at all; with all those dreadful accidents, and the exposure and bad food as you go from place to place, you are sure to get killed or lose your health."

"I could be private secretary to a literary man; but the salary is small, and may end any time."

"That would be better, and more what I want. It isn't that I object to honest work of any kind; but I don't want my son to spend his best years grubbing for a little money in a dark office, or be knocked about in a rough-and-tumble scramble to get on. I want to see you in some business where your tastes and talents can be developed and made useful; where you can go on rising, and in time put in your little fortune and be a partner; so that your years of apprenticeship will not be wasted, but fit you to take your place among the honorable men who make their lives and work useful and respected. I talked it all over with your dear father when you were a child; and if he had lived he would have shown you what I mean, and helped you to be what he was."

Mrs. Meg wiped away a quiet tear as she spoke; for the memory of her husband was a very tender one, and the education of his children had been a sacred task to which she gave all her heart and life, and so far had done wonderfully well—as her good son and loving daughters tried to prove. Demi's arm was round her now, as he said, in a voice so like his father's that it was the sweetest music to her ear, "Mother dear, I think I have got just what you want for me; and it shall not be my fault if I don't become the man you hope to see me. Let me tell you all about it. I didn't say anything till it was sure, because it would only worry you; but Aunt Jo and I have been on the lookout for it some time, and now it has come. You know her publisher, Mr. Tiber, is one of the most successful men in the business; also generous, kind, and the soul of honor—as his treatment of Aunty proves. Well, I've rather hankered for that place; for I love books, and as I can't make them I'd like to publish them. That needs some literary taste and judgment, it brings you in contact with fine people, and is an education in itself. Whenever I go into that large, handsome room to see Mr. Tiber for Aunt Jo, I always want to stay; for it's lined with books and pictures, famous men and women come and go, and Mr. Tiber sits at his desk like a sort of king, receiving his subjects; for the greatest authors are humble to him, and wait his Yes or No with anxiety. Of course I've nothing to do with all that, and may never have; but I like to see it, and the atmosphere is so different from the dark offices and hurly-burly of many other trades, where nothing but money is talked about, that it seems another world; and I feel at home in it. Yes, I'd rather beat the doormats and make fires there than be head clerk in the great hide and leather store at a big salary."

Here Demi paused for breath; and Mrs. Meg, whose face had been growing brighter and brighter, exclaimed eagerly, "Just what I should like! Have you got it? Oh, my dear boy! Your fortune is made if you go to that well-established and flourishing place, with those good men to help you along!"

"I think I have, but we mustn't be too sure of anything yet. I may not suit; I'm only on trial, and must begin at the beginning and work my way up faithfully. Mr. Tiber was very kind, and will push me on as fast as is fair to the other fellows, and as I prove myself fit to go up. I'm to begin the first of next month in the book room, filling orders; and I go round and get orders, and do various other things of the sort. I like it. I am ready to do anything about books, if it's only to dust them," laughed Demi, well pleased with his prospects; for, after trying various things,

he seemed at last to have found the sort of work he liked, and a
prospect that was very inviting to him.

"You inherit that love of books from Grandpa; he can't live
without them. I'm glad of it. Tastes of that kind show a refined
nature, and are both a comfort and a help all one's life. I am
truly glad and grateful, John, that at last you want to settle, and
have got such an entirely satisfactory place. Most boys begin
much earlier; but I don't believe in sending them out to face the
world so young, just when body and soul need home care and
watchfulness. Now you are a man, and must begin your life for
yourself. Do your best, and be as honest, useful, and happy as
your father, and I won't care about making a fortune."

"I'll try, Mother. Couldn't have a better chance; for Tiber &
Co. treat their people like gentlemen, and pay generously for
faithful work. Things are done in a business-like way there, and
that suits me. I hate promises that are not kept, and shiftless or
tyrannical ways anywhere. Mr. Tiber said, 'This is only to teach
you the ropes, Brooke; I shall have other work for you by and
by.' Aunty told him I had done book notices, and had rather a
fancy for literature; so though I can't produce any 'works of
Shakespeare,' as she says, I may get up some little things later.
If I don't, I think it a very honorable and noble profession to
select and give good books to the world; and I'm satisfied to be
a humble helper in the work."

"I'm glad you feel so. It adds so much to one's happiness to
love the task one does. I used to hate teaching; but housekeep-
ing for my own family was always sweet, though much harder in
many ways. Isn't Aunt Jo pleased about all this?" asked Mrs.
Meg, already seeing in her mind's eye a splendid sign with "Tiber, Brooke, & Co." over the door of a famous publishing
house.

"So pleased that I could hardly keep her from letting the cat
out of the bag too soon. I've had so many plans, and disappointed you so often, I wanted to be very sure this time. I had to
bribe Rob and Ted to keep her at home tonight till I'd told my

news, she was so eager to rush down and tell you herself. The castles that dear woman has built for me would fill all Spain, and have kept us jolly while we waited to know our fate. Mr. Tiber doesn't do things in a hurry; but when he makes up his mind, you are all right; and I feel that I am fairly launched."

"Bless you, dear, I hope so! It is a happy day for me, because I've been so anxious lest, with all my care, I had been too easy and indulgent, and my boy, with his many good gifts, might fritter his time away in harmless but unsatisfactory things. Now I am at ease about you. If only Daisy can be happy, and Josie give up her dream, I shall be quite contented."

Demi let his mother enjoy herself for a few minutes, while he smiled over a certain little dream of his own, not ready yet for the telling; then he said, in the paternal tone which he unconsciously used when speaking of his sisters, "I'll see to the girls; but I begin to think Grandpa is right in saying we must each be what God and nature make us. We can't change it much—only help to develop the good and control the bad elements in us. I have fumbled my way into my right place at last, I hope. Let Daisy be happy in her way, since it is a good and womanly one. If Nat comes home all right, I'd say, 'Bless you, my children,' and give them a nest of their own. Then you and I will help little Jo to find out if it is to be 'All the world's a stage' or 'Home, sweet home,' for her."

"I suppose we must, John; but I can't help making plans, and hoping they will come to pass. I see that Daisy is bound up in Nat; and if he is worthy of her, I shall let them be happy in their own way, as my parents let me. But Josie will be a trial, I foresee; and much as I love the stage, and always did, I don't see how I can ever let my little girl be an actress, though she certainly has great talent for it."

"Whose fault is that?" asked Demi, smiling, as he remembered his mother's early triumphs and unquenchable interest in the dramatic efforts of the young people round her.

"Mine, I know. How could it be otherwise when I acted

'Babes in the Wood' with you and Daisy before you could speak, and taught Josie to declaim 'Mother Goose' in her cradle. Ah, me! The tastes of the mother come out in her children, and she must atone for them by letting them have their own way, I suppose." And Mrs. Meg laughed, even while she shook her head over the undeniable fact that the Marches were a theatrical family.

"Why not have a great actress of our name, as well as an authoress, a minister, and an eminent publisher? We don't choose our talents but we needn't hide them in a napkin because they are not just what we want. I say, let Jo have her way, and do what she can. Here am I to take care of her; and you can't deny you'd enjoy fixing her furbelows, and seeing her shine before the footlights, where you used to long to be. Come, Mother, better face the music and march gaily, since your willful children will 'gang their ain gait.'"

"I don't see but I must, and 'leave the consequences to the Lord,' as Marmee used to say when she had to decide, and only saw a step of the road. I *should* enjoy it immensely, if I could only feel that the life would not hurt my girl, and leave her unsatisfied when it was too late to change; for nothing is harder to give up than the excitements of that profession. I know something of it; and if your blessed father had not come along, I'm afraid I should have been an actress, in spite of Aunt March and all our honored ancestors."

"Let Josie add new honor to the name, and work out the family talent in its proper place. I'll play dragon to her, and you play nurse, and no harm can come to our little Juliet, no matter how many Romeos spoon under her balcony. Really, ma'am, opposition comes badly from an old lady who is going to wring the hearts of our audience in the heroine's part in Aunty's play next Christmas. It's the most pathetic thing I ever saw, Mother; and I'm sorry you didn't become an actress, though we should be nowhere if you had."

Demi was on his legs now, with his back to the fire, in the

lordly attitude men like to assume when things go well with them, or they want to lay down the law on any subject.

Mrs. Meg actually blushed at her son's hearty praise, and could not deny that the sound of applause was as sweet now as when she played the "Witch's Curse" and "The Moorish Maiden's Vow" long years ago.

"It's perfectly absurd for me to do it, but I couldn't resist when Jo and Laurie made the part for me, and you children were to act in it. The minute I get on the old mother's dress I forget myself and feel the same thrill at the sound of the bell that I used to feel when we got up plays in the garret. If Daisy would only take the daughter's part it would be so complete; for with you and Josie I am hardly acting, it is all so real."

"Especially the hospital scene, where you find the wounded son. Why, Mother, do you know when we did that at last rehearsal my face was wet with real tears as you cried over me. It will bring down the house; but don't forget to wipe 'em off, or I shall sneeze," said Demi, laughing at the recollection of his mother's hit.

"I won't, but it almost broke my heart to see you so pale and dreadful. I hope there will never be another war in my time, for I should have to let you go; and I never want to live through the same experience we had with Father."

"Don't you think Alice does the part better than Daisy would? Daisy hasn't a bit of the actress in her, and Alice puts life into the dullest words she speaks. I think the Marquise is just perfect in our piece," said Demi, strolling about the room as if the warmth of the fire sent a sudden color to his face.

"So do I. She is a dear girl, and I'm proud and fond of her. Where is she tonight?"

"Pegging away at her Greek, I suppose. She usually is in the evening. More's the pity," added Demi, in a low tone, as he stared intently at the bookcase, though he couldn't read a title.

"Now, there is a girl after my own heart. Pretty, well-bred, well-educated, and yet domestic, a real companion as well as helpmate for some good and intelligent man. I hope she will find one."

"So do I," muttered Demi.

Mrs. Meg had taken up her work again, and was surveying a half-finished buttonhole with so much interest that her son's face escaped her eye. He shed a beaming smile upon the rows of poets, as if even in their glass prison they could sympathize and rejoice with him at the first rosy dawn of the great passion which they knew so well. But Demi was a wise youth, and never leaped before looking carefully. He hardly knew his own heart yet, and was contented to wait till the sentiment, the fluttering of whose folded wings he began to feel, should escape from the chrysalis and be ready to soar away in the sunshine to seek and claim its lovely mate. He had said nothing; but the brown eyes were eloquent, and there was an unconscious underplot to all the little plays he and Alice Heath acted so well together. She was busy with her books, bound to graduate with high honors, and he was trying to do the same in that larger college open to all, and where each man has his own prize to win or lose. Demi had nothing but himself to offer and, being a modest youth, considered that a poor gift till he had proved his power to earn his living and the right to take a woman's happiness into his keeping.

No one guessed that he had caught the fever except sharp-eyed Josie, and she, having a wholesome fear of her brother—who could be rather awful when she went too far—wisely contented herself with watching him like a little cat, ready to pounce on the first visible sign of weakness. Demi had taken to playing pensively upon his flute after he was in his room for the night, making this melodious friend his confidante, and breathing into it all the tender hopes and fears that filled his heart. Mrs. Meg, absorbed in domestic affairs, and Daisy, who cared for no music but Nat's violin, paid no heed to these chamber concerts; but Josie always murmured to herself, with a naughty chuckle, "Dick Swiveller is thinking of his Sophy Wackles," and bided her time to revenge certain wrongs inflicted upon her by Demi, who always took Daisy's side when she tried to curb the spirits of her unruly little sister.

This evening she got her chance, and made the most of it. Mrs. Meg was just rounding off her buttonhole, and Demi still strolling restlessly about the room, when a book was heard to slam in the study, followed by an audible yawn and the appearance of the student looking as if sleep and a desire for mischief were struggling which should be master.

"I heard my name. Have you been saying anything bad about me?" she demanded, perching on the arm of an easy chair.

Her mother told the good news, over which Josie duly rejoiced, and Demi received her congratulations with a benignant air which made her feel that too much satisfaction was not good for him, and incited her to put a thorn into his bed of roses at once.

"I caught something about the play just now, and I want to tell you that I'm going to introduce a song into my part to liven it up a bit. How would this do?" And seating herself at the piano she began to sing these words to the air of "Kathleen Mavourneen"—

"Sweetest of maidens, oh, how can I tell
    The love that transfigures the whole earth to me?
The longing that causes my bosom to swell,
    When I dream of a life all devoted to thee?"

She got no further, for Demi, red with wrath, made a rush at her, and the next moment a very agile young person was seen dodging round tables and chairs with the future partner of Tiber & Co. in hot pursuit. "You monkey, how dare you meddle with my papers?" cried the irate poet, making futile grabs at the saucy girl who skipped to and fro, waving a bit of paper tantalizingly before him.

"Didn't. Found it in the big 'Dic.' Serves you right if you

leave your rubbish about. Don't you like my song? It's very pretty."

"I'll teach you one that you won't like if you don't give me my property."

"Come and get it if you can." And Josie vanished into the study to have out her squabble in peace, for Mrs. Meg was already saying, "Children, children! Don't quarrel."

The paper was in the fire by the time Demi arrived, and he at once calmed down, seeing that the bone of contention was out of the way.

"I'm glad it's burnt; I don't care for it, only some verses I was trying to set to music for one of the girls. But I'll trouble you to let my papers alone, or I shall take back the advice I gave mother tonight about allowing you to act as much as you like."

Josie was sobered at once by this dire threat, and in her most wheedling tone begged to know what he had said. By way of heaping coals of fire on her head he told her, and this diplomatic performance secured him an ally on the spot.

"You dear old boy! I'll never tease you again though you moon and spoon both day and night. If you stand by me, I'll stand by you and never say a word. See here! I've got a note for you from Alice. Won't that be a peace offering and soothe your little feelings?"

Demi's eyes sparkled as Josie held up a paper cocked hat, but as he knew what was probably in it, he took the wind out of Josie's sails, and filled her with blank astonishment by saying carelessly, "That's nothing. It's only to say whether she will go to the concert with us tomorrow night. You can read it if you like."

With the natural perversity of her sex Josie ceased to be curious the moment she was told to read it, and meekly handed it over; but she watched Demi as he calmly read the two lines it contained and then threw it into the fire.

"Why, Jack, I thought you'd treasure every scrap the 'sweetest maid' touched. Don't you care for her?"

"Very much; we all do; but 'mooning and spooning,' as you elegantly express it, is not in my line. My dear little girl, your plays make you romantic, and because Alice and I act lovers sometimes you take it into your silly head that we are really so. Don't waste time hunting mare's nests, but attend to your own affairs and leave me to mine. I forgive you, but don't do it again; it's bad taste, and tragedy queens don't romp."

That last cut finished Josie; she humbly begged pardon and went off to bed, while Demi soon followed, feeling that he had not only settled himself but his too inquisitive little sister also. But if he had seen her face as she listened to the soft wailing of his flute he would not have been so sure, for she looked as cunning as a magpie as she said, with a scornful sniff, "Pooh, you can't deceive me; I *know* Dick is serenading Sophy Wackles."

CHAPTER 11

EMIL'S THANKSGIVING

THE "BRENDA" was scudding along with all sail set to catch the rising wind, and everyone on board was rejoicing, for the long voyage was drawing toward an end.

"Four weeks more, Mrs. Hardy, and we'll give you a cup of tea such as you never had before," said second mate Hoffmann, as he paused beside two ladies sitting in a sheltered corner of the deck.

"I shall be glad to get it, and still gladder to put my feet on solid ground," answered the elder lady, smiling for our friend Emil was a favorite, as well he might be, since he devoted himself to the captain's wife and daughter, who were the only passengers on board.

"So shall I, even if I have to wear a pair of shoes like Chinese junks. I've tramped up and down the deck so much, I shall be barefooted if we don't arrive soon," laughed Mary, the daughter, showing two shabby little boots as she glanced up at the companion of these tramps, remembering gratefully how pleasant he had made them.

"Don't think there are any small enough in China," answered

Emil, with a sailor's ready gallantry, privately resolving to hunt
up the handsomest shoes he could find the moment they
landed.

"I don't know what you would have done for exercise, dear, if
Mr. Hoffmann had not made you walk every day. This lazy life
is bad for young people, though it suits an old body like me well
enough in calm weather. Is this likely to be a gale, think ye?"
added Mrs. Hardy, with an anxious glance at the west, where
the sun was setting redly.

"Only a capful of wind, ma'am, just enough to send us along
lively," answered Emil, with a comprehensive glance aloft and
alow.

"Please sing, Mr. Hoffmann, it's so pleasant to have music at
this time. We shall miss it very much when we get ashore," said
Mary, in a persuasive tone which would have won melody from
a shark, if such a thing were possible.

Emil had often blessed his one accomplishment during these
months, for it cheered the long days, and made the twilight
hour his happiest time, wind and weather permitting. So now he
gladly tuned his pipe, and leaning on the taffrail near the girl,
watched the brown locks blowing in the wind as he sang her
favorite song—

> "Give me a freshening breeze, my boys,
>   A white and swelling sail,
> A ship that cuts the dashing waves,
>   And weathers every gale.
> What life is like a sailor's life,
>   So free, so bold, so brave?
> His home the ocean's wide expanse,
>   A coral bed his grave."

Just as the last notes of the clear, strong voice died away,
Mrs. Hardy suddenly exclaimed, "What's that?"

Emil's quick eye saw at once the little puff of smoke coming up a hatchway where no smoke should be, and his heart seemed to stand still for an instant as the dread word "Fire!" flashed through his mind. Then he was quite steady, and strolled away, saying quietly, "Smoking not allowed there, I'll go and stop it." But the instant he was out of sight his face changed, and he leaped down that hatchway, thinking with a queer smile on his lips, "If we *are* afire, shouldn't wonder if I did make 'a coral bed my grave.'"

He was gone a few minutes, and when he came up, half stifled with smoke, he was as white as a very brown man could be, but calm and cool as he went to report to the captain.

"Fire in the hold, sir."

"Don't frighten the women," was Captain Hardy's first order; then both bestirred themselves to discover how strong the treacherous enemy was, and to rout it if possible.

The "Brenda's" cargo was a very combustible one, and in spite of the streams of water poured into the hold it was soon evident that the ship was doomed. Smoke began to ooze up between the planks everywhere, and the rising gale soon fanned the smouldering fire to flames that began to break out here and there, telling the dreadful truth too plainly for anyone to hide. Mrs. Hardy and Mary bore the shock bravely when told to be ready to quit the ship at a minute's notice; the boats were hastily prepared, and the men worked with a will to batten down every loophole whence the fire might escape. Soon the poor "Brenda" was a floating furnace, and the order to "Take the boats!" came for all. The women first, of course; and it was fortunate that, being a merchantman, there were no more passengers on board, so there was no panic, and one after the other the boats pushed off. That in which the women were lingered near, for the brave captain would be the last to leave his ship.

Emil stayed by him till ordered away, and reluctantly obeyed; but it was well for him he went, for just as he had regained the boat, rocking far below, half hidden by a cloud of smoke, a mast, undermined by the fire now raging in the bowels of the ship, fell with a crash, knocking Captain Hardy overboard. The boat soon reached him as he floated out from the wreck, and Emil sprung into the sea to rescue him, for he was wounded and senseless. This accident made it necessary for the young man to take command, and he at once ordered the men to pull for their lives, as an explosion might occur at any moment.

The other boats were out of danger and all lingered to watch the splendid yet awesome spectacle of the burning ship alone on the wide sea, reddening the night sky and casting a lurid glare upon the water, where floated the frail boats filled with pale faces, all turned for a last look at the fated "Brenda," slowly settling to her watery grave. No one saw the end, however, for the gale soon swept the watchers far away and separated them, some never to meet again till the sea gives up its dead.

The boat whose fortunes we must follow was alone when dawn came up, showing these survivors all the dangers of their situation. Food and water had been put in, and such provision for comfort and safety as time allowed; but it was evident that with a badly wounded man, two women, and seven sailors, their supply would not last long, and help was sorely needed. Their only hope was in meeting a ship, although the gale, which had raged all night, had blown them out of their course. To this hope all clung, and whiled away the weary hours, watching the horizon and cheering one another with prophecies of speedy rescue.

Second mate Hoffmann was very brave and helpful, though this unexpected responsibility weighed heavily on his shoulders; for the captain's state seemed desperate, the poor wife's grief wrung his heart, and the blind confidence of the young girl in his power to save them, made him feel that no sign of doubt or fear must lessen it. The men did their part readily now, but Emil knew that if starvation and despair made brutes of them, his task might be a terrible one. So he clutched his courage with both hands, kept up a manly front, and spoke so cheerily of their good chances, that all instinctively turned to him for guidance and support.

The first day and night passed in comparative comfort, but when the third came, things looked dark and hope began to fail. The wounded man was delirious, the wife worn out with anxiety and suspense, the girl weak for want of food, having put away half her biscuit for her mother, and given her share of water to wet her father's feverish lips. The sailors ceased rowing and sat grimly waiting, some openly reproaching their leader for not following their advice, others demanding more food, all waxing dangerous as privation and pain brought out the animal instincts lurking in them. Emil did his best, but mortal man was helpless there, and he could only turn his haggard face from the pitiless sky, that dropped no rain for their thirst, to the boundless sea where no sail appeared to gladden their longing eyes. All day he tried to cheer and comfort them, while hunger gnawed, thirst parched, and growing fear lay heavy at his heart. He told stories to the men, implored them to bear up for the helpless women's sake, and promised rewards if they would pull while they had strength to regain the lost route, as nearly as he could make it out, and increase their chance of rescue. He rigged an awning of sailcloth over the suffering man and tended him like a son, comforted the wife, and tried to make the pale girl forget herself, by singing every song he knew or recounting his adventures by land and sea, till she smiled and took heart; for all ended well.

The fourth day came and the supply of food and water was nearly gone. Emil proposed to keep it for the sick man and the women, but two of the men rebelled, demanding their share. Emil gave up his as an example, and several of the good fellows followed it, with the quiet heroism which so often crops up in rough but manly natures. This shamed the others, and for another day an ominous peace reigned in that little world of suffering and suspense. But during the night, while Emil, worn out with fatigue, left the watch to the most trustworthy sailor, that he might snatch an hour's rest, these two men got at the stores and stole the last of the bread and water, and the one bottle of brandy, which was carefully hoarded to keep up their strength and make the brackish water drinkable. Half mad with thirst, they drank greedily and by morning one was in a stupor, from which he never woke; the other so crazed by the strong stimulant, that when Emil tried to control him, he leaped overboard and was lost. Horror-stricken by this terrible scene, the other men were submissive henceforth, and the boat floated on and on with its sad freight of suffering souls and bodies.

Another trial came to them that left all more despairing than before. A sail appeared, and for a time a frenzy of joy prevailed, to be turned to bitterest disappointment when it passed by, too far away to see the signals waved to them or hear the frantic cries for help that rung across the sea. Emil's heart sunk then, for the captain seemed dying, and the women could not hold out much longer. He kept up till night came; then in the darkness, broken only by the feeble murmuring of the sick man, the whispered prayers of the poor wife, the ceaseless swash of the waves, Emil hid his face, and had an hour of silent agony that aged him more than years of happy life could have done. It was not the physical hardship that daunted him, though want and weakness tortured him; it was his dreadful powerlessness to conquer the cruel fate that seemed hanging over them. The men he cared little for, since these perils were but a part of the life they chose; but the master he loved, the good woman who had been so kind to him, the sweet girl whose winsome presence had made the long voyage so pleasant for them all—if he could only save these dear and innocent creatures from a cruel death, he felt that he could willingly give his life for them.

As he sat there with his head in his hands, bowed down by the first great trial of his young life, the starless sky overhead, the restless sea beneath, and all around him suffering, for which he had no help, a soft sound broke the silence, and he listened like one in a dream. It was Mary singing to her mother, who lay sobbing in her arms, spent with this long anguish. A very faint and broken voice it was, for the poor girl's lips were parched with thirst; but the loving heart turned instinctively to the great Helper in this hour of despair, and He heard her feeble cry. It was a sweet old hymn often sung at Plumfield; and as he listened, all the happy past came back so clearly that Emil forgot the bitter present, and was at home again. His talk on the housetop with Aunt Jo seemed but yesterday, and, with a pang of self-reproach, he thought, "The scarlet strand! I must remember it, and do my duty to the end. Steer straight, old boy; and if you can't come into port, go down with all sail set."

Then, as the soft voice crooned on to lull the weary woman to a fitful sleep, Emil for a little while forgot his burden in a dream of Plumfield. He saw them all, heard the familiar voices, felt the grip of welcoming hands, and seemed to say to himself, "Well, they shall not be ashamed of me if I never see them anymore."

A sudden shout startled him from that brief rest, and a drop on his forehead told him that the blessed rain had come at last, bringing salvation with it; for thirst is harder to bear than hunger, heat, or cold. Welcomed by cries of joy, all lifted up their parched lips, held out their hands, and spread their garments to catch the great drops that soon came pouring down to cool the sick man's fever, quench the agony of thirst, and bring refreshment to every weary body in the boat. All night it fell, all night the castaways reveled in the saving shower, and took heart again, like dying plants revived by heaven's dew. The clouds broke away at dawn, and Emil sprung up, wonderfully braced and cheered by those hours of silent gratitude for this answer to their cry for help. But this was not all: as his eye swept the horizon, clear against the rosy sky shone the white sails of a ship, so near that they could see the pennon at her masthead and black figures moving on the deck.

One cry broke from all those eager throats, and rung across the sea, as every man waved hat or handkerchief and the women stretched imploring hands toward this great white angel of deliverance, coming down upon them as if the fresh wind filled every sail to help her on.

No disappointment now; answering signals assured them of help; and in the rapture of that moment the happy women fell on Emil's neck, giving him his reward in tears and blessings as their grateful hearts overflowed. He always said that was the proudest moment of his life, as he stood there holding Mary in his arms; for the brave girl, who had kept up so long, broke down then, and clung to him half fainting; while her mother busied herself about the invalid, who seemed to feel the joyful stir, and gave an order, as if again on the deck of his lost ship.

It was soon over; and when all were safely aboard the good "Urania," homeward bound, Emil saw his friends in tender hands, his men among their mates, and told the story of the wreck before he thought of himself. The savory odor of the soup, carried by to the cabin for the ladies, reminded him that he was starving, and a sudden stagger betrayed his weakness. He was instantly borne away, to be half killed by kindness, and being fed, clothed, and comforted, was left to rest. Just as the surgeon left the stateroom, he asked in his broken voice, "What day is this? My head is so confused, I've lost my reckoning."

"Thanksgiving Day, man! And we'll give you a regular New England dinner, if you'll eat it," answered the surgeon, heartily.

But Emil was too spent to do anything, except lie still and give thanks, more fervently and gratefully than ever before, for the blessed gift of life, which was the sweeter for a sense of duty faithfully performed.

CHAPTER 12

DAN'S CHRISTMAS

WHERE WAS Dan? In prison. Alas for Mrs. Jo! How her heart would have ached if she had known that while old Plum shone with Christmas cheer her boy sat alone in his cell, trying to read the little book she gave him, with eyes dimmed now and then by the hot tears no physical suffering had ever wrung from him, and longing with a homesick heart for all that he had lost.

Yes, Dan was in prison; but no cry for help came from him as he faced the terrible strait he was in with the dumb despair of an Indian at the stake; for his own bosom sin had brought him there, and this was to be the bitter lesson that tamed the lawless spirit and taught him self-control.

The story of his downfall is soon told; for it came, as so often happens, just when he felt unusually full of high hopes, good resolutions, and dreams of a better life. On his journey he met a pleasant young fellow, and naturally felt an interest in him, as Blair was on his way to join his elder brothers on a ranch in Kansas. Card playing was going on in the smoking car, and the lad—for he was barely twenty—tired with the long journey, beguiled the way with such partners as appeared, being full of

171

spirits, and a little intoxicated with the freedom of the West.
Dan, true to his promise, would not join, but watched with intense interest the games that went on, and soon made up his
mind that two of the men were sharpers anxious to fleece the
boy, who had imprudently displayed a well-filled pocketbook.
Dan always had a soft spot in his heart for any younger, weaker
creature whom he met, and something about the lad reminded
him of Teddy! So he kept an eye on Blair, and warned him
against his new friends.

Vainly, of course; for when all stopped over night in one of
the great cities, Dan missed the boy from the hotel whither he
had taken him for safekeeping; and learning who had come for
him, went to find him, calling himself a fool for his pains, yet
unable to leave the confiding boy to the dangers that surrounded him.

He found him gambling in a low place with the men, who
were bound to have his money; and by the look of relief on
Blair's anxious face when he saw him Dan knew without words
that things were going badly with him, and he saw the peril too
late.

"I can't come yet—I've lost; it's not my money; I must get it
back, or I dare not face my brothers," whispered the poor lad,
when Dan begged him to get away without further loss. Shame
and fear made him desperate; and he played on, sure that he
could recover the money confided to his care. Seeing Dan's
resolute face, keen eye, and traveled air, the sharpers were
wary, played fair, and let the boy win a little; but they had no
mind to give up their prey, and finding that Dan stood sentinel
at the boy's back, an ominous glance was exchanged between
them, which meant, "We must get this fellow out of the way."

Dan saw it, and was on his guard; for he and Blair were
strangers, evil deeds are easily done in such places, and no tales
told. But he would not desert the boy, and still kept watch of
every card till he plainly detected false play, and boldly said so.
High words passed, Dan's indignation overcame his prudence;

and when the cheat refused to restore his plunder with insulting words and drawn pistol, Dan's hot temper flashed out, and he knocked the man down with a blow that sent him crashing headfirst against a stove, to roll senseless and bleeding to the floor. A wild scene followed, but in the midst of it Dan whispered to the boy, "Get away, and hold your tongue. Don't mind me."

Frightened and bewildered, Blair quitted the city at once, leaving Dan to pass the night in the lockup, and a few days later to stand in court charged with manslaughter; for the man was dead. Dan had no friends, and having once briefly told the story, held his peace, anxious to keep all knowledge of this sad affair from those at home. He even concealed his name—giving that of David Kent, as he had done several times before in emergencies. It was all over very soon; but as there were extenuating circumstances his sentence was a year in prison, with hard labor.

Dazed by the rapidity with which this horrible change in his life came upon him, Dan did not fully realize it till the iron door clanged behind him and he sat alone in a cell as narrow, cold, and silent as a tomb. He knew that a word would bring Mr. Laurie to help and comfort him; but he could not bear to tell of this disgrace, or see the sorrow and the shame it would cause the friends who hoped so much for him.

"No," he said, clinching his fist, "I'll let them think me dead first. I shall be if I am kept here long." And he sprung up to pace the stone floor like a caged lion, with a turmoil of wrath and grief, rebellion and remorse, seething in heart and brain, till he felt as if he should go mad and beat upon the walls that shut him away from the liberty which was his life. For days he suffered terribly, then worn out, sunk into a black melancholy sadder to see than his excitement.

The warden of this prison was a rough man who had won the ill will of all by unnecessary harshness, but the chaplain was full of sympathy, and did his hard duty faithfully and tenderly. He labored with poor Dan, but seemed to make no impression, and was forced to wait till work had soothed the excited nerves and captivity tamed the proud spirit that would suffer but not complain.

Dan was put in the brush shop, and feeling that activity was his only salvation, worked with a feverish energy that soon won the approval of the master and the envy of less skillful mates. Day after day he sat in his place, watched by an armed overseer, forbidden any but necessary words, no intercourse with the men beside him, no change but from cell to shop, no exercise but the dreary marches to and fro, each man's hand on the other's shoulder, keeping step with the dreary tramp so different from the ringing tread of soldiers. Silent, gaunt, and grim, Dan did his daily task, ate his bitter bread, and obeyed commands with a rebellious flash of the eye, that made the warden say, "That's a dangerous man—watch him. He'll break out some day."

There were others more dangerous than he, because older in crime and ready for any desperate outbreak to change the monotony of long sentences. These men soon divined Dan's mood, and in the mysterious way convicts invent, managed to convey to him before a month was over that plans were being made for a mutiny at the first opportunity. Thanksgiving Day was one of the few chances for them to speak together as they enjoyed an hour of freedom in the prisonyard. Then all would be settled and the rash attempt made if possible, probably to end in bloodshed and defeat for most, but liberty for a few. Dan had already planned his own escape and bided his time, growing more and more moody, fierce, and rebellious, as loss of liberty wore upon soul and body; for this sudden change from his free, healthy life to such a narrow, gloomy, and miserable one, could not but have a terrible effect upon one of Dan's temperament and age. He brooded over his ruined life, gave up all his happy hopes and plans, felt that he could never face dear old Plumfield again, or touch those friendly hands, with the stain of blood upon his own. He did not care for the wretched man whom he had killed, for such a life was better ended, he thought; but the disgrace of prison would never be wiped out of his memory, though the cropped hair would grow again, the gray suit easily be replaced, and the bolts and bars left far behind.

"It's all over with me; I've spoilt my life, now let it go. I'll give up the fight and get what pleasure I can anywhere, anyhow. They shall think me dead and so still care for me, but never know what I am. Poor Mother Bhaer! She tried to help me, but it's no use; the firebrand can't be saved."

And dropping his head in his hand as he sat on his low bed, Dan would mourn over all he had lost in tearless misery, till merciful sleep would comfort him with dreams of the happy days when the boys played together, or those still later and happier ones when all smiled on him, and Plumfield seemed to have gained a new and curious charm.

There was one poor fellow in Dan's shop whose fate was harder than his, for his sentence expired in the spring, but there was little hope of his living till that time; and the coldest-hearted man pitied poor Mason as he sat coughing his life away in that close place and counting the weary days yet to pass before he could see his wife and little child again. There was some hope that he might be pardoned out, but he had no friends to bestir themselves in the matter, and it was evident that the great Judge's pardon would soon end his patient pain forever.

Dan pitied him more than he dared to show, and this one tender emotion in that dark time was like the little flower that sprung up between the stones of the prison yard and saved the captive from despair, in the beautiful old story. Dan helped Mason with his work when he was too feeble to finish his task, and the grateful look that thanked him was a ray of sunshine to cheer his cell when he was alone. Mason envied the splendid health of his neighbor, and mourned to see it wasting there. He was a peaceful soul and tried, as far as a whispered word or a warning glance could do it, to deter Dan from joining the "bad lot," as the rebels were called. But having turned his face from the light, Dan found the downward way easy, and took a grim satisfaction in the prospect of a general outbreak during which he might revenge himself upon the tyrannical warden, and strike a blow for his own liberty, feeling that an hour of insurrection would be a welcome vent for the pent-up passions that tormented him. He had tamed many a wild animal, but his own lawless spirit was too much for him, till he found the curb that made him master of himself.

The Sunday before Thanksgiving, as he sat in chapel, Dan observed several guests in the seats reserved for them, and looked anxiously to see if any familiar face was there; for he had a mortal fear that someone from home would suddenly confront him. No, all were strangers, and he soon forgot them in listening to the chaplain's cheerful words, and the sad singing of many heavy hearts. People often spoke to the convicts, so it caused no surprise when, on being invited to address them, one of the ladies rose and said she would tell them a little story; which announcement caused the younger listeners to prick up their ears, and even the older ones to look interested; for any change in their monotonous life was welcome.

The speaker was a middle-aged woman in black, with a sympathetic face, eyes full of compassion, and a voice that seemed to warm the heart, because of certain motherly tones in it. She reminded Dan of Mrs. Jo, and he listened intently to every word, feeling that each was meant for him, because by chance, they came at the moment when he needed a softening memory to break up the ice of despair which was blighting all the good impulses of his nature.

It was a very simple little story, but it caught the men's attention at once, being about two soldiers in a hospital during the late war, both badly wounded in the right arm, and both anxious to save these breadwinners and go home unmaimed. One was patient, docile, and cheerfully obeyed orders, even when told that the arm must go. He submitted and after much suffering recovered, grateful for life, though he could fight no more. The other rebelled, would listen to no advice, and having delayed too long, died a lingering death, bitterly regretting his folly when it was too late. "Now, as all stories should have a little moral, let me tell you mine," added the lady, with a smile, as she looked at the row of young men before her, sadly wondering what brought them there.

"This is a hospital for soldiers wounded in life's battle; here are sick souls, weak wills, insane passions, blind consciences, all the ills that come from broken laws, bringing their inevitable pain and punishment with them. There is hope and help for everyone, for God's mercy is infinite and man's charity is great; but penitence and submission must come before the cure is possible. Pay the forfeit manfully, for it is just; but from the suffering and shame wring new strength for a nobler life. The scar will remain, but it is better for a man to lose both arms than his soul; and these hard years, instead of being lost, may be made the most precious of your lives, if they teach you to rule yourselves. O friends, try to outlive the bitter past, to wash the sin away, and begin anew. If not for your own sakes, for that of the dear mothers, wives, and children, who wait and hope so patiently for you. Remember them, and do not let them love and long in vain. And if there be any here so forlorn that they have no friend to care for them, never forget the Father whose arms are always open to receive, forgive, and comfort His prodigal sons, even at the eleventh hour."

There the little sermon ended; but the preacher of it felt that her few hearty words had not been uttered in vain, for one boy's head was down, and several faces wore the softened look which told that a tender memory was touched. Dan was forced to set his lips to keep them steady, and drop his eyes to hide the sudden dew that dimmed them when waiting, hoping friends were spoken of. He was glad to be alone in his cell again, and sat thinking deeply, instead of trying to forget himself in sleep. It seemed as if those words were just what he needed to show him where he stood and how fateful the next few days might be to him. Should he join the "bad lot," and perhaps add another crime to the one already committed, lengthen the sentence already so terrible to bear, deliberately turn his back on all that was good, and mar the future that might yet be redeemed? Or should he, like the wiser man in the story, submit, bear the just punishment, try to be the better for it; and though the scar would remain, it might serve as a reminder of a battle not wholly lost, since he had saved his soul though innocence was gone? Then he would dare go home, perhaps, confess, and find fresh strength in the pity and consolation of those who never gave him up.

Good and evil fought for Dan that night as did the angel and the devil for Sintram, and it was hard to tell whether lawless nature or loving heart would conquer. Remorse and resentment, shame and sorrow, pride and passion, made a battlefield of that narrow cell, and the poor fellow felt as if he had fiercer enemies to fight now than any he had met in all his wanderings. A little thing turned the scale, as it so often does in these mysterious hearts of ours, and a touch of sympathy helped Dan decide the course which would bless or ban his life.

In the dark hour before the dawn, as he lay wakeful on his bed, a ray of light shone through the bars, the bolts turned softly, and a man came in. It was the good chaplain, led by the same instinct that brings a mother to her sick child's pillow; for long experience as nurse of souls had taught him to see the signs of hope in the hard faces about him, and to know when the moment came for a helpful word and the cordial of sincere prayer that brings such comfort and healing to tried and troubled hearts. He had been to Dan before at unexpected hours, but always found him sullen, indifferent, or rebellious, and had

gone away to patiently bide his time. Now it had come; a look of
relief was in the prisoner's face as the light shone on it, and the
sound of a human voice was strangely comfortable after listening to the whispers of the passions, doubts, and fears which had
haunted the cell for hours, dismaying Dan by their power, and
showing him how much he needed help to fight the good fight,
since he had no armor of his own.

"Kent, poor Mason has gone. He left a message for you, and
I felt impelled to come and give it now, because I think you
were touched by what we heard today, and in need of the help
Mason tried to give you," said the chaplain, taking the one seat
and fixing his kind eyes on the grim figure in the bed.

"Thank you, sir, I'd like to hear it," was all Dan's answer; but
he forgot himself in pity for the poor fellow dead in prison, with
no last look at wife or child.

"He went suddenly, but remembered you, and begged me to
say these words, 'Tell him *not to do it,* but to hold on, do his
best, and when his time is out go right to Mary, and she'll make
him welcome for my sake. He's got no friends in these parts and
will feel lonesome, but a woman's always safe and comfortable
when a fellow's down on his luck. Give him my love and good-
bye; for he was kind to me, and God will bless him for it.' Then
he died quietly, and tomorrow will go home with God's pardon,
since man's came too late."

Dan said nothing, but laid his arm across his face and lay
quite still. Seeing that the pathetic little message had done its
work even better than he hoped, the chaplain went on, unconscious how soothing his paternal voice was to the poor prisoner
who longed to "go home," but felt he had forfeited the right.

"I hope you won't disappoint this humble friend whose last
thought was for you. I know that there is trouble brewing, and
fear that you may be tempted to lend a hand on the wrong side.
Don't do it, for the plot will not succeed—it never does—and it
would be a pity to spoil your record which is fair so far. Keep up
your courage, my son, and go out at the year's end better, not

worse, for this hard experience. Remember a grateful woman waits to welcome and thank you if you have no friends of your own; if you have, do your best for their sake, and let us ask God to help you as He only can."

Then waiting for no answer the good man prayed heartily, and Dan listened as he never had before; for the lonely hour, the dying message, the sudden uprising of his better self, made it seem as if some kind angel had come to save and comfort him.

After that night there was a change in Dan, though no one knew it but the chaplain; for to all the rest he was the same silent, stern, unsocial fellow as before, and turning his back on the bad and the good alike, found his only pleasure in the books his friend brought him. Slowly, as the steadfast drop wears away the rock, the patient kindness of this man won Dan's confidence, and led by him he began to climb out of the Valley of Humiliation toward the mountains, whence, through the clouds, one can catch glimpses of the Celestial City whither all true pilgrims sooner or later turn their wistful eyes and stumbling feet. There were many backslidings, many struggles with Giant Despair and fiery Apollyon, many heavy hours when life did not seem worth living and Mason's escape the only hope. But through all, the grasp of a friendly hand, the sound of a brother's voice, the unquenchable desire to atone for the past by a better future, and win the right to see home again, kept poor Dan to his great task as the old year drew to its end, and the new waited to turn another leaf in the book whose hardest lesson he was learning now.

At Christmas he yearned so for Plumfield that he devised a way to send a word of greeting to cheer their anxious hearts, and comfort his own. He wrote to Mary Mason, who lived in another state, asking her to mail the letter he enclosed. In it he merely said he was well and busy, had given up the farm, and had other plans which he would tell later; would not be home before autumn probably, nor write often, but was all right, and sent love and merry Christmas to everyone.

Then he took up his solitary life again, and tried to pay his forfeit manfully.

CHAPTER 13

NAT'S NEW YEAR

"I DON'T expect to hear from Emil yet, and Nat writes regularly, but where is Dan? Only two or three postals since he went. Such an energetic fellow as he is could buy up all the farms in Kansas by this time," said Mrs. Jo one morning when the mail came in and no card or envelope bore Dan's dashing hand.

"He never writes often, you know, but does his work and then comes home. Months and years seem to mean little to him, and he is probably prospecting in the wilderness, forgetful of time," answered Mr. Bhaer, deep in one of Nat's long letters from Leipzig.

"But he promised he would let me know how he got on, and Dan keeps his word if he can. I'm afraid something has happened to him." And Mrs. Jo comforted herself by patting Don's head, as he came at the sound of his master's name to look at her with eyes almost human in their wistful intelligence.

"Don't worry, Mum dear, nothing ever happens to the old fellow. He'll turn up all right, and come stalking in some day with a gold mine in one pocket and a prairie in the other, as jolly as a grig," said Ted, who was in no haste to deliver Octoo to her rightful owner.

"Perhaps he has gone to Montana and given up the farm plan. He seemed to like the Indians best, I thought." And Rob went to help his mother with her pile of letters and his cheerful suggestions.

"I hope so, it would suit him best. But I am sure he would have told us his change of plan and sent for some money to work with. No, I feel in my prophetic bones that something is wrong," said Mrs. Jo, looking as solemn as Fate in a breakfast cap.

"Then we shall hear; ill news always travels fast. Don't borrow trouble, Jo, but hear how well Nat is getting on. I'd no idea the boy would care for anything but music. My good friend Baumgarten has launched him well, and it will do him good if he lose not his head. A good lad, but new to the world, and Leipzig is full of snares for the unwary. Gott be with him!"

The Professor read Nat's enthusiastic account of certain literary and musical parties he had been to, the splendors of the opera, the kindness of his new friends, the delight of studying under such a master as Bergmann, his hopes of rapid gain, and his great gratitude to those who had opened this enchanted world to him.

"That, now, is satisfactory and comfortable. I felt that Nat had unsuspected power in him before he went away; he was so manly and full of excellent plans," said Mrs. Jo, in a satisfied tone.

"We shall see. He will doubtless get his lesson and be the better for it. That comes to us all in our young days. I hope it will not be too hard for our good jüngling," answered the Professor, with a wise smile, remembering his own student life in Germany.

He was right; and Nat was already getting his lesson in life with a rapidity which would have astonished his friends at home. The manliness over which Mrs. Jo rejoiced was devel-

oping in unexpected ways, and quiet Nat had plunged into the
more harmless dissipations of the gay city with all the ardor of
an inexperienced youth taking his first sip of pleasure. The entire freedom and sense of independence was delicious, for many
benefits began to burden him, and he longed to stand on his
own legs and make his own way. No one knew his past here;
and with a well-stocked wardrobe, a handsome sum at his
banker's, and the best teacher in Leipzig, he made his debut as
a musical young gentleman, presented by the much-respected
Professor Bhaer and the wealthy Mr. Laurence, who had many
friends glad to throw open their houses to his protégé. Thanks
to these introductions, his fluent German, modest manners, and
undeniable talent, the stranger was cordially welcomed and
launched at once into a circle which many an ambitious young
man strove in vain to enter.

All this rather turned Nat's head; and as he sat in the brilliant
opera house, chatted among the ladies at some select coffee
party, or whisked an eminent professor's amiable daughter
down the room, trying to imagine she was Daisy, he often asked
himself if this gay fellow could be the poor homeless little street
musician who once stood waiting in the rain at the gates of
Plumfield. His heart was true, his impulses good, and his ambitions high; but the weak side of his nature came uppermost
here; vanity led him astray, pleasure intoxicated him, and for a
time he forgot everything but the delights of this new and
charming life. Without meaning to deceive, he allowed people
to imagine him a youth of good family and prospects; he
boasted a little of Mr. Laurie's wealth and influence, of Professor Bhaer's eminence, and the flourishing college at which he
himself had been educated. Mrs. Jo was introduced to the sentimental *Fräuleins* who read her books, and the charms and virtues of his own dear *Mädchen* confided to sympathetic mammas. All these boyish boastings and innocent vanities were duly
circulated among the gossips, and his importance much

increased thereby, to his surprise and gratification, as well as some shame.

But they bore fruit that was bitter in the end; for, finding that he was considered one of the upper class, it very soon became impossible for him to live in the humble quarters he had chosen, or to lead the studious, quiet life planned for him. He met other students, young officers, and fellows of all sorts, and was flattered at being welcomed among them; though it was a costly pleasure, and often left a thorn of regret to vex his honest conscience. He was tempted to take better rooms in a more fashionable street, leaving good Frau Tetzel to lament his loss, and his artist neighbor, Fräulein Vogelstein, to shake her gray ringlets and predict his return, a sadder and a wiser man.

The sum placed at his disposal for expenses and such simple pleasures as his busy life could command seemed a fortune to Nat, though it was smaller than generous Mr. Laurie first proposed. Professor Bhaer wisely counseled prudence, as Nat was unused to the care of money, and the good man knew the temptations that a well-filled purse makes possible at this pleasure-loving age. So Nat enjoyed his handsome little apartment immensely, and insensibly let many unaccustomed luxuries creep in. He loved his music, and never missed a lesson; but the hours he should have spent in patient practice were too often wasted at theater, ball, beer garden, or club—doing no harm beyond that waste of precious time, and money not his own; for he had no vices, and took his recreation like a gentleman, so far. But slowly a change for the worse was beginning to show itself, and he felt it. These first steps along the flowery road were downward, not upward; and the constant sense of disloyalty which soon began to haunt him made Nat feel, in the few quiet hours he gave himself, that all was not well with him, in spite of the happy whirl in which he lived.

"Another month, and then I will be steady," he said more than once, trying to excuse the delay by the fact that all was new to him, that his friends at home wished him to be happy, and that society was giving him the polish he needed. But as each month slipped away it grew harder to escape; he was inevitably drawn on, and it was so easy to drift with the tide that he deferred the evil day as long as possible. Winter festivities followed the more wholesome summer pleasures, and Nat found them more costly; for the hospitable ladies expected some return from the stranger; and carriages, bouquets, theater tickets, and all the little expenses a young man cannot escape at such times, told heavily on the purse which had seemed bottomless at first. Taking Mr. Laurie for his model, Nat became quite a gallant, and was universally liked; for through all the newly acquired airs and graces the genuine honesty and simplicity of his character plainly shone, winning confidence and affection from all who knew him.

Among these was a certain amiable old lady with a musical daughter—well-born but poor, and very anxious to marry the aforesaid daughter to some wealthy man. Nat's little fictions concerning his prospects and friends charmed the *gnädige Frau* as much as his music and devoted manners did the sentimental Minna. Their quiet parlor seemed homelike and restful to Nat, when tired of gayer scenes; and the motherly interest of the elder lady was sweet and comfortable to him; while the tender blue eyes of the pretty girl were always so full of welcome when he came, of regret when he left, and of admiration when he played to her, that he found it impossible to keep away from this attractive spot. He meant no harm, and feared no danger, having confided to the Frau Mamma that he was betrothed; so he continued to call, little dreaming what ambitious hopes the old lady cherished, nor the peril there was in receiving the adoration of a romantic German girl, till it was too late to spare her pain and himself great regret.

Of course some inkling of these new and agreeable experiences got into the voluminous letters he never was too gay, too busy, or too tired to write each week; and while Daisy rejoiced over his happiness and success, and the boys laughed at the idea

of "old Chirper coming out as a society man," the elders looked
sober, and said among themselves, "He is going too fast; he
must have a word of warning, or trouble may come."

But Mr. Laurie said, "Oh, let him have his fling; he's been
dependent and repressed long enough. He can't go far with the
money he has, and I've no fear of his getting into debt. He's too
timid and too honest to be reckless. It is his first taste of freedom; let him enjoy it, and he'll work the better by and by; I
know—and I'm sure I'm right."

So the warnings were very gentle, and the good people waited
anxiously to hear more of hard study, and less of "splendid
times." Daisy sometimes wondered, with a pang at her faithful
heart, if one of the charming Minnas, Hildegardes, and Lottch-
ens mentioned were not stealing her Nat away from her; but she
never asked, always wrote calmly and cheerfully, and looked in
vain for any hint of change in the letters that were worn out
with much reading.

Month after month slipped away, till the holidays came with
gifts, good wishes, and brilliant festivities. Nat expected to enjoy
himself very much, and did at first; for a German Christmas is a
spectacle worth seeing. But he paid dearly for the abandon with
which he threw himself into the gaieties of that memorable
week; and on New Year's Day the reckoning came. It seemed as
if some malicious fairy had prepared the surprises that arrived,
so unwelcome were they, so magical the change they wrought,
turning his happy world into a scene of desolation and despair
as suddenly as a transformation at the pantomime.

The first came in the morning, when duly armed with costly
bouquets and bonbons, he went to thank Minna and her mother
for the braces embroidered with forget-me-nots and the silk
socks knit by the old lady's nimble fingers, which he had found
upon his table that day. The Frau Mamma received him gra-
ciously; but when he asked for the daughter the good lady
frankly demanded what his intentions were, adding that certain
gossip which had reached her ear made it necessary for him to

declare himself or come no more, as Minna's peace must not be compromised.

A more panic-stricken youth was seldom seen than Nat as he received this unexpected demand. He saw too late that his American style of gallantry had deceived the artless girl, and might be used with terrible effect by the artful mother, if she chose to do it. Nothing but the truth could save him, and he had the honor and honesty to tell it faithfully. A sad scene followed; for Nat was obliged to strip off his fictitious splendor, confess himself only a poor student, and humbly ask pardon for the thoughtless freedom with which he had enjoyed their too confiding hospitality. If he had had any doubts of Frau Schomburg's motives and desires, they were speedily set at rest by the frankness with which she showed her disappointment, the vigor with which she scolded him, and the scorn with which she cast him off when her splendid castles in the air collapsed.

The sincerity of Nat's penitence softened her a little, and she consented to a farewell word with Minna, who had listened at the keyhole, and was produced drenched in tears, to fall on Nat's bosom, crying, "Ah, thou dear one, never can I forget thee, though my heart is broken!"

This was worse than the scolding; for the stout lady also wept, and it was only after much German gush and twaddle that he escaped, feeling like another Werther; while the deserted Lotte consoled herself with the bonbons, her mother with the more valuable gifts.

The second surprise arrived as he dined with Professor Baumgarten. His appetite had been effectually taken away by the scene of the morning, and his spirits received another damper when a fellow student cheerfully informed him that he was about to go to America, and should make it his agreeable duty to call on the "lieber Herr Professor Bhaer" to tell him how gaily his protégé was disporting himself at Leipzig. Nat's heart died within him as he imagined the effect these glowing tales would have at Plumfield—not that he had willfully

deceived them, but in his letters many things were left untold;
and when Carlsen added, with a friendly wink, that he would
merely hint at the coming betrothal of the fair Minna and his
"heart's friend," Nat found himself devoutly hoping that this
other inconvenient heart's friend might go to the bottom of the
sea before he reached Plumfield to blast all his hopes by these
tales of a misspent winter. Collecting his wits, he cautioned
Carlsen with what he flattered himself was Mephistophelian art,
and gave him such confused directions that it would be a miracle if he ever found Professor Bhaer. But the dinner was spoilt
for Nat, and he got away as soon as possible, to wander discon-
solately about the streets, with no heart for the theater or the
supper he was to share with some gay comrades afterward. He
comforted himself a little by giving alms to sundry beggars,
making two children happy with gilded gingerbread, and drinking a lonely glass of beer, in which he toasted his Daisy and
wished himself a better year than the last had been.

Going home at length, he found a third surprise awaiting him
in the shower of bills which had descended upon him like a
snowstorm, burying him in an avalanche of remorse, despair,
and self-disgust. These bills were so many and so large that he
was startled and dismayed; for, as Mr. Bhaer wisely predicted,
he knew little about the value of money. It would take every
dollar at the banker's to pay them all at once, and leave him
penniless for the next six months, unless he wrote home for
more. He would rather starve than do that, and his first impulse
was to seek help at the gaming table, whither his new friends
had often tempted him. But he had promised Mr. Bhaer to
resist what then had seemed an impossible temptation; and now
he would not add another fault to the list already so long. Borrow he would not, nor beg. What could he do? For these appall-
ing bills must be paid, and the lessons go on; or his journey was
an ignominious failure. But he must live meantime. And how?
Bowed down with remorse for the folly of these months, he saw
too late whither he was drifting, and for hours paced up and

down his pretty rooms, floundering in a Slough of Despond, with no helping hand to pull him out—at least he thought so till letters were brought in, and among fresh bills lay one well-worn envelope with an American stamp in the corner.

Ah, how welcome it was! How eagerly he read the long pages full of affectionate wishes from all at home! For everyone had sent a line, and as each familiar name appeared, his eyes grew dimmer and dimmer till, as he read the last—"God bless my boy! Mother Bhaer"—he broke down; and laying his head on his arms, blistered the paper with a rain of tears that eased his heart and washed away the boyish sins that now lay so heavy on his conscience.

"Dear people, how they love and trust me! And how bitterly they would be disappointed if they knew what a fool I've been! I'll fiddle in the streets again before I'll ask for help from them!" cried Nat, brushing away the tears, of which he was ashamed, although he felt the good they had done.

Now he seemed to see more clearly what to do; for the helping hand had been stretched across the sea, and Love, the dear Evangelist, had lifted him out of the slough and shown him the narrow gate, beyond which deliverance lay. When the letter had been re-read, and one corner where a daisy was painted, passionately kissed, Nat felt strong enough to face the worst and conquer it. Every bill should be paid, every salable thing of his own sold, these costly rooms given up; and once back with the thrifty Frau Tetzel, he would find work of some sort by which to support himself, as many another student did. He must give up the new friends, turn his back on the gay life, cease to be a butterfly, and take his place again among the grubs. It was the only honest thing to do, but very hard for the poor fellow to crush his little vanities, renounce the delights so dear to the young, own his folly, and step down from his pedestal to be pitied, laughed at, and forgotten.

It took all Nat's pride and courage to do this, for his was a sensitive nature; esteem was very precious to him, failure very bitter, and nothing but the inborn contempt for meanness and deceit kept him from asking help or trying to hide his need by some dishonest device. As he sat alone that night, Mr. Bhaer's words came back to him with curious clearness, and he saw himself a boy again at Plumfield, punishing his teacher as a lesson to himself, when timidity had made him lie.

"He shall not suffer for me again, and I won't be a sneak if I am a fool. I'll go and tell Professor Baumgarten all about it and ask his advice. I'd rather face a loaded cannon; but it must be done. Then I'll sell out, pay my debts, and go back where I belong. Better be an honest pauper than a jackdaw among peacocks." And Nat smiled in the midst of his trouble, as he looked about him at the little elegancies of his room, remembering what he came from.

He kept his word manfully, and was much comforted to find that his experience was an old story to the professor, who approved his plan, thinking wisely that the discipline would be good for him, and was very kind in offering help and promising to keep the secret of his folly from his friend Bhaer till Nat had redeemed himself.

The first week of the new year was spent by our prodigal in carrying out his plan with penitent dispatch, and his birthday found him alone in the little room high up at Frau Tetzel's, with nothing of his former splendor but sundry unsalable keepsakes from the buxom maidens, who mourned his absence deeply. His male friends had ridiculed, pitied, and soon left him alone, with one or two exceptions, who offered their purses generously and promised to stand by him. He was lonely and heavy-hearted, and sat brooding over his small fire as he remembered the last New Year's Day at Plumfield, when at this hour he was dancing with his Daisy.

A tap at the door roused him, and with a careless "Herein," he waited to see who had climbed so far for his sake. It was the good Frau proudly bearing a tray, on which stood a bottle of wine and an astonishing cake bedecked with sugarplums of

every hue, and crowned with candles. Fräulein Vogelstein followed, embracing a blooming rose tree, above which her gray
curls waved and her friendly face beamed joyfully as she cried,
"Dear Herr Blak, we bring you greetings and a little gift or two
in honor of this ever-to-be-remembered day. Best wishes! And
may the new year bloom for you as beautifully as we your
heartwarm friends desire."

"Yes, yes, in truth we do, dear Herr," added Frau Tetzel. "Eat
of this with-joy-made Kuchen, and drink to the health of the
faraway beloved ones in the good wine."

Amused, yet touched by the kindness of the good souls, Nat
thanked them both, and made them stay to enjoy the humble
feast with him. This they gladly did, being motherly women full
of pity for the dear youth, whose straits they knew, and having
substantial help to offer, as well as kind words and creature
comforts.

Frau Tetzel, with some hesitation, mentioned a friend of hers
who, forced by illness to leave his place in the orchestra of a
second-rate theater, would gladly offer it to Nat, if he could
accept so humble a position. Blushing and toying with the roses
like a shy girl, good old Vogelstein asked if in his leisure moments he could give English lessons in the young ladies' school
where she taught painting, adding that a small but certain salary
would be paid him.

Gratefully Nat accepted both offers, finding it less humiliat-
ing to be helped by women than by friends of his own sex. This
work would support him in a frugal way, and certain musical
drudgery promised by his master assured his own teaching. Delighted with the success of their little plot, these friendly neighbors left him with cheery words, warm handclasps, and faces
beaming with feminine satisfaction at the hearty kiss Nat put on
each faded cheek, as the only return he could make for all this
helpful kindness.

It was strange how much brighter the world looked after that;
for hope was a better cordial than the wine, and good resolu-

tions bloomed as freshly as the little rose tree that filled the room with fragrance, as Nat woke the echoes with the dear old airs, finding now as always his best comforter in music, to whom henceforth he swore to be a more loyal subject.

CHAPTER 14

PLAYS AT PLUMFIELD

As IT IS as impossible for the humble historian of the March family to write a story without theatricals in it as for our dear Miss Yonge to get on with less than twelve or fourteen children in her interesting tales, we will accept the fact, and at once cheer ourselves after the last afflicting events, by proceeding to the Christmas plays at Plumfield; for they influence the fate of several of our characters, and cannot well be skipped.

When the college was built Mr. Laurie added a charming little theater which not only served for plays, but declamations, lectures, and concerts. The drop curtain displayed Apollo with the Muses grouped about him; and as a compliment to the donor of the hall the artist had given the god a decided resemblance to our friend, which was considered a superb joke by everyone else. Home talent furnished stars, stock company, orchestra, and scene-painter; and astonishing performances were given on this pretty little stage.

Mrs. Jo had been trying for some time to produce a play which should be an improvement upon the adaptations from the French then in vogue, curious mixtures of fine toilettes,

false sentiment, and feeble wit, with no touch of nature to
redeem them. It was easy to plan plays full of noble speeches
and thrilling situations, but very hard to write them; so she
contented herself with a few scenes of humble life in which the
comic and pathetic were mingled; and as she fitted her characters to her actors, she hoped the little venture would prove that
truth and simplicity had not entirely lost their power to charm.
Mr. Laurie helped her, and they called themselves Beaumont
and Fletcher, enjoying their joint labor very much; for Beaumont's knowledge of dramatic art was of great use in curbing
Fletcher's too-aspiring pen, and they flattered themselves that
they had produced a neat and effective bit of work as an experiment.

All was ready now; and Christmas Day was much enlivened
by last rehearsals, the panics of timid actors, the scramble for
forgotten properties, and the decoration of the theater. Ever-
green and holly from the woods, blooming plants from the hothouse on Parnassus, and the flags of all nations made it very gay
that night in honor of the guests who were coming, chief among
them, Miss Cameron, who kept her promise faithfully. The
orchestra tuned their instruments with unusual care, the scene-
shifters set their stage with lavish elegance, the prompter hero-
ically took his seat in the stifling nook provided for him, and the
actors dressed with trembling hands that dropped the pins, and
perspiring brows whereon the powder wouldn't stick. Beaumont
and Fletcher were everywhere, feeling that their literary reputa-
tion was at stake; for sundry friendly critics were invited, and
reporters, like mosquitoes, cannot be excluded from any earthly
scene, be it a great man's deathbed or a dime museum.

"Has she come?" was the question asked by every tongue
behind the curtain; and when Tom, who played an old man,
endangered his respectable legs among the footlights to peep,
announced that he saw Miss Cameron's handsome head in the
place of honor, a thrill pervaded the entire company, and Josie

declared with an excited gasp that she was going to have stage fright for the first time in her life.

"I'll shake you if you do," said Mrs. Jo, who was in such a wild state of dishevelment with her varied labors that she might have gone on as Madge Wildfire, without an additional rag or crazy elflock.

"You'll have time to get your wits together while we do our piece. We are old stagers and calm as clocks," answered Demi, with a nod toward Alice, ready in her pretty dress and all her properties at hand.

But both clocks were going rather faster than usual, as heightened color, brilliant eyes, and a certain flutter under the laces and velvet coat betrayed. They were to open the entertainment with a gay little piece which they had played before and did remarkably well. Alice was a tall girl, with dark hair and eyes, and a face which intelligence, health, and a happy heart made beautiful. She was looking her best now, for the brocades, plumes, and powder of the Marquise became her stately figure; and Demi in his court suit, with sword, three-cornered hat, and white wig, made as gallant a Baron as one would wish to see. Josie was the maid, and looked her part to the life, being as pretty, pert, and inquisitive as any French soubrette. These three were all the characters; and the success of the piece depended on the spirit and skill with which the quickly changing moods of the quarrelsome lovers were given, their witty speeches made to tell, and the by-play suited to the courtly period in which the scene was laid.

Few would have recognized sober John and studious Alice in the dashing gentleman and coquettish lady, who kept the audience laughing at their caprices; while they enjoyed the brilliant costumes, and admired the ease and grace of the young actors. Josie was a prominent figure in the plot, as she listened at keyholes, peeped into notes, and popped in and out at all the most inopportune moments, with her nose in the air, her hands in her apron pockets, and curiosity pervading her little figure from the topmost bow of her jaunty cap to the red heels of her slippers. All went smoothly; and the capricious Marquise, after tormenting the devoted Baron to her heart's content, owned herself conquered in the war of wits, and was just offering the hand he had fairly won, when a crash startled them, and a heavily decorated side-scene swayed forward, ready to fall upon Alice. Demi saw it, and sprung before her to catch and hold it up, standing like a modern Samson with the wall of a house on his back. The danger was over in a moment, and he was about to utter his last speech, when the excited young scene-shifter, who had flown up a ladder to repair the damage, leaned over to whisper, "All right," and release Demi from his spread-eagle attitude; as he did so, a hammer slipped out of his pocket, to fall upon the upturned face below, inflicting a smart blow and literally knocking the Baron's part out of his head.

A quick curtain' robbed the audience of a pretty little scene not down on the bill; for the Marquise flew to stanch the blood with a cry of alarm: "Oh! John, you are hurt! Lean on me"— which John gladly did for a moment, being a trifle dazed, yet quite able to enjoy the tender touch of the hands busied about him and the anxiety of the face so near his own; for both told him something which he would have considered cheaply won by a rain of hammers and the fall of the whole college on his head.

Nan was on the spot in a moment with the case, that never left her pocket; and the wound was neatly plastered up by the time Mrs. Jo arrived, demanding tragically, "Is he too much hurt to go on again? If he is, my play is lost!"

"I'm all the fitter for it, Aunty; for here's a real instead of a painted wound. I'll be ready; don't worry about me." And catching up his wig, Demi was off, with only a very eloquent look of thanks to the Marquise, who had spoilt her gloves for his sake, but did not seem to mind it at all, though they reached above her elbows, and were most expensive.

"How are your nerves, Fletcher?" asked Mr. Laurie as they

stood together during the breathless minute before the last bell rings.

"About as calm as yours, Beaumont," answered Mrs. Jo, gesticulating wildly to Mrs. Meg to set her cap straight.

"Bear up, partner! I'll stand by you whatever comes!"

"I feel that it ought to go; for, though it's a mere trifle, a good deal of honest work and truth have gone into it. Doesn't Meg look the picture of a dear old country woman?"

She certainly did, as she sat in the farmhouse kitchen by a cheery fire, rocking a cradle and darning stockings as if she had done nothing else all her life. Gray hair, skillfully drawn lines on the forehead, and a plain gown, with cap, little shawl, and check apron, changed her into a comfortable, motherly creature who found favor the moment the curtain went up and discovered her rocking, darning, and crooning an old song. In a short soliloquy about Sam, her boy, who wanted to enlist; Dolly, her discontented little daughter, who longed for city ease and pleasures; and poor "Elizy," who had married badly, and come home to die, bequeathing her baby to her mother, lest its bad father should claim it, the little story was very simply opened, and made effective by the real boiling of the kettle on the crane, the ticking of a tall clock, and the appearance of a pair of blue worsted shoes which waved fitfully in the air to the soft babble of a baby's voice. Those shapeless little shoes won the first applause; and Mr. Laurie, forgetting elegance in satisfaction, whispered to his coadjutor, "I thought the baby would fetch them!"

"If the dear thing won't squall in the wrong place, we are saved. But it is risky. Be ready to catch it if all Meg's cuddlings prove in vain," answered Mrs. Jo, adding, with a clutch at Mr. Laurie's arm as a haggard face appeared at the window, "Here's Demi! I hope no one will recognize him when he comes on as the son. I'll never forgive you for not doing the villain yourself."

"Can't run the thing and act too. He's capitally made up, and likes a bit of melodrama."

"This scene ought to have come later; but I wanted to show that the mother was the heroine as soon as possible. I'm tired of lovesick girls and runaway wives. We'll prove that there's romance in old women also. Now he's coming!"

And in slouched a degraded-looking man, shabby, unshaven, and evil-eyed, trying to assume a masterful air as he dismayed the tranquil old woman by demanding his child. A powerful scene followed; and Mrs. Meg surprised even those who knew her best by the homely dignity with which she at first met the man she dreaded; then, as he brutally pressed his claim, she pleaded with trembling voice and hands to keep the little creature she had promised the dying mother to protect; and when he turned to take it by force, quite a thrill went through the house as the old woman sprung to snatch it from the cradle, and holding it close, defied him in God's name to tear it from that sacred refuge. It was really well done; and the round of applause that greeted the fine tableau of the indignant old woman, the rosy, blinking baby clinging to her neck, and the daunted man who dared not execute his evil purpose with such a defender for helpless innocence, told the excited authors that their first scene was a hit.

The second was quieter, and introduced Josie as a bonny country lass setting the supper table in a bad humor. The pettish way in which she slapped down the plates, hustled the cups, and cut the big brown loaf, as she related her girlish trials and ambitions, was capital. Mrs. Jo kept her eye on Miss Cameron, and saw her nod approval several times at some natural tone or gesture, some good bit of by-play, or a quick change of expression in the young face, which was as variable as an April day. Her struggle with the toasting fork made much merriment; so did her contempt for the brown sugar, and the relish with which she sweetened her irksome duties by eating it; and when she sat, like Cinderella, on the hearth, tearfully watching the flames dance on the homely room, a girlish voice was heard to exclaim impulsively, "Poor little thing! she ought to have *some* fun!"

The old woman enters; and mother and daughter have a pretty scene, in which the latter coaxes and threatens, kisses and cries, till she wins the reluctant consent of the former to visit a rich relation in the city; and from being a little thundercloud Dolly becomes bewitchingly gay and good, as soon as her willful wish is granted. The poor old soul has hardly recovered from this trial when the son enters, in army blue, tells he has enlisted, and must go. That is a hard blow; but the patriotic mother bears it well, and not till the thoughtless young folks have hastened away to tell their good news elsewhere does she break down. Then the country kitchen becomes pathetic, as the old mother sits alone mourning over her children, till the gray head is hidden in the hands as she kneels down by the cradle to weep and pray, with only Baby to comfort her fond and faithful heart.

Sniffs were audible all through the latter part of this scene; and when the curtain fell, people were so busy wiping their eyes that for a moment they forgot to applaud. That silent moment was more flattering than noise; and as Mrs. Jo wiped the real tears off her sister's face, she said as solemnly as an unconscious dab of rouge on her own nose permitted, "Meg, you have saved my play! Oh, why aren't you a real actress, and I a real playwright?"

"Don't gush now, dear, but help me dress Josie; she's in such a quiver of excitement, I can't manage her, and this is her best scene, you know."

So it was; for her aunt had written it especially for her, and little Jo was happy in a gorgeous dress, with a train long enough to satisfy her wildest dreams. The rich relation's parlor was in festival array, and the country cousin sails in, looking back at her sweeping flounces with such artless rapture that no one had the heart to laugh at the pretty jay in borrowed plumes. She has confidences with herself in the mirror, from which it is made evident that she has discovered all is not gold that glitters, and has found greater temptations than those a girlish love of pleasure, luxury, and flattery bring her. She is sought by a rich lover;

but her honest heart resists the allurements he offers, and in its innocent perplexity wishes "mother" was there to comfort and counsel.

A gay little dance, in which Dora, Nan, Bess, and several of the boys took part, made a good background for the humble figure of the old woman in her widow's bonnet, rusty shawl, big umbrella, and basket. Her naive astonishment, as she surveys the spectacle, feels the curtains, and smooths her old gloves during the moment she remains unseen, was very good; but Josie's unaffected start when she sees her, and the cry, "Why, there's Mother!" was such a hearty little bit of nature, it hardly needed the impatient tripping over her train as she ran into the arms that seemed now to be her nearest refuge.

The lover plays his part; and ripples of merriment greeted the old woman's searching questions and blunt answers during the interview which shows the girl how shallow his love is, and how near she has been to ruining her life as bitterly as poor "Elizy" did. She gives her answer frankly, and when they are alone, looks from her own bedizened self to the shabby dress, work-worn hands, and tender face, crying with a repentant sob and kiss, "Take me home, Mother, and keep me safe. I've had enough of this!"

"That will do you good, Maria; don't forget it," said one lady to her daughter as the curtain went down; and the girl answered, "Well, I'm sure I don't see why it's touching; but it is," as she spread her lace handkerchief to dry.

Tom and Nan came out strong in the next scene; for it was a ward in an army hospital, and surgeon and nurse went from bed to bed, feeling pulses, administering doses, and hearing complaints with an energy and gravity which convulsed the audience. The tragic element, never far from the comic at such times and places, came in when, while they bandaged an arm, the doctor told the nurse about an old woman who was searching through the hospital for her son, after days and nights on battlefields, through ambulances, and among scenes which would have killed most women.

"She will be here directly, and I dread her coming; for I'm afraid the poor lad who has just gone is her boy. I'd rather face a cannon than these brave women, with their hope and courage and great sorrow," says the surgeon.

"Ah, these poor mothers break my heart!" adds the nurse, wiping her eyes on her big apron; and with the words Mrs. Meg came in.

There was the same dress, the basket and umbrella, the rustic speech, the simple manners; but all were made pathetic by the terrible experience which had changed the tranquil old woman to that haggard figure with wild eyes, dusty feet, trembling hands, and an expression of mingled anguish, resolution, and despair which gave the homely figure a tragic dignity and power that touched all hearts. A few broken words told the story of her vain search, and then the sad quest began again. People held their breath as, led by the nurse, she went from bed to bed, showing in her face the alternations of hope, dread, and bitter disappointment as each was passed. On a narrow cot was a long figure covered with a sheet, and here she paused to lay one hand on her heart and one on her eyes, as if to gather courage to look at the nameless dead. Then she drew down the sheet, gave a long shivering sigh of relief, saying softly, "Not my son, thank God! But some mother's boy." And stooping down, she kissed the cold forehead tenderly.

Somebody sobbed there, and Miss Cameron shook two tears out of her eyes, anxious to lose no look or gesture as the poor soul, nearly spent with the long strain, struggled on down the long line. But her search was happily ended; for, as if her voice had roused him from his feverish sleep, a gaunt, wild-eyed man sat up in his bed, and stretching his arms to her, cried in a voice that echoed through the room, "Mother, Mother! I knew you'd come to me!"

She did go to him, with a cry of love and joy that thrilled

every listener, as she gathered him in her arms with the tears and prayers and blessing such as only a fond and faithful old mother could give.

The last scene was a cheerful contrast to this; for the country kitchen was bright with Christmas cheer, the wounded hero, with black patch and crutches well displayed, sat by the fire in the old chair, whose familiar creak was soothing to his ear; pretty Dolly was stirring about, gaily trimming dresser, settle, high chimney piece, and old-fashioned cradle with mistletoe and holly; while the mother rested beside her son, with that blessed baby on her knee. Refreshed by a nap and nourishment, this young actor now covered himself with glory by his ecstatic prancings, incoherent remarks to the audience, and vain attempts to get the footlights, as he blinked approvingly at these brilliant toys. It was good to see Mrs. Meg pat him on the back, cuddle the fat legs out of sight, and appease his vain longings with a lump of sugar, till Baby embraced her with a grateful ardor that brought him a round of applause all for his little self.

A sound of singing outside disturbs the happy family, and, after a carol in the snowy moonlight, a flock of neighbors troop in with Christmas gifts and greetings. Much by-play made this a lively picture; for Sam's sweetheart hovered round him with a tenderness the Marquise did not show the Baron; and Dolly had a pretty bit under the mistletoe with her rustic adorer, who looked so like Ham Peggotty in his cowhide boots, rough jacket, and dark beard and wig, that no one would have recognized Ted but for the long legs, which no extent of leather could disguise. It ended with a homely feast, brought by the guests; and as they sat round the table covered with doughnuts and cheese, pumpkin pie, and other country delicacies, Sam rises on his crutches to propose the first toast, and holding up his mug of cider, says, with a salute, and a choke in his voice, "Mother, God bless her!" All drink it standing, Dolly with her arm round the old woman's neck, as she hides her happy tears on her daughter's breast; while the irrepressible baby beat rapturously on the table with a spoon, and crowed audibly as the curtain went down.

They had it up again in a jiffy to get a last look at the group about that central figure, which was showered with bouquets, to the great delight of the infant Roscius; till a fat rosebud hit him on the nose, and produced the much-dreaded squall, which, fortunately, only added to the fun at that moment.

"Well, that will do for a beginning," said Beaumont, with a sigh of relief, as the curtain descended for the last time, and the actors scattered to dress for the closing piece.

"As an experiment, it is a success. Now we can venture to begin our great American drama," answered Mrs. Jo, full of satisfaction and grand ideas for the famous play—which, we may add, she did not write that year, owing to various dramatic events in her own family.

"The Owlsdark Marbles" closed the entertainment, and, being something new, proved amusing to this very indulgent audience. The gods and goddesses on Parnassus were displayed in full conclave; and, thanks to Mrs. Amy's skill in draping and posing, the white wigs and cotton-flannel robes were classically correct and graceful, though sundry modern additions somewhat marred the effect, while adding point to the showman's learned remarks. Mr. Laurie was Professor Owlsdark, in cap and gown; and, after a high-flown introduction, he proceeded to exhibit and explain his marbles. The first figure was a stately Minerva; but a second glance produced a laugh, for the words "Woman's Rights" adorned her shield, a scroll bearing the motto "Vote early and often" hung from the beak of the owl perched on her lance, and a tiny pestle and mortar ornamented her helmet. Attention was drawn to the firm mouth, the piercing eye, the awe-inspiring brow, of the strong-minded woman of antiquity, and some scathing remarks made upon the degeneracy of her modern sisters who failed to do their duty. Mercury came next, and was very fine in his airy attitude, though the winged legs quivered as if it was difficult to keep the lively

god in his place. His restless nature was dilated upon, his
mischievous freaks alluded to, and a very bad character given to
the immortal messenger-boy; which delighted his friends, and
caused the marble nose of the victim to curl visibly with scorn
when derisive applause greeted a particularly hard hit. A
charming little Hebe stood next, pouring nectar from a silver
teapot into a blue china teacup. She also pointed a moral; for
the Professor explained that the nectar of old was the beverage
which cheers but does not inebriate, and regretted that the ex-
cessive devotion of American women to this classic brew proved
so harmful, owing to the great development of brain their culture produced. A touch at modern servants, in contrast to this
accomplished table girl, made the statue's cheeks glow under
the chalk, and brought her a hearty round as the audience recognized Dolly and the smart soubrette.

Jove in all his majesty followed, as he and his wife occupied
the central pedestals in the half-circle of immortals. A splendid
Jupiter, with hair well set up off the fine brow, ambrosial beard,
silver thunderbolts in one hand, and a well-worn ferule in the
other. A large stuffed eagle from the museum stood at his feet;
and the benign expression of his august countenance showed
that he was in a good humor—as well he might be, for he was
paid some handsome compliments upon his wise rule, the
peaceful state of his kingdom, and the brood of all-accom-
plished Pallases that yearly issued from his mighty brain. Cheers
greeted this and other pleasant words, and caused the thun-
derer to bow his thanks; for "Jove nods," as everyone knows,
and flattery wins the heart of gods and men.

Mrs. Juno, with her peacocks, darning needle, pen, and cooking spoon, did not get off so easily; for the Professor was down
on her with all manner of mirth-provoking accusations, criti-
cisms, and insults even. He alluded to her domestic infelicity,
her meddlesome disposition, sharp tongue, bad temper, and
jealousy, closing, however, with a tribute to her skill in caring
for the wounds and settling the quarrels of belligerent heroes,

as well as her love for youths in Olympus and on earth. Gales of laughter greeted these hits, varied by hisses from some indignant boys, who would not bear, even in joke, any disrespect to dear Mother Bhaer, who, however, enjoyed it all immensely, as the twinkle in her eye and the irrepressible pucker of her lips betrayed.

A jolly Bacchus astride of his cask took Vulcan's place, and appeared to be very comfortable with a beer mug in one hand, a champagne bottle in the other, and a garland of grapes on his curly head. He was the text of a short temperance lecture, aimed directly at a row of smart young gentlemen who lined the walls of the auditorium. George Cole was seen to dodge behind a pillar at one point, Dolly nudged his neighbor at another, and there was slaughter all along the line as the Professor glared at them through his big glasses, and dragged their bacchanalian orgies to the light and held them up to scorn.

Seeing the execution he had done, the learned man turned to the lovely Diana, who stood as white and still as the plaster stag beside her, with sandals, bow, and crescent; quite perfect, and altogether the best piece of statuary in the show. She was very tenderly treated by the paternal critic, who, merely alluding to her confirmed spinsterhood, fondness for athletic sports, and oracular powers, gave a graceful little exposition of true art and passed on to his last figure.

This was Apollo in full fig, his curls skilfully arranged to hide a well-whitened patch over the eye, his handsome legs correctly poised, and his gifted fingers about to draw divine music from the silvered gridiron which was his lyre. His divine attributes were described, as well as his little follies and failings, among which were his weakness for photography and flute playing, his attempts to run a newspaper, and his fondness for the society of the Muses; which latter slap produced giggles and blushes among the girl graduates, and much mirth among the stricken youths; for misery loves company, and after this they began to rally.

Then, with a ridiculous conclusion, the Professor bowed his thanks; and after several recalls the curtain fell, but not quickly enough to conceal Mercury, wildly waving his liberated legs, Hebe dropping her teapot, Bacchus taking a lively roll on his barrel, and Mrs. Juno rapping the impertinent Owlsdark on the head with Jove's ruler.

While the audience filed out to supper in the hall, the stage was a scene of dire confusion as gods and goddesses, farmers and barons, maids and carpenters, congratulated one another on the success of their labors. Assuming various costumes, actors and actresses soon joined their guests, to sip bounteous draughts of praise with their coffee, and cool their modest blushes with ice cream. Mrs. Meg was a proud and happy woman when Miss Cameron came to her as she sat by Josie, with Demi serving both, and said, so cordially that it was impossible to doubt the sincerity of her welcome words, "Mrs. Brooke, I no longer wonder where your children get their talent. I make my compliments to the Baron, and next summer you must let me have little 'Dolly' as a pupil when we are at the beach."

One can easily imagine how this offer was received, as well as the friendly commendation bestowed by the same kind critic on the work of Beaumont and Fletcher, who hastened to explain that this trifle was only an attempt to make nature and art go hand in hand, with little help from fine writing or imposing scenery. Everybody was in the happiest mood, especially "little Dolly," who danced like a will-o'-the wisp with light-footed Mercury, and Apollo as he promenaded with the Marquise on his arm, who seemed to have left her coquetry in the green room with her rouge.

When all was over, Mrs. Juno said to Jove, to whose arm she clung as they trudged home along the snowy paths, "Fritz dear, Christmas is a good time for new resolutions, and I've made one never to be impatient or fretful with my beloved husband again. I know I am, though you won't own it; but Laurie's fun had some truth in it, and I felt hit in a tender spot. Henceforth I am a model wife, else I don't deserve the dearest, best man ever born." And being in a dramatic mood, Mrs. Juno tenderly embraced her excellent Jove in the moonlight, to the great amusement of sundry lingerers behind them.

So all three plays might be considered successes, and that merry Christmas night a memorable one in the March family; for Demi got an unspoken question answered, Josie's fondest wish was granted, and, thanks to Professor Owlsdark's jest, Mrs. Jo made Professor Bhaer's busy life quite a bed of roses by the keeping of her resolution. A few days later she had her reward for this burst of virtue in Dan's letter, which set her fears at rest and made her very happy, though she was unable to tell him so, because he sent her no address.

CHAPTER 15

WAITING

"MY WIFE, I have bad news for thee," said Professor Bhaer, coming in one day early in January.

"Please tell it at once. I can't bear to wait, Fritz," cried Mrs. Jo, dropping her work and standing up as if to take the shot bravely.

"But we *must* wait and hope, heart's dearest. Come and let us bear it together. Emil's ship is lost, and as yet no news of him."

It was well Mr. Bhaer had taken his wife into his strong arm, for she looked ready to drop, but bore up after a moment, and sitting by her good man, heard all that there was to tell. Tidings had been sent to the ship owners at Hamburg by some of the survivors, and telegraphed at once by Franz to his uncle. As one boatload was safe, there was hope that others might also escape, though the gale had sent two to the bottom. A swift-sailing steamer had brought these scanty news, and happier ones might come at any hour; but kind Franz had not added that the sailors reported the captain's boat as undoubtedly wrecked by the falling mast, since the smoke hid its escape, and the gale soon drove all far asunder. But this sad rumor reached

Plumfield in time; and deep was the mourning for the happy-hearted Commodore, never to come singing home again.

Mrs. Jo refused to believe it, stoutly insisting that Emil would outlive any storm and yet turn up safe and gay. It was well she clung to this hopeful view, for poor Mr. Bhaer was much afflicted by the loss of his boy, because his sister's sons had been his so long he scarcely knew a different love for his very own. Now was a chance for Mrs. Juno to keep her word; and she did, speaking cheerily of Emil, even when hope waxed faint and her heart was heavy. If anything could comfort the Bhaers for the loss of one boy, it would have been the affection and the sorrow shown by all the rest. Franz kept the cable busy with his varying messages, Nat sent loving letters from Leipzig, and Tom harassed the shipping agents for news. Even busy Jack wrote them with unusual warmth; Dolly and George came often, bearing the loveliest flowers and the daintiest bonbons to cheer Mrs. Bhaer and sweeten Josie's grief; while good-hearted Ned traveled all the way from Chicago to press their hands and say, with a tear in his eye, "I was so anxious to hear all about the dear old boy, I couldn't keep away."

"That's right comfortable, and shows me that if I didn't teach my boys anything else, I did give them the brotherly love that will make them stand by one another all their lives," said Mrs. Jo, when he had gone.

Rob answered reams of sympathizing letters, which showed how many friends they had; and the kindly praises of the lost man would have made Emil a hero and a saint, had they all been true. The elders bore it quietly, having learned submission in life's hard school; but the younger people rebelled; some hoped against hope and kept up, others despaired at once, and little Josie, Emil's pet cousin and playmate, was so broken-hearted, nothing could comfort her. Nan dosed in vain, Daisy's cheerful words went by like the wind, and Bess's devices to amuse her all failed utterly. To cry in Mother's arms and talk about the wreck, which haunted her even in her sleep, was all she cared to do; and Mrs. Meg was getting anxious when Miss Cameron sent Josie a kind note bidding her learn bravely her first lesson in real tragedy, and *be* like the self-sacrificing heroines she loved to *act*. That did the little girl good, and she made an effort, in which Teddy and Octoo helped her much; for the boy was deeply impressed by this sudden eclipse of the firefly whose light and life all missed when they were gone, and lured her out every day for long drives behind the black mare, who shook her silvery bells till they made such merry music Josie could not help listening to it, and whisked her over the snowy roads at a pace which set the blood dancing in her veins and sent her home strengthened and comforted by sunshine, fresh air, and congenial society—three aids young sufferers seldom can resist.

As Emil was helping nurse Captain Hardy, safe and well aboard the steamer, all this sorrow would seem wasted; but it was not, for it drew many hearts more closely together by a common grief, taught some patience, some sympathy, some regret for faults that lie heavy on the conscience when the one sinned against is gone, and all of them the solemn lesson to be ready when the summons comes. A hush lay over Plumfield for weeks, and the studious faces on the hill reflected the sadness of those in the valley. Sacred music sounded from Parnassus to comfort all who heard; the brown cottage was besieged with gifts for the little mourner, and Emil's flag hung at half mast on the roof where he last sat with Mrs. Jo.

So the weeks went heavily by till suddenly, like a thunderbolt out of a clear sky, came the news, "All safe, letters on the way." Then up went the flag, out rang the college bells, bang went Teddy's long-unused cannon, and a chorus of happy voices cried, "Thank God," as people went about, laughing, crying, and embracing one another in a rapture of delight. By and by the longed-for letters came, and all the story of the wreck was told; briefly by Emil, eloquently by Mrs. Hardy, gratefully by the captain, while Mary added a few tender words that went straight to their hearts and seemed the sweetest of all. Never were letters so read, passed round, admired, and cried over as these; for Mrs. Jo carried them in *her* pocket when Mr. Bhaer did not have them in his, and both took a look at them when they said their prayers at night. Now the Professor was heard humming like a big bee again as he went to his classes, and the lines smoothed out of Mother Bhaer's forehead, while she wrote this real story to anxious friends and let her romances wait. Now messages of congratulation flowed in, and beaming faces showed everywhere. Rob amazed his parents by producing a poem which was remarkably good for one of his years, and Demi set it to music that it might be sung when the sailor boy returned. Teddy stood on his head literally, and tore about the neighborhood on Octoo, like a second Paul Revere—only *his* tidings were good. But best of all, little Josie lifted up her head as the snowdrops did, and began to bloom again, growing tall and quiet, with the shadow of past sorrow to tone down her former vivacity and show that she *had* learned a lesson in trying to act well her part on the real stage, where all have to take their share in the great drama of life.

Now another sort of waiting began; for the travelers were on their way to Hamburg, and would stay there awhile before coming home, as Uncle Hermann owned the "Brenda," and the captain must report to him. Emil must remain to Franz's wedding, deferred till now because of the season of mourning, so happily ended. These plans were doubly welcome and pleasant after the troublous times which went before, and no spring ever seemed so beautiful as this one; for, as Teddy put it,

> "Now is the winter of our discontent
> Made glorious summer by these sons of Bhaer!"

—Franz and Emil being regarded in the light of elder brothers by the real "sons of Bhaer."

There was great scrubbing and dusting among the matrons as

they set their houses in order not only for Class Day, but to receive the bride and groom, who were to come to them for the honeymoon trip. Great plans were made, gifts prepared, and much joy felt at the prospect of seeing Franz again; though Emil, who was to accompany them, would be the greater hero. Little did the dear souls dream what a surprise was in store for them, as they innocently laid their plans and wished all the boys could be there to welcome home their eldest and their Casabianca.

While they wait and work so happily, let us see how our other absent boys are faring as they too wait and work and hope for better days. Nat was toiling steadily along the path he had wisely chosen, though it was by no means strewn with flowers— quite thorny was it, in fact, and hard to travel, after the taste of ease and pleasure he had got when nibbling at forbidden fruit. But his crop of wild oats was a light one, and he resolutely reaped what he had sowed, finding some good wheat among the tares. He taught by day; he fiddled night after night in the dingy little theater, and he studied so diligently that his master was well pleased, and kept him in mind as one to whom preferment was due, if any chance occurred. Gay friends forgot him; but the old ones stood fast, and cheered him up when *Heinweh* and weariness made him sad. As spring came on things mended— expenses grew less, work pleasanter, and life more bearable than when wintry storms beat on his thinly clad back, and frost pinched the toes that patiently trudged in old boots. No debts burdened him; the year of absence was nearly over; and if he chose to stay, Herr Bergmann had hopes for him that would bring independence for a time at least. So he walked under the lindens with a lighter heart, and in the May evenings went about the city with a band of strolling students, making music before houses where he used to sit as guest. No one recognized him in the darkness, though old friends often listened to the band; and once Minna threw him money, which he humbly received as part of his penance, being morbid on the subject of his sins.

His reward came sooner than he expected, and was greater
than he deserved, he thought, though his heart leaped with joy
when his master one day informed him that he was chosen, with
several other of his most promising pupils, to join the musical
society which was to take part in the great festival in London
the next July. Here was not only honor for the violinist but
happiness for the man, as it brought him nearer home, and
would open a chance of further promotion and profit in his
chosen profession.

"Make thyself useful to Bachmeister there in London with
thy English, and if all goes well with him, he will be glad to take
thee to America, whither he goes in the early autumn for winter
concerts. Thou hast done well these last months, and I have
hopes of thee."

As the great Bergmann seldom praised his pupils, these
words filled Nat's soul with pride and joy, and he worked yet
more diligently than before to fulfill his master's prophecy. He
thought the trip to England happiness enough, but found room
for more when, early in June, Franz and Emil paid him a flying
visit, bringing all sorts of good news, kind wishes, and comfortable gifts for the lonely fellow, who could have fallen on their
necks and cried like a girl at seeing his old mates again. How
glad he was to be found in his little room busy at his proper
work, not living like an idle gentleman on borrowed money!
How proud he was to tell his plans, assure them that he had no
debts, and receive their praises for his improvement in music,
their respect for his economy and steadfastness in well-doing!
How relieved when, having honestly confessed his shortcomings, they only laughed, and owned that they also had known
like experiences, and were the wiser for them. He was to go to
the wedding late in June, and join his comrades in London. As
best man, he could not refuse the new suit Franz insisted on
ordering for him; and a check from home about that time made
him feel like a millionaire—and a happy one; for this was accompanied by such kind letters full of delight in his success, he

felt that he had earned it, and waited for his joyful holiday with the impatience of a boy.

Dan meantime was also counting the weeks till August, when he would be free. But neither marriage bells nor festival music awaited him; no friends would greet him as he left the prison; no hopeful prospect lay before him; no happy homegoing was to be his. Yet his success was far greater than Nat's, though only God and one good man saw it. It was a hard-won battle; but he would never have to fight so terrible a one again; for, though enemies would still assail him from within and from without, he had found the little guidebook that Christian carried in his bosom, and Love, Penitence, and Prayer, the three sweet sisters, had given him the armor which would keep him safe. He had not learned to wear it yet, and chafed against it, though he felt its value, thanks to the faithful friend who had stood by him all that bitter year.

Soon he was to be free again, worn and scarred in the fray, but out among men in the blessed sun and air. When he thought of it Dan felt as if he could not wait, but must burst that narrow cell and fly away, as the caddis-worms he used to watch by the brookside shed their stony coffins, to climb the ferns and soar into the sky. Night after night he lulled himself to sleep with planning how, when he had seen Mary Mason according to his promise, he would steer straight for his old friends, the Indians, and in the wilderness hide his disgrace and heal his wounds. Working to save the many would atone for the sin of killing one, he thought; and the old free life would keep him safe from the temptations that beset him in cities.

"By and by, when I'm all right again, and have something to tell that I'm not ashamed of, I'll go home," he said, with a quicker beat of the impetuous heart that longed to be there so intensely, he found it as hard to curb as one of his unbroken horses on the plains. "Not yet. I must get over this first. They'd see and smell and feel the prison taint on me, if I went now, and I couldn't look them in the face and hide the truth. I *can't* lose

Ted's love, Mother Bhaer's confidence, and the respect of—of
—the girls—for they did respect my strength, anyway; but now
they wouldn't touch me." And poor Dan looked with a shudder
at the brown fist he clinched involuntarily as he remembered
what it had done since a certain little white hand had laid in it
confidingly. "I'll make 'em proud of me yet; and no one shall
ever know of this awful year. I *can* wipe it out, and I will, so
help me God!" And the clinched hand was held up as if to take
a solemn oath that this lost year should yet be made good, if
resolution and repentance could work the miracle.

CHAPTER 16

IN THE TENNIS COURT

ATHLETIC SPORTS were in high favor at Plumfield; and the river, where the old punt used to wobble about with a cargo of small boys, or echo to the shrill screams of little girls trying to get lilies, now was alive with boats of all kinds, from the slender wherry to the trim pleasure craft, gay with cushions, awnings, and fluttering pennons. Everyone rowed, and the girls as well as the youths had their races, and developed their muscles in the most scientific manner. The large, level meadow near the old willow was now the college playground, and here baseball battles raged with fury, varied by football, leaping, and kindred sports fitted to split the fingers, break the ribs, and strain the backs of the too-ambitious participants. The gentler pastimes of the damsels were at a safe distance from this Champ de Mars; croquet mallets clicked under the elms that fringed the field, racquets rose and fell energetically in several tennis courts, and gates of different heights were handy to practice the graceful bound by which every girl expected to save her life someday when the mad bull, which was always coming but never seemed to arrive, should be bellowing at her heels.

One of these tennis grounds was called "Jo's Court," and
here the little lady ruled like a queen; for she was fond of the
game, and being bent on developing her small self to the highest degree of perfection, she was to be found at every leisure
moment with some victim hard at it. On a certain pleasant Saturday afternoon she had been playing with Bess and beating
her; for, though more graceful, the Princess was less active than
her cousin, and cultivated her roses by quieter methods.

"Oh, dear! You are tired, and every blessed boy is at that
stupid baseball match. What shall I do?" sighed Josie, pushing
back the great red hat she wore, and gazing sadly round her for
more worlds to conquer.

"I'll play presently, when I'm a little cooler. But it is dull work
for me, as I never win," answered Bess, fanning herself with a
large leaf.

Josie was about to sit down beside her on the rustic seat and
wait, when her quick eye saw afar off two manly forms arrayed
in white flannel; their blue legs seemed bearing them toward
the battle going on in the distance; but they never reached the
fray; for, with a cry of joy, Jo raced away to meet them, bent on
securing this heaven-sent reinforcement. Both paused as she
came flying up, and both raised their hats; but oh, the difference
there was in the salutes! The stout youth pulled his off lazily
and put it on again at once, as if glad to get the duty over; the
slender being, with the crimson tie, lifted his with a graceful
bend, and held it aloft while he accosted the rosy, breathless
maid, thus permitting her to see his raven locks smoothly
parted, with one little curl upon the brow. Dolly prided himself
upon that bow, and practiced it before his glass, but did not
bestow it upon all alike, regarding it as a work of art, fit only for
the fairest and most favored of his female admirers; for he was
a pretty youth, and fancied himself an Adonis.

Eager Josie evidently did not appreciate the honor he did
her, for with a nod she begged them both to "come along and
play tennis, not go and get all hot and dirty with the boys."

These two adjectives won the day; for Stuffy was already warmer than he liked to be, and Dolly had on a new suit which he desired to keep immaculate as long as possible, conscious that it was very becoming.

"Charmed to oblige," answered the polite one, with another bend.

"You play, I'll rest," added the fat boy, yearning for repose and gentle converse with the Princess in the cooling shade.

"Well, you can comfort Bess, for I've beaten her all to bits and she needs amusing. I know you've got something nice in your pocket, George; give her some, and 'Dolphus can have her racquet. Now then, fly round." And driving her prey before her, Josie returned in triumph to the court.

Casting himself ponderously upon the bench, which creaked under his weight, Stuffy—as we will continue to call him, though no one else dared use the old name now—promptly produced the box of confectionery, without which he never traveled far, and regaled Bess with candied violets and other dainties, while Dolly worked hard to hold his own against a most accomplished antagonist. He would have beaten her if an unlucky stumble, which produced an unsightly stain upon the knee of those new shorts, had not distracted his mind and made him careless. Much elated at her victory, Josie permitted him to rest, and offered ironical consolation for the mishap which evidently weighed upon his mind.

"Don't be an old Betty; it can be cleaned. You must have been a cat in some former state, you are so troubled about dirt; or a tailor, and lived for clothes."

"Come now, don't hit a fellow when he is down," responded Dolly from the grass where he and Stuffy now lay to make room for both girls on the seat. One handkerchief was spread under him, and his elbow leaned upon another, while his eyes were sadly fixed upon the green and brown spot which afflicted him. "I like to be neat; don't think it civil to cut about in old shoes and gray flannel shirts before ladies. *Our* fellows are gentlemen, and dress as such," he added, rather nettled at the word "tailor," for he owed one of those too attractive persons an uncomfortably big bill.

"So are ours; but good clothes alone don't make a gentleman *here*. We require a good deal more," flashed Josie, in arms at once to defend her college. "You will hear of some of the men in 'old boots and gray flannel' when you and your fine gentlemen are twiddling your ties and scenting your hair in obscurity. I *like* old boots and wear them, and I hate dandies. Don't you, Bess?"

"Not when they are kind to me, and belong to our old set," answered Bess, with a nod of thanks to Dolly, who was carefully removing an inquisitive caterpillar from one of her little russet shoes.

"*I* like a lady who is always polite, and doesn't snap a man's head off if he has a mind of his own. Don't you, George?" asked Dolly, with his best smile for Bess and a Harvard stare of disapprobation for Josie.

A tranquil snore was Stuffy's sole reply, and a general laugh restored peace for the moment. But Josie loved to harass the lords of creation who asserted themselves too much, and bided her time for another attack till she had secured more tennis. She got another game; for Dolly was a sworn knight of dames, so he obeyed her call, leaving Bess to sketch George as he lay upon his back, his stout legs crossed, and his round red face partially eclipsed by his hat. Josie got beaten this time, and came back rather cross, so she woke the peaceful sleeper by tickling his nose with a straw till he sneezed himself into a sitting posture, and looked wrathfully about for "that confounded fly."

"Come, sit up and let us have a little elegant conversation; you 'howling swells' ought to improve our minds and manners, for we are only poor 'country girls in dowdy gowns and hats,'" began the gadfly, opening the battle with a sly quotation from one of Dolly's unfortunate speeches about certain studious damsels who cared more for books than finery.

"I didn't mean you! Your gowns are all right, and those hats the latest thing out," began poor 'Dolphus, convicting himself by that incautious exclamation.

"Caught you that time; I thought you fellows were all *gentlemen*, civil as well as nice. But you are always sneering at girls who don't dress well, and that is a very unmanly thing to do; my mother said so." And Josie felt that she had dealt a shrewd blow at the elegant youth who bowed at many shrines if they were well-decorated ones.

"Got you there, old boy, and she's right. You never hear *me* talk about clothes and such twaddle," said Stuffy, suppressing a yawn, and feeling for another bonbon wherewith to refresh himself.

"You talk about eating, and that is even worse for a man. You will marry a cook and keep a restaurant someday," laughed Josie, down on him at once.

This fearful prediction kept him silent for several moments; but Dolly rallied, and wisely changing the subject, carried the war into the enemy's camp.

"As you wanted us to improve your manners, allow me to say that young ladies in good society don't make personal remarks or deliver lectures. Little girls who are not out do it, and think it witty; but I assure you it's not good form."

Josie paused a moment to recover from the shock of being called "a little girl," when all the honors of her fourteenth birthday were fresh upon her; and Bess said, in the lofty tone which was infinitely more crushing than Jo's impertinence, "That is true; but we have lived all our lives with superior people, so we have no society talk like your young ladies. We are so accustomed to sensible conversation, and helping one another by telling our faults, that we have no gossip to offer you."

When the Princess reproved, the boys seldom resented it; so Dolly held his peace, and Josie burst out, following her cousin's lead, which she thought a happy one, *"Our* boys like to have us talk with them, and take kindly any hints we give. *They* don't think they know everything and are quite perfect at eighteen, as I've observed the Harvard men do, especially the *very young* ones."

Josie took immense satisfaction in that return shot; and Dolly showed that he was hit, by the nettled tone in which he answered, with a supercilious glance at the hot, dusty, and noisy crowd on the baseball ground, "The class of fellows you have here need all the polish and culture you can give them; and I'm glad they get it. Our men are largely from the best families all over the country, so we don't need girls to teach us anything."

"It's a pity you don't have more of such 'fellows' as ours. They value and use well what college gives them, and aren't satisfied to slip through, getting all the fun they can and shirking the work. Oh, I've heard you 'men' talk, and heard your fathers say they wish they hadn't wasted time and money just that you might say you'd been through college. As for the girls, you'll be much better off in all ways when they do get in, and keep you lazy things up to the mark, as we do here."

"If you have such a poor opinion of us, why do you wear our color?" asked Dolly, painfully conscious that he was not improving the advantages his Alma Mater offered him, but bound to defend her.

"I don't. My hat is scarlet, not crimson. Much you know about color," scoffed Josie.

"I know that a cross cow would soon set you scampering, if you flaunted that red tile under her nose," retorted Dolly.

"I'm ready for her. Can your fine young ladies do this—or you either?" And burning to display her latest accomplishment, Josie ran to the nearest gate, put one hand on the top rail, and vaulted over as lightly as a bird.

Bess shook her head, and Stuffy laughingly applauded; but Dolly, scorning to be braved by a girl, took a flying leap and landed on his feet beside Josie, saying calmly, "Can you do that?"

"Not yet, but I will by and by."

As his foe looked a little crestfallen, Dolly relented, and affably added sundry feats of a like nature, quite unconscious that he had fallen into a dreadful snare; for the dull red paint on the gate, not being used to such vigorous handling, came off in streaks upon his shoulders when he turned a backward swing and came up smiling, to be rewarded with the aggravating remark, "If you want to know what crimson is, look at your back; it's nicely stamped on and won't wash out, I think."

"The deuce it won't!" cried Dolly, trying to get an impossible view, and giving it up in great disgust.

"I guess we'd better be going, Dolf," said peaceable Stuffy, feeling that it would be wise to retreat before another skirmish took place, as his side seemed to be getting the worst of it.

"Don't hurry, I beg; stay and rest; you must need it after the tremendous amount of brain work you've done this week. It is time for our Greek. Come, Bess. Good afternoon, *gentlemen.*" And, with a sweeping courtesy, Josie led the way, with her hat belligerently cocked up, and her racquet borne like a triumphal banner over one shoulder; for having had the last word, she felt that she could retire with the honors of war.

Dolly gave Bess his best bow, with the chill on; and Stuffy subsided luxuriously, with his legs in the air, murmuring in a dreamy tone, "Little Jo is as cross as two sticks today. I'm going in for another nap: too hot to play anything."

"So it is. Wonder if Spitfire was right about these beastly spots?" And Dolly sat down to try dry cleansing with one of his handkerchiefs. "Asleep?" he asked, after a few moments of this cheerful occupation, fearing that his chum might be too comfortable when he was in a fume himself.

"No. I was thinking that Jo wasn't far wrong about shirking. 'Tis a shame to get so little, when we ought to be grinding like Morton and Torry and that lot. I never wanted to go to college;

but my governor made me. Much good it will do either of us!"
answered Stuffy, with a groan; for he hated work, and saw two
more long years of it before him.

"Gives a man prestige, you know. No need to dig. I mean to
have a gay old time, and be a 'howling swell,' if I choose. Between you and me though, it *would* be no end jolly to have the
girls along. Study be hanged! But if we've got to turn the grind-
stone, it would be mighty nice to have some of the little dears to
lend a hand. Wouldn't it now?"

"I'd like three this minute—one to fan me, one to kiss me,
and one to give me some iced lemonade!" sighed Stuffy, with a
yearning glance toward the house, whence no succor appeared.

"How would root beer do?" asked a voice behind them,
which made Dolly spring to his feet and Stuffy roll over like a
startled porpoise.

Sitting on the stile that crossed the wall nearby was Mrs. Jo,
with two jugs slung over her shoulder by a strap, several tin
mugs in her hand, and an old-fashioned sunbonnet on her head.

"I knew the boys would be killing themselves with ice water;
so I strolled down with some of my good, wholesome beer. They
drank like fishes. But Silas was with me; so my cruse still holds
out. Have some?"

"Yes, thanks, very much. Let us pour it." And Dolly held the
cup while Stuffy joyfully filled it; both very grateful, but rather
afraid she had heard what went before the wish she fulfilled.

She proved that she had by saying, as they stood drinking her
health, while she sat between them, looking like a middle-aged
vivandière, with her jugs and mugs, "I was glad to hear you say
you would like to have girls at your college; but I hope you will
learn to speak more respectfully of them before they come; for
that will be the first lesson they will teach you."

"Really, ma'am, I was only joking," began Stuffy, gulping
down his beer in a hurry.

"So was I. I'm sure I—I'm devoted to 'em," stuttered Dolly,

panic-stricken; for he saw that he was in for a lecture of some sort.

"Not in the right way. Frivolous girls may like to be called 'little dears' and things of that sort; but the girls who love study wish to be treated like reasonable beings, not dolls to flirt with. Yes, I'm going to preach; that's my business; so stand up and take it like men."

Mrs. Jo laughed; but she was in earnest; for by various hints and signs during the past winter she knew that the boys were beginning to "see life" in the way she especially disapproved. Both were far from home, had money enough to waste, and were as inexperienced, curious, and credulous as most lads of their age. Not fond of books, therefore without the safeguard which keeps many studious fellows out of harm; one self-indulgent, indolent, and so used to luxury that pampering of the senses was an easy thing; the other vain—as all comely boys are —full of conceit, and so eager to find favor in the eyes of his comrades that he was ready for anything which would secure it. These traits and foibles made both peculiarly liable to the temptations which assail pleasure-loving and weak-willed boys. Mrs. Jo knew them well, and had dropped many a warning word since they went to college; but till lately they seemed not to understand some of her friendly hints; now she was sure they would, and meant to speak out; for long experience with boys had made her both bold and skillful in handling some of the dangers usually left to silence, till it is too late for anything but pity and reproach.

"I'm going to talk to you like a mother, because yours are far away; and there are things that mothers can manage best, if they do their duty," she solemnly began from the depths of the sunbonnet.

"Great Scott! We're in for it now!" thought Dolly, in secret dismay; while Stuffy got the first blow by trying to sustain himself with another mug of beer.

"That won't hurt you; but I must warn you about drinking

other things, George. Overeating is an old story; and a few
more fits of illness will teach you to be wise. But drinking is a
more serious thing, and leads to worse harm than any that can
afflict your body alone. I hear you talk about wines as if you
knew them and cared more for them than a boy should; and
several times I've heard jokes that meant mischief. For heaven's
sake, don't begin to play with this dangerous taste 'for fun,' as
you say, or because it's the fashion, and the other fellows do.
Stop at once, and learn that temperance in all things is the only
safe rule."

"Upon my honor, I only take wine and iron. I need a tonic,
mother says, to repair the waste of brain tissue while I'm studying," protested Stuffy, putting down the mug as if it burnt his
fingers.

"Good beef and oatmeal will repair your tissues much better
than any tonic of that sort. Work and plain fare are what you
want; and I wish I had you here for a few months out of harm's
way. I'd Banting you, and fit you to run without puffing, and get
on without four or five meals a day. What an absurd hand that
is for a man! You ought to be ashamed of it!" And Mrs. Jo
caught up the plump fist, with deep dimples at each knuckle,
which was fumbling distressfully at the buckle of the belt girt
about a waist far too large for a youth of his age.

"I can't help it—we all grow fat; it's in the family," said Stuffy
in self-defense.

"All the more reason you should live carefully. Do you want
to die early, or be an invalid all your life?"

"No, ma'am!"

Stuffy looked so scared that Mrs. Jo could not be hard upon
his budding sins, for they lay at his over-indulgent mother's
door in a great measure; so she softened the tone of her voice,
and added, with a little slap on the fat hand, as she used to do
when it was small enough to pilfer lumps of sugar from her
bowl, "Then be careful; for a man writes his character in his

face; and you don't want gluttony and intemperance in yours, I know."

"I'm sure I don't! Please make out a wholesome bill of fare, and I'll stick to it, if I can. I *am* getting stout, and I don't like it; and my liver's torpid, and I have palpitations and headache. Overwork, mother says; but it may be overeating." And Stuffy gave a sigh of mingled regret for the good things he renounced, and relief as he finished loosening his belt as soon as his hand was free.

"I will. Follow it, and in a year you'll be a man and not a meal bag. Now, Dolly." And Mrs. Jo turned to the other culprit, who shook in his shoes and wished he hadn't come.

"Are you studying French as industriously as you were last winter?"

"No, ma'am. I don't care for it—that is, I—I'm busy with G-Greek just now," answered Dolly, beginning bravely, quite in the dark as to what that odd question meant till a sudden memory made him stutter and look at his shoes with deep interest.

"Oh, he doesn't study it; only reads French novels and goes to the theater when the Opera Bouffe is here," said Stuffy, innocently confirming Mrs. Jo's suspicions.

"So I understood; and that is what I want to speak about. Ted had a sudden desire to learn French in that way, from something you said, Dolly; so I went myself, and was quite satisfied that it was no place for a decent boy. Your men were out in full force; and I was glad to see that some of the younger ones looked as ashamed as I felt. The older fellows enjoyed it, and when we came out were waiting to take those painted girls to supper. Did you ever go with them?"

"Once."

"Did you like it?"

"No'm. I—I came away early," stammered Dolly, with a face as red as his splendid tie.

"I'm glad you have not lost the grace of blushing yet; but you will soon, if you keep up this sort of study and forget to be ashamed. The society of such women will unfit you for that of good ones, and lead you into trouble and sin and shame. Oh, why don't the city fathers stop that evil thing, when they know the harm it does? It made my heart ache to see those boys, who ought to be at home and in their beds, going off for a night of riot which would help to ruin some of them forever."

The youths looked scared at Mrs. Jo's energetic protest against one of the fashionable pleasures of the day, and waited in conscience-stricken silence—Stuffy glad that he never went to those gay suppers, and Dolly deeply grateful that he "came away early." With a hand on either shoulder, and all the terrors smoothed from her brow, Mrs. Jo went on in her most motherly tone, anxious to do for them what no other woman would, and do it kindly, "My dear boys, if I didn't love you, I would not say these things. I know they are not pleasant; but my conscience won't let me hold my peace when a word may keep you from two of the great sins that curse the world and send so many young men to destruction. You are just beginning to feel the allurement of them, and soon it will be hard to turn away. Stop now, I beg of you, and not only save yourselves but help others by a brave example. Come to me if things worry you; don't be afraid or ashamed; I have heard many sadder confessions than any you are ever likely to bring me, and been able to comfort many poor fellows, gone wrong for want of a word in time. Do this, and you will be able to kiss your mothers with clean lips, and by and by have the right to ask innocent girls to love you."

"Yes'm, thank you. I suppose you're right. But it's pretty hard work to toe the mark when ladies give you wine and gentlemen take their daughters to see Aimée," said Dolly, foreseeing tribulations ahead, though he knew it was time to "pull up."

"So it is; but all the more honor to those who are brave and wise enough to resist public opinion, and the easygoing morals of bad or careless men and women. Think of the persons whom you respect most, and in imitating them you will secure the respect of those who look up to you. I'd rather my boys should be laughed at and cold-shouldered by a hundred foolish fellows than lose what, once gone, no power can give them back—innocence and self-respect. I don't wonder you find it 'hard to toe the mark,' when books, pictures, ballrooms, theaters, and streets offer temptations; yet you *can* resist, if you try. Last winter Mrs. Brooke used to worry about John's being out so late reporting; but when she spoke to him about the things he must see and hear on his way to and from the office at midnight, he said in his sober way, 'I know what you mean, Mother; but no fellow need to go wrong unless he *wants* to.'"

"That's like the Deacon!" exclaimed Stuffy, with an approving smile on his fat face.

"I'm glad you told me that. He's right; and it's because he doesn't want to go wrong we all respect him so," added Dolly, looking up now with an expression which assured his Mentor that the right string had been touched, and a spirit of emulation roused, more helpful, perhaps, than any words of hers. Seeing this, she was satisfied, and said, as she prepared to leave the bar before which her culprits had been tried and found guilty, but recommended to mercy, "Then be to others what John is to you —a good example. Forgive me for troubling you, my dear lads, and remember my little preachment. I think it will do you good, though I may never know it. Chance words spoken in kindness often help amazingly; and that's what old people are here for—else their experience is of little use. Now, come and find the young folk. I hope I shall never have to shut the gates of Plumfield upon *you,* as I have on some of your 'gentlemen.' I mean to keep my boys and girls safe if I can, and this a wholesome place where the good old-fashioned virtues are lived and taught."

Much impressed by that dire threat, Dolly helped her from her perch with deep respect; and Stuffy relieved her of her empty jugs, solemnly vowing to abstain from all fermented beverages except root beer, as long as feeble flesh could hold out. Of course they made light of "Mother Bhaer's lecture" when they were alone—that was to be expected of "the men of our class." But in their secret souls they thanked her for giving their boyish consciences a jog, and more than once afterward had cause to remember gratefully that half-hour in the tennis court.

CHAPTER 17

AMONG THE MAIDS

ALTHOUGH THIS story is about Jo's boys, her girls cannot be neglected, because they held a high place in this little republic, and especial care was taken to fit them to play their parts worthily in the great republic which offered them wider opportunities and more serious duties. To many the social influence was the better part of the training they received; for education is not confined to books, and the finest characters often graduate from no college, but make experience their master, and life their book. Others cared only for the mental culture, and were in danger of over-studying, under the delusion which pervades New England that learning must be had at all costs, forgetting that health and real wisdom are better. A third class of ambitious girls hardly knew what they wanted, but were hungry for whatever could fit them to face the world and earn a living, being driven by necessity, the urgency of some half-unconscious talent, or the restlessness of strong young natures to break away from the narrow life which no longer satisfied.

At Plumfield all found something to help them; for the growing institution had not yet made its rules as fixed as the laws of

the Medes and Persians, and believed so heartily in the right of
all sexes, colors, creeds, and ranks to education, that there was
room for everyone who knocked, and a welcome to the shabby
youths from up country, the eager girls from the West, the awkward freedman or woman from the South, or the well-born
student whose poverty made this college a possibility when
other doors were barred. There still was prejudice, ridicule, neglect in high places, and prophecies of failure to contend
against; but the Faculty was composed of cheerful, hopeful men
and women who had seen greater reforms spring from smaller
roots, and after stormy seasons blossom beautifully, to add
prosperity and honor to the nation. So they worked on steadily
and bided their time, full of increasing faith in their attempt as
year after year their numbers grew, their plans succeeded, and
the sense of usefulness in this most vital of all professions
blessed them with its sweet rewards.

Among the various customs which had very naturally sprung
up was one especially useful and interesting to "the girls," as
the young women liked to be called. It all grew out of the old
sewing hour still kept up by the three sisters long after the little
workboxes had expanded into big baskets full of household
mending. They were busy women, yet on Saturdays they tried to
meet in one of the three sewing rooms; for even classic Parnassus had its nook where Mrs. Amy often sat among her servants,
teaching them to make and mend, thereby giving them a respect
for economy, since the rich lady did not scorn to darn her hose,
and sew on buttons. In these household retreats, with books and
work, and their daughters by them, they read and sewed and
talked in the sweet privacy that domestic women love, and can
make so helpful by a wise mixture of cooks and chemistry, table
linen and theology, prosaic duties and good poetry.

Mrs. Meg was the first to propose enlarging this little circle;
for as she went her motherly rounds among the young women
she found a sad lack of order, skill, and industry in this branch
of education. Latin, Greek, the higher mathematics, and science

of all sorts prospered finely; but dust gathered on the work-baskets, frayed elbows went unheeded, and some of the blue stockings sadly needed mending. Anxious lest the usual sneer at learned women should apply to "our girls," she gently lured two or three of the most untidy to her house, and made the hour so pleasant, the lesson so kindly, that they took the hint, were grateful for the favor, and asked to come again. Others soon begged to make the detested weekly duty lighter by joining the party, and soon it was a privilege so much desired that the old museum was refitted with sewing machines, tables, rocking chairs, and a cheerful fireplace, so that, rain or shine, the needles might go on undisturbed.

Here Mrs. Meg was in her glory, and stood wielding her big shears like a queen as she cut out white work, fitted dresses, and directed Daisy, her special aide, about the trimming of hats, and completing the lace and ribbon trifles which add grace to the simplest costume and save poor or busy girls so much money and time. Mrs. Amy contributed taste, and decided the great question of colors and complexions; for few women, even the most learned, are without that desire to look well which makes many a plain face comely, as well as many a pretty one ugly for want of skill and knowledge of the fitness of things. She also took her turn to provide books for the readings, and as art was her forte she gave them selections from Ruskin, Hamerton, and Mrs. Jameson, who is never old. Bess read these aloud as her contribution, and Josie took her turn at the romances, poetry, and plays her uncles recommended. Mrs. Jo gave little lectures on health, religion, politics, and the various questions in which all should be interested, with copious extracts from Miss Cobbe's "Duties of Women," Miss Brackett's "Education of American Girls," Mrs. Duffy's "No Sex in Education," Mrs. Woolson's "Dress Reform," and many of the other excellent books wise women write for their sisters, now that they are waking up and asking, "What shall we do?"

It was curious to see the prejudices melt away as ignorance

was enlightened, indifference change to interest, and intelligent minds set thinking, while quick wits and lively tongues added spice to the discussions which inevitably followed. So the feet that wore the neatly mended hose carried wiser heads than before, the pretty gowns covered hearts warmed with higher purposes, and the hands that dropped the thimbles for pens, lexicons, and celestial globes, were better fitted for life's work, whether to rock cradles, tend the sick, or help on the great work of the world.

One day a brisk discussion arose concerning careers for women. Mrs. Jo had read something on the subject and asked each of the dozen girls sitting about the room, what she intended to do on leaving college. The answers were as usual: "I shall teach, help Mother, study medicine, art," etc.; but nearly all ended with, "Till I marry."

"But if you don't marry, what then?" asked Mrs. Jo, feeling like a girl again as she listened to the answers, and watched the thoughtful, gay, or eager faces.

"Be old maids, I suppose. Horrid, but inevitable, since there are so many superfluous women," answered a lively lass, too pretty to fear single blessedness unless she chose it.

"It is well to consider that fact, and fit yourselves to be useful, not superfluous women. That class, by the way, is largely made up of widows, I find; so don't consider it a slur on maidenhood."

"That's a comfort! Old maids aren't sneered at half as much as they used to be, since some of them have grown famous and proved that woman isn't a half but a whole human being, and can stand alone."

"Don't like it all the same. We can't all be like Miss Cobbe, Miss Nightingale, Miss Phelps, and the rest. So what can we do but sit in a corner and look on?" asked a plain girl with a dissatisfied expression.

"Cultivate cheerfulness and content, if nothing else. But there are so many little odd jobs waiting to be done that nobody need 'sit idle and look on,' unless she chooses," said Mrs. Meg, with a smile, laying on the girl's head the new hat she had just trimmed.

"Thank you very much. Yes, Mrs. Brooke, I see; it's a little job, but it makes me neat and happy—and grateful," she added, looking up with brighter eyes as she accepted the labor of love and the lesson as sweetly as they were given.

"One of the best and most beloved women I know has been doing odd jobs for the Lord for years, and will keep at it till her dear hands are folded in her coffin. All sorts of things she does —picks up neglected children and puts them in safe homes, saves lost girls, nurses poor women in trouble, sews, knits, trots, begs, works for the poor day after day with no reward but the thanks of the needy, the love and honor of the rich who make Saint Matilda their almoner. That's a life worth living; and I think that quiet little woman will get a higher seat in Heaven than many of those of whom the world has heard."

"I know it's lovely, Mrs. Bhaer, but it's dull for young folks. We do want a little fun before we buckle to," said a Western girl with a wide-awake face.

"Have your fun, my dear; but if you must earn your bread, try to make it sweet with cheerfulness, not bitter with the daily regret that it isn't cake. I used to think mine was a very hard fate because I had to amuse a somewhat fretful old lady; but the books I read in that lonely library have been of immense use to me since, and the dear old soul bequeathed me Plumfield for my 'cheerful service and affectionate care.' I didn't deserve it, but I did use to try to be jolly and kind, and get as much honey out of duty as I could, thanks to my dear mother's help and advice."

"Gracious! If I could earn a place like this, I'd sing all day and be an angel; but you have to take your chance, and get nothing for your pains, perhaps. I never do," said the Westerner, who had a hard time with small means and large aspirations.

"Don't do it for the reward, but be sure it will come, though not in the shape you expect. I worked hard for fame and money one winter, but I got neither, and was much disappointed. A year afterward I found I had earned two prizes: skill with my pen, and—Professor Bhaer."

Mrs. Jo's laugh was echoed blithely by the girls, who liked to have these conversations enlivened by illustrations from life.

"You are a very lucky woman," began the discontented damsel, whose soul soared above new hats, welcome as they were, but did not quite know where to steer.

"Yet her name used to be 'Luckless Jo,' and she never had what she wanted till she had given up hoping for it," said Mrs. Meg.

"I'll give up hoping, then, right away, and see if my wishes will come. I only want to help my folks, and get a good school."

"Take this proverb for your guide: 'Get the distaff ready, and the Lord will send the flax,' " answered Mrs. Jo.

"We'd better all do that, if we are to be spinsters," said the pretty one, adding gaily, "I think I should like it, on the whole—they are so independent. My Aunt Jenny can do just what she likes, and ask no one's leave; but Ma has to consult Pa about everything. Yes, I'll give you my chance, Sally, and be a 'superfluum,' as Mr. Plock says."

"You'll be one of the first to go into bondage, see if you aren't. Much obliged, all the same."

"Well, I'll get my distaff ready, and take whatever flax the Fates send—single, or double-twisted, as the powers please."

"That is the right spirit, Nelly. Keep it up, and see how happy life will be with a brave heart, a willing hand, and plenty to do."

"No one objects to plenty of domestic work or fashionable pleasure, I find; but the minute we begin to study, people tell us we can't bear it, and warn us to be very careful. I've tried the other things, and got so tired I came to college; though my people predict nervous exhaustion and an early death. Do you think there is any danger?" asked a stately girl, with an anxious glance at the blooming face reflected in the mirror opposite.

"Are you stronger or weaker than when you came two years ago, Miss Winthrop?"

"Stronger in body, and much happier in mind. I think I was dying of ennui; but the doctors called it inherited delicacy of constitution. That is why Mamma is so anxious, and I wish not to go too fast."

"Don't worry, my dear; that active brain of yours was starving for good food; it has a plenty now, and plain living suits you better than luxury and dissipation. It is all nonsense about girls not being able to study as well as boys. Neither can bear cramming; but with proper care both are better for it; so enjoy the life your instinct led you to, and we will prove that wise head work is a better cure for that sort of delicacy than tonics, and novels on the sofa, where far too many of our girls go to wreck nowadays. They burn the candle at both ends; and when they break down they blame the books, not the balls."

"Dr. Nan was telling me about a patient of hers who thought she had a heart complaint, till Nan made her take off her corsets, stopped her coffee and dancing all night, and made her eat, sleep, walk, and live regularly for a time; and now she's a brilliant cure. Common-sense versus custom, Nan said."

"I've had no headaches since I came here, and can do twice as much studying as I did at home. It's the air, I think, and the fun of going ahead of the boys," said another girl, tapping her big forehead with her thimble, as if the lively brain inside was in good working order and enjoyed the daily gymnastics she gave it.

"Quality, not quantity, wins the day, you know. Our brains may be smaller, but I don't see that they fall short of what is required of them; and if I'm not mistaken, the largest-headed man in our class is the dullest," said Nelly, with a solemn air which produced a gale of merriment; for all knew that the young Goliath she mentioned had been metaphorically slain by this quick-witted David on many a battlefield, to the great disgust of himself and mates.

"Mrs. Brooke, do I gauge on the right or the wrong side?" asked the best Greek scholar of her class, eyeing a black silk apron with a lost expression.

"The right, Miss Pierson; and leave a space between the tucks; it looks prettier so."

"I'll never make another; but it will save my dresses from inkstains, so I'm glad I've got it." And the erudite Miss Pierson labored on, finding it a harder task than any Greek root she ever dug up.

"We paper stainers must learn how to make shields, or we are lost. I'll give you a pattern of the pinafore I used to wear in my 'blood-and-thunder days,' as we call them," said Mrs. Jo, trying to remember what became of the old tin kitchen which used to hold her works.

"Speaking of writers reminds me that my ambition is to be a George Eliot, and thrill the world! It must be so splendid to know that one has such power, and to hear people own that one possesses a 'masculine intellect'! I don't care for most women's novels, but hers are immense; don't you think so, Mrs. Bhaer?" asked the girl with the big forehead, and torn braid on her skirt.

"Yes. But they don't thrill me as little Charlotte Brontë's books do. The brain is there, but the heart seems left out. I admire, but I don't love, George Eliot; and her life is far sadder to me than Miss Brontë's, because, in spite of the genius, love, and fame, she missed the light without which no soul is truly great, good, or happy."

"Yes'm, I know; but still it's so romantic and sort of new and mysterious, and she *was* great in one sense. Her nerves and dyspepsia do rather destroy the illusion; but I adore famous people and mean to go and see all I can scare up in London someday."

"You will find some of the best of them busy about just the work I recommend to you; and if you want to see a great lady, I'll tell you that Mrs. Laurence means to bring one here today. Lady Ambercrombie is lunching with her, and after seeing the college is to call on us. She especially wanted to see our sewing school, as she is interested in things of this sort, and gets them up at home."

"Bless me! I always imagined lords and ladies did nothing but ride round in a coach and six, go to balls, and be presented to the Queen in cocked hats and trains and feathers," exclaimed an artless young person from the wilds of Maine, whither an illustrated paper occasionally wandered.

"Not at all. Lord Ambercrombie is over here studying up our American prison system, and my lady is busy with the schools— both very high-born, but the simplest and most sensible people I've met this long time. They are neither of them young or handsome, and dress very plainly; so don't expect anything splendid. Mr. Laurence was telling me last night about a friend of his who met my lord in the hall, and owing to a rough great-coat and a red face, mistook him for a coachman, and said, 'Now, my man, what do you want here?' Lord Ambercrombie mildly mentioned who he was, and that he had come to dinner. And the poor host was much afflicted, saying afterward, 'Why didn't he wear his stars and garters? Then a fellow would know he was a lord.'"

The girls laughed again, and a general rustle betrayed that each was prinking a bit before the titled guest arrived. Even Mrs. Jo settled her collar, and Mrs. Meg felt if her cap was right, while Bess shook out her curls, and Josie boldly consulted the glass; for they were women, in spite of philosophy and philanthropy.

"Shall we all rise?" asked one girl, deeply impressed by the impending honor.

"It would be courteous."

"Shall we shake hands?"

"No, I'll present you *en masse,* and your pleasant faces will be introduction enough."

"I wish I'd worn my best dress. Ought to have told us," whispered Sally.

"Won't my folks be surprised when I tell them we have had a real lady to call on us?" said another.

"Don't look as if you'd never seen a gentlewoman before, Milly. We are not all fresh from the wilderness," added the stately damsel who, having Mayflower ancestors, felt that she was the equal of all the crowned heads of Europe.

"Hush, she's coming! Oh, my heart, what a bonnet!" cried the gay girl in a stage whisper; and every eye was demurely fixed upon the busy hands as the door opened to admit Mrs. Laurence and her guest.

It *was* rather a shock to find, after the general introduction was over, that this daughter of a hundred earls was a stout lady in a plain gown, and a rather weather-beaten bonnet, with a bag of papers in one hand and a notebook in the other. But the face was full of benevolence, the sonorous voice very kind, the genial manners very winning, and about the whole person an indescribable air of high breeding which made beauty of no consequence, costume soon forgotten, and the moment memorable to the keen-eyed girls whom nothing escaped.

A little chat about the rise, growth, and success of this particular class, and then Mrs. Jo led the conversation to the English lady's work, anxious to show her pupils how rank dignifies labor, and charity blesses wealth.

It was good for these girls to hear of the evening schools supported and taught by women whom they knew and honored; of Miss Cobbe's eloquent protest winning the protection of the law for abused wives; Mrs. Butler saving the lost; Mrs. Taylor, who devoted one room in her historic house to a library for her servants; Lord Shaftesbury, busy with his new tenement houses in the slums of London; of prison reforms; and all the brave work being done in God's name by the rich and great for the humble and the poor. It impressed them more than many quiet home lectures would have done, and roused an ambition to help when their time should come, well knowing that even in glorious America there is still plenty to be done before she is what she should be—truly just, and free, and great. They were also quick to see that Lady Ambercrombie treated all there as her equals, from stately Mrs. Laurence to little Josie, taking notes of everything and privately resolving to have some thick-soled English boots as soon as possible. No one would have guessed that she had a big house in London, a castle in Wales, and a grand countryseat in Scotland, as she spoke of Parnassus with admiration, Plumfield as a "dear old home," and the college as an honor to all concerned in it. At that, of course every head went up a little, and when my lady left, every hand was ready for the hearty shake the noble Englishwoman gave them, with words they long remembered, "I am very pleased to see this much-neglected branch of a woman's education so well conducted here, and I have to thank my friend Mrs. Laurence for one of the most charming pictures I've seen in America—Penelope among her maids."

A group of smiling faces watched the stout boots trudge away, respectful glances followed the shabby bonnet till it was out of sight, and the girls felt a truer respect for their titled guest than if she had come in the coach and six, with all her diamonds on.

"I feel better about the 'odd jobs' now. I only wish I could do them as well as Lady Ambercrombie does," said one.

"I thanked my stars my buttonholes were nice, for she looked at them and said, 'Quite workmanlike, upon me word,'" added another, feeling that her gingham gown had come to honor.

"Her manners were as sweet and kind as Mrs. Brooke's. Not a bit stiff or condescending, as I expected. I see now what you meant, Mrs. Bhaer, when you said once that well-bred people were the same all the world over."

Mrs. Meg bowed her thanks for the compliment, and Mrs. Bhaer said, "I know them when I see them, but never shall be a model of deportment myself. I'm glad you enjoyed the little visit. Now, if you young people don't want England to get ahead of us in many ways, you must bestir yourselves and keep abreast; for our sisters are in earnest, you see, and don't waste time worrying about their sphere, but make it wherever duty calls them."

"We will do our best, ma'am," answered the girls heartily, and trooped away with their workbaskets, feeling that though they might never be Harriet Martineaus, Elizabeth Brownings, or George Eliots, they might become noble, useful, and independent women, and earn for themselves some sweet title from the grateful lips of the poor, better than any a queen could bestow.

CHAPTER 18

CLASS DAY

THE CLERK of the weather evidently has a regard for young people, and sends sunshine for class days as often as he can. An especially lovely one shone over Plumfield as this interesting anniversary came round, bringing the usual accompaniments of roses, strawberries, white-gowned girls, beaming youths, proud friends, and stately dignitaries full of well-earned satisfaction with the yearly harvest. As Laurence College was a mixed one, the presence of young women as students gave to the occasion a grace and animation entirely wanting where the picturesque half of creation appear merely as spectators. The hands that turned the pages of wise books also possessed the skill to decorate the hall with flowers; eyes tired with study shone with hospitable warmth on the assembling guests; and under the white muslins beat hearts as full of ambition, hope, and courage as those agitating the broadcloth of the ruling sex.

College Hill, Parnassus, and old Plum swarmed with cheery faces, as guests, students, and professors hurried to and fro in the pleasant excitement of arriving and receiving. Everyone was welcomed cordially, whether he rolled up in a fine carriage, or trudged afoot to see the good son or daughter come to honor on the happy day that rewarded many a mutual sacrifice. Mr. Laurie and his wife were on the reception committee, and their lovely house was overflowing. Mrs. Meg, with Daisy and Jo as aides, was in demand among the girls, helping on belated toilettes, giving an eye to spreads, and directing the decorations. Mrs. Jo had her hands full as President's lady, and the mother of Ted; for it took all the power and skill of that energetic woman to get her son into his Sunday best.

Not that he objected to being well arrayed; far from it; he adored good clothes, and owing to his great height already reveled in a dress suit, bequeathed him by a dandy friend. The effect was very funny; but he would wear it in spite of the jeers of his mates, and sighed vainly for a beaver, because his stern parent drew the line there. He pleaded that English lads of ten wore them and were "no end nobby." But his mother only answered, with a consoling pat of the yellow mane, "My child, you are absurd enough now; if I let you add a tall hat, Plumfield wouldn't hold either of us, such would be the scorn and derision of all beholders. Content yourself with looking like the ghost of a waiter, and don't ask for the most ridiculous headgear in the known world."

Denied this noble badge of manhood, Ted soothed his wounded soul by appearing in collars of an amazing height and stiffness, and ties which were the wonder of all female eyes. This freak was a sort of vengeance on his hard-hearted mother; for the collars drove the laundress to despair, never being just right, and the ties required such art in the tying that three women sometimes labored long before—like Beau Brummel— he turned from a heap of "failures" with the welcome words, "That will do." Rob was devoted on these trying occasions, his own toilet being distinguished only by its speed, simplicity, and neatness. Ted was usually in a frenzy before he was suited, and roars, whistles, commands, and groans were heard from the den wherein the Lion raged and the Lamb patiently toiled. Mrs. Jo bore it till boots were hurled and a rain of hairbrushes set in, then, fearing for the safety of her eldest, she would go to the rescue, and by a wise mixture of fun and authority finally succeed in persuading Ted that he was, "a thing of beauty," if not "a joy forever." At last he would stalk majestically forth, imprisoned in collars compared to which those worn by Dickens's afflicted Biler were trifles not worth mentioning. The dress coat was a little loose in the shoulders, but allowed a noble expanse of glossy bosom to be seen, and with a delicate handkerchief negligently drooping at the proper angle, had a truly fine effect. Boots that shone, and likewise pinched, appeared at one end of the "long, black clothespin"—as Josie called him—and a youthful but solemn face at the other, carried at an angle which, if long continued, would have resulted in spinal curvature. Light gloves, a cane, and—oh, bitter drop in the cup of joy!—an ignominious straw hat, not to mention a choice floweret in the buttonhole, and a festoon of watch-guard below, finished off this impressive boy.

"How's that for style?" he asked, appearing to his mother and cousins whom he was to escort to the hall on this particular occasion.

A shout of laughter greeted him, followed by exclamations of horror; for he had artfully added the little blond moustache he often wore when acting. It was very becoming, and seemed the only balm to heal the wound made by the loss of the beloved hat.

"Take it off this moment, you audacious boy! What *would* your father say to such a prank on this day when we must all behave our best?" said Mrs. Jo, trying to frown, but privately thinking that among the many youths about her none was so beautiful and original as her long son.

"Let him wear it, Aunty; it's so becoming. No one will ever guess he isn't eighteen at least," cried Josie, to whom disguise of any sort was always charming.

"Father won't observe it; he'll be absorbed in his bigwigs

and the girls. No matter if he does, he'll enjoy the joke and introduce me as his oldest son. Rob is nowhere when I'm in full fig." And Ted took the stage with a tragic stalk, like Hamlet in a tail coat and choker.

"My son, obey me!" And when Mrs. Jo spoke in that tone her word was law. Later, however, the moustache appeared, and many strangers firmly believed that there were three young Bhaers. So Ted found one ray of joy to light his gloom.

Mr. Bhaer was a proud and happy man when, at the appointed hour, he looked down upon the parterre of youthful faces before him, thinking of the "little gardens" in which he had hopefully and faithfully sowed good seed years ago, and from which this beautiful harvest seemed to have sprung. Mr. March's fine old face shone with the serenest satisfaction, for this was the dream of his life fulfilled after patient waiting; and the love and reverence in the countenances of the eager young men and women looking up at him plainly showed that the reward he coveted was his in fullest measure. Laurie always effaced himself on these occasions as much as courtesy would permit; for everyone spoke gratefully in ode, poem, and oration of the founder of the college and the noble dispenser of his beneficence. The three sisters beamed with pride as they sat among the ladies, enjoying, as only women can, the honor done the men they loved; while "the original Plums," as the younger ones called themselves, regarded the whole affair as their work, receiving the curious, admiring, or envious glances of strangers with a mixture of dignity and delight rather comical to behold.

The music was excellent, and well it might be when Apollo waved the baton. The poems were—as usual on such occasions —of varied excellence, as the youthful speakers tried to put old truths into new words, and made them forceful by the enthusiasm of their earnest faces and fresh voices. It was beautiful to see the eager interest with which the girls listened to some brilliant brother student, and applauded him with a rustle as of wind over a bed of flowers. It was still more significant and

pleasant to watch the young men's faces when a slender white
figure stood out against the background of black-coated dignitaries, and with cheeks that flushed and paled, and lips that
trembled till earnest purpose conquered maiden fear, spoke to
them straight out of a woman's heart and brain concerning the
hopes and doubts, the aspirations and rewards all must know,
desire, and labor for. This clear, sweet voice seemed to reach
and rouse all that was noblest in the souls of these youths, and
to set a seal upon the years of comradeship which made them
sacred and memorable forever.

Alice Heath's oration was unanimously pronounced the success of the day; for without being flowery or sentimental, as is
too apt to be the case with these first efforts of youthful orators,
it was earnest, sensible, and so inspiring that she left the stage
in a storm of applause, the good fellows being as much fired by
her stirring appeal to "march shoulder to shoulder," as if she
had chanted the "Marseillaise" then and there. One young man
was so excited that he nearly rushed out of his seat to receive
her as she hastened to hide herself among her mates, who welcomed her with faces full of tender pride and tearful eyes. A
prudent sister detained him, however, and in a moment he was
able to listen with composure to the President's remarks.

They were worth listening to, for Mr. Bhaer spoke like a
father to the children whom he was dismissing to the battle of
life; and his tender, wise, and helpful words lingered in their
hearts long after the praise was forgotten. Then came other
exercises peculiar to Plumfield, and the end. Why the roof did
not fly off when the sturdy lungs of the excited young men
pealed out the closing hymn will forever be a mystery; but it
remained firm, and only the fading garlands vibrated as the
waves of music rolled up and died away, leaving sweet echoes to
haunt the place for another year.

Dinners and spreads consumed the afternoon, and at sunset
came a slight lull as everyone sought some brief repose before
the festivities of the evening began. The President's reception

was one of the enjoyable things in store, also dancing on Parnassus, and as much strolling, singing, and flirting, as could be compressed into a few hours by youths and maidens just out of school.

Carriages were rolling about, and gay groups on piazzas, lawns, and windowseats idly speculated as to who the distinguished guests might be. The appearance of a very dusty vehicle loaded with trunks at Mr. Bhaer's hospitably open door caused much curious comment among the loungers, especially as two rather foreign-looking gentlemen sprung out, followed by two young ladies, all four being greeted with cries of joy and much embracing by the Bhaers. Then they all disappeared into the house, the luggage followed, and the watchers were left to wonder who the mysterious strangers were, till a fair collegian declared that they must be the Professor's nephews, one of whom was expected on his wedding journey.

She was right. Franz proudly presented his blonde and buxom bride, and she was hardly kissed and blessed when Emil led up his bonny English Mary, with the rapturous announcement, "Uncle, Aunt Jo, here's another daughter! Have you room for *my* wife, too?"

There could be no doubt of that; and Mary was with difficulty rescued from the glad embraces of her new relatives, who, remembering all the young pair had suffered together, felt that this was the natural and happy ending of the long voyage so perilously begun.

"But why not tell us, and let us be ready for two brides instead of one?" asked Mrs. Jo, looking as usual rather demoralized in a wrapper and crimping pins, having rushed down from her chamber, where she was preparing for the labors of the evening.

"Well, I remember what a good joke you all considered Uncle Laurie's marriage, and I thought I'd give you another nice little surprise," laughed Emil. "I'm off duty, and it seemed best to take advantage of wind and tide, and come along as convoy to the old boy here. We hoped to get in last night, but couldn't fetch it, so here we are in time for the end of the jollification, anyway."

"Ah, my sons, it is too feeling-full to see you both so happy and again in the old home. I haf no words to outpour my gratitude, and can only ask of the dear Gott in Himmel to bless and keep you all," cried Professor Bhaer, trying to gather all four into his arms at once, while tears rolled down his cheeks, and his English failed him.

An April shower cleared the air and relieved the full hearts of the happy family; then of course everyone began to talk—Franz and Ludmilla in German with the uncle, Emil and Mary with the aunts; and round this group gathered the young folk, clamoring to hear all about the wreck, and the rescue, and the homeward voyage. It was a very different story from the written one; and as they listened to Emil's graphic words, with Mary's soft voice breaking in now and then to add some fact that brought out the courage, patience, and self-sacrifice he so lightly touched upon, it became a solemn and pathetic thing to see and hear these happy creatures tell of that great danger and deliverance.

"I never hear the patter of rain now that I don't want to say my prayers; and as for women, I'd like to take my hat off to every one of 'em, for they are braver than any man I ever saw," said Emil, with the new gravity that was as becoming to him as the new gentleness with which he treated everyone.

"If women are brave, some men are as tender and self-sacrificing as women. I know one who in the night slipped his share of food into a girl's pocket, though starving himself, and sat for hours rocking a sick man in his arms that he might get a little sleep. No, love, I will tell, and you must let me!" cried Mary, holding in both her own the hand he laid on her lips to silence her.

"Only did my duty. If that torment had lasted much longer I might have been as bad as poor Barry and the boatswain.

Wasn't that an awful night?" And Emil shuddered as he recalled it.

"Don't think of it, dear. Tell about the happy days on the 'Urania,' when Papa grew better and we were all safe and homeward bound," said Mary, with the trusting look and comforting touch which seemed to banish the dark and recall the bright side of that terrible experience.

Emil cheered up at once, and sitting with his arm about his "dear lass," in true sailor fashion told the happy ending of the tale.

"Such a jolly old time as we had at Hamburg. Uncle Hermann couldn't do enough for the captain, and while Mamma took care of him, Mary looked after me. I had to go into dock for repairs; fire hurt my eyes, and watching for a sail and want of sleep made 'em as hazy as a London fog. She was pilot and brought me in all right, you see, only I couldn't part company, so she came aboard as first mate, and I'm bound straight for glory now."

"Hush! That's silly, dear," whispered Mary, trying in her turn to stop him, with English shyness about tender topics. But he took the soft hand in his, and proudly surveying the one ring it wore, went on with the air of an admiral aboard his flagship.

"The captain proposed waiting a spell; but I told him we weren't likely to see any rougher weather than we'd pulled through together, and if we didn't know one another after such a year as this, we never should. I was sure I shouldn't be worth my pay without this hand on the wheel; so I had my way, and my brave little woman has shipped for the long voyage. God bless her!"

"Shall you really sail with him?" asked Daisy, admiring her courage, but shrinking with cat-like horror from the water.

"I'm not afraid," answered Mary, with a loyal smile. "I've proved my captain in fair weather and in foul, and if he is ever wrecked again, I'd rather be with him than waiting and watching ashore."

· "A true woman, and a born sailor's wife! You are a happy man, Emil, and I'm sure *this* trip will be a prosperous one," cried Mrs. Jo, delighted with the briny flavor of this courtship. "Oh, my dear boy, I always felt you'd come back, and when everyone else despaired I never gave up, but insisted that you were clinging to the main-top jib somewhere on that dreadful sea." And Mrs. Jo illustrated her faith by grasping Emil with a truly Pillycoddian gesture.

"Of course I was!" answered Emil, heartily. "And my 'main-top jib' in this case was the thought of what you and Uncle said to me. That kept me up; and among the million thoughts that came to me during those lone nights none was clearer than the idea of the red strand, you remember—English navy, and all that. I liked the notion, and resolved that if a bit of my cable was left afloat, the red stripe should be there."

"And it was, my dear, it was! Captain Hardy testifies to that, and here is your reward." And Mrs. Jo kissed Mary with a maternal tenderness which betrayed that she liked the English rose better than the blue-eyed German *Korn-blumen,* sweet and modest though it was.

Emil surveyed this little ceremony with complacency, saying, as he looked about the room which he never thought to see again, "Odd isn't it, how clearly trifles come back to one in times of danger? As we floated there, half-starved and in despair, I used to think I heard the bells ringing here, and Ted tramping downstairs, and you calling, 'Boys, boys, it's time to get up!' I actually smelt the coffee we used to have, and one night I nearly cried when I woke from a dream of Asia's ginger cookies. I declare, it was one of the bitterest disappointments of my life to face hunger with that spicy smell in my nostrils. If you've got any, do give me one!"

A pitiful murmur broke from all the aunts and cousins, and Emil was at once borne away to feast on the desired cookies, a supply always being on hand. Mrs. Jo and her sister joined the other group, glad to hear what Franz was saying about Nat.

"The minute I saw how thin and shabby he was, I knew that something was wrong; but he made light of it, and was so happy over our visit and news that I let him off with a brief confession, and went to Professor Baumgarten and Bergmann. From them I learned the whole story of his spending more money than he ought and trying to atone for it by unnecessary work and sacrifice. Baumgarten thought it would do him good, so kept his secret till I came. It did do him good, and he's paid his debts and earned his bread by the sweat of his brow, like an honest fellow."

"I like that much in Nat. It is, as I said, a lesson, and he learns it well. He proves himself a man, and has deserved the place Bergmann offers him," said Mr. Bhaer, looking well pleased as Franz added some facts already recorded.

"I told you, Meg, that he had good stuff in him, and love for Daisy would keep him straight. Dear lad, I wish I had him here this moment!" cried Mrs. Jo, forgetting in delight the doubts and anxieties which had troubled her for months past.

"I am very glad, and suppose I shall give in as I always do, especially now that the epidemic rages so among us. You and Emil have set all their heads in a ferment, and Josie will be demanding a lover before I can turn round," answered Mrs. Meg, in a tone of despair.

But her sister saw that she was touched by Nat's trials, and hastened to add the triumphs, that the victory might be complete; for success is always charming.

"This offer of Herr Bergmann is a good one, isn't it?" she asked, though Mr. Laurie had already satisfied her on that point when Nat's letter brought the news.

"Very fine in every way. Nat will get capital drill in Bachmeister's orchestra, see London in a delightful way, and if he suits come home with them, well started among the violins. No great honor, but a sure thing and a step up. I congratulated him, and he was very jolly over it, saying, like the true lover he is, 'Tell Daisy. Be sure and tell her all about it.' I'll leave that to you, Aunt Meg, and you can also break it gently to her that the old boy has a fine blond beard. Very becoming; hides his weak mouth, and gives a noble air to his big eyes and 'Mendelssohnian brow,' as a gushing girl called it. Ludmilla has a photo of it for you."

This amused them; and they listened to many other interesting bits of news which kind Franz, even in his own happiness, had not forgotten to remember for his friend's sake. He talked so well, and painted Nat's patient and pathetic shifts so vividly, that Mrs. Meg was half won; though if she had learned of the Minna episode and the fiddling in beer gardens and streets, she might not have relented so soon. She stored up all she heard, however, and, womanlike, promised herself a delicious talk with Daisy, in which she would allow herself to melt by degrees, and perhaps change the doubtful "We shall see" to a cordial "He has done well; be happy, dear."

In the midst of this agreeable chat the sudden striking of a clock recalled Mrs. Jo from romance to reality, and she exclaimed, with a clutch at her crimping pins, "My blessed people, you must eat and rest; and I must dress, or receive in this disgraceful rig. Meg, will you take Ludmilla and Mary upstairs and see to them! Franz knows the way to the dining room. Fritz, come with me and be made tidy, for what with heat and emotion, we are both perfect wrecks."

CHAPTER 19

WHITE ROSES

WHILE THE travelers refreshed, and Mrs. President struggled into her best gown, Josie ran into the garden to gather flowers for the brides. The sudden arrival of these interesting beings had quite enchanted the romantic girl, and her head was full of heroic rescues, tender admiration, dramatic situations, and feminine wonder as to whether the lovely creatures would wear their veils or not. She was standing before a great bush of white roses, culling the most perfect for the bouquets which she meant to tie with the white ribbon festooned over her arm, and lay on the toilette tables of the new cousins, as a delicate attention. A step startled her, and looking up she saw her brother coming down the path with folded arms, bent head, and the absent air of one absorbed in deep thought.

"Sophy Wackles," said the sharp child, with a superior smile, as she sucked her thumb just pricked by a too eager pull at the thorny branches.

"What are you at here, Mischief?" asked Demi, with an Irvingesque start, as he felt rather than saw a disturbing influence in his daydream.

"Getting flowers for 'our brides.' Don't you wish you had one?" answered Josie, to whom the word "mischief" suggested her favorite amusement.

"A bride or a flower?" asked Demi, calmly, though he eyed the blooming bush as if it had a sudden and unusual interest for him.

"Both. You get the one, and I'll give you the other."

"Wish I could!" and Demi picked a little bud, with a sigh that went to Josie's warm heart.

"Why don't you then? It's lovely to see people so happy. Now's a good time to do it if you ever mean to. *She* will be going away forever soon."

"Who?" And Demi pulled a half-opened bud, with a sudden color in his own face, which sign of confusion delighted little Jo.

"Don't be a hypocrite. You know I mean Alice. Now, Jack, I'm fond of you, and want to help; it's so interesting—all these lovers and weddings and things, and we ought to have our share. So you take my advice and speak up like a man, and make sure of Alice before she goes."

Demi laughed at the seriousness of the small girl's advice; but he liked it, and showed that it suited him by saying blandly, instead of snubbing her as usual, "You are very kind, child. Since you are so wise, could you give me a hint how I'd better 'speak up,' as you elegantly express it?"

"Oh, well, there are various ways, you know. In plays the lovers go down on their knees; but that's awkward when they have long legs. Ted never does it well, though I drill him for hours. You could say, 'Be mine, be mine!' like the old man who threw cucumbers over the wall to Mrs. Nickleby, if you want to be gay and easy; or you could write a poetical pop. You've tried it, I dare say."

"But seriously, Jo, I do love Alice, and I think she knows it. I want to tell her so; but I lose my head when I try, and don't care to make a fool of myself. Thought you might suggest some pretty way; you read so much poetry and are so romantic."

Demi tried to express clearly, but forgot his dignity and his usual reserve in the sweet perplexity of his love, and asked his little sister to teach him how to put the question which a single word can answer. The arrival of his happy cousins had scattered all his wise plans and brave resolutions to wait still longer. The Christmas play had given him courage to hope, and the oration today had filled him with tender pride; but the sight of those blooming brides and beaming grooms was too much for him, and he panted to secure his Alice without an hour's delay. Daisy was his confidante in all things but this; a brotherly feeling of sympathy had kept him from telling her his hopes, because her own were forbidden. His mother was rather jealous of any girl he admired; but knowing that she liked Alice, he loved on and enjoyed his secret alone, meaning soon to tell her all about it.

Now suddenly Josie and the rosebush seemed to suggest a speedy end to his tender perplexities; and he was moved to accept her aid as the netted lion did that of the mouse.

"I think I'll write," he was slowly beginning, after a pause during which both were trying to strike out a new and brilliant idea.

"I've got it! Perfectly lovely—just suit her, and you too, being a poet!" cried Josie, with a skip.

"What is it? Don't be ridiculous, please," begged the bashful lover, eager, but afraid of this sharp-tongued bit of womanhood.

"I read in one of Miss Edgeworth's stories about a man who offers three roses to his lady—a bud, a half-blown, and a full-blown rose. I don't remember which she took; but it's a pretty way, and Alice knows about it because she was there when we read it. Here are all kinds; you've got the two buds, pick the sweetest rose you can find, and I'll tie them up and put them in her room. She is coming to dress with Daisy, so I can do it nicely."

Demi mused a moment with his eyes on the bridal bush, and a smile came over his face so unlike any it had ever worn before, that Josie was touched, and looked away as if she had no right to see the dawn of the great passion which, while it lasts, makes a young man as happy as a god.

"Do it," was all he said, and slowly gathered a full-blown rose to finish his floral love message.

Charmed to have a finger in this romantic pie, Josie tied a graceful bow of ribbon about the stems and finished her last nosegay with much content, while Demi wrote upon a card—

DEAR ALICE—You know what the flowers mean. Will you wear one or all tonight, and make me still prouder, fonder, and happier than I am?

Yours entirely,   JOHN

Offering this to his sister, he said in a tone that made her feel the deep importance of her mission—"I trust you, Jo. This means everything to me. No jokes, dear, if you love me."

Josie's answer was a kiss that promised all things; and then she ran away to do her "gentle spiriting," like Ariel, leaving Demi to dream among the roses like Ferdinand.

Mary and Ludmilla were charmed with their bouquets; and the giver had the delight of putting some of the flowers into the dark hair and the light as she played maid at the toilettes of "our brides," which consoled her for a disappointment in the matter of veils.

No one helped Alice dress; for Daisy was in the next room with her mother; and not even their loving eyes saw the welcome which the little posy received, nor the tears and smiles and blushes that came and went as she read the note and pondered what answer she should give. There was no doubt about the one she *wished* to give; but duty held her back; for at home there were an invalid mother and an old father. She was needed there, with all the help she could now bring by the acquirements four years of faithful study had given her. Love looked very sweet, and a home of her own with John a little heaven on earth

—but not yet. And she slowly laid away the full-blown rose as she sat before the mirror, thinking over the great question of her life.

Was it wise and kind to ask him to wait, to bind him by any promise, or even to put into words the love and honor she felt for him? No—it would be more generous to make the sacrifice alone, and spare him the pain of hope deferred. He was young; he would forget; and she could do her duty better, perhaps, if no impatient lover waited for her. With eyes that saw but dimly, and a hand that lingered on the stem he had stripped of thorns, she laid the half-blown flower by the rose, and asked herself if even the little bud might be worn. It looked very poor and pale beside the others; yet being in the self-sacrificing mood which real love brings, she felt that even a small hope was too much to give, if she could not follow it up with more.

As she sat looking sadly down on the symbols of an affection that grew dearer every moment, she listened half unconsciously to the murmur of voices in the adjoining room. Open windows, thin partitions, and the stillness of summer twilight made it impossible to help hearing, and in a few moments more she could not refrain; for they were talking of John.

"So nice of Ludmilla to bring us all bottles of real German cologne! Just what we need after this tiring day! Be sure John has his! He likes it so!"

"Yes, Mother. Did you see him jump up when Alice ended her oration? He'd have gone to her if I hadn't held him back. I don't wonder he was pleased and proud. I spoilt my gloves clapping, and quite forgot my dislike of seeing women on platforms, she was so earnest and unconscious and sweet after the first moment."

"Has he said anything to you, dear?"

"No; and I guess why. The kind boy thinks it would make me unhappy. It wouldn't. But I know his ways; so I wait, and hope all will go well with him."

"It must. No girl in her senses would refuse our John, though he isn't rich, and never will be. Daisy, I've been longing to tell you what he did with his money. He told me last night, and I've had no time since to tell you. He sent poor young Barton to the hospital, and kept him there till his eyes were saved—a costly thing to do. But the man can work now and care for his old parents. He was in despair, sick and poor, and too proud to beg; and our dear boy found it out, and took every penny he had, and never told even his mother till she made him."

Alice did not hear what Daisy answered, for she was busy with her own emotions—happy ones now, to judge from the smile that shone in her eyes and the decided gesture with which she put the little bud in her bosom, as if she said, "He deserves some reward for that good deed, and he shall have it."

Mrs. Meg was speaking, and still of John, when she could hear again, "Some people would call it unwise and reckless, when John has so little; but *I* think his first investment a safe and good one, for 'he who giveth to the poor lendeth to the Lord.' And I was so pleased and proud, I wouldn't spoil it by offering him a penny."

"It is his having nothing to offer that keeps him silent, I think. He is so honest, he won't ask till he has much to give. But he forgets that love is everything. I know he's rich in that. I see and feel it. And any woman should be glad to get it."

"Right, dear. I felt just so, and was willing to work and wait with and for *my* John."

"So she will be, and I hope they will find it out. But she is so dutiful and good, I'm afraid she won't let herself be happy. You would like it, Mother?"

"Heartily, for a better, nobler girl doesn't live. She is all I want for my son, and I don't mean to lose the dear, brave creature if I can help it. Her heart is big enough for both love and duty; and they can wait more happily if they do it together —for wait they must, of course."

"I'm so glad *his* choice suits you, mother, and *he* is spared the saddest sort of disappointment."

Daisy's voice broke there; and a sudden rustle, followed by a soft murmur, seemed to tell that she was in her mother's arms, seeking and finding comfort there.

Alice heard no more, and shut her window with a guilty feeling but a shining face; for the proverb about listeners failed here, and she had learned more than she dared to hope. Things seemed to change suddenly. She felt that her heart *was* large enough for both love and duty; she knew now that she would be welcomed by mother and sister; and the memory of Daisy's less happy fate, Nat's weary probation, the long delay, and possible separation forever—all came before her so vividly that prudence seemed cruelty; self-sacrifice, sentimental folly, and anything but the whole truth, disloyalty to her lover. As she thought thus, the half-blown rose went to join the bud; and then, after a pause, she slowly kissed the perfect rose, and added it to the telltale group, saying to herself with a sort of sweet solemnity, as if the words were a vow, "I'll love and work and wait with and for my John."

It was well for her that Demi was absent when she stole down to join the guests who soon began to flow through the house in a steady stream. The new brightness which touched her usually thoughtful face was easily explained by the congratulations she received as orator, and the slight agitation observable when a fresh batch of gentlemen approached soon passed, as none of them noticed the flowers she wore over a very happy heart.

Demi meantime was escorting certain venerable personages about the college, and helping his grandfather entertain them with discussions of the Socratic method of instruction, Pythagoras, Pestalozzi, Froebel, and the rest, whom he devoutly wished at the bottom of the Red Sea; and no wonder, for his head and heart were full of love and roses, hopes and fears. He piloted the "potent, grave, and reverend seigniors" safely down to Plumfield at last, and landed them before his uncle and aunt Bhaer, who were receiving in state, the one full of genuine delight in all men and things, the other suffering martyrdom with a smile, as she stood shaking hand after hand, and affecting utter unconsciousness of the sad fact that ponderous Professor Plock had camped upon the train of her state and festival velvet gown.

With a long sigh of relief Demi glanced about him for the beloved girl. Most persons would have looked some time before any particular angel could be discovered among the white-robed throng in parlors, hall, and study; but his eye went—like the needle to the pole—to the corner where a smooth dark head, with its braided crown, rose like a queen's, he thought, above the crowd which surrounded her. Yes, she had a flower at her throat; one, two, oh, blessed sight! He saw it all across the room, and gave a rapturous sigh which caused Miss Perry's frizzled crop to wave with a sudden gust. He did *not* see the rose, for it was hidden by a fold of lace; and it was well, perhaps, that bliss came by installments, or he might have electrified the assembled multitude by flying to his idol, there being no Daisy to clutch him by the coattail. A stout lady, thirsting for information, seized him at that thrilling moment, and he was forced to point out celebrities with a saintly patience which deserved a better reward than it received; for a certain absence of mind and incoherence of speech at times caused the ungrateful dowager to whisper to the first friend she met after he had escaped, "I saw no wine at any of the spreads, but it is plain that young Brooke has had too much. Quite gentlemanly, but evidently a trifle intoxicated, my dear."

Ah, so he was—but with a diviner wine than any that ever sparkled at a class-day lunch, though many collegians know the taste of it; and when the old lady was disposed of, he gladly turned to find the young one, bent on having a single word. He saw her standing by the piano now, idly turning over music as she talked with several gentlemen. Hiding his impatience under an air of scholastic repose, Demi hovered near, ready to advance when the happy moment came, wondering meantime why elderly persons persisted in absorbing young ones instead of sensibly sitting in corners with their contemporaries. The elderly persons in question retired at length, but only to be replaced by two impetuous youths who begged Miss Heath to accompany them to Parnassus and join the dance. Demi thirsted for their blood, but was appeased by hearing George and Dolly say, as they lingered a moment after her refusal, "Really, you know, I'm quite converted to coeducation and almost wish I'd remained here. It gives a grace to study, a sort of relish even to Greek, to see charming girls at it," said Stuffy, who found the feast of learning so dry, any sauce was welcome; and he felt as if he had discovered a new one.

"Yes, by Jove! We fellows will have to look out or you'll carry off all the honors. You were superb today, and held us all like magic, though it was so hot there, I really think I couldn't have stood it for anyone else," added Dolly, laboring to be gallant and really offering a touching proof of devotion; for the heat melted his collar, took the curl out of his hair, and ruined his gloves.

"There is room for all, and if you will leave us the books, we will cheerfully yield the baseball, boating, dancing, and flirting, which seem to be the branches you prefer," answered Alice, sweetly.

"Ah, now you are too hard upon us! We can't grind all the time, and you ladies don't seem to mind taking a turn at the two latter 'branches' you mention," returned Dolly, with a glance at George which plainly said, "I had her there."

"Some of us do in our first years. Later we give up childish things, you see. Don't let me keep you from Parnassus." And a smiling nod dismissed them, smarting under the bitter consciousness of youth.

"You got it there, Doll. Better not try to fence with these superior girls. Sure to be routed, horse, foot, and dragoons,"

said Stuffy, lumbering away, somewhat cross with too many
spreads.

"So deuced sarcastic! Don't believe she's much older than we
are. Girls grow up quicker, so she needn't put on airs and talk
like a grandmother," muttered Dolly, feeling that he had sacri-
ficed his kids upon the altar of an ungrateful Pallas.

"Come along and let's find something to eat. I'm faint with so
much talking. Old Plock cornered me and made my head spin
with Kant and Hegel and that lot."

"I promised Dora West I'd give her a turn. Must look her up;
she's a jolly little thing, and doesn't bother about anything but
keeping step."

And arm in arm the boys strolled away, leaving Alice to read
music as diligently as if society had indeed no charms for her.
As she bent to turn a page, the eager young man behind the
piano saw the rose and was struck speechless with delight. A
moment he gazed, then hastened to seize the coveted place
before a new detachment of bores arrived.

"Alice, I can't believe it—did you understand—how shall I
ever thank you?" murmured Demi, bending as if he, too, read
the song, not a note or word of which did he see, however.

"Hush! Not now. I understood—I don't deserve it—we are
too young, we must wait. But—I'm very proud and happy,
John!"

What would have happened after that tender whisper I tremble to think, if Tom Bangs had not come bustling up, with the
cheerful remark, "Music? Just the thing. People are thinning
out, and we all want a little refreshment. My brain fairly reels
with the 'ologies and 'isms I've heard discussed tonight. Yes,
give us this, sweet thing! Scotch songs are always charming."

Demi glowered, but the obtuse boy never saw it, and Alice,
feeling that this would be a safe vent for sundry unruly emotions, sat down at once, and sung the song which gave her
answer better than she could have done—

BIDE A WEE

"The puir auld folk at home, ye mind,
  Are frail and failing sair;
And weel I ken they'd miss me, lad,
  Gin I come hame nae mair.
The grist is out, the times are hard,
  The kine are only three;
I canna leave the auld folk now.
  We'd better bide a wee.

"I fear me sair they're failing baith;
  For when I sit apart,
They talk o' Heaven so earnestly,
  It well nigh breaks my heart.
So, laddie, dinna urge me now,
  It surely winna be;
I canna leave the auld folk yet.
  We'd better bide a wee."

The room was very still before the first verse ended, and Alice skipped the next, fearing she could not get through; for John's eyes were on her, showing that he knew she sang for him and let the plaintive little ballad tell what her reply must be. He took it as she meant it, and smiled at her so happily that her heart got the better of her voice, and she rose abruptly, saying something about the heat.

"Yes, you are tired. Come out and rest, my dearest." And with a masterful air Demi took her into the starlight, leaving Tom to stare after them, winking as if a skyrocket had suddenly gone off under his nose.

"Bless my soul! The Deacon really meant business last summer and never told me. Won't Dora laugh?" And Tom departed in hot haste to impart and exult over his discovery.

What was said in the garden was never exactly known; but the Brooke family sat up very late that night, and any curious eye at the window would have seen Demi receiving the homage of his womankind as he told his little romance. Josie took great credit to herself in the matter, insisting that she had made the match; Daisy was full of the sweetest sympathy and joy; and Mrs. Meg so happy that when Jo had gone to dream of bridal veils, and Demi sat in his room blissfully playing the air of "Bide a Wee," she had her talk about Nat, ending with her arms round her dutiful daughter and these welcome words as her reward, "Wait till Nat comes home, and then my good girl shall wear white roses too."

CHAPTER 20

LIFE FOR LIFE

THE SUMMER DAYS that followed were full of rest and pleasure for young and old, as they did the honors of Plumfield to their happy guests. While Franz and Emil were busy with the affairs of Uncle Hermann and Captain Hardy, Mary and Ludmilla made friends everywhere; for, though very unlike, both were excellent and charming girls. Mrs. Meg and Daisy found the German bride a *Hausfrau* after their own hearts, and had delightful times learning new dishes, hearing about the semiyearly washes and the splendid linen room at Hamburg, or discussing domestic life in all its branches. Ludmilla not only taught, but learned, many things, and went home with many new and useful ideas in her blond head.

Mary had seen so much of the world that she was unusually lively for an English girl, while her various accomplishments made her a most agreeable companion. Much good sense gave her ballast; and the late experiences of danger and happiness added a sweet gravity at times, which contrasted well with her natural gaiety. Mrs. Jo was quite satisfied with Emil's choice, and felt sure this true and tender pilot would bring him safe to

269

port through fair or stormy weather. She had feared that Franz
would settle down into a comfortable, money-making burgher,
and be content with that; but she soon saw that his love of
music and his placid Ludmilla put much poetry into his busy
life, and kept it from being too prosaic. So she felt at rest about
these boys, and enjoyed their visit with real, maternal satisfaction, parting with them in September most regretfully, yet hopefully, as they sailed away to the new life that lay before them.

Demi's engagement was confided to the immediate family
only, as both were pronounced too young to do anything but
love and wait. They were so happy that time seemed to stand
still for them, and after a blissful week they parted bravely—
Alice to home duties, with a hope that sustained and cheered
her through many trials; and John to his business, full of a new
ardor which made all things possible when such a reward was
offered.

Daisy rejoiced over them, and was never tired of hearing her
brother's plans for the future. Her own hope soon made her
what she used to be—a cheery, busy creature, with a smile, kind
word, and helping hand for all; and as she went singing about
the house again, her mother felt that the right remedy for past
sadness had been found. The dear Pelican still had doubts and
fears, but kept them wisely to herself, preparing sundry searching tests to be applied when Nat came home, and keeping a
sharp eye on the letters from London; for some mysterious hint
had flown across the sea, and Daisy's content seemed reflected
in Nat's present cheerful state of mind.

Having passed through the Werther period, and tried a little
Faust—of which experience he spoke to his Marguerite as if it
had included an acquaintance with Mephistopheles, Block-
sburg, and Auerbach's wine cellar—he now felt that he was
a Wilhelm Meister, serving his apprenticeship to the great
masters of life. As she knew the truth of his small sins and
honest repentance, Daisy only smiled at the mixture of love and
philosophy he sent her, knowing that it was impossible for a

young man to live in Germany without catching the German spirit.

"His heart is all right; and his head will soon grow clear when he gets out of the fog of tobacco, beer, and metaphysics he's been living in. England will wake up his common sense, and good salt air blow his little follies all away," said Mrs. Jo, much pleased with the good prospects of her violinist—whose return was delayed till spring, to his private regret, but professional advancement.

Josie had a month with Miss Cameron at the seaside, and threw herself so heartily into the lessons given her that her energy, promise, and patience laid the foundation of a friendship which was of infinite value to her in the busy, brilliant years to come; for little Jo's instincts were right; and the dramatic talent of the Marches was to blossom by and by into an actress famous, virtuous, and beloved.

Tom and his Dora were peacefully ambling altarward; for Bangs senior was so afraid his son would change his mind again, and try a third profession, that he gladly consented to an early marriage, as a sort of anchor to hold the mercurial Thomas fast. Aforesaid Thomas could not complain of cold shoulders now; for Dora was a most devoted and adoring little mate, and made life so pleasant to him that his gift for getting into scrapes seemed lost, and he bade fair to become a thriving man, with undeniable talent for the business he had chosen.

"We shall be married in the autumn, and live with my father for a while. The governor is getting on, you know, and my wife and I must look after him. Later we shall have an establishment of our own," was a favorite speech of his about this time, and usually received with smiles; for the idea of Tommy Bangs at the head of an "establishment" was irresistibly funny to all who knew him.

Things were in this flourishing condition, and Mrs. Jo was beginning to think her trials were over for that year, when a new excitement came. Several postcards had arrived at long intervals

from Dan, who gave them "Care of M. Mason, etc.," as his
address. By this means he was able to gratify his longing for
home news, and to send brief messages to quiet their surprise at
his delay in settling. The last one, which came in September,
was dated "Montana," and simply said—

Here at last, trying mining again; but not going to stay long.
All sorts of luck. Gave up the farm idea. Tell plans soon.
Well, busy, and very <u>happy</u>.

D. K.

If they had known what the heavy dash under "happy"
meant, that postcard would have been a very eloquent bit of
pasteboard; for Dan was free, and had gone straight away to the
liberty he panted for. Meeting an old friend by accident, he
obliged him at a pinch by acting as overseer for a time, finding
the society even of rough miners very sweet, and something in
the muscular work wonderfully pleasant, after being cooped up
in the brush shop so long. He loved to take a pick and wrestle
with rock and earth till he was weary—which was very soon; for
that year of captivity had told upon his splendid physique. He
longed to go home, but waited week after week to get the
prison taint off him and the haggard look out of his face. Meanwhile he made friends of masters and men; and as no one knew
his story, he took his place again in the world gratefully and
gladly—with little pride now, and no plans but to do some good
somewhere, and efface the past.

Mrs. Jo was having a grand clearing-out of her desk one Oc-
tober day, while the rain poured outside, and peace reigned in
her mansion. Coming across the postcards, she pondered over
them, and then put them carefully away in the drawer labelled
"Boys' Letters," saying to herself, as she bundled eleven requests for autographs into the wastepaper basket, "It is quite
time for another card, unless he is coming to tell his plans. I'm

really curious to know what he has been about all this year, and how he's getting on now."

That last wish was granted within an hour; for Ted came rushing in, with a newspaper in one hand, a collapsed umbrella in the other, and a face full of excitement, announcing, all in one breathless jumble, "Mine caved in—twenty men shut up—no way out—wives crying—water rising—Dan knew the old shaft—risked his life—got 'em out—most killed—papers full of it—I knew he'd be a hero—hurray for old Dan!"

"What? Where? When? Who? Stop roaring, and let me read!" commanded his mother, entirely bewildered.

Relinquishing the paper, Ted allowed her to read for herself, with frequent interruptions from him—and Rob, who soon followed, eager for the tale. It was nothing new; but courage and devotion always stir generous hearts, and win admiration; so the account was both graphic and enthusiastic; and the name of Daniel Kean, the brave man who saved the lives of others at the risk of his own, was on many lips that day. Very proud were the faces of these friends as they read how their Dan was the only one who, in the first panic of the accident, remembered the old shaft that led into the mine—walled up, but the only hope of escape, if the men could be got out before the rising water drowned them; how he was lowered down alone, telling the others to keep back till he saw if it was safe; how he heard the poor fellows picking desperately for their lives on the other side, and by knocks and calls guided them to the right spot; then headed the rescue party, and working like a hero, got the men out in time. On being drawn up last of all, the worn ropes broke, and he had a terrible fall, being much hurt, but was still alive. How the grateful women kissed his blackened face and bloody hands, as the men bore him away in triumph, and the owners of the mine promised a handsome reward, if he lived to receive it!

"He must live; he *shall,* and come home to be nursed as soon as he can stir, if I go and bring him myself! I always knew he'd do something fine and brave, if he didn't get shot or hung for some wild prank instead," cried Mrs. Jo, much excited.

"Do go, and take me with you, Mum. I ought to be the one, Dan's so fond of me and I of him," began Ted, feeling that this would be an expedition after his own heart.

Before his mother could reply, Mr. Laurie came in, with almost as much noise and flurry as Teddy the second, exclaiming as he waved the evening paper, "Seen the news, Jo? What do you think? Shall I go off at once, and see after that brave boy?"

"I wish you would. But the thing may not be all true—rumor lies so. Perhaps a few hours will bring an entirely new version of the story."

"I've telephoned to Demi for all he can find out; and if it's true, I'll go at once. Should like the trip. If he's able, I'll bring him home; if not, I'll stay and see to him. He'll pull through. Dan will never die of a fall on his head. He's got nine lives, and not lost half of them yet."

"If you do go, Uncle, mayn't I go with you? I'm just spoiling for a journey; and it would be such larks to go out there with you, and see the mines and Dan, and hear all about it, and help. I can nurse. Can't I, Rob?" cried Teddy, in his most wheedlesome tones.

"Pretty well. But if Mother can't spare you, I'm ready if Uncle needs anyone," answered Rob, in his quiet way, looking much fitter for the trip than excitable Ted.

"I can't spare either of you. My boys get into trouble, unless I keep them close at home. I've no right to hold the others; but I won't let you out of my sight, or something will happen. Never saw such a year, with wrecks and weddings and floods and engagements, and every sort of catastrophe!" exclaimed Mrs. Jo.

"If you deal in girls and boys, you must expect this sort of thing, ma'am. The worst is over, I hope, till these lads begin to go off. Then I'll stand by you, for you'll need every kind of support and comfort, specially if Ted bolts early," laughed Mr. Laurie, enjoying her lamentations.

"I don't think anything can surprise me now; but I am anxious about Dan, and feel that someone had better go to him. It's a rough place out there, and he may need careful nursing. Poor lad, he seems to get a good many hard knocks! But perhaps he needs them as 'a mellerin' process,' as Hannah used to say."

"We shall hear from Demi before long, and then I'll be off." With which cheerful promise Mr. Laurie departed; and Ted, finding his mother firm, soon followed, to coax his uncle to take him.

Further inquiry confirmed and added interest to the news. Mr. Laurie was off at once; and Ted went into town with him, still vainly imploring to be taken to his Dan. He was absent all day; but his mother said, calmly, "Only a fit of the sulks because he is thwarted. He's safe with Tom or Demi, and will come home hungry and meek at night. I know him."

But she soon found that she *could* still be surprised; for evening brought no Ted, and no one had seen him. Mr. Bhaer was just setting off to find his lost son, when a telegram arrived, dated at one of the way-stations on Mr. Laurie's route—

Found Ted in the cars. Take him along. Write tomorrow.

T. LAURENCE

"Ted bolted sooner than you expected, Mother. Nevermind— Uncle will take good care of him, and Dan be very glad to see him," said Rob, as Mrs. Jo sat, trying to realize that her youngest was actually on his way to the wild West.

"Disobedient boy! He shall be severely punished, if I ever get him again. Laurie winked at this prank; I know he did. Just like him. Won't the two rascals have a splendid time? Wish I was with them! Don't believe that crazy boy took even a nightgown with him, or an overcoat. Well, there will be two patients for us to nurse when they get back, if they ever do. Those reckless express trains always go down precipices, and burn up, or telescope. Oh! My Ted, my precious boy, how can I let him go so far away from me?"

And mother-like, Mrs. Jo forgot the threatened chastisement in tender lamentations over the happy scapegrace, now whizzing across the continent in high feather at the success of his first revolt. Mr. Laurie was much amused at his insisting that those words, "when Ted bolts," put the idea into his head; and therefore the responsibility rested upon his shoulders. He assumed it kindly from the moment he came upon the runaway asleep in a car, with no visible luggage but a bottle of wine for Dan and a blacking brush for himself; and as Mrs. Jo suspected, the "two rascals" did have a splendid time. Penitent letters arrived in due season, and the irate parents soon forgot to chide in their anxiety about Dan, who was very ill, and did not know his friends for several days. Then he began to mend; and everyone forgave the bad boy when he proudly reported that the first conscious words Dan said were "Hullo, Ted!" with a smile of pleasure at seeing a familiar face bent over him.

"Glad he went, and I won't scold anymore. Now, what shall we put in the box for Dan?" And Mrs. Jo worked off her impatience to get hold of the invalid by sending comforts enough for a hospital.

Cheering accounts soon began to come, and at length Dan was pronounced able to travel, but seemed in no haste to go home, though never tired of hearing his nurses talk of it.

"Dan is strangely altered," wrote Laurie to Jo, "not by this illness alone, but by something which has evidently gone before. I don't know what, and leave you to ask; but from his ravings when delirious I fear he has been in some serious trouble the past year. He seems ten years older, but improved, quieter, and so grateful to us. It is pathetic to see the hunger in his eyes as they rest on Ted, as if he couldn't see enough of him. He says Kansas was a failure, but can't talk much; so I bide my time. The people here love him very much, and he cares for that sort of thing now; used to scorn any show of emotion, you know;

now he wants everyone to think well of him, and can't do enough to win affection and respect. I may be all wrong. You will soon find out. Ted is in clover, and the trip has done him a world of good. Let me take him to Europe when we go? Apron strings don't agree with him any better than they did with me when I proposed to run away to Washington with you some century ago. Aren't you sorry you didn't?"

This private letter set Mrs. Jo's lively fancy in a ferment, and she imagined every known crime, affliction, and complication which could possibly have befallen Dan. He was too feeble to be worried with questions now, but she promised herself most interesting revelations when she got him safe at home; for the "firebrand" was her most interesting boy. She begged him to come, and spent more time in composing a letter that should bring him, than she did over the most thrilling episodes in her "works."

No one but Dan saw the letter; but it did bring him, and one November day Mr. Laurie helped a feeble man out of a carriage at the door of Plumfield, and Mother Bhaer received the wanderer like a recovered son; while Ted, in a disreputable-looking hat and an astonishing pair of boots, performed a sort of war dance round the interesting group.

"Right upstairs and rest; I'm nurse now, and this ghost must eat before he talks to anyone," commanded Mrs. Jo, trying not to show how shocked she was at this shorn and shaven, gaunt and pallid shadow of the stalwart man she parted with.

He was quite content to obey, and lay on the long lounge in the room prepared for him, looking about as tranquilly as a sick child restored to its own nursery and mother's arms, while his new nurse fed and refreshed him, bravely controlling the questions that burned upon her tongue. Being weak and weary, he soon fell asleep; and then she stole away to enjoy the society of the "rascals," whom she scolded and petted, pumped and praised, to her heart's content.

"Jo, I think Dan has committed some crime and suffered for

it," said Mr. Laurie, when Ted had departed to show his boots
and tell glowing tales of the dangers and delights of miners' life
to his mates. "Some terrible experience has come to the lad,
and broken his spirit. He was quite out of his head when we
arrived, and I took the watching, so I heard more of those sad
wanderings than anyone else. He talked of the 'warden,' some
trial, a dead man, and Blair and Mason, and would keep offering me his hand, asking me if I would take it and forgive him.
Once, when he was very wild, I held his arms, and he quieted in
a moment, imploring me not to 'put the handcuffs on.' I declare, it was quite awful sometimes to hear him in the night talk
of old Plum and you, and beg to be let out and go home to die."

"He isn't going to die, but live to repent of anything he may
have done; so don't harrow me up with these dark hints, Teddy.
I don't care if he's broken the Ten Commandments, I'll stand by
him, and so will you, and we'll set him on his feet and make a
good man of him yet. I know he's not spoilt, by the look in his
poor face. Don't say a word to anyone, and I'll have the truth
before long," answered Mrs. Jo, still loyal to her bad boy,
though much afflicted by what she heard.

For some days Dan rested, and saw few people; then good
care, cheerful surroundings, and the comfort of being at home
began to tell, and he seemed more like himself, though still very
silent as to his late experiences, pleading the doctor's orders not
to talk much. Everyone wanted to see him; but he shrunk from
any but old friends, and "wouldn't lionize worth a cent," Ted
said, much disappointed that he could not show off his brave
Dan.

"Wasn't a man there who wouldn't have done the same, so
why make a row over me?" asked the hero, feeling more
ashamed than proud of the broken arm, which looked so interesting in a sling.

"But isn't it pleasant to think that you saved twenty lives,
Dan, and gave husbands, sons, and fathers back to the women

who loved them?" asked Mrs. Jo one evening as they were alone together after several callers had been sent away.

"Pleasant! It's all that kept me alive, I do believe. Yes, I'd rather have done it than be made president or any other big thing in the world. No one knows what a comfort it is to think I've saved twenty men to more than pay for—" There Dan stopped short, having evidently spoken out of some strong emotion to which his hearer had no key.

"I thought you'd feel so. It is a splendid thing to save life at the risk of one's own, as you did, and nearly lost it," began Mrs. Jo, wishing he had gone on with that impulsive speech which was so like his old manner.

" 'He that loseth his life shall gain it,' " muttered Dan, staring at the cheerful fire which lighted the room, and shone on his thin face with a ruddy glow.

Mrs. Jo was so startled at hearing such words from his lips that she exclaimed joyfully, "Then you *did* read the little book I gave you, and kept your promise?"

"I read it a good deal after a while. I don't know much yet, but I'm ready to learn; and that's something."

"It's everything. Oh, my dear, tell me about it! I know something lies heavy on your heart; let me help you bear it, and so make the burden lighter."

"I know it would; I want to tell; but some things even *you* couldn't forgive; and if *you* let go of me, I'm afraid I can't keep afloat."

"Mothers can forgive *anything!* Tell me all, and be sure that I will *never* let you go, though the whole world should turn from you."

Mrs. Jo took one of the big wasted hands in both of hers and held it fast, waiting silently till that sustaining touch warmed poor Dan's heart, and gave him courage to speak. Sitting in his old attitude, with his head in his hands, he slowly told it all, never once looking up till the last words left his lips.

"Now you know. Can you forgive a murderer, and keep a jailbird in your house?"

Her only answer was to put her arms about him, and lay the shorn head on her breast, with eyes so full of tears they could but dimly see the hope and fear that made his own so tragical.

That was better than any words; and poor Dan clung to her in speechless gratitude, feeling the blessedness of mother love—that divine gift which comforts, purifies, and strengthens all who seek it. Two or three great, bitter drops were hidden in the little woolen shawl where Dan's cheek rested, and no one ever knew how soft and comfortable it felt to him after the hard pillows he had known so long. Suffering of both mind and body had broken will and pride, and the lifted burden brought such a sense of relief that he paused a moment to enjoy it in dumb delight.

"My poor boy, how you have suffered all this year, when we thought you free as air! Why didn't you tell us, Dan, and let us help you? Did you doubt your friends?" asked Mrs. Jo, forgetting all other emotions in sympathy, as she lifted up the hidden face, and looked reproachfully into the great hollow eyes that met her own frankly now.

"I was ashamed. I tried to bear it alone rather than shock and disappoint you, as I know I have, though you try not to show it. Don't mind; I must get used to it." And Dan's eyes dropped again as if they could not bear to see the trouble and dismay his confession painted on his best friend's face.

"I *am* shocked and disappointed by the sin, but I am also very glad and proud and grateful that my sinner has repented, atoned, and is ready to profit by the bitter lesson. No one but Fritz and Laurie need ever know the truth; we owe it to them, and they will feel as I do," answered Mrs. Jo, wisely thinking that entire frankness would be a better tonic than too much sympathy.

"No, they won't. Men never forgive like women. But it's right. Please tell 'em for me, and get it over. Mr. Laurence knows it, I guess. I blabbed when my wits were gone; but he was very kind

all the same. I can bear their knowing it; but oh, not Ted and
the girls!" Dan clutched her arm with such an imploring face
that she hastened to assure him no one should know except the
two old friends, and he calmed down as if ashamed of his sudden panic.

"It wasn't murder, mind you, it was in self-defense; he drew
first, and I had to hit him. Didn't mean to kill him; but it doesn't
worry me as much as it ought, I'm afraid. I've more than paid
for it, and such a rascal is better out of the world than in it,
showing boys the way to hell. Yes, I know you think that's awful
in me; but I can't help it. I hate a scamp as I do a skulking
coyote, and always want to get a shot at 'em. Perhaps it would
have been better if he had killed me; my life is spoilt."

All the old prison gloom seemed to settle like a black cloud
on Dan's face as he spoke, and Mrs. Jo was frightened at the
glimpse it gave her of the fire through which he had passed to
come out alive, but scarred for life. Hoping to turn his mind to
happier things, she said cheerfully, "No, it isn't. You have
learned to value it more and use it better for this trial. It is not a
lost year, but one that may prove the most helpful of any you
ever know. Try to think so, and begin again; we will help, and
have all the more confidence in you for this failure. We all do
the same and struggle on."

"I never can be what I was. I feel about sixty, and don't care
for anything now I've got here. Let me stay till I'm on my legs,
then I'll clear out and never trouble you anymore," said Dan,
despondently.

"You are weak and low in your mind; that will pass, and by
and by you will go to your missionary work among the Indians
with all the old energy and the new patience, self-control, and
knowledge you have gained. Tell me more about that good
chaplain and Mary Mason and the lady whose chance word
helped you so much. I want to know all about the trials of my
poor boy."

Won by her tender interest, Dan brightened up and talked on

till he had poured out all the story of that bitter year, and felt the better for the load he lifted off.

If he had known how it weighed upon his hearer's heart, he would have held his peace; but she hid her sorrow till she had sent him to bed, comforted and calm; then she cried her heart out, to the great dismay of Fritz and Laurie, till they heard the tale and could mourn with her; after which they all cheered up and took counsel together how best to help this worst of all the "catastrophes" the year had brought them.

CHAPTER 21

ASLAUGA'S KNIGHT

IT WAS curious to see the change which came over Dan after
that talk. A weight seemed off his mind; and though the old
impetuous spirit flashed out at times, he seemed intent on trying to show his gratitude and love and honor to these true
friends by a new humility and confidence very sweet to them,
very helpful to him. After hearing the story from Mrs. Jo, the
Professor and Mr. Laurie made no allusion to it beyond the
hearty handgrasp, the look of compassion, the brief word of
good cheer in which men convey sympathy, and a redoubled
kindness which left no doubt of pardon. Mr. Laurie began at
once to interest influential persons in Dan's mission, and set in
motion the machinery which needs so much oiling before anything can be done where government is concerned. Mr. Bhaer,
with the skill of a true teacher, gave Dan's hungry mind something to do, and helped him understand himself by carrying on
the good chaplain's task so paternally that the poor fellow often
said he felt as if he had found a father. The boys took him to
drive, and amused him with their pranks and plans; while the
women, old and young, nursed and petted him till he felt like a

sultan with a crowd of devoted slaves, obedient to his lightest
wish.

A very little of this was enough for Dan, who had a masculine
horror of "mollycoddling," and so brief an acquaintance with
illness that he rebelled against the doctor's orders to keep quiet;
and it took all Mrs. Jo's authority and the girls' ingenuity to
keep him from leaving his sofa long before strained back and
wounded head were well. Daisy cooked for him; Nan attended
to his medicines; Josie read aloud to while away the long hours
of inaction that hung so heavily on his hands; while Bess
brought all her pictures and casts to amuse him, and, at his
special desire, set up a modeling stand in his parlor and began
to mold the buffalo head he gave her. Those afternoons seemed
the pleasantest part of his day; and Mrs. Jo, busy in her study
close by, could see the friendly trio and enjoy the pretty pictures
they made. The girls were much flattered by the success of their
efforts, and exerted themselves to be very entertaining, consult-
ing Dan's moods with the feminine tact most woman creatures
learn before they are out of pinafores. When he was gay, the
room rang with laughter; when gloomy, they read or worked in
respectful silence till their sweet patience cheered him up again;
and when in pain they hovered over him like "a couple of angels," as he said. He often called Josie "Little Mother," but
Bess was always "Princess"; and his manner to the two cousins
was quite different. Josie sometimes fretted him with her fussy
ways, the long plays she liked to read, and the maternal scold-
ings she administered when he broke the rules; for having a lord
of creation in her power was so delightful to her that she would
have ruled him with a rod of iron if he had submitted. To Bess,
in her gentler ministrations, he never showed either impatience
or weariness, but obeyed her least word, exerted himself to
seem well in her presence, and took such interest in her work
that he lay looking at her with unwearied eyes; while Josie read
to him in her best style unheeded.

Mrs. Jo observed this, and called them "Una and the Lion,"

which suited them very well, though the lion's mane was shorn,
and Una never tried to bridle him. The elder ladies did their
part in providing delicacies and supplying all his wants; but Mrs.
Meg was busy at home, Mrs. Amy preparing for the trip to
Europe in the spring, and Mrs. Jo hovering on the brink of a
"vortex"—for the forthcoming book had been sadly delayed by
the late domestic events. As she sat at her desk, settling papers
or meditatively nibbling her pen while waiting for the divine
afflatus to descend upon her, she often forgot her fictitious heroes and heroines in studying the live models before her, and
thus by chance looks, words, and gestures discovered a little
romance unsuspected by anyone else.

The *portière* between the rooms was usually drawn aside, giving a view of the group in the large bay window—Bess at one
side, in her gray blouse, busy with her tools; Josie at the other
side with her book; and between, on the long couch, propped
with many cushions, lay Dan in a many-hued Eastern dressing
gown presented by Mr. Laurie and worn to please the girls,
though the invalid much preferred an old jacket "with no confounded tail to bother over." He faced Mrs. Jo's room, but
never seemed to see her, for his eyes were on the slender figure
before him, with the pale winter sunshine touching her golden
head, and the delicate hands that shaped the clay so deftly.
Josie was just visible, rocking violently in a little chair at the
head of the couch, and the steady murmur of her girlish voice
was usually the only sound that broke the quiet of the room,
unless a sudden discussion arose about the book or the buffalo.

Something in the big eyes, bigger and blacker than ever in the
thin white face, fixed so steadily on one object, had a sort of
fascination for Mrs. Jo after a time, and she watched the
changes in them curiously; for Dan's mind was evidently not on
the story, and he often forgot to laugh or exclaim at the comic
or exciting crisis. Sometimes they were soft and wistful, and the
watcher was very glad that neither damsel caught that dangerous look, for when they spoke it vanished; sometimes it was full

of eager fire, and the color came and went rebelliously, in spite of his attempt to hide it with an impatient gesture of hand or head; but oftenest it was dark, and sad, and stern, as if those gloomy eyes looked out of captivity at some forbidden light or joy. This expression came so often that it worried Mrs. Jo, and she longed to go and ask him what bitter memory overshadowed those quiet hours. She knew that his crime and its punishment must lie heavy on his mind; but youth, and time, and new hopes would bring comfort, and help to wear away the first sharpness of the prison brand. It lifted at other times, and seemed almost forgotten when he joked with the boys, talked with old friends, or enjoyed the first snows as he drove out every fair day. Why should the shadow always fall so darkly on him in the society of these innocent and friendly girls? They never seemed to see it, and if either looked or spoke, a quick smile came like a sunburst through the clouds to answer them. So Mrs. Jo went on watching, wondering, and discovering, till accident confirmed her fears.

Josie was called away one day, and Bess, tired of working, offered to take her place if he cared for more reading.

"I do; your reading suits me better than Jo's. She goes so fast my stupid head gets in a muddle and soon begins to ache. Don't tell her; she's a dear little soul, and so good to sit here with a bear like me."

The smile was ready as Bess went to the table for a new book, the last story being finished.

"You are not a bear, but very good and patient, we think. It is always hard for a man to be shut up, Mamma says, and must be terrible for you, who have always been so free."

If Bess had not been reading titles she would have seen Dan shrink as if her last words hurt him. He made no answer; but other eyes saw and understood why he looked as if he would have liked to spring up and rush away for one of his long races up the hill, as he used to do when the longing for liberty grew uncontrollable. Moved by a sudden impulse, Mrs. Jo caught up her workbasket and went to join her neighbors, feeling that a non-conductor might be needed; for Dan looked like a thunder-cloud full of electricity.

"What shall we read, Aunty? Dan doesn't seem to care. You know his taste; tell me something quiet and pleasant and short. Josie will be back soon," said Bess, still turning over the books piled on the center table.

Before Mrs. Jo could answer, Dan pulled a shabby little vol-ume from under his pillow, and handing it to her said, "Please read the third one; it's short and pretty—I'm fond of it."

The book opened at the right place, as if the third story had been often read, and Bess smiled as she saw the name.

"Why, Dan, I shouldn't think you'd care for this romantic German tale. There is fighting in it; but it is very sentimental, if I remember rightly."

"I know it. But I've read so few stories, I like the simple ones best. Had nothing else to read sometimes; I guess I know it all by heart, and never seem to be tired of those fighting fellows, and the fiends and angels and lovely ladies. You read 'Aslauga's Knight,' and see if you don't like it. Edwald was rather too soft for my fancy; but Froda was first rate, and the spirit with the golden hair always reminded me of you."

As Dan spoke Mrs. Jo settled herself where she could watch him in the glass, and Bess took a large chair facing him, saying, as she put up her hands to retie the ribbon that held the cluster of thick, soft curls at the back of her head, "I hope Aslauga's hair wasn't as troublesome as mine, for it's always tumbling down. I'll be ready in a minute."

"Don't tie it up; please let it hang. I love to see it shine that way. It will rest your head, and be just right for the story, Goldi-locks," pleaded Dan, using the childish name and looking more like his boyish self than he had done for many a day.

Bess laughed, shook down her pretty hair, and began to read, glad to hide her face a little; for compliments made her shy, no matter who paid them. Dan listened intently now; and Mrs. Jo,

with eyes that went often from her needle to the glass, could
see, without turning, how he enjoyed every word as if it had
more meaning for him than for the other listeners. His face
brightened wonderfully, and soon wore the look that came
when anything brave or beautiful inspired and touched his better self. It was Fouqué's charming story of the knight Froda and
the fair daughter of Sigurd, who was a sort of spirit, appearing
to her lover in hours of danger and trial, as well as triumph and
joy, till she became his guide and guard, inspiring him with
courage, nobleness, and truth, leading him to great deeds in the
field, sacrifices for those he loved, and victories over himself by
the gleaming of her golden hair, which shone on him in battle,
dreams, and perils by day and night, till after death he finds the
lovely spirit waiting to receive and to reward him.

Of all the stories in the book this was the last one would have
supposed Dan would like best, and even Mrs. Jo was surprised
at his perceiving the moral of the tale through the delicate im-
agery and romantic language by which it was illustrated. But as
she looked and listened she remembered the streak of sentiment and refinement which lay concealed in Dan like the gold
vein in a rock, making him quick to feel and to enjoy fine color
in a flower, grace in an animal, sweetness in women, heroism in
men, and all the tender ties that bind heart to heart; though he
was slow to show it, having no words to express the tastes and
instincts which he inherited from his mother. Suffering of soul
and body had tamed his stronger passions, and the atmosphere
of love and pity now surrounding him purified and warmed his
heart till it began to hunger for the food neglected or denied so
long. This was plainly written in his too-expressive face, as, fan-
cying it unseen, he let it tell the longing after beauty, peace, and
happiness embodied for him in the innocent fair girl before
him.

The conviction of this sad yet natural fact came to Mrs. Jo
with a pang, for she felt how utterly hopeless such a longing

was; since light and darkness were not farther apart than snow-
white Bess and sin-stained Dan. No dream of such a thing disturbed the young girl, as her entire unconsciousness plainly
showed. But how long would it be before the eloquent eyes
betrayed the truth? And then what disappointment for Dan,
what dismay for Bess, who was as cool and high and pure as her
own marbles, and shunned all thought of love with maidenly
reserve.

"How hard everything is made for my poor boy! How can I
spoil his little dream, and take away the spirit of good he is
beginning to love and long for? When my own dear lads are
safely settled I'll never try another, for these things are heart-
breaking, and I can't manage anymore," thought Mrs. Jo, as she
put the lining into Teddy's coatsleeve upside down, so perplexed
and grieved was she at this new catastrophe.

The story was soon done, and as Bess shook back her hair
Dan asked as eagerly as a boy, "Don't you like it?"

"Yes, it's very pretty, and I see the meaning of it; but Undine
was always my favorite."

"Of course, that's like you—lilies and pearls and souls and
pure water. Sintram used to be mine; but I took a fancy to this
when I was—ahem—rather down on my luck one time, and it
did me good, it was so cheerful and sort of spiritual in its meaning, you know."

Bess opened her blue eyes in wonder at this fancy of Dan's
for anything "spiritual"; but she only nodded, saying, "Some of
the little songs are sweet and might be set to music."

Dan laughed; "I used to sing the last one to a tune of my own
sometimes at sunset—

> Listening to celestial lays,
> Bending thy unclouded gaze
> On the pure and living light,
> Thou art blest, Aslauga's Knight!

And I was," he added, under his breath, as he glanced toward the sunshine dancing on the wall.

"This one suits you better now." And glad to please him by her interest, Bess read in her soft voice:

> "Heal fast, heal fast, ye hero wounds;
> O knight, be quickly strong!
>   Beloved strife
>   For fame and life,
> Oh, tarry not too long!"

"I'm no hero, never can be, and 'fame and life' can't do much for me. Never mind, read me the paper, please. This knock on the head has made a regular fool of me."

Dan's voice was gentle; but the light was gone out of his face now, and he moved restlessly as if the silken pillows were full of thorns. Seeing that his mood had changed, Bess quietly put down the book, took up the paper, and glanced along the columns for something to suit him.

"You don't care for the money market, I know, nor musical news. Here's a murder; you used to like those; shall I read it? One man kills another—"

"No!"

Only a word, but it gave Mrs. Jo a thrill, and for a moment she dared not glance at the telltale mirror. When she did Dan lay motionless with one hand over his eyes, and Bess was happily reading the art news to ears that never heard a word. Feeling like a thief who has stolen something very precious, Mrs. Jo slipped away to her study, and before long Bess followed to report that Dan was fast asleep.

Sending her home, with the firm resolve to keep her there as much as possible, Mother Bhaer had an hour of serious thought all alone in the red sunset; and when a sound in the next room led her there, she found that the feigned sleep had become real repose; for Dan lay breathing heavily, with a scarlet spot on either cheek, and one hand clinched on his broad breast. Yearning over him with a deeper pity than ever before, she sat in the little chair beside him, trying to see her way out of this tangle, till his hand slipped down, and in doing so snapped a cord he wore about his neck and let a small case drop to the floor.

Mrs. Jo picked it up, and as he did not wake, sat looking at it, idly wondering what charm it held; for the case was of Indian workmanship, and the broken cord, of closely woven grass, sweet scented and pale yellow.

"I won't pry into any more of the poor fellow's secrets. I'll mend and put it back, and never let him know I've seen his talisman."

As she spoke she turned the little wallet to examine the fracture, and a card fell into her lap. It was a photograph, cut to fit its covering, and two words were written underneath the face, "My Aslauga." For an instant Mrs. Jo fancied that it might be one of herself, for all the boys had them; but as the thin paper fell away, she saw the picture Demi took of Bess that happy summer day. There was no doubt now, and with a sigh she put it back, and was about to slip it into Dan's bosom so that not even a stitch should betray her knowledge, when, as she leaned toward him, she saw that he was looking straight at her with an expression that surprised her more than any of the strange ones she had ever seen in that changeful face before.

"Your hand slipped down; it fell; I was putting it back," explained Mrs. Jo, feeling like a naughty child caught in mischief.

"You saw the picture?"

"Yes."

"And know what a fool I am?"

"Yes, Dan, and am so grieved—"

"Don't worry about me. I'm all right—glad you know, though I never meant to tell you. Of course it is only a crazy fancy of mine, and nothing can ever come of it. Never thought there would. Good Lord! What could that little angel ever be to me but what she is—a sort of dream of all that's sweet and good?"

More afflicted by the quiet resignation of his look and tone than by the most passionate ardor, Mrs. Jo could only say, with a face full of sympathy—

"It is very hard, dear, but there is no other way to look at it. You are wise and brave enough to see that, and to let the secret be ours alone."

"I swear I will! Not a word nor a look if I can help it. No one guesses, and if it troubles no one, is there any harm in my keeping this, and taking comfort in the pretty fancy that kept me sane in that cursed place?"

Dan's face was eager now, and he hid away the little worn case as if defying any hand to take it from him. Anxious to know everything before giving counsel or comfort, Mrs. Jo said quietly—"Keep it, and tell me all about the 'fancy.' Since I have stumbled on your secret, let me know how it came, and how I can help to make it lighter to bear."

"You'll laugh, but I don't mind. You always did find out our secrets and give us a lift. Well, I never cared much for books, you know; but down yonder when the devil tormented me I had to do something or go stark mad, so I read both the books you gave me. One was beyond me, till that good old man showed me how to read it, but the other, this one, was a comfort, I tell you. It amused me, and was as pretty as poetry. I liked 'em all, and most wore out Sintram. See how used up he is! Then I came to this, and it sort of fitted that other happy part of my life, last summer—here."

Dan stopped for a moment as the words lingered on his lips; then, with a long breath, went on, as if it was hard to lay bare the foolish little romance he had woven about a girl, a picture, and a child's story there in the darkness of the place which was as terrible to him as Dante's Inferno, till he found his Beatrice.

"I couldn't sleep, and *had* to think about something, so I used to fancy I was Folko, and see the shining of Aslauga's hair in the

sunset on the wall, the glim of the watchman's lamp, and the
light that came in at dawn. My cell was high. I could see a bit of
sky. Sometimes there was a star in it, and that was 'most as good
as a face. I set great store by that patch of blue, and when a
white cloud went by, I thought it was the prettiest thing in all
this world. I guess I was pretty near a fool; but those thoughts
and things helped me through, so they are all solemn true to
me, and I can't let them go. The dear shiny head, the white
gown, the eyes like stars, and the sweet, calm ways that set her
as high above me as the moon in heaven. Don't take it away!
It's only a fancy, but a man must love something, and I'd better
love a spirit like her than any of the poor common girls who
would care for me."

The quiet despair in Dan's voice pierced Mrs. Jo to the heart,
but there was no hope and she gave none. Yet she felt that he
was right, and that this hapless affection might do more to uplift
and purify him than any other he might know. Few women
would care to marry Dan now, except such as would hinder, not
help, him in the struggle which life would always be to him; and
it was better to go solitary to his grave than become what she
suspected his father had been—a handsome, unprincipled, and
dangerous man, with more than one broken heart to answer for.

"Yes, Dan, it *is* wise to keep this innocent fancy, if it helps
and comforts you, till something more real and possible comes
to make you happier. I wish I could give you any hope; but we
both know that the dear child is the apple of her father's eye,
the pride of her mother's heart, and that the most perfect lover
they can find will hardly seem to them worthy of their precious
daughter. Let her remain for you the high, bright star that leads
you up and makes you believe in heaven."

Mrs. Jo broke down there; it seemed so cruel to destroy the
faint hope Dan's eyes betrayed, that she could not moralize
when she thought of his hard life and lonely future. Perhaps it
was the wisest thing she could have done, for in her hearty
sympathy he found comfort for his own loss, and very soon was

able to speak again in the manly tone of resignation to the inevitable that showed how honest was his effort to give up everything but the pale shadow of what, for another, might have been a happy possibility.

They talked long and earnestly in the twilight; and this second secret bound them closer than the first; for in it there was neither sin nor shame—only the tender pain and patience which has made saints and heroes of far worse men than our poor Dan. When at length they rose at the summons of a bell, all the sunset glory had departed, and in the wintry sky there hung one star, large, soft, and clear, above a snowy world. Pausing at the window before she dropped the curtain, Mrs. Jo said cheerfully, "Come and see how beautiful the evening star is, since you love it so." And as he stood behind her, tall and pale, like the ghost of his former self, she added softly, "And remember, dear, if the sweet girl is denied you, the old friend is always here to love and trust and pray for you."

This time she was not disappointed; and had she asked any reward for many anxieties and cares, she received it when Dan's strong arm came round her, as he said, in a voice which showed her that she had not labored in vain to pluck her firebrand from the burning, "I never can forget that; for she's helped to save my soul, and make me dare to look up there and say, 'God bless her!' "

CHAPTER 22

POSITIVELY LAST APPEARANCE

"Upon my word, I feel as if I lived in a powder magazine, and don't know which barrel will explode next, and send me flying," said Mrs. Jo to herself next day, as she trudged up to Parnassus to suggest to her sister that perhaps the most charming of the young nurses had better return to her marble gods before she unconsciously added another wound to those already won by the human hero. She told no secrets; but a hint was sufficient; for Mrs. Amy guarded her daughter as a pearl of great price, and at once devised a very simple means of escape from danger. Mr. Laurie was going to Washington on Dan's behalf, and was delighted to take his family with him when the idea was carelessly suggested. So the conspiracy succeeded finely; and Mrs. Jo went home, feeling more like a traitor than ever. She expected an explosion; but Dan took the news so quietly, it was plain that he cherished no hope; and Mrs. Amy was sure her romantic sister had been mistaken. If she had seen Dan's face when Bess went to say good-bye, her maternal eye would have discovered far more than the unconscious girl did. Mrs. Jo trembled lest he should betray himself; but he had learned self-

control in a stern school, and would have got through the hard
moment bravely, only, when he took both her hands, saying
heartily, "Good-bye, Princess. If we don't meet again, remember your old friend Dan sometimes," she, touched by his late
danger and the wistful look he wore, answered with unusual
warmth, "How can I help it, when you make us all so proud of
you? God bless your mission, and bring you safely home to us
again!"

As she looked up at him with a face full of frank affection
and sweet regret, all that he was losing rose so vividly before
him that Dan could not resist the impulse to take the "dear
goldy head" between his hands and kiss it, with a broken
"Good-bye," then hurried back to his room, feeling as if it were
the prison cell again, with no glimpse of heaven's blue to comfort him.

This abrupt caress and departure rather startled Bess; for she
felt with a girl's quick instinct that there was something in that
kiss unknown before, and looked after him with sudden color in
her cheeks and new trouble in her eyes. Mrs. Jo saw it, and
fearing a very natural question, answered it before it was put.

"Forgive him, Bess. He has had a great trouble, and it makes
him tender at parting with old friends; for you know he may
never come back from the wild world he is going to."

"You mean the fall and danger of death?" asked Bess, innocently.

"No, dear; a greater trouble than that. But I cannot tell you
any more—except that he has come through it bravely; so you
may trust and respect him, as I do."

"He has lost someone he loved. Poor Dan! We must be very
kind to him."

Bess did not ask the question, but seemed content with her
solution of mystery—which was so true that Mrs. Jo confirmed
it by a nod, and let her go away believing that some tender loss
and sorrow wrought the great change all saw in Dan, and made
him so slow to speak concerning the past year.

But Ted was less easily satisfied, and this unusual reticence
goaded him to desperation. His mother had warned him not to
trouble Dan with questions till he was quite well; but this prospect of approaching departure made him resolve to have a full,
clear, and satisfactory account of the adventures which he felt
sure must have been thrilling, from stray words Dan let fall in
his fever. So one day when the coast was clear, Master Ted
volunteered to amuse the invalid, and did so in the following
manner: "Look here, old boy, if you don't want me to read,
you've got to talk, and tell me all about Kansas, and the farms,
and that part. The Montana business I know, but you seem to
forget what went before. Brace up, and let's have it," he began,
with an abruptness which roused Dan from a brown study most
effectually.

"No, I don't forget; it isn't interesting to anyone but myself. I
didn't see any farms—gave it up," he said slowly.

"Why?"

"Other things to do."

"What?"

"Well, brush making for one thing."

"Don't chaff a fellow. Tell true."

"I truly did."

"What for?"

"To keep out of mischief, as much as anything."

"Well, of all the queer things—and you've done a lot—that's
the queerest," cried Ted, taken aback at this disappointing discovery. But he didn't mean to give up yet, and began again.

"What mischief, Dan?"

"Never you mind. Boys shouldn't bother."

"But I do want to know, awfully, because I'm your pal, and
care for you no end. Always did. Come, now, tell me a good
yarn. I love scrapes. I'll be mum as an oyster if you don't want it
known."

"Will you?" and Dan looked at him, wondering how the boyish face would change if the truth were suddenly told him.

"I'll swear it on locked fists, if you like. I know it was jolly, and I'm aching to hear."

"You are as curious as a girl. More than some—Josie and—and Bess never asked a question."

"They don't care about rows and things; they liked the mine business, heroes, and that sort. So do I, and I'm as proud as Punch over it; but I see by your eyes that there was something else before that, and I'm bound to find out who Blair and Mason are, and who was hit and who ran away, and all the rest of it."

"What!" cried Dan, in a tone that made Ted jump.

"Well, you used to mutter about 'em in your sleep, and Uncle Laurie wondered. So did I; but don't mind, if you can't remember, or would rather not."

"What else did I say? Queer, what stuff a man will talk when his wits are gone."

"That's all I heard; but it seemed interesting, and I just mentioned it, thinking it might refresh your memory a bit," said Teddy, very politely; for Dan's frown was heavy at that moment.

It cleared off at this reply, and after a look at the boy squirming with suppressed impatience in his chair, Dan made up his mind to amuse him with a game of cross-purposes and half-truths, hoping to quench his curiosity, and so get peace.

"Let me see; Blair was a lad I met in the cars, and Mason a poor fellow who was in a—well, a sort of hospital where I happened to be. Blair ran off to his brothers, and I suppose I might say Mason was hit, because he died there. Does that suit you?"

"No, it doesn't. Why did Blair run? And who hit the other fellow? I'm sure there was a fight somewhere, wasn't there?"

"Yes."

"I guess I know what it was about."

"The devil, you do! Let's hear you guess. Must be amusing," said Dan, affecting an ease he did not feel.

Charmed to be allowed to free his mind, Ted at once

unfolded the boyish solution of the mystery which he had been cherishing, for he felt that there was one somewhere.

"You needn't say yes, if I guess right and you are under oath to keep silent. I shall know by your face, and never tell. Now see if I'm not right. Out there they have wild doings, and it's my belief you were in some of 'em. I don't mean robbing mails, and Ku-Kluxing, and that sort of thing; but defending the settlers, or hanging some scamp, or even shooting a few, as a fellow must sometimes, in self-defense. Ah, ha! I've hit it, I see. Needn't speak; I know the flash of your old eye, and the clinch of your big fist." And Ted pranced with satisfaction.

"Drive on, smart boy, and don't lose the trail," said Dan, finding a curious sense of comfort in some of these random words, and longing, but not daring, to confirm the true ones. He might have confessed the crime, but not the punishment that followed, the sense of its disgrace was still so strong upon him.

"I knew I should get it; can't deceive me long," began Ted, with such an air of pride Dan could not help a short laugh.

"It's a relief, isn't it, to have it off your mind? Now, just confide in me and it's all safe, unless you've sworn not to tell."

"I have."

"Oh, well, then don't;" and Ted's face fell, but he was himself again in a moment and said, with the air of a man of the world, "It's all right—I understand—honor binds—silence to death, etc. Glad you stood by your mate in the hospital. How many did you kill?"

"Only one."

"Bad lot, of course?"

"A damned rascal."

"Well, don't look so fierce; I've no objection. Wouldn't mind popping at some of those bloodthirsty blackguards myself. Had to dodge and keep quiet after it, I suppose."

"Pretty quiet for a long spell."

"Got off all right in the end, and headed for your mines and

did that jolly brave thing. Now, I call that all decidedly interesting and capital. I'm glad to know it; but I won't blab."

"Mind you don't. Look here, Ted, if you'd killed a man,
would it trouble you—a bad one, I mean?"

The lad opened his mouth to say, "Not a bit," but checked
that answer as if something in Dan's face made him change his
mind. "Well, if it was my duty in war or self-defense, I suppose I
shouldn't; but if I'd pitched into him in a rage, I guess I should
be very sorry. Shouldn't wonder if he sort of haunted me, and
remorse gnawed me as it did Aram and those fellows. *You* don't
mind, do you? It was a fair fight, wasn't it?"

"Yes, I was in the right; but I wish I'd been out of it. Women
don't see it that way, and look horrified at such things. Makes it
hard; but it don't matter."

"Don't tell 'em; then they can't worry," said Ted, with the nod
of one versed in the management of the sex.

"Don't intend to. Mind you keep your notions to yourself, for
some of 'em are wide of the mark. Now you may read if you
like." And there the talk ended; but Ted took great comfort in
it, and looked as wise as an owl afterward.

A few quiet weeks followed, during which Dan chafed at the
delay; and when at length word came that his credentials were
ready, he was eager to be off, to forget a vain love in hard work,
and live for others, since he might not for himself.

So one wild March morning our Sintram rode away, with
horse and hound, to face again the enemies who would have
conquered him, but for Heaven's help and human pity.

"Ah, me! It does seem as if life was made of partings, and
they get harder as we go on," sighed Mrs. Jo, a week later, as
she sat in the long parlor at Parnassus one evening, whither the
family had gone to welcome the travelers back.

"And meetings too, dear; for here we are, and Nat is on his
way at last. Look for the silver lining, as Marmee used to say,
and be comforted," answered Mrs. Amy, glad to be at home
and find no wolves prowling near her sheepfold.

"I've been so worried lately, I can't help croaking. I wonder what Dan thought at not seeing you again? It was wise; but he would have enjoyed another look at home faces before he went into the wilderness," said Mrs. Jo, regretfully.

"Much better so. We left notes and all we could think of that he might need, and slipped away before he came. Bess really seemed relieved; I'm sure I was." And Mrs. Amy smoothed an anxious line out of her white forehead, as she smiled at her daughter, laughing happily among her cousins.

Mrs. Jo shook her head as if the silver lining of that cloud was hard to find; but she had no time to croak again, for just then Mr. Laurie came in looking well pleased at something.

"A new picture has arrived; face toward the music room, good people, and tell me how you like it. I call it 'Only a fiddler,' after Andersen's story. What name will you give it?"

As he spoke he threw open the wide doors, and just beyond they saw a young man standing, with a beaming face, and a violin in his hand. There was no doubt about the name to this picture, and with the cry "Nat! Nat!" there was a general uprising. But Daisy reached him first, and seemed to have lost her usual composure somewhere on the way, for she clung to him, sobbing with the shock of a surprise and joy too great for her to bear quietly. Everything was settled by that tearful and tender embrace, for, though Mrs. Meg speedily detached her daughter, it was only to take her place; while Demi shook Nat's hand with brotherly warmth, and Josie danced round them like Macbeth's three witches in one, chanting in her most tragic tones, "Chirper thou wast; second violin thou art; first thou shalt be. Hail, all hail!"

This caused a laugh, and made things gay and comfortable at once. Then the usual fire of questions and answers began, to be kept up briskly while the boys admired Nat's blond beard and foreign clothes, the girls his improved appearance—for he was ruddy with good English beef and beer, and fresh with the seabreezes which had blown him swiftly home—and the older folk rejoiced over his prospects. Of course all wanted to hear him play; and when tongues tired, he gladly did his best for them, surprising the most critical by his progress in music even more than by the energy and self-possession which made a new man of bashful Nat. By and by when the violin—that most human of all instruments—had sung to them the loveliest songs without words, he said, looking about him at these old friends with what Mr. Bhaer called a "feeling-full" expression of happiness and content, "Now let me play something that you will all remember, though you won't love it as I do." And standing in the attitude which Ole Bull has immortalized, he played the street melody he gave them the first night he came to Plumfield. They remembered it, and joined in the plaintive chorus, which fitly expressed his own emotions—

> "Oh, my heart is sad and weary
> Everywhere I roam,
> Longing for the old plantation
> And for the old folks at home."

"Now I feel better," said Mrs. Jo, as they all trooped down the hill soon after. "Some of our boys are failures, but I think this one is going to be a success, and patient Daisy a happy girl at last. Nat is your work, Fritz, and I congratulate you heartily."

"Ach, we can but sow the seed and trust that it falls on good ground. I planted, perhaps, but you watched that the fowls of the air did not devour it, and brother Laurie watered generously; so we will share the harvest among us, and be glad even for a small one, heart's dearest."

"I thought the seed had fallen on very stony ground with my poor Dan; but I shall not be surprised if he surpasses all the rest in the real success of life, since there is more rejoicing over one repentant sinner than many saints," answered Mrs. Jo, still clinging fast to her black sheep although a whole flock of white ones trotted happily before her.

*   *   *

It is a strong temptation to the weary historian to close the present tale with an earthquake which should engulf Plumfield and its environs so deeply in the bowels of the earth that no youthful Schliemann could ever find a vestige of it. But as that somewhat melodramatic conclusion might shock my gentle readers, I will refrain, and forestall the usual question, "How did they end?" by briefly stating that all the marriages turned out well. The boys prospered in their various callings; so did the girls, for Bess and Josie won honors in their artistic careers, and in the course of time found worthy mates. Nan remained a busy, cheerful, independent spinster, and dedicated her life to her suffering sisters and their children, in which true woman's work she found abiding happiness. Dan never married, but lived, bravely and usefully, among his chosen people till he was shot defending them, and at last lay quietly asleep in the green wilderness he loved so well, with a lock of golden hair upon his breast, and a smile on his face which seemed to say that Aslauga's Knight had fought his last fight and was at peace. Stuffy became an alderman, and died suddenly of apoplexy after a public dinner. Dolly was a society man of mark till he lost his money, when he found congenial employment in a fashionable tailoring establishment. Demi became a partner, and lived to see his name above the door, and Rob was a professor at Laurence College; but Teddy eclipsed them all by becoming an eloquent and famous clergyman, to the great delight of his astonished mother. And now, having endeavored to suit everyone by many weddings, few deaths, and as much prosperity as the eternal fitness of things will permit, let the music stop, the lights die out, and the curtain fall forever on the March family.